continued . . .

A Place Called Home

Secret Shadows

Judie Aitken

BERKLEY SENSATION, NEW YORK

THE BERKLEY PUBLISHING GROUP
Published by the Penguin Group
Penguin Group (USA) Inc.
375 Hudson Street, New York, New York 10014, USA
Penguin Group (Canada), 10 Alcorn Avenue, Toronto, Ontario M4V 3B2, Canada
(a division of Pearson Penguin Canada Inc.)
Penguin Books Ltd., 80 Strand, London WC2R 0RL, England
Penguin Group Ireland, 25 St. Stephen's Green, Dublin 2, Ireland (a division of Penguin Books Ltd.)
Penguin Group (Australia), 250 Camberwell Road, Camberwell, Victoria 3124, Australia
(a division of Pearson Australia Group Pty. Ltd.)
Penguin Books India Pvt. Ltd., 11 Community Centre, Panchsheel Park, New Delhi—110 017, India
Penguin Group (NZ), Cnr. Airborne and Rosedale Roads, Albany, Auckland 1310, New Zealand
(a division of Pearson New Zealand Ltd.)
Penguin Books (South Africa) (Pty.) Ltd., 24 Sturdee Avenue, Rosebank, Johannesburg 2196, South
Africa

Penguin Books Ltd., Registered Offices: 80 Strand, London WC2R 0RL, England

This is a work of fiction. Names, characters, places, and incidents either are the product of the author's
imagination or are used fictitiously, and any resemblance to actual persons, living or dead, business es-
tablishments, events, or locales is entirely coincidental.

SECRET SHADOWS

A Berkley Sensation Book / published by arrangement with the author

PRINTING HISTORY
Berkley Sensation edition / December 2004

Copyright © 2004 by Judie Aitken.
Interior text design by Stacy Irwin.

ISBN: 0-425-19941-X

BERKLEY® SENSATION
Berkley Sensation Books are published by The Berkley Publishing Group,
a division of Penguin Group (USA) Inc.,
375 Hudson Street, New York, New York 10014.
BERKLEY SENSATION and the "B" design
are trademarks belonging to Penguin Group (USA) Inc.

PRINTED IN THE UNITED STATES OF AMERICA

10 9 8 7 6 5 4 3 2 1

For my sister Elizabeth, who has many, many more talents than she has ever realized. She can make ballet costumes out of crepe paper that fulfill every little girl's fantasy. She knits sweaters that feel like warm hugs and recycles plastic bags as though it were an art form. She isn't afraid to send her husband (hi, Paul) off alone to buy the groceries, and she keeps solid friendships for years and years and years. She tenderly nurses the sick, brings laughter into a room, and she's an incomparable mother and grandma. She can still fit into her wedding gown, remembers everyone's birthday, and has the best recipe for curried fruit compote that you've ever tasted. But her greatest talent is always being there—steady as a rock—like a shining beacon—for those she loves.

IV

Dear Reader,

Once again I will take you into the culture of the Native American people, specifically the Lakota of the northern plains. In many ways the culture is changing, and in just as many ways the old traditions, the old beliefs, remain. I hope that you enjoy your journey with me down the Red Road.

I have often mentioned frybread in my books. Frybread became a staple food for Indian families during the time of relocation, and it has remained a staple due to the commodities provided in some areas and due to family custom. Frybread booths at Indian gatherings are numerous and a favorite place to pick up a snack. Many of you have asked for the recipe, and the one below is just one of many. Recipes for frybread often differ from family to family or from tribe to tribe. There are also some commercially produced frybread mixes available. Some of the best frybread I have ever eaten was made by one of the Lakota inmates at the federal prison in Illinois while my family and I visited for their annual prison powwow. The following basic recipe is typical. This recipe makes 12 to 15 small pieces or 7 large flat ones for Indian tacos.

FRYBREAD
(*Wigli uη Kagapi*)

3 cups flour	1 cup powdered milk
3 tsp. baking powder	2 tbsp. melted shortening
1 1/2 tsp. salt	1 1/2 cups water
2 tbsp. sugar	

Put all dry ingredients in a bowl, add shortening and water and mix with hands until a soft dough. Dump onto a floured board and knead for a minute or two. Pinch off apple-sized lumps and shape into a disk. Poke an indentation in the center to help the dough to cook evenly. Shape does affect the taste or the way the dough fries. For Indian tacos, the disk must be flat, with the depression in the center on both sides. Fry in fat (about 375°) until golden and done on both sides, about 5 minutes. Drain on absorbent paper.

Frybread can be eaten plain; with honey, butter, or jam on it; and some folks like to cook it with bacon. Indian tacos, another favorite meal that features frybread, are made with a large flat piece of frybread layered with taco-seasoned ground beef, chopped onions, tomatoes and lettuce, and hot sauce. Enjoy!

I have also often mentioned powwows. A powwow is not a ceremony or a spiritual event. It is a social gathering where Indian people come together to sing, to dress in their Indian clothes and dance, to celebrate, and to have a good time. In Indian country families have kept the same campsite at the powwow grounds for years and years. Powwows can range anywhere from a small family dance to celebrate a birthday or the return of a family member from the service, to an annual tribe-sponsored dance such as Comanche Homecoming, or to the huge commercial contest dances such as Red Earth or Gathering of the Nations that are held in coliseums and offer thousands and thousands of dollars in prize money.

In this book one of my characters talks about a *49*. A 49 is a spontaneous social event that takes place after a powwow has ended for the evening. Usually considered a gathering of young adults, the 49 is held away from the dance arbor and away from the campground. The singers beat the rhythm on a small, handheld hide drum and sing songs with predominantly English and often humorous lyrics to a round-dance beat. The attendees dance in a side step around the singers. A 49 sometimes goes on until dawn. It's a place where boys meet girls, where they can "snag" a romance for the night or longer. The melodies of the 49 songs were originally sung by the southern plains tribes as war journey songs, but through the years they have spread throughout Indian country as part of the powwow culture.

Many stories exist that try to explain why this gathering is called a 49. Some say it was begun by the Kiowa who, in 1849 after the government banned large social gatherings, got together secretly in the dark of night. Other stories say that the name comes from an old story about fifty warriors who went off to battle and only forty-nine returned, and the gathering was held to honor the forty-nine. However they got their name, 49s are as traditional at a powwow as the frybread stands.

One added note: Cold Creek Indian Reservation only exists in my imagination, but I have tried to combine the elements of many reservations that exist across the country. Poverty remains on most, diabetes and alcoholism are major health problems, and yet pride is everpresent, educational opportunities are increasing, financial opportunities have bloomed for some, and public awareness of the culture—its beauty and its needs—is growing.

I hope that you enjoy *Secret Shadows*. I would love to hear from you. Please visit my Web site at www.judieaitken.com.

Best wishes, always . . .

Judie Aitken

1

Mid-December

DANE WHITE EAGLE LOATHED THE HOUR-LONG DRIVE
from his home in the city to Cold Creek Lakota Reservation. He had traveled the route so many times he knew he
could make it in the middle of a blizzard with his eyes
closed. From the weather report he'd heard earlier on the
radio, he just might have the chance to put his boast to the
test. But no matter how much he hated the trip, he gladly
made it as often as he could—at least twice a month, sometimes more. Today the trip was extra special.

As he left the main highway and drove onto reservation
land, a cold wind raced across the scrub-brush South
Dakota hills, kicking up dirt and snow along its way. The
DOT's line of snow fence that kept the state highway clear
stopped at the edge of the reservation. No snow fence had
been strung along the Cold Creek two-lane, and drifts were
quickly building. It wouldn't be long before they'd creep
out onto the road.

In Rapid City the temperature had been hovering just
above freezing, but on a day like today on the reservation,

without many buildings to break the unrelenting wind, the wind chill would probably be somewhere around five below. The wind rarely slowed to a gentle breeze on this stretch of land, and even the trees, what few there were, had given up, growing bent and twisted in their defeat. Looking out over the desolate hills, Dane couldn't see a single speck of bright color. The landscape was an expansive palette of whites and grays and browns. Winter had come hard to the rez.

Cold Creek Reserve wasn't as large as Pine Ridge or Rosebud, but it was just as poor. On the west side of the reservation, a group of about forty houses, a general store, the Broken Arrow restaurant, two gas stations, a smoke shop, and a tourist shop made up the small town of Red Star where Dane had been raised.

In two weeks it would be Christmas. When he'd left the city, shiny decorations and Christmas lights had dappled the snow-crested streets with bright splashes of color. On the rez few families had the extra money to pay for twinkling lights and holiday gewgaws. For the most part, Christmas on Cold Creek looked like just another bleak stretch of winter.

No matter what time of year it was, nothing ever got better on Cold Creek, it just got worse. Everything got worse. Kylee's last trip to the cancer clinic in the city had certainly proven that to be true.

His little sister's bravery humbled him. At thirteen years of age she stood on the exciting brink of womanhood, but she would never complete her journey. For the last two years Kylee had been battling what the doctors called a glioblastoma multiforme, a damned fancy name for an inoperable brain tumor.

He didn't know how Kylee managed to keep her spirits high. She always had a smile. No one ever heard her feel sorry for herself, not even when the chemo made her gut-wrenching sick or the radiation stole her energy and her beautiful long hair. No one ever heard her whine or complain, and no one ever heard her resent the kids who lived their young and healthy lives just outside her world. If anything, Kylee always went out of her way to soothe everyone else's discomforts.

Jerked from his thoughts, Dane jammed on the brakes as a pack of dogs broke from a tall stand of buffalo grass and dashed across the ice-slicked road in front of him.

His truck skidded, fishtailed, and then spun to a stop, the rear end embedded in a snowdrift.

"Son of a bitch! You know better than hitting the brakes on ice." Frustrated, knowing he'd lose time with Kylee while he tried to get out of the drift, he hit the steering wheel with the heel of his hand. "Damn good-for-nothing rez dogs!"

He watched the dogs lope ragtag across the open field. Every reservation had them, dogs so far removed from any purebred ancestors that you couldn't tell what bloodlines filled their veins. But it was a safe bet that coyote ran strong in all of them.

His mouth shifted into a wry smile. *Now, there's a hell of a potential moneymaker.* He chuckled aloud at the idea. *The tribal council ought to register the damned ugly mutts with the AKC as a new breed.* He watched the dogs as they eagerly circled a clump of bushes, their noses to the ground. *I bet some rich, white New York City or Hollywood bleeding heart would love to help the downtrodden noble Indians by paying top dollar to own the first genuine, registered rez dog on the block.*

Dane grinned and shook his head. The idea was ludicrous, but even more absurd was the fact that the foolish scheme would probably work.

Whatever critter had tempted the mutts had skeddadled, and the dogs quickly regrouped, dashed over the next rise, and were soon out of sight.

"Okay, White Eagle," he muttered, "let's see you get your ass out of the snow." Dane grabbed the gearshift, slipping it into drive and then reverse, drive and reverse, rocking the truck back and forth. At first the rear wheels just spun in the deep snow, but after a few more tries the tires hit dirt and the pickup eased out of the drift and back onto the road.

Three and a half miles later, the small reservation town of Red Star came into view. After another half mile, Dane turned into the driveway that ran beside his mother's house. It wasn't really a driveway, just a patch of hard-packed dirt where four generations of White Eagles had parked their third- and fourth-hand, rusted-out Indian cars. The grass had given up fighting oil leaks and bald tires years ago and no longer tried to sprout on the narrow strip of land. At least ten inches of snow now covered the ground and almost every inch of his mother's old blue Ford.

Looking at the house brought a smile to Dane's lips and made him feel good. The strings of colored Christmas lights that he'd hung along the eaves the week before twinkled like bright little stars, a sad contrast to the dismal neighborhood and gloomy afternoon. His mother had complained about the extra cost of electricity, and Dane had gently reminded her that he'd been paying her utility bills for the past few years. He'd finally convinced her that the few extra pennies spent for Christmas lights weren't going to empty his wallet.

The lights stayed on. In fact, the lights stayed on twenty-four hours a day. It was his mother's way of getting in the last word, her way of letting him know she thought he was acting like some big shot, show-off city Indian, foolishly throwing his money around.

The day he'd brought the lights, he'd also brought a bushy pine tree from a corner Christmas tree lot in the city. The look of excitement on Kylee's face had been well worth the hassle of getting the darned crooked thing upright in the stand in the corner of the living room. The rest of the evening had been spent helping her decorate the tree. They'd hung pretty paper snowflakes and tiny colorful God's eyes made with yarn. His mother had helped by adding little red tassels she'd made with fringe from an old powwow shawl.

The lopsided star on the top of the tree was nothing more than a cardboard cutout that Kylee had covered with a couple of pieces of tinfoil. They'd all laughed at the silly decoration but agreed that the reflection of the tree lights on the crinkled foil made the star twinkle just as well as one of the twenty-dollar store-bought ones.

Kylee had hung the final decorations on the tree, six or seven pure white eagle plumes. On her last birthday some of the tribal elders had come and said healing prayers over her. They had smudged her with cedar smoke and sang some of the old healing songs. Before they'd left, each had given her a puffy plume, a breath-of-life feather. Tied on the tree they looked like little soft mounds of snow.

The thought that had struck him that night still caused a tight ache in his chest each time he remembered it. Everything about the Christmas tree was like Kylee: beautiful, traditional, and innocent.

Christmas. How many more Christmases would Kylee have?

Her last CAT scan and MRI had shown the worst news possible. In the last three months the tumor had grown, causing her headaches to worsen. The paralysis that had started in July now claimed the left side of her body. How could something so ugly and cruel be flourishing inside such a beautiful child?

The reality was that in all likelihood, this would be her last Christmas. It had become the unspoken dark truth in their small family.

Yeah, he had good reason to make the monotonous drive out to Cold Creek as often as he could.

He'd promised Kylee a special weekend. This evening he'd take her to the Christmas party powwow in the city at the Indian Center, and then she'd spend the night at his apartment. In the morning before he brought her home, they'd go to Saint Mark's for the late service so she could see the living nativity complete with a donkey, a few sheep, and three camels the church had borrowed from the zoo. She'd been talking about nothing else for weeks, and he'd be damned if he was going to disappoint her. She asked for so little.

Dane knew his time with Kylee was quickly melting away, and there was nothing he could do to slow it down. He took as much time away from his job as he could, but working undercover on a drug sting with the FBI wasn't like putting in an average eight-hour day. He'd given up almost every waking hour for the past nine months working on the case, time he resented not being spent with Kylee. His job ate up not only time but his private life as well. Hell, even his own mother didn't know what he was doing or who he really worked for.

Infiltrating the Big Elk gang had been easy for him. It was why he'd been chosen for the job. The gang leader had grown up in Red Star and had been Dane's father's best friend. Bobby Big Elk had started out dealing pot and crack, but he wasn't happy to discover his suppliers were the ones making all the money. With a recipe he'd paid five thousand dollars for and a few more thousands spent for chemicals and a custom-made mold, Bobby Big Elk was in the designer drug business. Making and selling his own brand of ecstasy proved far more lucrative than dealing pot and crack cocaine, and it was a hell of a lot more profitable than Indian allotment money or a paycheck from an honest job.

With information Dane had already passed on to Special Agents Gaines and Pardue at the FBI, they'd nailed Bobby with a sentence for possession with the intent to sell. They'd hoped with Bobby Big Elk facing an eight- to twelve-year stretch in the federal penitentiary at Wakefield that he'd make a deal and tell them where he was making the stuff. Bobby had refused to talk.

Being in prison hadn't slowed the Big Elks' business down at all. Bobby, the smart one in the family, still ran his business from inside, telling his older brother, Leland, what to do and when to do it.

Selling the stuff and getting kids hooked on ecstasy was bad enough, but the big problem was that some of the Big Elks' dope was killing their customers. The FBI lab had found high concentrations of PMA—paramethoxyamphetamine—in some of the pills they'd confiscated from users and a couple of Bobby's dealers. The chemical increased the highs that drew kids in flocks to buy the Big Elks' brand of ecstasy, but it also could cause some ghastly side effects. The list read like a menu for a nightmare. PMA attacked the body's core temperature, pushing it sky high. With a kid's temperature hitting 108 degrees and higher, their blood pressure and heart rate would shoot off the high end of the chart, and convulsions, organ failure, coma, and death would soon follow.

Going undercover in Bobby Big Elk's mob put Dane in a lot of danger. If things started going wrong, Dane knew that whatever friendship Bobby had had with his father wouldn't mean spit. And although he loved the adrenaline rush that working undercover gave him, Dane hated the lies he had to tell his family and friends.

His mother thought he'd thrown his college education away. She didn't know he'd been recruited by the FBI, that he'd graduated from law school, or that he'd spent a little over sixteen weeks at the FBI Academy at Quantico, Virginia. She didn't know he was now an undercover special agent for the Bureau. The year she thought he'd been wandering around the country working whatever odd jobs he could get, he was actually in the FBI field office in Oklahoma City picking up more experience and training.

Connie White Eagle, like everyone else in Red Star and on Cold Creek, believed her son had quit his chance for an education. She believed he'd come home a failure and that the best job he could get was as a night security guard at the abandoned Bronson Industries property. But Bronson wasn't what it appeared to be. Bronson Industries was a front, a sham business set up by the FBI that did little more than give Dane the reason to carry a gun. The Bronson logo was printed on his paycheck, but the money was actually his FBI salary. It provided the health insurance that covered Kylee's treatments.

Dane shut off the motor and stepped out of his truck, turning his head as the cold wind whipped his hair across his face. Even keeping his hair long had been an order from the Bureau. They liked the look because it was pure Lakota and pure antiestablishment.

From the time he'd applied to the academy, the Bureau had had a specific plan for his future. Indian reservations fell under the jurisdiction of the FBI, and relations between the government and the Indians had always been filled with distrust. Controlling illegal activities on the reservations had almost been impossible. Having an undercover agent who fit right into the community, an agent who not only looked the part but *was* the part, seemed the best solution.

Some of his assignments had left Dane feeling like a Judas, but this case . . . this case wasn't one of them. The ecstasy that Bobby Big Elk and his brother Leland were selling was far from what the name implied.

Dane shook his head. *Enough thinking about work. For the next two days I'm just Kylee's big brother.*

Dodging snowdrifts and carefully climbing the icy porch steps, Dane pushed open the front door and stepped into the house.

He'd grown up in this little government-built, shotgun bungalow, and it didn't matter whenever he showed up, Connie White Eagle's house was always immaculately neat and clean. Heat blasted out of the woodstove in the living room, and the smell of frybread and onions hung heavy on the air.

"Anybody here want to go to a Christmas party with me?" He winked at his mother, who stood in the kitchen turning frybread in the skillet. They both listened to the halting steps coming down the short hallway.

"I do! I do! Take me!" Kylee shuffled into the small living room, leaning heavily on her cane with each step. Excitement put a smile on her lips and a bright gleam in her dark eyes.

"That's why I'm here." Dane crossed the room in three strides and caught her up in his arms.

Dropping her cane on the floor, Kylee giggled and wrapped her right arm around Dane's neck and clung to him. He could feel the ridge of each rib and the heave of every breath her frail body took. Tears pushed into his eyes, but he battled against their spill with all the grit he possessed. Kylee worked too hard at being brave. He'd rather be skinned alive than let her see his tears. He'd save them for the middle of the night when all the lights were out, when he couldn't sleep, and when the sense of helplessness overtook him and tore into his gut.

Kylee nuzzled at his neck through the fall of his hair. "You smell yummy." She giggled again. "Do you smell this good for all your dates?"

"Nope." He laughed, delighted that she felt well enough to tease him. "Just when I take out my favorite girl." He swung her around and kissed her cheek. "Where's your coat, *Taŋski?*"

"Don't. Don't call me little sister," Kylee complained, a slight pout taking shape on her lips. "I'm thirteen, that's almost grown up, and I'm almost as tall as Mom."

He kissed her again, his lips making a loud, comical smacking sound on her cheek. "You can be ninety-two and ten feet taller than Mom, and you'll still be my *Taŋski.*" He gently put her down and handed her the cane. "Are you ready to go, princess?"

"You ain't gonna take time to eat?" Connie White Eagle stepped away from the stove. "Old Clement Runs After brought me some deer."

"The old man's sweet on you," Dane teased.

His mother shot him an exasperated glare. "He's sweet on my frybread." She lifted a golden piece of bread from the skillet and dropped it into the grease-stained cardboard box on the countertop. "I made a good stew, thick gravy with carrots, potatoes, and onions . . . like you like it." She pointed at the stove with a slight lift of her chin. "I got some blueberry *wojapi* and fresh frybread, too."

Guilt gave Dane's conscience a hard jab. His mother had gone to the trouble of cooking for him, but he'd given his promise to Kylee. "Sorry, *Ina,* I told my date we'd hit every McDonald's between here and Rapid City."

With a slight shrug, his mother turned back to the stove and, using the long-handled fork, turned the piece of frybread in the skillet. "It'll keep till supper tomorrow when you bring her back." She glanced out the window over the sink. "Looks like it's gonna start snowin' again. Ain't no way you wanna get caught out here in a bliz—damn it! Damn it!" She dropped the fork on the countertop. "That crazy *suŋgmanitu* is back again. It's out there messin' with Kylee's pup."

Connie rapped her knuckles against the kitchen window as if that would be noise enough to scare off the brazen coyote. "It got every one of Mattie Old Horn's chickens last week. Ate 'em down to nothing but feathers and beaks. Yesterday it chased after her granddaughter . . . the little one, Debbie's baby." She shook her head. "Some kid's gonna get hurt . . . or worse." She turned and looked at Dane. "You got your gun?"

"Yeah." He brushed back the right side of his jacket and placed his hand over the Beretta in the holster clipped to his belt.

Connie White Eagle nodded. "Can ya . . . you know?" She cocked her finger as if pointing a pistol.

Dane glanced at Kylee, worried that seeing him shoot the coyote might upset her.

"Dane, please." Leaning on her cane, Kylee took an unsteady step toward him. "Don't let it hurt Pirate."

"I won't, *Taŋski.* Don't worry." He lightly touched the tip of her nose with his index finger. "No good-for-nothing coyote is going to mess with our champion, pure-bred rez dog."

Stepping out the back door and onto the small concrete stoop, Dane drew the Beretta from the holster. The balance and weight of the gun felt comfortable and familiar in his hand. For a few moments he watched the coyote circle around the doghouse, moving in closer and closer. The white pup with the black patch around its eye was smart enough to stay just out of range of the coyote's snapping jaws.

A gust of wind slid beneath Dane's collar. Ignoring its bite, he gauged the distance to the coyote. Holding the gun in both hands, he raised it to eye level, took careful aim, and squeezed off a single round. The coyote yelped once and then dropped, dead before it hit the snow-covered ground.

"No more chicken dinners for you, or puppy picnics," Dane breathed, looking to his right for the ejected shell. It had disappeared into the snow. He slid a new round into the clip and settled the Beretta back in the holster. Shooting the animal brought him no pleasure, but at least Kylee's pup didn't have to worry about becoming a coyote snack.

Connie White Eagle stepped out onto the stoop beside him. Wiping her hands on her apron, she looked at the dead coyote. "I'll tell Leland Big Elk to come get it. He says he's puttin' together a new set of dance clothes for powwow season. Maybe he'll want the pelt."

Dane stiffened but didn't look at his mother. "You still seeing him?"

"Yeah. He comes over a couple of times a week." She paused for a moment and then continued. "I know you don't like him, but we get along good. I like the idea of a man bein' interested in me." She drew a long, deep breath. "I ain't as young as I used to be." She paused again, pushing her hands down into the pockets of her sweater. "Besides, he does nice things for Kylee. He bought her a boom box to play her tapes on and a pretty red collar with fake diamonds on it for her pup. He treats me good, too."

Dane fought the urge to look at his mother, but he didn't want to see the defiant expression he knew he'd find on her face. "From the new television in the living room, I'd say he's treating you real good." The son in him wanted to warn his mother about the other things he knew about Leland Big Elk and his brother, Bobby. He wanted to tell her where the extra money came from so a jobless reservation Indian could buy televisions, flashy new pickup trucks, and fancy high-priced cowboy boots. But the undercover cop in him wouldn't allow it.

"You tryin' to make me feel guilty 'cause I took a present from Leland, went to a movie in town with him, or like bein' with him?" She punctuated her pique with a small snort. "Eyee, it won't work, Dane." She drew a deep breath. "You don't know what it's like staying with Kylee all the time." The hard edge left her voice. "She's my baby, and God knows I love her with all my heart, but I deserve some good times and some happiness, too. I never got it with your father." She stared out over the snow-covered hills, and her voice softened further. "Just so you know, last week Leland asked me to marry him."

Unable to stop himself, Dane shot a hard glance at his mother and wasn't surprised to find her jaw set in a firm and stubborn line. She'd almost been a baby herself when he'd been born; married at fifteen and a mother six months later. There'd been little happiness in her life, but at fifty, Connie White Eagle still had a pretty and youthful look about her. Only a few lines creased the corners of her eyes, her thick hair still held its coal-black color, and she'd kept her girlish figure. She could easily pass for someone in her late thirties, even for his older sister. When she turned and looked at him, her dark eyes were bright and challenging.

Marry Leland Big Elk? Damn! A sudden rush of cold hit Dane's gut, a chill that had nothing to do with the winter wind that numbed his skin. He couldn't help himself. He couldn't wait for her next words. He had to ask. "And what was your answer?"

She raised her chin, giving it a defiant tilt. "You'll be happy to know that I told him no, that I couldn't. I told him I couldn't . . . because of Kylee . . . because she needs me." She moved her shoulders in a slight shrug. "Leland wasn't very happy. He said he'd help with Kylee, that he had lots of money and could help pay for her treatment, that he could take care of both of us. But I still said no." Her voice cracked with emotion. "I told him my time with my baby was too short to share with anyone who ain't family." She looked up at Dane. "Is that what you wanted to hear?"

It was exactly what he'd wanted to hear. Although Bobby Big Elk was in Wakefield Penitentiary, Leland was following his brother's orders and keeping the family business going. Since Dane had infiltrated the gang, Leland was Dane's contact. Dane had already been able to pass on a lot of information to the FBI that had come from Leland's bragging about drug drops in the city, raves held at the powwows, or the parties held out in the hills. He'd learned who some of the dealers were, but he still hadn't found out where the brothers' lab was, where they made their ecstasy. Finding the lab was at the top of Dane's "things to do" list, but the last place he wanted Leland Big Elk was in his private life, in his family, and in his mother's bed.

Yeah, he wanted to hear that his mother wasn't going to marry Leland Big Elk. *My God, what a damned mess that'd be!*

Dane offered his mother the only warning he could give. "I want you to be happy, Mom, but you know Leland's been in and out of trouble with the law. Just promise me you'll take things slow, real slow, until you know if that part of his life is over. Okay?"

"Big-shot security guard, eh?" She shook her head. "You gonna get your cop friends to run a rap sheet on every man who comes calling?"

Not waiting for his answer and without another word, Connie turned to go back into the house. Dane took her arm.

"*Ina,* wait. I need to talk to you about something else, and I don't want Kylee to hear."

Connie pulled her sweater across her breasts and snuggled down into its warmth. "Hurry up. My bones are freezing out here."

Now that he had her attention, Dane didn't know where to begin. The words kept balking on his tongue. Looking down at the snow-covered stoop, he idly began clearing a small space with his boot. "She's fading away." The words sounded odd, and he barely recognized his own voice. "She's thinner today than when I was here last week." He glanced up and found tears filling his mother's eyes.

Connie's voice trembled. "Ain't nothing we can do 'bout it 'cept keep her comfortable and . . . wait."

Dane looked back down at the crescent-shaped ridge his boot had left in the snow. "She's still getting treatment, right?"

"You mean chemo? Yeah. Not that it's doin' any damned good." Connie shivered and clutched the top of her sweater, drawing both sides together at her neck. "It makes her sick, and she can't eat. She tries hard to make me think there's no pain and she's having a good day or she's slept through the night. She thinks I can't hear her . . . but I do." She scrubbed the back of her hand across her cheeks, wiping away her tears. "Her breathin' gets heavy, and she makes little moaning sounds. Last night was bad." She shuddered and burrowed further into her sweater. "A mother ain't supposed to see her baby die before she goes herself . . . especially not like this, not inch by inch."

Looking at his mother, Dane watched a fresh wash of tears slide down her cheeks. He took her face between his hands, lightly brushed her tears away with a gentle sweep of his thumbs, and then drew her into his arms. "You're a strong woman, *Ina.* You've passed that strength on to your daughter, but I think you're both playing games with each other." He tipped her chin up with his index finger. "I think you should sit down and cry . . . together."

"You do, eh?" Connie stiffened in his arms. "And that's gonna solve all our problems?"

"No, of course it won't, but I think things need to be open between you two. She's got to stop hiding her pain, and you've got to stop letting her."

"Fine talk for someone who ain't here all the time, who don't see what it's like every day." She pulled away. "You know them doctors at the clinic the last time I took her? Big city know-it-alls. They said I was stressed out." A cynical laugh left her unsmiling lips. "They tried to give me some kind of pills to make me feel better 'bout all this." She gave a soft snort. "Ain't no hundred pills a day gonna do that."

"Mom, I . . ."

She reached up and gently stroked down the side of Dane's face. Her fingers toyed with a strand of his long hair, and then she drew his head down and kissed his cheek. "I know you do your very best, we all do, but no matter how good it is, it ain't ever gonna be enough." She gave him a light pat where she'd just kissed him, then turned to open the door. "Come on, you two have a big time planned. Don't keep her waiting."

"Did you pack all her medicine . . . her chemo?" Just like *glioblastoma multiforme,* he hated saying the words *chemo* or *chemotherapy.* His throat always tightened as though he were allergic to them. "Is there anything I need to know?"

"Just make sure she don't forget to take her pills. It's easier for her with food." Connie turned away from the door and looked far out across the snowy field, beyond the white and black pup, beyond the doghouse, and beyond the dead coyote. "That stuff for her headaches is in there, too. It comes already in the needles, and if she needs it, she knows how to give herself the shot. Don't let her double up. Too much is worse'n not enough."

Connie shivered again, and Dane put his arm around her. "Come on, *Ina.* Let's get back inside before we both freeze up solid till spring."

In fifteen minutes Dane had loaded Kylee's small suitcase with her clothes and medicines in the backseat of his truck. Before carrying her out from the house, he unclipped his holster from his belt and set it on the console between the two front seats. The last time he'd carried her, the butt of his Beretta had caught on her jacket, and the gun and holster had been pulled off his belt and landed in the dirt. With the hair trigger setting on the gun, he wasn't about to let that happen again.

Back in the house Dane bundled Kylee in a brightly colored Pendleton blanket. With a final good-bye to his mother, he carried Kylee out to his truck. Settling her in the passenger seat, he tucked the blanket around her legs and up under her chin. Although the truck heater pumped out enough heat to roast a goose, he wanted to keep her from getting even the slightest chill.

The first few minutes of their trip back to town were made in uneasy silence. Kylee wasn't chattering like she usually did. Instead, she stared out the window, the expression on her face unreadable. Mile after mute mile passed before she turned away from the window.

"I know you and Mom were talkin' about me when you were outside," Kylee said, her voice soft yet accusing. She didn't look at him. "I'm not a baby, you know."

So that was her problem. "I know, *Taŋski*, I know. I just wanted to make sure that I knew about the medicines you're supposed to take. That's all. No big secrets."

"*I* know all about my medicines. You could've asked me instead of whisperin' with Mom." She glanced at him. "The doctors and nurses do that, too. It's like I'm not there . . . like I'm already gone." She paused for a moment, then let her breath out in a big sigh. "You should've asked me."

"Yeah. You're right," Dane replied. "I should've asked you." He reached over and patted her knee. "I'm sorry, *Taŋski*. I won't do it again. I promise."

Kylee turned away and stared out the window again.

Another silence spread out between them, and then she quietly added, "Your pitiful apology is accepted."

"Good. I'm glad." A smile lifted the corners of his mouth. She might be within months of losing the biggest battle in her life, but no one could say that his little sister wasn't intent on winning her smaller ones.

Traffic was light. Folks were staying home and keeping warm and cozy instead of fighting the snow. Only one other car, an older dark Chevy about a hundred yards behind, followed them off the rez.

Dane pushed a cassette into the tape player, and pow-wow music blasted out of the speakers. He'd brought all of Kylee's favorites, the Black Lodge Singers, Elk Whistle, and Red Thunder. The miles sped by as they sang along. By the time they'd hit the outskirts of Rapid City, she had sung herself out. Nestled deep into the warm folds of the blanket, she'd fallen asleep.

Dane glanced at her. Even in the early evening light he could see the dark circles under her eyes, the sharp outline of her cheekbones, and the delicate translucency of her skin. She'd lost all of her beautiful, long, dark hair during her last course of radiation treatments, but it had grown back just enough to hold the pretty beaded barrettes he'd bought her for her birthday. He decided to let her sleep. She'd need her energy later to enjoy the party at the Indian Center.

He pulled off I-90 and into the city limits, heading west toward the center of town. The dark Chevy that had followed him from Cold Creek turned off the interstate as well.

Dane shrugged away the uneasy feeling that rippled through him and mentally chided himself. Working undercover kept him edgy, but being suspicious of every coincidence was ridiculous. This was the main exit to the city; anybody heading into town would turn off here. He wasn't about to let his professional paranoia ruin Kylee's time at the party.

"Damn . . . the party!" Slowing down, he turned right at the next stoplight. He'd forgotten the presents he'd bought for the kids at the center. As he pulled away from the stoplight, a quick glance in the rearview mirror settled his other concern. The old Chevy wasn't behind him anymore.

Six blocks later, Dane drove into the parking lot and stopped in front of his apartment. He looked over at Kylee. She still slept. Deciding not to disturb her, he cracked the window an inch and left the motor running. He'd only be gone a moment or two.

Dane bounded up the stairs to his apartment, unlocked the door, and began stacking the brightly wrapped parcels on his arm. There wasn't anything expensive, just some toys and games to put in Santa's sack at the party. As he bent to pick up the last package, he heard the sound. An unmistakable flat pop. Every cop knew the sound too well. Every cop dreaded the sound.

A gunshot.

Adrenaline blasted through his body, burning like hot acid everywhere it went. He pitched the boxes to the floor and raced out the door. Taking the stairs two and three at a time, he grabbed at his waist for the Beretta. His fingers found only his jeans pocket and his belt.

"Jesus!"

The gun was still in the truck. He'd left it on the console.

Dane pushed through the front doors, his eyes quickly scanning the parking lot. The only noise was the slight rumble of his pickup's motor and the faint strains of "Oh Holy Night" playing on somebody's radio. The only movement was the soft fall of cotton-ball-sized snowflakes and the wisp of exhaust from the tailpipe of his truck.

He slipped in the deepening drifts, and the cold night air burned in his chest as he raced to his truck. Fresh tire tracks and footprints dented the snow beside his pickup, and his feet slid in the grooves as he yanked open the door on the driver's side.

Thank God, Kylee was still asleep. Although the blanket

had fallen from around her shoulders, everything seemed all right.

Then it hit him. The realization punched his gut, robbing his breath and attacking his sanity. The strong stench of burnt gunpowder proved that absolutely nothing was all right.

Kylee lay slouched against the passenger door, and her left arm, her paralyzed arm, lay partway onto the console with the palm of her hand facing up. A metallic glint led his gaze to her right hand. His Beretta.

The foul taste of fear filled his mouth, and the hard pounding in his chest expanded and grew until he thought his heart would explode.

Frantic, his cop's objectivity almost gone, Dane dove into the truck. The beam of light cast by the streetlamp and the overhead interior light in the truck highlighted the truth. The star-shaped wound in Kylee's left temple. A trail of blood trickled down the side of her face, and the dark blood splatter on the shattered passenger window only added to the truth.

An anguished wail pushed its way up from deep within his gut and shattered the cold and snowy, quiet holiday evening.

"Taηski!"

2

Mid-April—Pennington County Courthouse

"WOULD THE WITNESS PLEASE GIVE THE COURT HER name and address?"

"Claire Anne Colby, 1438 Sheridan Lake Road, Rapid City."

"And Miss Colby, what is your profession?"

"Actually, it's Dr. Colby. I'm an emergency and trauma specialist at Pennington General Hospital."

The prosecuting attorney stepped closer to the witness stand. "Dr. Colby, please, let me get something absolutely clear for the jury. When you say you're an emergency and trauma specialist, does this mean that you are considered to be an expert in this field?"

"Emergency and trauma patients are the only patients I treat." She turned toward the jury. "Following my internship and residency at Indiana University and Methodist Hospitals in Indianapolis, I also completed a four-year fellowship. I've been in practice for over two years."

"And you are now employed by Pennington General?"

"Yes. I'm currently the assistant director of Emergency and Trauma Services at Pennington."

"So it's safe to assume that with these credentials, Dr. Colby, you know an emergency when you see one?"

A light ripple of laughter trickled through the gallery, only to be silenced by two sharp blows of the judge's gavel.

"Objection," Dickie Buford said, a beat off of being timely. He hefted his bulk from his chair, wheezing with the effort. "Asked and answered, Your Honor. Does Mr. Chisholm have to belabor the point, asking the same question in two different ways? I'm sure the jury understands Dr. Colby's expertise." He pulled a limp, dingy handkerchief from his pocket and wiped the coating of sweat from his brow. He turned toward the jury and offered them a condescending smile. "Even *I* understood her answer the first time he asked the question."

The sound of chair legs scraping against the tiled floor as his lawyer rose to his feet startled Dane. The noise wrested his attention away from the attractive, husky-voiced brunette on the witness stand. He hadn't remembered her being so pretty. He hadn't remembered the sound of her voice being so captivating, either. In fact, he hadn't remembered too much about Dr. Claire Colby at all. Too many other memories about that night were crammed into his head.

Dane looked up as Dickie Buford settled back into his chair. Damn it, what was the idiot doing? He'd told Buford when he'd hired him to just sit, keep his mouth shut, and let the situation ride. The last thing Dane wanted was this broken-down ambulance chaser thinking he was some kind of hot-dog attorney who could win this case. Even if Dane wanted to win, which he didn't, Dickie Buford certainly wasn't the man to get the job done. That's exactly why he'd been hired.

"Sustained," Judge Hamill pronounced. "Move on, Mr. Chisholm. Ask your witness another question."

"Yes, Your Honor." Ray Chisholm turned away from the bench and back to Claire Colby. "Doctor, where were you at approximately seven-thirty on Saturday, December thirteenth, of last year?"

"I was on duty in the ER at Pennington General."

"And how is it that you can be so sure of your whereabouts on that date?" Ray Chisholm stepped closer to the witness stand.

"Not only do I remember the night clearly, but the daily roster and the notes that I made in my patients' charts confirm that I worked that evening."

Dane watched Claire Colby coolly give her testimony. Knowing she would accurately relate each moment of that night brought him more pain than he'd expected. His throat tightened against the ache. He knew the only way to ease the pain was to stop the whole damned charade, and he wasn't going to do that.

Easy . . . just take it easy. Damn, he couldn't lose his cool now. He'd sold his soul to sit in this courtroom and be convicted.

Dane placed his hands on his knees, and, hidden by the table, tightened them into fists, digging his fingernails into his palms. He hadn't expected this reaction to seeing Claire Colby again, but he supposed it was understandable. She was the strongest link that he had to that night. No wonder each word she spoke cut deeper and deeper into his heart.

There had hardly been a day since December when he hadn't thought about Kylee, or dreamed about her, or blamed himself for her death. She existed in every breath he took, every nuance of his life. Denied bail and kept in lockup since he'd been arrested for her murder, there'd been little else to do while waiting out the days and months until his trial.

Aided by Special Agents Gaines and Pardue, the state's case against him was solid. It wasn't any surprise that forensics had matched his prints to those on the Beretta and to the spent shell casing they'd found in his truck. Hell, of course the prints matched—the gun was his. The gun-powder residue, left on his hand when he'd shot the coyote, provided even more damning evidence. The FBI had taken advantage of every bit of information, twisting it, embellishing it, until his conviction was a sure thing.

The empty shell casing in his mother's backyard had disappeared as though it had never existed, and Connie White Eagle had conveniently never been questioned. When the dead coyote couldn't be found, whispers on the rez said that like *Iktomi* the trickster, it had just stood up and trotted away.

No matter how the evidence was manipulated, one question always remained in Dane's mind. Why had some-one shot an innocent child? He'd looked at the question from every possible angle, and only one answer seemed to make any sense. Somehow, some way, his connection with the Big Elks was involved.

The FBI forensics team had found gunpowder residue on Kylee's left hand, her paralyzed hand. This information had been suppressed as well, but Dane believed it was the most important clue he had in his search for Kylee's killer. Was it possible that the shooter had known she couldn't use her left hand? Had the killer first put the gun in Kylee's left hand and then remembered her paralysis and moved it to her right?

Although Gaines and Pardue weren't too keen on the theory, no doubt remained in Dane's mind. The scene had been staged.

Someone had gone to a lot of trouble to make Kylee's death look like a suicide . . . a phony suicide. But why? Who had the opportunity? Who had the motive? The questions had plagued him for weeks. And then in a flash, the insidious reason became clear. The whole scheme had been devised to frame him.

One name kept sliding into Dane's mind. Leland Big Elk. But that didn't make any sense. Dane knew his cover hadn't been blown, and he was outselling every other dealer the Big Elks supplied. Why get rid of the golden goose? But Gaines and Pardue didn't think Leland was involved. They thought Kylee's killer was a rival drug dealer warning Dane to stay off his turf.

To insure his trial and guilty verdict, the FBI added another twist to the charade. The words *mercy killing* were leaked to the press, and then a nasty rumor about Dane being tired of paying for all of Kylee's medical bills sent the TV reporters rushing to film their top breaking news spots. Every intentional twist and turn of the plan had brought Dane to Pennington County Courthouse.

Outside the jail, spring had begun to bloom. Just this morning as the guards were bringing him to court, he'd thought he'd smelled the sweet fragrance of lilacs. The scent had come through an open window, bringing memories of Kylee along with it.

Lilacs. Kylee had loved lilacs. She'd asked him to plant lilac bushes by her bedroom window . . . as if they'd ever grow in the fallow reservation dirt. But he'd planted them anyway, and somehow they'd survived for four hardscrapple years, growing taller and stronger and bursting forth in the spring with their grape-hued clusters of fragrant blossoms. Night after spring night Kylee would leave her bedroom window open so the breeze would carry their scent to her bed. She'd even dried the blooms and wrapped them in little pieces of cloth so she'd have their sweet smell all year long. He wondered if the bushes had survived through the winter and, if so, was his mother still taking care of them . . . for Kylee?

The sound of Ray Chisholm's voice bore into Dane's head and cruelly yanked his attention back to the courtroom.

"Dr. Colby, is this the man who attacked your nurse that night?" Chisholm pointed toward Dane.

"Objection, Your Honor. Inflammatory. No, uh . . . leading. Whatever it is, I object, Your Honor." Dickie Buford half-rose from his chair before Dane could grab his arm and pull him back down. Struggling to be heard, Buford added, "There's no evidence that my client *attacked* anyone."

"Sustained," Judge Hamill ruled. "Mr. Chisholm, I'm getting tired of your attempts to lead this witness."

"Yes, Your Honor. My apologies to the court." Chisholm spread his hands, gesturing as if he'd made an honest mistake and was embarrassed.

Dane knew better.

Chisholm theatrically paused for a moment and then re-phrased his question. "Dr. Colby, do you see the individual in this courtroom who created a disturbance in the emergency department on the evening of December thirteenth?"

"Yes. Yes, I do."

"Would you point him out to the jury, please?"

"Yes. He is sitting at the table over there in the dark blue shirt."

Dane watched Claire Colby lift her hand, a hand that saved lives every day, and point at him. He flinched, feeling the damning touch of her accusing finger jab his conscience.

"Let the record show that Dr. Colby has identified the defendant, Dane White Eagle."

Ray Chisholm was an up-and-comer in the DA's office. Dane had seen him work a few times. Chisholm didn't have all the facts, just the ones the FBI wanted him to have, but he would solidly establish each and every point of the prosecution's case and then try to leave absolutely no room for reasonable doubt. Good. Dane definitely wanted Chisholm to do his job, just as much as he wanted good old Dickie Buford to sit in his chair and keep his mouth shut.

Dane leaned forward, placed his forearms on the table, and clasped his hands. He felt the weight of his braids against his chest, and a bitter sigh fled his lips. Even his long hair bore witness to his guilt. He'd been raised with traditional values and should have cut his hair to show his mourning for Kylee, but the plan—the damned grand plan—wouldn't allow even that.

He turned and glanced over his shoulder at the gallery

behind him. There wasn't an empty seat in the courtroom.
The case had been covered on every television station and
reported in every newspaper throughout the state. Thank
God his mother had decided to stay away from the trial, but
he really hadn't expected her to come. She hadn't come to
see him in jail and had hung up on him the few times he'd
tried to call. Connie White Eagle clearly believed what the
police and the FBI had told her. She clearly believed he
was guilty. He couldn't imagine the pain she was feeling,
pain he was adding to. He could only pray that someday
she would understand and forgive him.

He scanned the gallery again. Not a red brother in the
bunch. *That's no surprise.* Security would probably take
every safeguard against possible problems and keep them
out, or more likely, his own people had decided to shun
him. He recognized a few faces, two of the guys he'd
played on an open hockey league with and one of the girls
from O'Malley's Pub, Megan or Maggie—he couldn't remember which—that he'd dated once or twice. The rest
were courtroom groupies.

Five rows back he found the two men he was looking
for. Gaines and Pardue.

Without any acknowledgment, Dane turned back to
watch Ray Chisholm continue to win the case. The hell of
it was Chisholm didn't know that the outcome of this trial
had already been decided. Chisholm would win, even if he
presented his closing argument in pig Latin.

"Dr. Colby," Chisholm continued, "would you please
tell the court what happened the night of December thirteenth in the emergency room at Pennington General?" He
turned his attention toward the jury, obviously wanting to
gauge their reactions to her testimony for himself.

Claire Colby looked up from her neatly folded hands
resting on the lip of the witness stand and moved them to
her lap. Dane watched her straighten her back and sit taller
in the chair, an apparent attempt to bolster her courage.
Her breasts rose and fell as she took one deep breath after

another, as if to steady her nerves. Then she surprised him. She totally shook him to the core. She turned and looked directly at him, and her gaze locked with his. The moment seemed to stretch, the air between them becoming as taut as an overtuned piano wire. Dane held his breath for a heartbeat or two before slowly exhaling.

"Doctor, would you please answer the question?"

God, she's not just pretty, she's beautiful. The unexpected thought seemed ludicrous coming at this time. Hell, he was in the middle of being tried and convicted for killing his sister, but the thought wouldn't leave his head. In the next instant, he felt a sudden twinge of regret for getting Claire Colby mixed up in this mess, but he couldn't apologize. More than that, he *wouldn't* apologize. There was nothing to apologize for. She'd chosen to work in a hospital ER. If it hadn't been her, it would have been some other doctor.

Why the hell did an exquisite woman like this want to spend her days and nights facing blood and pain and mayhem? Why hadn't she just found herself a rich husband and spent her days doing whatever the beautiful wives of rich husbands did?

He didn't stop the ironic chuckle that suddenly pushed up his throat. That was a damn fool thought. Wasn't he the one who'd always told Kylee that she could do whatever she wanted to do, be whatever she wanted to be?

Had Claire Colby heard his laugh? He didn't think so, but he met her slight frown with a curt nod of his head. He watched her eyes for a reaction. They widened with surprise. Smoky blue. He could see their dusky color and the lush sweep of her dark lashes from where he sat. Her gaze never left his. *Just tell it like it happened, Doc. Just tell Chisholm what he wants the jury to hear.*

He watched her throat constrict in a dry swallow and wished he could offer her a glass of sweet, fresh ice water to soothe her discomfort. At another time, in another place maybe he would have . . . hell, no damned point going there . . . not now, not ever. She hadn't turned away from him; her gaze still met his, and for a moment the courtroom ceased to exist. There was no plausible reason why he felt this attraction to her, unless it was nothing more than realizing that she was probably the last good-looking woman he'd see in a long time.

"Dr. Colby?" Judge Hamill tapped the gavel. "Are you all right?"

"Yes, I'm sorry." She slowly turned away to answer Ray Chisholm's question. "Saturdays are usually very busy in the ER."

Dane immediately felt the loss of the connection between them, and the room suddenly seemed empty.

"I had just finished with a patient," she continued. "I was completing his chart when I heard a disturbance at the triage desk."

"Triage?" Chisholm continued to watch the jury.

She gave a silent nod. "That is where the seriousness of an ER walk-in's case is evaluated, and that in turn determines which patients are seen first."

Chisholm turned back to face his witness. "I see. So, Dr. Colby, is that where you first saw the defendant, Mr. White Eagle . . . at triage?"

"Yes, it was."

Dane bowed his head and stared at the striated patterns of the wood grain on the tabletop. With the tip of his finger he traced along a scar left by someone's errant ballpoint pen, anything to distract himself. The ache in his chest increased. He tried to breathe, but the pain turned into a steel band that coiled around his heart and tightened inch by inch. In the next moment all the words that filled the courtroom would be about his *taηski*, about his beautiful little Kylee.

"Would you please tell the court what you saw, Dr. Colby?"

Dane couldn't stop the impulse and looked up. Claire Colby was staring at him again. He could see the look of pity in her eyes. He'd expected contempt, even disgust, but certainly not pity. Damn her. He didn't want her pity. He didn't want anyone's pity. He'd made the decision months ago to go through this . . . no matter what it cost him. He wanted his guilty verdict, and he wanted it now.

As if she had heard him, she glanced at the jury. *That's it, sweetheart, sell it to them. Sell it to those twelve people who are supposed to be my peers.* Another sarcastic chuckle erupted. *Yeah, they're my peers, all right . . . not a red brother among 'em.*

Dane slumped down in his chair and tried to close his ears and his mind to Claire Colby's testimony. He stared out the window to the sunny April day and willed his mind to go to other places, to think about anything but a cold and snowy December night that ended at Pennington General Hospital.

He failed.

He failed because it was his job to keep his wits about him. He failed because it was spring, and the lilacs were blooming. He failed because he could smell their subtle fragrance all the way through to his soul.

Resigned to the probability that hearing Claire Colby's testimony was part of his punishment for leaving Kylee alone in the truck, he surrendered and listened.

"When I approached the triage desk, I saw Mr. White Eagle."

"Was he alone?"

"No. He was carrying a child, a young girl. She was wrapped in a blanket . . . a bloodstained blanket."

Ray Chisholm turned and lifted a plastic-wrapped package from the bailiff's table. He pulled the Pendleton from the bag, unfolded it, and held it up, showing the large, dark, rust-colored bloodstain. A gasp rolled from the lips of a lady juror in the front row. "Is this the blanket, Dr. Colby?"

"Yes . . . well, it looks like the same one."

Chisholm dramatically held the blanket up toward the jury. The woman juror gasped again. For Dane, the display seemed to last for hours, and he turned away, trying desperately to remember the scent of lilacs instead.

Chisholm dropped the blanket back on the bailiff's table and continued his line of questioning. "Had Mr. White Eagle and the girl come by ambulance?"

"No. Ambulance patients arrive through another door that leads directly into the treatment area of the ER. As I said, he came in at the triage desk. I later learned that he had driven to the hospital, himself."

"Hearsay," Dickie Buford interrupted. "Hearsay, Your Honor."

"Sustained," Judge Hamill replied. He turned toward the court clerk. "Delete the last sentence of Dr. Colby's response from the record." He looked up. "The jury is to disregard it, as well."

Dane leaned closer to Dickie Buford. "Quit doing me any favors, Buford. You're wasting time."

Before Buford could respond, Chisholm asked another question. "Did Mr. White Eagle say who the child was?"

"Yes. He said she was his sister."

"And did he say what was wrong with his sister?"

Claire Colby's voice took on a hollow sound. "Yes. He said that she'd been shot." She tentatively raised her hand and touched her left temple. "In the head."

"Those were the defendant's exact words?'

Claire Colby nodded.

"Please speak up, Dr. Colby."

Dane looked up and found she'd lifted her blue-eyed gaze to him once more. He turned away.

"Did the defendant say who had shot his sister?"

"No, he did not."

"Did he say how she had been shot?"

"No, he did not."

"Was he agitated?"

Chisholm's question surprised Dane, and he quickly looked over at him. *Where the hell is he going with that?*

A frown creased Claire Colby's brow. "No, I wouldn't

say *agitated* is the correct word to describe his emotional state."

"All right, what would you say was the defendant's emotional state that night?"

Dickie Buford's chair legs scraped the floor again as he pushed himself to his feet. "Objection, Your Honor," he rasped. "Dr. Colby is an ER physician, not a psychiatrist . . . or a psychic." His belly beneath his coffee- and breakfast-stained shirt jiggled as he chuckled at what he apparently thought was a clever comment. "Dr. Colby had never met my client before and had no way of knowing what his emotional state was."

One more outburst like that, and Dane vowed he'd let Dickie Buford know exactly what his emotional state was.

"Withdrawn," Ray Chisholm responded with a patronizing smile. He stepped back from the witness stand. "Doctor, would you please describe your personal perception of Mr. White Eagle's demeanor when you first saw him?"

Dane looked at Claire just as she slowly brushed aside a lock of her polished brunette hair from her cheek. Another painful jolt hit him as he watched her fingers tuck the stray tendrils behind her ear. He'd watched those fingers before. Long, slender, and graceful, even when hidden in blood-covered surgical gloves, their actions had been swift, deliberate, and yet compassionate while caring for Kylee. His gaze shifted from her hand to her face, and once again he found himself under her inspection.

Without looking away, she began her answer. "He seemed . . . almost detached."

"Didn't you find that odd?" Chisholm asked, moving closer to the witness stand.

Dane returned Claire's direct gaze. Why didn't she just keep her mind on her testimony and quit staring at him? He stretched his legs out under the defense table and crossed his arms over his chest. *Just look disinterested. Show her, and the jury, that you don't give a damn what they think about you and what you have or haven't done.*

She settled her hands in her lap and finally looked away, her gaze settling on Chisholm. "Mr. Chisholm, from my observations while working in the ER, no two people react the same when they're involved in an emergency. Some, at the extreme, become hysterical, while others seem almost untouched or detached, as though they don't care." She glanced at the jury, then back at Chisholm. "I thought this might be Mr. White Eagle's usual manner of handling an emergency."

"So you think he was uncaring?"

"No, that is definitely not what I said."

Dane tried to keep from smiling. *You lost that round, Chisholm.*

Apparently undaunted, Chisholm continued. "What happened next?"

"He demanded to be immediately taken back to a treatment room. One of the triage nurses tried to examine the child, but he pushed her aside."

"Did he knock the nurse to the floor?"

"Yes, he did, but I don't believe it was on purpose."

Dane watched the stretch of her rose-colored silk blouse across her breasts as she drew a deep breath. For someone who worked in a job that demanded a certain hardness of character to face trauma every day, there was an incredible softness and vulnerability about her. He found the dichotomy intriguing. The phrase *iron butterfly* came to mind.

Aside from her natural beauty, Claire Colby showed a strong cache of integrity. She was the kind of woman who would have attracted his attention anywhere . . . any time.

As if he had spoken his thoughts out loud, she glanced at him once again, only to turn away when she found him looking at her.

"What happened next, Dr. Colby?"

"He shouted that he wanted a doctor." She paused and took a sip from the glass of water that the bailiff had finally set on the witness stand in front of her.

"And?"

"I stepped forward and identified myself. Mr. White Eagle then pushed by me and carried the girl into one of the treatment stations and put her on the gurney."

"Aren't there usually security officers on duty at all times in the ER?"

"Yes."

"Did they respond in any way to the defendant's actions?"

"They began to, but stopped."

"Stopped? Why did they stop?"

She met Dane's gaze once again. "They stopped because Mr. White Eagle told them to call the police, a Detective Stedman at the main downtown precinct."

Dane almost smiled but quickly checked himself. He had been the one to come up with the idea for the code name for Gaines and Pardue. It had come in handy a couple of times when he needed to contact them. *I certainly never thought I'd need it for anything like this.*

"Is it not the law, Dr. Colby, that all gunshot wounds coming into the ER have to be reported to the police?"

"Yes."

"Didn't you think it odd that it was the defendant who told the security officers to call them?"

"No, not really. At the time I didn't think about it one way or another. People pick up a lot of information from TV shows."

Chisholm's questions continued. "When you examined the girl, what did you find?"

Claire dropped her head, looking down at her hands in her lap. Her thick brunette hair swept forward, creating a curtain on either side of her face. "She had been shot."

Judge Hamill leaned toward Claire. "Could you speak up, please."

She glanced up, nodded, then moved closer to the microphone. "I said . . . she'd been shot. There was a single gunshot wound, an entry wound, to her left temple. The exit wound on the right side of her head was . . ." She quickly looked over at Dane, then just as quickly looked away. "The exit wound was much larger."

Dane tightly folded his arms over his chest. His breath shallowed. Each beat of his heart pounded like an excruciating punch to his ribs. He'd never believed that words or emotions could cause physical pain, but he had certainly learned differently in the past hour or so.

Once again he pushed his mind to travel elsewhere, willing the courtroom and everyone in it to disappear into thin air. All he wanted . . . all he needed was to turn the clock back and hold Kylee in his arms again, warm and alive.

"At any time up to this point had the defendant explained how his sister had been shot?"

"No, he had not."

"Did you ask?"

"Yes. I asked because I'd noticed gunpowder stippling around the entrance wound."

"And what would this indicate?"

Claire Colby paused, obviously choosing her words very carefully. "I'm not a forensics expert, but stippling like I saw on the patient, or tattooing as it is sometimes called, generally indicates that the gun has been fired at a very close range."

"You've seen this before in your medical career?"

"Unfortunately, yes."

"Where was Mr. White Eagle at this time?" Chisholm turned and pointed at Dane.

"He was in the treatment station with his sister the whole time."

"Isn't this unusual?" Chisholm turned back to Claire.

"Yes. We usually ask family members to wait in the waiting room."

"And why was the defendant not asked to leave?"

"Because his sister's condition was so grave, so very

grave. There was no chance for survival. She died within five minutes of being brought in."

"When did the police arrive?"

"Shortly after that." Claire slowly lifted the glass and took another sip of water.

"What happened after the police arrived?"

"They took Mr. White Eagle into my office to question him."

"Did he go willingly?"

"No. He didn't want to leave his sister."

"And then?"

"Two other detectives arrived. I think they had been examining Mr. White Eagle's truck."

"Objection, objection." Dickie Buford slapped the top of the table and rose from his chair. "Miss . . . er . . . Dr. Colby did not see them examine my client's truck. Hearsay . . . supposition . . ."

Dane grabbed Buford's wrist and pulled the lawyer back into his seat. Leaning closer, close enough to have the stench of Buford's cheap aftershave and hair oil make his eyes water, Dane hoarsely whispered, "Shut up. I told you before, no heroics."

"Mr. Buford, is there a problem with your client?" Judge Hamill's booming voice filled the courtroom.

Buford looked up at the judge, then shot an uneasy glance at Dane. "N-no sir. N-no problem."

"Good. I'll allow the question. Continue, Mr. Chisholm."

"Thank you, Your Honor." Ray Chisholm turned away from the judge, and his attention zeroed in on Claire Colby. "Doctor, did you hear the detectives say that they had been examining Mr. White Eagle's truck?"

"Yes, yes I did."

"And what did you hear the detectives say they had found?"

"They said they had found a gun and an empty shell casing."

Once more Dane found himself faced with Claire Colby's blue eyes, only this time their look was cold and judgmental. *Good. The lady's made up her mind, and the jury will see that.*

"What happened next, Dr. Colby?"

"One officer stayed with Kylee White Eagle's body to wait for the medical examiner while the two officers took Mr. White Eagle into my office. I soon heard what sounded like a scuffle, a chair overturning, and some shouting. I stepped into the room and saw the detectives restraining him." She paused, looking down at her folded hands in her lap. "They were holding him against the wall and putting handcuffs on him."

"And then?"

From the look on Ray Chisholm's face, Dane knew the DA realized that he was just about to win the case. There was only one last bit of business, and he knew Claire Colby was going to deliver it. Every nerve in his body tightened and zinged with apprehension. He'd given Buford his instructions: no heroics, no TV lawyer-show moves, not that Buford was smart enough to showboat, but he was stupid enough to try.

"Dr. Colby . . . what then?" Chisholm repeated his question.

Tears rimmed her eyes, and when she spoke, her voice filled with the sound of regret. "I heard Mr. White Eagle say that his sister's death, her murder, was . . . his fault."

3

Late April—Pennington County Courthouse

DANE SLOUCHED DOWN AT THE TABLE IN ONE OF THE
straightbacked chairs. Comfort was not an option.

Two police officers had brought him over to the courthouse from lockup, and both now stood guard on the other
side of the door. Before they'd left the room, they had removed the cumbersome manacles from his ankles and unlocked his handcuffs.

"Small favors," he muttered, rubbing his wrists.

He loathed the confines of the small interview room that
was usually reserved for attorneys and their clients. Little
more than ten feet square, just enough space for a small
table and three chairs, it was the only place he could talk
privately with Jack Gaines and Gil Pardue.

His cell in city lockup was awful enough, but this room,
windowless and painted an institutional green, smelled of
vending machine coffee and sour sweat mixed with fear. In
defiance of the No Smoking sign on the wall, the room also
reeked of stale cigarette smoke. The longer he sat in the
ugly box, the smaller it seemed to become. The table and

chairs crowded the space, leaving little room to move around. He chuckled, the sound cold and bitter even to his own ears. *I guess I'd damn well better get used to small spaces . . . quick.*

Dane glanced at the clock on the wall. Three-ten. At three-thirty he'd be sitting in front of Judge Hamill and the jury for his sentencing. There'd be no surprises. There'd be no one pleading for his life or for leniency. It was, as the expression went, all cut and dried.

He propped his elbows on the table, buried his face in his hands, and closed his eyes. "What in the hell am I doing?"

He'd asked himself the same question at least a thousand times in the past few months. It always twisted his gut and caused him to break out in a cold sweat, but it had become a daily mantra since he'd agreed to take the fall for Kylee's murder.

Special Agents Gaines and Pardue had cooked up the bizarre scheme the night Kylee had died. They'd taken him into Claire Colby's office at the hospital, and he'd fought them, not wanting to leave Kylee. He remembered going crazy, knocking over a chair and a lamp before Pardue had restrained him, holding him against the wall while Gaines continued to tell him the plan. The plan. The damn magnificent plan.

Dane raised his head and stared at his hands. When had they begun to shake? *The moment you got smart enough to be scared.* He had good reason to be scared. Being locked up in Wakefield Penitentiary to get close enough to Bobby Big Elk and find out as much as he could about where the batches of bright pink ecstasy tablets were being made could cost him his life. Even if he were able to get the information the FBI wanted, his life would be changed forever. Sure, he'd be cleared of Kylee's murder, and it was possible that his role in putting the Big Elk gang out of business would be exposed, but there would always be folks who'd believe he'd gone against his own people, and worse . . . who would still believe he'd killed his own sister.

His life had already been threatened at least a dozen times in city lockup. There'd be more threats in Wakefield. Some would be just words, but some inmates would try to make good on those words. Asking for secure housing wasn't an option; that would make it impossible for him to get to Bobby Big Elk. If he got in trouble, there wouldn't be anyone in Wakefield who could help him; not even the warden or the staff would be told who he really was or why he was there. He'd be on his own.

Staying alert and watching his back twenty-four/seven was the only way to stay alive. Drug dealers were as common as cockroaches in the federal penitentiary, but you didn't kill a child and expect to stay alive in the pen for very long. Even the worst criminals had their code of ethics.

The sound of voices outside of the room pulled Dane from his thoughts. Special Agent Jack Gaines pushed through the door, assuring the guards he'd be okay alone in the room with the prisoner. He took a seat across the table from Dane and shoved a Styrofoam cup of coffee toward him.

"What's this? A peace offering?" Dane removed the lid and lifted the cup to his lips, grimacing as the hot, bitter liquid insulted his tongue. He set the cup back on the table and pushed it away, ignoring the dark brew that splashed over the rim and puddled on the table.

"Peace offering? What do I need a peace offering for?" Gaines reached in his pocket, took out a pack of cigarettes, and tossed it on the table.

"I figured I'd be in Wakefield by now. Instead, I've been sitting on my ass here for four months."

"If we could've moved this thing along any faster, don't you think we would've, Dane? After all the time that's gone into setting this up, we can't risk anyone outside the Bureau knowing what's going on. It has to look real." Gaines pried the lid off his own coffee cup, and for a moment, watched the steam rise into the air. "Sure, it might've helped if the judge or prosecutor had been in on it, but we couldn't take the chance that somebody would talk." Gaines slurped a mouthful of coffee. "Besides, we didn't want it to look as though the FBI had any formal involvement in this. No matter how we handled the investigation, we'd get accused of going onto the rez and pushing folks around looking for answers. You know as well as I do what would happen then. Everyone would clam up or those AIM guys would come out of the bushes, stick their big collective nose into this, and stir up everybody." He set his cup down on the table. "These things take finesse and time."

"Yeah, time for Big Elk's boys to make a lot more lethal drugs. Time for them to get it out in the city and the rez and ruin more lives and families. Time for more kids to die." Dane fisted his hand and struck the top of the table. "Damn it, Jack. We've lost so much time with me sitting in the slammer, and they've had the same amount of time to run the streets."

"Hey," Gaines protested. "We've picked up a couple of Big Elk's dealers, his gang's getting smaller by the minute."

"Hell, that isn't enough! That's just a drop in the bucket as long as the stuff is out there."

"I know, I know. But beginning today that's gonna change." Gaines reached for the crumpled pack of cigarettes. Withdrawing one, he stuck it in his mouth but made no attempt to light it. Looking up, he saw Dane watching him and gave a slight shrug. "I'm trying to quit."

"You ought to do four months in lockup," Dane replied, unwilling to keep the sarcastic edge from his voice. "It's cold turkey all the way."

Gaines's lips curved around the unlit cigarette in a smile. "It's a good thing you didn't have the habit, eh?"

The flippant remark gave Dane's temper a nudge. *This guy's out there walking around a free man, and I'm in a sweatbox, wearing a damned orange jumpsuit with Pris-*

oner stenciled on the back and eating God knows what with a plastic spoon.

He knew there wasn't a thing he could do about it now or for the next two or three months . . . not until the charade played out. It would be a long time before he'd be free, before he could walk the bleak back hills of Cold Creek Reserve, before he would taste his mother's frybread and *wojapi* again . . . before he could visit Kylee's grave.

Getting her killer would make it all worthwhile.

Another thought elbowed its way into his brain, changing the direction his mind had been taking. Claire Colby. It would be a long time before he would see a woman as pretty. Where in the hell had that come from? He shook his head as if the simple movement would dislodge the thought. No way. It stuck, hard and fast, and mocked him. He closed his eyes, and she immediately materialized in his mind, just like she had almost every night since his trial. Sometimes he could almost smell the subtle vanilla scent of her perfume. The fragrance had lightly ridden on an air current in the courtroom, the smell sweet and pure like lilacs.

Lilacs. The heavy ache returned and filled his soul. It didn't do a damn bit of good to go there, either.

Dane glanced up at Gaines. "Just remember, I'm not doing this for you or for the Bureau. You've known from the beginning that I've had one goal." He pushed away from the table and stood. "We made a deal. I promised I'd go down for *Taŋski*'s murder and spend enough time in Wakefield with Bobby Big Elk to get any info I can about his lab and—"

"And what if you don't get anything from Bobby?" Jack Gaines's words stopped Dane cold. "You gonna bail out? You gonna leave us hanging?"

Dane placed both hands flat on the table and leaned over Gaines. "That's a damned cheap shot, Jack. Remember, it was you white guys who kept breaking your promises, not

us savage redskins." His laughter held a bitter sound. He
straightened up, his eyes never leaving Jack Gaines. "I'll
see this job through, but like I said, you know what I want
out of it." The muscle along the edge of his jaw tightened,
and he drew a ragged breath. "Time's running out. You
guys know as well as I do that the longer it takes to close a
murder case, the colder it gets. We've got to get the bastard
who killed Kylee." Frustration burned throughout his body.
"That's all that matters. And then, as the old song goes, you
can take this job and shove it." He sat down, folded his
arms across his chest, and closed himself off from further
discussion.

Looking somewhat contrite, Gaines took the unlit ciga-
rette from his mouth and rolled it between his fingers. "The
Bureau is gonna keep that promise, Dane." He looked up.
"With no fingerprints in your truck or on the gun but yours
and Kylee's, we're at a dead end, but we're still digging.
And I promise you, we won't stop."

Dane nodded. He still wasn't convinced that the outra-
geous ruse would work, but he was also unwilling to con-
cede that he may have already wasted four months of his
life in jail for it. He could have spent that time looking for
Kylee's killer himself. Hell, what if he never found the bastard? Wakefield wasn't a Boy Scout camp. What if *he* came
out of this scheme dead?

He'd wondered for months whether the Big Elk case
and Kylee's death were somehow linked. The idea
wouldn't go away. And if the Big Elk brothers knew he
hadn't shot Kylee, he'd bet the last breath in his body they
knew who had. He just had to play the innocent, wrongly
convicted prisoner, keep his eyes and ears open, and stay
alive.

He'd already proven himself to Bobby Big Elk out on
the streets. Although the dealing he'd done had been a
sham, selling only to FBI plants, he'd set himself up as one
of the gang's top dealers. Dane figured that for as long as
he worked the sting, the FBI and the U.S. government

would probably be the Big Elks' best customers. Now he'd have to get close to Bobby in Wakefield and get him to spill the information the FBI wanted. But, even when this was all over, nothing could ever go back to the way it was before that December evening.

"Word travels fast on the prison grapevine; you know that," Jack Gaines said, swirling the remaining dregs of coffee around and around in the bottom of his cup. "I guarantee Bobby-boy knows where you are and that you're heading his way." His hand stilled. "And, I'd guarantee that his brother Leland has kept him up to date on you, too."

"Speaking of Leland, you guys better keep harassing the hell out of *that* son of a bitch so he doesn't have any time with my mother. The last thing I need is for Leland Big Elk to become my new stepdaddy." Ignoring Gaines's laughter and changing his mind about the coffee, Dane drew his cup back to his side of the table, lifted it to his lips, and drank.

"The wait'll be over today, and you'll be on your way to Wakefield," Gaines said.

"You make it sound like a damn vacation."

"Quit your grumbling. This is a helluva good thing you're doing . . . for the public and the victims' families . . . for your people, and for the Bureau."

Dane snorted and placed his hand over his heart. "What, no flags, marching bands, and balloons? How about a cheerleader or two?" He shook his head. "Cut it out, Jack, you're killing me."

"You can be a horse's ass about this all you want, but we couldn't have gotten this close without you. Being Lakota gave you the perfect advantage. You knew the Big Elk boys, and you fit perfectly into their gang because you're from their home rez. Nobody would ever guess you were undercover. They haven't yet . . . have they?" Gaines's mood sobered. "I know what you've given up for this: your reputation, your physical freedom . . . and the freedom to mourn your sister's death." Jack Gaines pointed his index finger at Dane. "Whether you like it or not, the Bureau is appreciative, and a lot of other folks will be, too. Don't you think your sister would be?" Gaines dropped his hand back to the table and curled his fingers around his cup. "I don't know how you're dealing with that. I can't begin to imagine your pain."

"You're right. You can't," Dane replied, his voice barely louder than a whisper. "You don't have a friggin' clue."

"She was a beautiful kid," Jack Gaines added, lowering his gaze. "It's a damned pity. What a waste of life. She didn't deserve any of it . . . the cancer or the other."

If he was going to keep his sanity, Dane knew he had to get the conversation off of Kylee. Holding her memory in his own thoughts was hard enough, but talking about her to an outsider scraped cruelly on his soul. He stretched his legs out, crossed them ankle over ankle, and slouched further into the chair. He searched his mind for any topic to change the conversation. "The casinos, like the one on the Pine Ridge, are making a lot of good new turf for Big Elk to sell his poison. The kids have too much money in their pockets and can afford more than huffing paint for a thrill. I hope to hell you've got some guys watching for action there."

Gaines dropped his gaze and nodded. "Two more kids were found on the Pine Ridge last week. We lost one, and the other is still in critical condition."

"Jack, we've got to move faster. This has turned into a deadly epidemic."

"We're doing all we can until you find out where the damned lab is . . . where Big Elk is making the shit." Gaines looked up at Dane.

"I still think the lab is somewhere on Cold Creek," Dane said. "It makes sense to hide it somewhere where everybody knows you, where you fit in and don't stand out like a stranger . . . or an Indian in a white man's neighborhood."

"That's the theory we like best, too, and we're going with it," Gaines responded. "We've been following Leland.

The easy part is when he's in town, but a white guy sticks out in Leland's own neighborhood, on Cold Creek, like . . . well, like a white guy."

"I see your point." Dane grinned, taking in Jack Gaines's bright red hair and freckles. "But what makes you so sure that the Pine Ridge kids had Big Elk's ecstasy?"

"They were holding the same kinda tabs as these." Gaines reached into his pocket and withdrew a small clear plastic bag. Two pink triangular tablets lay in the bottom of the bag. "The lab is running the analysis today, but we're gonna come up with the same results." He dropped the bag onto the table. "Thing is, only a couple of the tablets we've recovered have been bad. The lab found the stuff that's the usual crap and then there's the other stuff that's lethal, the tabs with PMA. We're beginning to think maybe more than one person is mixing."

Dane nodded. "That sounds reasonable. And you're sure it's all Big Elks' dope?"

"It's all being pressed in the same custom mold."

"Waskuyeca wakan," Dane muttered, picking up the small plastic bag and holding it up to the light. "The rez kids call it *waskuyeca wakan,* strong candy."

Gaines nodded. "In town, the white kids are calling it a wedgy . . . 'cause of its shape, I guess. Like a wedge of pie."

"It's supposed to be a tipi, but I don't care if it's shaped like Anna Nicole Smith's ass, it's addicting kids and killing them." Dane tossed the bag back onto the table. It landed next to Gaines's hand.

For a few minutes silence took over the room, the bite of Dane's anger still heavy on the air. Finally Gaines took the unlit cigarette from his mouth again. "We got another kid last night . . . a white kid, here in town. The city cops took him to Pennington." He paused for a moment, obviously watching for Dane's reaction. "Claire Colby . . . Dr. Colby . . . worked on him for over an hour but . . ." He shrugged, then tapped the plastic bag with his index finger. "These were in the kid's pocket."

Claire Colby. Her name echoed through Dane's mind, bringing with it the memory of blue eyes and a mouth with an invitingly full lower lip and an attractive arched curve to the upper. He wearily rubbed his hands over his face. Dr. Claire Colby spent much too much time in his head, and attempts to evict her hadn't been very successful.

Gaines pocketed the plastic bag. "Are you sure you're up to this?"

"It's kinda late to ask me that, isn't it?" Dane replied, thankful to have Gaines interrupt his thoughts. "It's pretty much a done deal, or it will be when I'm sentenced."

"Just so you know, we're behind you one hundred percent."

"You'd better be one hundred percent ready to get me the hell out of Wakefield when the time comes."

Before Gaines could answer, the door opened, and Special Agent Gil Pardue stepped into the room; the two guards followed close behind. Dane could see Dickie Buford pacing back and forth in the hallway outside.

"It's time. The judge and the jury are coming in."

"YOU LOOK BEAT." Julie Jankowski rested her hand on Claire's shoulder. "Why don't you take a break? You've been here over ten hours."

A quick glance at the clock confirmed Claire's suspicions. "I came in about one this afternoon. It's more like thirteen." A tired sigh slipped from between her lips as she pushed away from the doorjamb she'd been leaning against. "And you've been beside me for just about every one of them." She shot a quick glance at Julie. "How do you stay looking so darned perky?"

Julie shrugged and grinned. "Oh, I don't know. Isn't that what a wonderful, great, and dedicated nurse is supposed to do . . . work hard for her favorite doc and be perky? If you haven't noticed, I'm all that and more."

"Oh yeah, you most definitely are." Her response to

Julie's joke may have held some teasing sarcasm, but Claire meant every word. Julie Jankowski was the best thing that had happened to her in a long, long time. *If it hadn't been for Julie, I wouldn't have . . . Don't go there, life's too short.*

She pushed the thought of her ex-husband away, knowing it would be gone for a while but would always return. If the memories didn't come on their own, any of the scars on her body would quickly bring them back.

"So, here it is, two A.M. on a Saturday," Julie declared. "We've had one car wreck, two myocardial infarctions, three brawls with broken noses, one stab wound, and an unusual impacted item in the lower orifice of a very effeminate young man."

"Ah, yes," Claire laughed. "Just another normal night in the ER, and there's not even a full moon." Her laugh turned into a yawn, and she quickly lifted her hand to cover her mouth.

"I saw that." Julie crossed her arms over her chest. "When are you going to learn to say no when our darling Dr. Danson asks you to cover his three-day shift so he can play bounce on the naked pony with his latest babe?" She shook her head, her disapproval clear. "You can barely keep your eyes open, and I bet you haven't eaten since you got here." She took Claire's arm and began steering her toward the door. "Come on, girlfriend. We're gonna take a break and go get something to eat in the hospital barfeteria."

"You mean the cafeteria, don't you?" Claire gave it a moment's thought and laughed. "No, I guess you don't." She hesitated, quickly glancing around the ER.

"They'll do fine without you for thirty minutes." Julie tugged on Claire's arm. "Come on. I'm buying."

A deep growl rumbled in Claire's stomach. She hadn't eaten anything since four o'clock that afternoon when she'd grabbed a tuna sandwich from the machine in the doctors' lounge. In a few short minutes between patients, she'd been able to eat half of the sandwich; the other half still sat on her desk and was probably as hard as concrete by now. The thought made her shudder. "Okay, you're on. I can't turn down a free meal."

As they headed for the door, a man who had just been wheeled up to the triage desk grabbed Claire's wrist. A deep cut marred his forehead, and the skin around his right eye was beginning to turn a dark purple.

"Hey, baby. I hope *you're* the one who's gonna fix me up." He winked with his good eye and leered at her. "I sure could use some tender lovin' care from a sweet doll baby like you. What's your name, honey?"

Claire tried to pull away.

"Come on, sweet cheeks, what's your first name?"

Julie pried the man's fingers from around Claire's wrist and leaned over, meeting the man face-to-face. "Her first name is Doctor." She motioned to the burly paramedic standing nearby. "And this is Duane. If you behave yourself, he'll make sure you get out of here without two black eyes." Julie propelled Claire out of the ER. She snorted. "Saturday night drunks. The worst. The species are better known as assholes."

The main corridor to the cafeteria was almost deserted. Visiting hours had long since passed, and the only traffic in the hallway was marked by the faint squeak of rubber-soled shoes as a few other employees went about their own business. The whir of a floor-buffing machine came from the alcove near the elevators, and the operator's voice on the overhead intercom reported a code blue in room A204. By seven-thirty in the morning, the corridors would be bustling with activity again.

Pennington General Hospital was like a small town. Everyone knew everyone else, and familiar faces always smiled with friendly greetings. It was quite a change from the huge hospital Claire had worked at in Indianapolis.

"Yummy," Julie declared, taking a deep whiff as she placed two trays on the serving rail. "It smells like braised loin of toad, this evening. The house specialty." She selected two pieces of chocolate cake from the display shelf, dropping one plate on her own tray and the other on Claire's. She pointed to the large pan of fried chicken on the steam table. "I'll have that, and mashed potatoes, carrots, and peas," she said to the server. She jerked her thumb toward Claire. "My anemic friend will have the same, but put lots of extra gravy on her potatoes."

"I can't eat all that."

"Well, you're gonna try." Julie plucked at Claire's loose scrubs. "You're getting too thin. I'm not saying you're ugly . . . just too thin." She performed a perfect pirouette. "Guys like a gal with a little substance . . . something they can hang on to." Julie motioned to the server to add another ladle of gravy to Claire's potatoes. "Some good old-fashioned greasy nourishment can help solve your problem." She wiggled, then patted her own hips. "See what I mean? Solid, round, and oh so enticing. Every inch of me is built for comfort, not for speed."

Claire's voice cracked with laughter. "I don't plan on enticing anyone, and besides, all I want is a salad—"

"Well, all you're getting is this." Julie took the heavily laden plate from the serving lady and plopped it on Claire's tray. *"Bon appétit."*

Tired beyond all reason, Claire gave up trying to change Julie's mind. She wouldn't win. Like it or not, a plate of fried chicken and gravy loomed in her immediate future.

They sat at a booth near the window, settled in, and placed their plates and glasses on the table. For a moment or two only the sound of cutlery clinking against the thick china plates broke the silence.

"So, when are you going to let me fix you up with that guy that I was telling you about?" Julie looked up from her plate. "My brother says he's really nice . . . a little shy, but definitely good dating material."

Claire shook her head. "Thanks, but no thanks. I've had my go at dating and marriage. Now I want to concentrate on my career and get my life completely back on course."

Julie reached across the table and patted Claire's hand. "Not all guys are rotten apples who like to hit women; besides, all that is over and done with, and that bastard will never touch you again. It's time to get out there and start dating again . . . if for no other reason than just to have a good time. Kenny and I will even double with you if that would help."

"Thanks, but no." Claire felt the familiar tightening in her stomach that even the most casual mention of her ex-husband could trigger.

"Okay, consider the topic closed . . . for now," Julie added.

"Thanks." Claire felt the knots in her stomach begin to ease, and she focused on her meal.

"Your boy got sentenced today," Julie said, gnawing on a chicken leg.

Every nerve in Claire's body switched onto high alert, making the unease in her stomach seem insignificant. Willing herself not to look up from her plate, she tightened her emotional reins and attempted to look nonchalant. She had tried to catch the news at six and then again at eleven, but one of the broken noses and the stab wound had chosen those times to show up.

For the three weeks since the trial ended, she had been unable to get Dane White Eagle out of her mind. No, if she was going to be truthful about it, it went back farther than that. A day hadn't gone by since the December night when he'd brought his sister into the ER that she hadn't thought about him. He slipped into her mind during the day, and he walked through her dreams at night. *If anyone knew I had this obsession, they'd think I was insane.* A slight groan vibrated in her throat. *Maybe I am.* It was best to keep her interest hidden. Even Julie didn't have an inkling. "What are you talking about? Who?"

Julie snickered. "Ah, so we're going to play that game, are we?" She gathered a fingertip dollop of dark icing from her chocolate cake and slipped it into her mouth. "You're not fooling me. I know you too well." Julie's finger pointed at Claire, then dipped and drew another groove through the icing on her cake before disappearing between her lips once again. "You may be Super Doc in the ER. You may be a wonderfully kind person who likes dogs and babies. But you, Dr. Colby, are a lousy liar." She reached for her lemonade. "I saw you pacing back and forth in front of the TV in the waiting room every chance you got."

Obviously Julie did have an inkling. Feeling very embarrassed, Claire looked up from her plate, her fork stalled midway to her mouth. "I still missed the newscast. We had patients come in."

Julie took a sip from her glass, her eyes never leaving Claire. "Twenty-five years. He got twenty-five years with the possibility of parole in fifteen."

"That's it? That's all?" Surprised, Claire shook her head, unsure if the feeling that washed over her was outrage or relief. "I was positive there'd be more. Life at least."

Julie drove her fork into the pile of mashed potatoes on her plate. "Me, too, but apparently the jury didn't think the prosecution had proved premeditation."

"But he'd told me the girl's death was his fault. I testified to that in court." The familiar and unwieldy weight of guilt settled on her as it had a thousand times before. She had doubted his confession, and yet she'd still testified against him. The thoughts had run through her mind time and time again, but the conclusion had always been the same. The night Dane White Eagle brought his sister to the ER, he certainly hadn't looked like a man hoping for death. He looked like a man who feared it. He looked like a man who desperately sought life.

"Well, whatever they call it, Mr. Cute-in-His-Tight-Jeans White Eagle is on his way to Wakefield Penitentiary to spend a few quiet years contemplating his sin." Julie's words sounded garbled as she spoke around the lump of mashed potatoes in her mouth. "He is a handsome devil,

though, isn't he? Can you imagine that man a hundred or
so years ago in nothing but a loincloth and a feather? Oh,
my Gawd!" She fanned her hand in front of her face. "It's
a horrible shame to take a prime piece of man-meat like
that off the market."

"Not if he's guilty." Claire squared her shoulders. "He's
going where he deserves to go. He committed a heinous
crime. My God, Julie, he killed his own sister."

Julie snorted. "You don't believe that for one minute."

"I testified at his trial, and—"

"You testified to what you saw and heard, not what you
feel. I saw the anguish that you went through. Remember?
I was with you the whole time." She reached across the
table and lightly patted Claire's hand. "The jury may have
chosen the guilty verdict, but neither of us believe the prosecution proved their case without reasonable doubt." Julie
picked up her knife to cut her chicken breast, then raised
and pointed it at Claire. "I guarantee that had he been
white, the outcome would have been a lot different, too."
She lowered her knife and began cutting into her chicken.
"Hmm . . . excuse me, that was my Lakota blood talking."

"What are you saying? Why would the fact he's Lakota
make a difference?"

Julie looked up, a stunned expression on her face.
"You're joking, right? You've been here what, two years?
Can you honestly say you haven't seen any prejudice in
that time?"

"Of course I have," Claire replied. "How can I not notice? But I certainly don't expect to find it in a court of law."

Julie shook her head. "Well, Miss Pollyanna from Indiana, you're gonna find it everywhere where there's Indians . . . or half bloods like me . . . even in this hospital."

DANE SHIFTED IN the backseat of the unmarked FBI car,
hoping to find a comfortable position where the cuffs that
bound his hands behind his back wouldn't dig into his

wrists. After one last night in lockup, he was on his way to Wakefield. Gaines and Pardue had shown up at the jail bright and early, his transport paperwork in hand. They'd taken custody of him about an hour ago, and now they both sat in the front seat of the car. The smell of cigarette smoke wafted back to him. Gaines had obviously decided he'd quit smoking long enough.

The trip out of the city had been made in silence, and as they'd passed Pennington General Hospital, Dane had been surprised to see Claire Colby pulling out of the parking lot. How ironic that she'd be the last person he'd see in Rapid City . . . the one person who had helped seal his fate. He supposed he should be grateful to her.

He didn't know if she'd seen him, but he hadn't taken his eyes off of her until she turned off to the right and drove out of sight. The driver's side window of her car had been rolled down, and the wind lifted and blew her hair back from her face, revealing her delicate profile. Maybe if the timing had been different, if their paths had crossed in a different way . . . *Don't even think of the maybes. White doctors and Lakota FBI agents just don't mix. Hell, white and Lakota anyone don't mix.* He took a deep breath. At least he'd have one more image of her to add to his secret collection.

"You okay back there?" Jack Gaines looked at him in the rearview mirror. "You got anything you want to go over again before we hit Wakefield?"

Dane slouched down and rested his head against the back of the seat. "Just get me there, and let's get this show on the road." He closed his eyes, willing himself to fall asleep.

CLAIRE DREW THE blinds in her bedroom windows, praying that she could keep enough daylight out of the room to get some sleep. Thank God she had the next two days off.

The sheets felt cool and soothing against her skin as she

snuggled into her favorite spot on the bed and closed her eyes. She hoped that sleep would come soon, but her mind was in a whirl, and thoughts of Dane White Eagle kept the sandman at bay. Something had been niggling at her since the trial, and she could never put her finger on it, but now it tapped her on her mental shoulder, taunting her with its simplicity.

Throughout his trial, Dane White Eagle had appeared to be totally disinterested in the proceedings. But anyone who closely watched could see he had been aware, acutely aware, of every word, every movement, and every nuance of his trial. And Dane White Eagle had done absolutely nothing to save himself from prison. After the initial plea of not guilty, he'd done nothing to back up that claim. He'd never taken the stand. He detained his own attorney from questioning any of the prosecution's witnesses except the fingerprint expert, whose testimony hadn't helped Dane White Eagle's case at all. And he hadn't allowed his lawyer to call any witnesses of his own.

Why? He'd pled not guilty. Why hadn't he tried to prove it?

Exhausted, she closed her eyes, pulled the covers up under her chin, and soon the weightless sensation of impending sleep caught her up and cradled her in its embrace.

Somewhere in that twilight journey a dream image floated across her mind and drew her into its depths. Movement stirred around her and caught her up, transporting her to a different time, a different place.

Night surrounded her, and hearing the rustling of long grasses, she turned toward the sound. Running across a wide-open field beneath a full silver moon, the image of a pack of dogs, different shapes, different sizes, different colors, filled her dream eyes. She heard their panting, their low growls, and she felt the rush of wind as they raced by. A slight movement drew her dream gaze to the top of a hill and there, standing with her arms outstretched, stood the child, Kylee White Eagle. The girl pointed at the dogs and spoke, and her single word rode the back of the wind and filled Claire's dream ears. *Iktomi.*

The dogs sped away from her and then, as though a silent command had been given, they slowed, stopped, and herded together. From the middle of the pack, a man rose and stood among them as moonlight gleamed on his naked skin.

His name softly left her lips. "Dane."

4

"YOU BEEN TO SEE YOUR BOY YET?" CLEMENT RUNS
after settled into the threadbare recliner in Connie White
Eagle's living room and set his coffee mug and piece of
frybread on the dinged-up TV table beside him.

"No."

"Ain't right you don't."

"Ain't right you keep poking your nose in my business."
Connie rose from the rocking chair where she'd spent
much of her time since Kylee had died. She slowly moved
to the window and looked out.

The dried-up Christmas tree still lay in the front of the
house where she'd dragged and left it on Christmas Day.
The skeletal branches had turned a dry, rusty brown, and
the needles lay in clumps on the ground beneath them. The
decorations were gone. She'd kept the eagle plumes, tucking them away in a box with some of Kylee's favorite trin-
kets. The paper snowflakes had blown away. The little
God's eyes and other ornaments had been picked off the
tree by Mattie Old Horn's grandkids.

Connie glanced up. The string of Christmas lights still

hung in precarious loops from the eaves. Her voice broke as a large lump rose and lodged in her throat. She fought the tears that came with it. "I ought to . . . yank them damn lights down and take 'em to the dump."

"You ought to take a hard look at what you're putting your boy through."

She wheeled around to face Clement, the flush of anger hot on her cheeks. "What *I'm* putting *him* through? What about what he's putting me through? What about what he put my daughter through?"

Clement shook his head. "You're wrong, *Cuŋski*. Ain't no way he did what they're sayin'."

A moment of silence filled the room, giving Connie the opportunity to respond. She didn't.

"He loved that child too much," Clement prodded.

"I'm sure he'd be happy to know that at least someone believes him."

"Dane needs to know *you* believe him." The chair creaked as Clement leaned back. "He told the court he weren't guilty. How come you don't believe him?"

Connie set her hands on her hips. "He didn't defend himself or let them lawyers ask him any questions." She shrugged. "I figure when you're guilty, you don't want to answer any questions."

"That's bunk. He'd have died before hurtin' that child in any way . . . and you know it."

Connie slowly shook her head. "Maybe he did it so she wouldn't have to suffer anymore. That's what some of them reporters on the TV said it could've been . . . they called it a 'mercy killing.' " She turned away and gazed out the window again. "Good thing *he* didn't get no mercy."

Clement heaved a sigh and then continued. "When did you turn so cold, *Cuŋski*?" Once more a silence spread out between them, seconds becoming minutes before Clement spoke again. "No matter what's been said, you've gotta feel deep down that Dane didn't do it."

Connie faced Clement again. She hit her chest over her

heart with her fisted hand. "You think you know what's deep inside me? You think you know it all, old man?" She dropped her hand to her side. "You come out of the hills and wander down here, what . . . once or twice a month. You got no TV, you got no newspapers. . . . How you know what's inside me or what they said in his trial?"

"How do you know what happened there?" Clement lifted his chin and pursed his lips at her. "Did you go?"

"You know I didn't." Connie folded her arms around her body, tightly hugged herself, and glowered at him. "There weren't no reason for me to go." The lump in her throat grew larger. "It was his gun, his truck, and his hand that left the fingerprints. . . . They got all the proof they needed."

"You call that proof? Bah. Ain't nothin' but smoke and shadows. Of course they were his fingerprints, woman, it was his gun, his truck. That don't take no fancy police work."

Connie laughed, the sound cynical to her own ears. "So now you're gonna tell the cops where they went wrong? It's too late; the trial's over."

"I ain't gonna tell the police nothin', but I'll tell you this: There's somethin' real fishy goin' on."

"Clement, stop it!" Connie could barely breathe. "Why can't you accept what's happened? Quit looking for answers where there ain't none."

Clement lifted his hand, silencing her argument. "Just listen to me." He moved forward in the chair, sitting near the edge of the seat. "Dane told the police that the gun had been in *Taηski*'s right hand when he found her. Why would he make a point to tell them that? Because it was the truth."

"How else was he gonna make it look like she'd done it to herself?" Saying the words brought physical pain to Connie. *My God, how long will it be before I can talk about this without it hurtin' so much?*

"Your son's no liar. No way." Clement snorted. "As tiny and sick as she was, Dane knows the kick from that pistol would've . . . she'd have dropped it. Ain't no way she could've held on to it." He lowered his gaze for a moment as if he knew his words were hurting her. "If he was guilty, he could've said the gun was on the floor of the truck or layin' on her lap." Clement shook his head. "No, he didn't. Hell, he didn't have to say nothin'. No one else but him saw her then." He rested his elbows on his knees and clasped his hands. "If he wanted her dead, he could've just called nine-one-one and let her die before the police and the ambulance got there. But he didn't. He got her to the hospital as fast as he could. That don't sound like no murder to me."

"Stop! Just stop it!" Tears burned in Connie's eyes. "She's gone. I've lost her forever. For God's sake, let her rest."

"If you don't listen to me, and you don't think this through, you're gonna lose your son, too." A harsh timbre that wasn't there earlier now filled Clement's voice.

Connie released a ragged sigh. It was too late for Clement's words to give her any concern. She'd already put Dane out of her life. She bit down on her tongue, refusing to put voice to her thoughts and give Clement Runs After any more ammunition.

"See, it's too awkward." Clement pointed to his left temple with the gnarled arthritic index finger on his right hand, then shook his head. "Nope. If Dane wanted to make it look like she'd shot herself, the wound would have been here." He pointed to his right temple. "Whoever done it weren't very smart. I don't know why anybody'd want to hurt a sweet child, but I think a big part of their plan was to make it look like Dane'd done it." Clement paused, his gaze meeting Connie's. "And maybe the killer figured Dane would look more guilty to the cops if it looked like he'd tried to fool 'em into thinkin' she'd . . . done it herself."

"If this is such a great theory, how come the cops didn't come up with this themselves?"

"I don't know, *Cuŋski*. Maybe 'cause they don't know your son."

"No. It's because the whole idea is ridiculous. That's why." Connie began to turn away, the dull pain in her chest growing with each word Clement spoke. She wished the old man would shut up.

"You think so? Well, how ridiculous is this?" He paused for a moment as if making sure he had her undivided attention. "Whoever it was, and it wasn't Dane, knew *Taŋski* couldn't use her left hand. Did ya ever think about that?"

No, she didn't want to think about that. She didn't want to think about anything, but the old man was working hard to put a wedge in what she believed. "Who are you? Columbo?"

Clement shook his head, and his thin white braids moved against the front of his flannel shirt. A frown creased his dark brow. "Columbo? Who's that? That messy lookin' squint-eyed guy in the trench coat on TV?"

Connie sighed. "See what I mean? You've been up in those hills too long . . . just you and those howlin' coyotes. Maybe we should start calling you *Suŋgmanitu Wacasa* . . . Coyote Man."

"Call me what you want, but I keep my eyes and ears open, *Cuŋski*. I see and hear a lot more than people think." He leaned out of the recliner and patted the seat of the rocker. "Come on. Sit down. We need to talk some more."

She reluctantly settled into the rocker, her eyes never leaving the old man. She'd known Clement Runs After all of her life. He'd been good to her, better than blood family. After Dane and Kylee's father had run off and then got himself killed in a bar brawl, and after she'd put both of her parents in the ground, Clement Runs After had helped her feed her children. He'd made sure they had enough firewood to make it through the winter, and he'd taught Dane how to hunt and fish . . . and helped him grow up to be proud of who he was, proud to be Lakota. Once or twice a month Clement would come out of the hills where he lived in an old two-room cabin, and he'd bring her meat: fresh venison, a few rabbits, or some fish. At Thanksgiving he always tried to get a nice wild turkey. There would be vegetables from his garden, wild apples and berries from the hills, and he'd even shared his commodity allotments of cheese and flour and sugar with her.

There was another thing about the old man that touched her heart. He was traditional to the bone, and he gave her daughter's spirit great honor. Since Kylee had died, he'd never spoken her name aloud again. To do so would keep her spirit earthbound. It was the old way, the old beliefs. He called her *Taŋski* instead, just like Dane always had.

Connie fought the spill of the tears that rimmed her eyes. "Say what you got to say, you old *Suŋgmanitu Wacasa,* and I'll listen. I owe you that much."

"*Hau,* you do." Clement slowly nodded, rubbed his hand over his age-creased face, then tore off a piece of frybread and thoughtfully chewed on it for a few minutes. "Who knew *Taŋski* couldn't move on the left side?"

She shrugged. "I guess just about everybody on the rez. It wasn't a secret." She didn't like where his reasoning was going. "So, now you're gonna send the police knockin' on every door in Red Star or every door on Cold Creek? And are you gonna tell them why you think somebody like Dibs Yellow Knife or Jackson Horse or Jerome Rabbit would want to shoot a thirteen-year-old girl? Or maybe it was old Eula Long Bow who did it. She don't have a car, but I bet she could hitch a ride to the city. Only trouble is, she's ninety and lost her leg last winter from the diabetes."

Clement snorted. "I won't even answer your foolishness. There are only two things that matter." He held up one finger. "Your boy didn't do it." He held up a second finger. "And someone who knows you did."

"You're the one talkin' foolish. If Dane is so innocent, why is he in Wakefield?"

"Why don't you go ask him?"

"Why don't you stop pushing? My mind's made up."

"If your car won't make the trip, I can borrow Sidney

Old Horn's truck and take you up to Wakefield sometime. It would be a good thing."

Connie set the rocker into motion. The rhythm soothed her. "Leland goes up to see his brother every week. Bobby's told him he's talked to Dane. I got all the news I need without having to go nowhere." She clenched her teeth, wishing Clement Runs After would drink his coffee, eat his jellied frybread, and go home.

"I don't know why you waste your time with that Leland Big Elk. He's been trouble all of his life . . . just like his brother." Clement licked a dab of grape jelly from his finger. "He's gonna end up where Bobby is, you watch it happen, and when it does, who you gonna have then?"

Connie's temper flared. "Leland is a good man, a good friend. Who do you think was here for me all the time when my daughter died? Who do you think paid for her coffin and bought that beautiful gravestone she's got?" She drew a deep breath, hoping it would calm her. It didn't. "Who do you think takes me up to the cemetery so I can put flowers on her grave? And who do you think holds me when I cry 'cause I miss my girl so much?" She shook her head, trading her anger for the pain that surged through her body from head to toe. "It sure ain't my son." She swiped at the tears rolling down her cheeks. "He's the one that put her there."

Clement bowed his head as though the fight had completely seeped out of him. "Your father was my best friend. We were like brothers, me and him." He looked up, his rheumy gaze meeting Connie's. "That makes me your *lek-ski,* your uncle, and you're my niece, my *cuŋski.* Your children have always called me Grandfather, *Tuŋkasila*, and in the old traditions that makes us family, *tiospaye.*"

"I don't need no lessons in Lakota, I been talkin' it all my life." Connie scowled at him.

"I'm just sayin' what gives me the right to say these things to you. That's all." The sound of his deep sigh filled the room. "A lot of other folks have been here for you . . . including me." He dropped his gaze and toyed with the dented copper bracelet that encircled his left wrist. "You're wrong about Dane . . . and you're wrong about Leland Big Elk, but you ain't gonna listen to what I got to say . . . at least not now." He looked up at her. "I don't understand you, *Cuηski*, I don't understand why you don't believe your son."

She stiffened. His voice had been soft, and she'd heard the sound of resignation in it. "Don't you think I want to believe him? Don't you know I'm torn apart inside? But what good does it do? There's no forgiveness in my heart. It's empty."

Clement bowed his head, sat silent and still for a moment, then gripped both arms of the recliner and slowly pushed himself up from the chair. He tottered for a second or two on his bowed legs before finding his balance. His gaze never left Connie. "Well, I guess this old Coyote Man is gonna go wander back up to the hills." He stopped in front of her. "Take a hard look at who your boy is, how he's been raised. He believes the way our old people taught him, how you taught him . . . and how I taught him. Killin' weren't any part of that. He's got pride in the old ways, and he honors his family and himself. He had the gumption to go off to school . . . law school, and—"

"And then threw it all away." She threw her arms up. "For what? A yearlong fling that took him to God knows where; the postcards came from all over . . . Virginia, Oklahoma City, Chicago. Then when he came home, the only work he could get was as a night security guard in an empty warehouse."

"That's an honest job," Clement quietly replied. "That's more'n your good friend Leland's got."

Clement's words cut through her argument like a knife, and Connie began to feel the strong touch of defeat. She wrapped her arms around herself. "I have no son."

The old man harrumphed and slowly shook his head. "You got no brain." He made his way to the front door and, opening it wide, stepped out on the front stoop. He looked up at the string of Christmas lights. "Yup, I think you oughta take these things down. They're too bright and cheery to belong to a woman who'd rather keep herself in the dark."

DANE LEANED AGAINST the high brick wall that surrounded the recreation yard. Keeping your back to the wall was a good way to stay alive in Wakefield. Maximum security, level five, Wakefield was home to some of the worst prisoners in the system. In the two months he'd been at Wakefield, he'd met some of these inmates head-to-head. Showing them you wouldn't back down was as important as breathing; it could mean the difference between life and death. There had been some tense moments. Being the new fish on the cellblock could be unhealthy, but most now knew he was one of Bobby Big Elk's boys. The majority of the threats and challenges had eased off, but Dane knew better than to let his guard down. There were always a few renegades in the tribe.

He glanced up, enjoying the touch of the hot July sun on his face. An hour a day in the yard was hardly enough to satisfy his love for being outdoors, but considering where he was . . . an hour was better than none.

He squinted against the sun's glare as it glinted off the three rolls of razor wire that topped the fifteen-foot wall. It amazed him to see the birds flitting in and out through the coils, never clipping a wing or nicking a foot. The birds might be able to survive the razored edges of the wire, but not too many prisoners would be stupid enough to take their chances going over it. The guards in the towers, every one a trained sharpshooter, also made a man think more than once about trying to escape.

"You've been keepin' yourself alone, homeboy," Bobby Big Elk said, settling next to Dane. "Some of the brothers are beginning to wonder if maybe you're bein' an apple—you know, red outside and white inside."

Dane had set his game up very carefully since he'd arrived at Wakefield. Take it slow. He knew if he rushed Bobby Big Elk, tried to get close too soon, it would make Bobby and the others suspicious. If he bided his time, he knew Bobby would seek him out. The plan was working.

"An apple, eh," Dane replied. He shot a hard glance at Bobby, only to see him shrug with an obviously counterfeit apology.

"Word gets out how many times your white pals come visitin'. So, what's with that?" Not looking at Dane, Bobby pulled a banana out of his back pocket and slowly began to strip the peel.

A burst of adrenaline sent Dane's pulse scrambling. The last thing he needed after all this work and time was for anyone to get wary or have his cover blown. He didn't answer. Maybe it would be safer to let Bobby come up with his own answers.

Half of the banana disappeared into Bobby's mouth. "I told 'em, like you said. You got new lawyers 'cause your first guy was so lousy." He chuckled. "But they could be cops pumpin' you for info about my little business." Bobby stepped closer and peered into Dane's face, pushing for an answer. "Am I right?"

"Right about which one? Lawyers or cops?" Dane pushed back. "What do you think, *kola?* I worked too damned hard out on the streets for you to call me a squealer. What makes you think the cops know about that? What makes you think I'd roll over on you?" Breathing a disgusted grunt, he shoved away from the wall and began to walk off. *Stay cool. Keep it cool.* Telling Bobby that Gaines and Pardue were his new attorneys was the only way he could meet with them without anyone getting too curious. After a few steps, he turned and confronted Bobby Big Elk again. "I made damned sure nobody knew who was supplying me."

Bobby slid the rest of the banana into his mouth. "No one else's pills look like mine."

"So? Who says yours were the only ones I was pushing? Besides," Dane continued, turning back to Bobby, "what put me in here doesn't have a damned thing to do with you."

Bobby looked at Dane for a few moments, then shrugged. "What put you in here was a bum rap. Everybody knows that." Bobby flipped the empty banana peel over the fence. It caught and dangled for a moment on the razor wire, then split in two and fell to the ground. "Ain't no way you did that shootin'."

"You think?" Dane snorted. "Maybe you know who killed her."

Bobby shook his head. "I'd like to help you, *kola,* but I ain't heard nothin'. I was in here when it happened."

"Maybe you ought to go tell the judge and jury that I'm innocent."

Dane turned and walked away, sticking to the perimeter of the yard.

"They hear it all the time, and don't pay no attention." Bobby kept stride with him. "Ask any one of us in here. Hell, we're all innocent." He laughed and slapped Dane on the shoulder. "Maybe your new lawyers can get ya an appeal."

"Yeah, maybe they can." Gaines and Pardue had everything in place for just that.

"Bad part of you bein' in here is that I'm losing good fast cash. Leland told me you'd set yourself up quite a good bunch of regulars."

"You're not losing anything. Users are users. If they can't find their usual supplier, they'll buy from someone else."

Bobby slid a sidelong glance at Dane. "So, if you're innocent, you got any idea who done it . . . your sister, I mean?"

Dane's step faltered, but he quickly caught himself. "I know what you mean." He fought to cover his emotions. He forced himself to relax, surprised how easy it was to re-gain the facade. *Maybe I've been doing it too well for too damn long.* He kept walking, deliberately not answering Bobby's question and finding that keeping quiet was one of the most difficult things he'd done since coming to Wakefield.

"Okay, *kola,* I get it," Bobby said. "The subject's off limits. That's cool."

They continued walking along the fence in silence, the hour in the yard almost over.

Bobby stopped when they reached the row of benches just outside the prison chapel and sat. He leaned forward, set his elbows on his knees, and clasped his hands. Dane joined him on the bench. Neither spoke for a moment. Bobby looked up at the guard towers, then his gaze swept the yard. "There's somethin' else I gotta ask you."

Again, Dane didn't let his guard down. "Ask me what?"

"I been hearin' word about some of our E causing trouble . . . big trouble. You know anything?"

"You don't know? Leland hasn't said anything?" *Tug the bait and catch the big fish.* Clement's words slid into Dane's mind as though the old man were standing next to him.

"No. It's somethin' I heard on the iron bar internet."

Dane laughed. "So, is that what they're calling the old grapevine, now?"

"Hey, this is serious shit. I got word that they're getting ready to give me some bus therapy and ship me off to the pen in Terre Haute. I gotta make sure things are tight here if they do. I gotta know what you've heard." Bobby Big Elk's voice had an apprehensive ring to it. "I don't got a TV like some guys here. Leland was supposed to bring one, but it never showed up. I got no way to get all the news."

Dane almost laughed aloud. Bobby Big Elk's TV was sitting in Connie White Eagle's living room. *It's time to set the hook.* "Before I came here I'd heard that a couple of kids died." Dane shrugged, trying to look as indifferent as possible. *Give the bait a good hard yank.* "I don't know how true it is, but the TV news said something about bright pink ecstasy pills being found in their pockets."

Bobby Big Elk looked like he'd been punched. "That don't mean nothin'. Could be anybody's pills."

"The news mentioned they were triangles, like a tipi."

Bobby dropped his head into his hands, then quietly asked, "How'd they die?"

Gotcha. Dane glanced at Bobby. "The cops tested the stuff. They found something called PMA in the pills."

Bobby straightened up and looked at Dane. "PMA? What the shit is that?"

Dane shrugged his shoulders. "Paramethoxyamphetamine."

"Where'd you learn that?"

"I read a lot," Dane replied.

"So, what the hell is it?" Bobby began to shuffle his feet.

"It's a chemical that's supposed to give a bigger and better high, but too much does something crazy to the user's temperature and blood pressure when they're wiggin'." He glanced at Bobby. "That's what they said killed them . . . the PMA." He looked out over the recreation yard. "It sure wasn't the touchy-feely kind of high the kids were lookin' for."

"Aw shit." Bobby Big Elk quickly stood and paced back and forth in front of Dane. "Son of a bitch! There weren't a damned thing wrong with the stuff I'd mixed up before I came in here, and I ain't never used that . . . that PMA shit." He punched at the air. "Leland! The fuckin' idiot." He stopped, turned, and looked down at Dane. "Damn Leland's been playin' big shot again, thinkin' he can take over and run the whole show. He's good out on the street, but he don't know crap about making the stuff." Bobby fisted his right hand and drove it into the palm of his left. "He's gonna take us all down. If he's messed with the recipe, they can get us on a murder rap . . . all of us." Bobby kicked at the dirt with his heel. "I'm gonna ream him a new one when he shows up here again."

The big fish is hooked, time to put him in the cooler. "Maybe he needs help in the lab. There's a guy I know on the outside, he can be trusted. He knows how to mix. Maybe he could—"

Bobby vigorously shook his head. "No. No way. Only Big Elks work the lab. It's hidden good, and we're the only ones who know where it is . . . and that's the way it's gonna stay. None of our guys know where it is, not even you, *kola,* and it ain't gonna change. I don't want no outsider poking in my business. Family doesn't snitch. Outsiders do." He paced a few steps, then returned to Dane. "I'll tell Leland to quit playin' big chief and dump the batches he's made." Bobby punched the air again. "Damn it, he's got shit for brains!"

Dane stood. "As long as you're in here and he's out there, you're losing control."

"So what am I supposed to do, fly over the damned razor wire and straighten everything out?"

Dane tried to look sympathetic. "Seems like you've got yourself a loose monkey." He stepped into line with the inmates filing out of the yard, leaving Bobby Big Elk to agonize about his problems on his own.

5

THE ORDER FOR LIGHTS OUT ALONG THE CELL ROWS
at Wakefield never meant complete darkness. The overhead lights were dimmed but never turned off, and those in
the guard stations stayed bright all night.

Wide awake, Dane lay on his cot. Sleep eluded him.
He'd tossed and turned on the narrow bed for what seemed
like hours and finally gave up. Lying on his back, his hands
clasped behind his head, he listened to the night sounds
echoing throughout Cellblock 3. There were always whispers and coughs, snoring, moans, and sometimes, like tonight, crying. *I bet it's the new kid they brought in this
afternoon.* He was probably no more than eighteen or
twenty, but his smooth-skinned baby face and slim body
made him look too young to be away from home. It also
made him fair game for . . . *When the hell did I become
such a bleeding heart? If he's in Wakefield, the maza tipi,
the iron house, he's been a bad boy.* A cynical chuckle
filled his throat. *And what's my excuse?* Young kids like
that had a real tough time in prison. *He's prime bait for*

some big daddy. Dane shuddered, hating what the system made of men . . . or did to them.

The faster he got out of Wakefield, the happier he'd be. The time he'd spent in the setup of the sting, waiting for his trial and sentencing, and in Wakefield itself hadn't paid off, but it had still been worthwhile. Bobby Big Elk had given him some of the information they wanted, but not all. Hearing about the kids who were dying from some of his ecstasy tabs had really knocked Bobby for a loop. He'd looked like a man facing death row, and if the FBI could make their case, both Bobby and his brother Leland would be.

Bobby had dropped the names of a couple of his chemical suppliers, he even told Dane whose recipe he used for the tabs, but he'd always stopped short of saying where his lab was. There'd been another piece of good information, though, that had made it all worthwhile. Dane now knew where Bobby Big Elk's weakest link was: Leland.

The corner of his mouth lifted in a slight smile. If Bobby wasn't going to crack, Leland would.

It was time to move, time to put the next phase of the plan in gear, time to use his Get Out of Jail Free card. Gaines and Pardue were coming to Wakefield in a couple of days to get things rolling, and both Leland and Bobby Big Elk were in for a big surprise.

"Hey, White Eagle, you awake?" The hoarse whisper came from the next cell; Lucien Primeaux, a two-time lifer for first-degree murder. A Cree from Turtle Mountain, Lucien's accent was a unique mixture of Indian, English, and French. "I got a message for you from up da row."

Dane didn't move. "Yeah? Who's sending me voice mail this time of night? Something sweet, I hope."

"Mon Dieu, but you da real smart-ass Injun. Maybe you jus' better watch dat mouth of yours 'fore it get you hurt."

"Thanks for the heartfelt concern, Primeaux. What's the word?"

"You got to give me somethin' 'fore I tell you."

Dane laughed quietly. "Yeah? Since when? Play your scam on someone else. I'm not a green fish anymore."

"Mais oui, but two months in dis place don't make you a long john, either."

"Just pass the damn message."

"Avec plaisir, mon ami, wit pleasure." Primeaux chuckled. "Somebody don't like you much. He say he gonna stick you for what you done to your sis. He say he got hisself a nice brand-new sharp shank he been makin'. He don't think da court done a good enough job for dat little girl, so he gonna take care of it here." He sniggered again. "Be careful, *mon bon ami,* it come any time, any place."

"You can pass *this* message back up the line. Tell whoever it is to fuck off and quit ruining my sleep."

Primeaux laughed. "Don't worry, big Injun, I'll send da mail, but if dat guy do his job, you be getting a lot of sleep real soon. You be takin' da dirt nap for a long time. *Bon chance, mon ami."*

Dane rolled over onto his side, stared at the gray concrete wall, and listened to his message being passed up the row. There was no way of knowing who had sent the original; not a single inmate on the message line would tell. It could even have come from another tier. It seemed ironic, but nothing was tighter than the prison code of ethics.

"To hell with it," Dane muttered. No point getting all bent out of shape about Primeaux's words. It wasn't the first threat he'd received in the two months he'd been in Wakefield, and he didn't expect it would be the last. He closed his eyes, tried to push all thoughts of anything from his mind, and waited for sleep.

When sleep finally came, it brought the dream, the dream that had come to him almost every night since he'd arrived at Wakefield . . . the dream of a pack of rez dogs running hard across the bleak and treeless hills of Cold Creek Reservation.

He was never an observer in the dream but always a participant. Completely surrounded by the dogs, he ran with them on four legs. His muscles burned with the speed, his body bent to the chase, and his mind totally melded with the pack.

Fog lay over the ground. It pocketed in the little hollows and gullies and filtered through the scrub brush and tall buffalo grasses. Its touch felt moist and cool on his body, and it carried the pungent scent of cedar.

The pack raced up the rise and down the other side, through a creek bed, and across an open field, the pace dizzying and relentless. Stragglers were not tolerated. The dogs pushed through the wispy haze, dividing it, and leaving a clear trail, distinct proof of their passage.

On the other side of the wide field, the pack hurtled up the slope of another hill, the muscles in their hindquarters bunching then stretching over and over again, driving them up the steep grade. As he ran, the wind whipped against his face, and he bared his teeth against its blast. His lungs burned as his panting breath drew air into his body and ached as the air left him in a pain-filled bay.

Suddenly returning to his human shape, he stumbled and fell. Splayed out on the ground, his hands grasped at the buffalo grass. The pack of rez dogs did not hesitate, nor did they notice he'd left them. Without even a backward glance, they continued up and over the crest of the hill and disappeared from sight. He lay still and alone in the dry buffalo grass. Even the wind had left him.

Looking up, where there had been nothing before, a single tree, dark and lonely, now stood shrouded in the fog-veiled sky. Twisted by time and weather, its branch tips reached out in all directions, crooked and gnarled like claws. Beneath the tree, becoming more visible as the mist shifted and swirled, a young Lakota girl stepped forward. Clad in white buckskins, she gazed down the slope at him. A light wind that did not touch him or move the grasses

around him teased at her long black hair and moved the
fringes on her dress. Her mouth lifted into a gentle smile,
and she reached her hand out to him.

His heartache returned. She was the sweet child he'd lost.

As his dream eyes watched, another form appeared on
the hilltop, a woman. She stepped out of the fog and joined
the girl beneath the tree. The phantom wind touched and
caressed her, too, lifting her long coffee-brown hair and
bringing a soft blush to her cheeks. Her blue-eyed gaze fell
on him, warmed him, and a swelling of hope filled his soul.

And then, their voices blending together, they spoke,
saying nothing more than a single whispered word. *"Iktomi."*

Dane bolted upright. Wide awake, he gasped for breath
as his heart frantically sought its normal rhythm. Leaning
forward, he buried his face in his hands and prayed that he
hadn't made a sound, and if he had, that no one on the cell
row had heard him. He shivered, the night air touching the
sweat that coated his chest and shoulders. *This is crazy.
This damned dream has come almost every night since I
got here.* He drew one steadying breath after another. *You'd
think I'd be used to it by now.*

Dane stood and, ignoring the cold touch of concrete on
the soles of his bare feet, began to pace his small cell. Five
steps, back and forth. He knew without a doubt who the
girl and the woman in his dream were. Kylee and Claire
Colby. And, no matter how many times the dream came to
him, the puzzle always remained. It would make sense if
his mother were in the dreams with Kylee, but Kylee and
Claire Colby? That didn't make any sense at all.

"Iktomi." He barely breathed the name. *The trickster.
The shapeshifter. What the hell is that all about?*

The dream always left him feeling uneasy when he
awoke, and no matter how hard he tried to erase it, the disquiet clung with a tenacious grip. He tried to put reason to
the dream and its persistence, but the explanation always
remained elusive.

Clement had once told him that the old people believed dreams had great meaning. The old ones said they could foretell the future, give answers to a problem, or provide a warrior with strength and knowledge. *Or drive the dreamer mad. Which is it with this dream, Clement, you old* tatanka? *Wisdom or madness?*

He sat on the edge of his bunk and drew his blanket across his lap. Divining dreams was certainly not covered in the FBI handbook. *Where are you when I need you, Tuηkasila?* He shook his head and softly laughed. *Where am I when I need you?*

HER ELBOWS RESTING on her desk, Claire rubbed her eyes, drove her fingers through her hair, then rested her forehead against the palms of her hands. She'd spent the last two hours at her desk trying to bring a stack of patient charts up to date. Exhaustion had seeped into her body with each passing minute. Being off for a few days had helped some, but she'd been having trouble sleeping, and another fourteen-hour shift had put her at the edge again.

"You got a few minutes?"

She looked up to find Julie at her office door. "Sure, of course." She waved her friend in. "Close the door and sit."

"Phew," Julie sighed, plopping down on the sofa that sometimes doubled as a bed when Claire pulled all-nighters. "We've had ourselves another busy night."

"What are you doing back? I thought you'd gone home hours ago."

"I did," Julie replied, propping her feet up on the couch. "I'm doing a split shift tonight."

Claire pushed the charts aside. There were only a few left to do, and she could finish them later. She wanted to talk with Julie about her plan, and now was as good a time as any. "I'm glad you came by. I have something I need to tell you. . . ." She hesitated, uncertain how to begin. *Straight up and direct is best, I guess.* "I'm leaving Pennington."

Julie swung her legs off the couch, dropped her feet to the floor, and leaned forward. "What? Why? Where are you going? When?"

Claire held up her hand. "Slow down. You know I've been wanting more than just trauma work. It doesn't satisfy me anymore."

"Claire, for God's sake, if you want satisfaction, get yourself a man!"

"Please, don't start that again, not now. This has nothing to do with my social life."

"Or lack of it," Julie gibed.

Choosing to ignore the remark, Claire continued, "It's all about what I do ten, twelve, fourteen hours a day."

"Okay, I'll be quiet and listen. Talk to me."

Claire drew a deep breath and began. "I don't know what happens to most of my patients. They come in, we patch them up, and then they go to surgery, ICU, or out on a nursing floor, and I never see them again."

"Yeah, so?"

Claire glanced at the stack of charts on her desk, then back to Julie. "Don't you ever wonder how they're doing when they leave the ER? Don't you miss seeing them get better and well enough to go home?"

"You're kidding, right?"

"No. No, I'm not."

"All you have to do is check on the computer to see what's going on with them or go up to the nursing units."

"That's not enough. It's not the same," Claire replied. "I want to see my patients more than just once in the ER. I want to get to know them, help heal them, feel satisfied when they're discharged and go home. I miss being part of that process. I want to be actively involved in patient care." She sighed. "I'm tired of bullet holes and knife wounds, smashed bodies from car wrecks . . . and the overall insanity of the trauma unit."

"But it's exciting. Claire, you're a fabulous ER doc; besides, you're at the cutting edge of everything."

"It's like that for you maybe, but I want to spend time with patients, see their daily progress."

Julie leaned back against the sofa cushions. "So, what's your plan? You buying into a private practice?"

"No. I don't have the kind of money that takes. I've decided to do something else." Knowing Julie wasn't going to like her idea, Claire's words came with hesitation. "For the last couple of months I've been looking at other possibilities here at the hospital and didn't find anything I wanted. So I began looking outside. I want to go back to a general type of practice."

"Where?"

"There's . . . a clinic job that opened up, and . . . I took it."

"Here? In town?"

"No."

"Are you going to make me drag every word and bit of information out of you, piece by piece? Where?"

"Indian Health Services. One of the reservations needed a doctor, and I applied . . . and got the job."

"What?" Julie quickly stood and, with her hands on her hips, moved to the edge of Claire's desk. "Are you nuts? You've got to be kidding, right? No one in their right mind voluntarily goes to work for Indian Health Services, especially not someone like you who already has a great job." She rolled her eyes and expelled an exasperated sigh. "With Dr. Porter retiring early next year, they'll probably move you up to his spot. You'll be director of ER and Trauma. My God, Claire, do you really want to throw that opportunity away for IHS? You'll ruin your career." She leaned forward and pressed both hands on Claire's desk. "They'll send you off in the boonies somewhere, and you'll constantly be fighting bureaucracy for supplies and equipment. Where are you going to find good, trustworthy employees . . . and keep them? You'll be responsible for everything."

"I know. I'm looking forward to it."

Julie straightened up, shook her head, paced a few steps, then turned back to face Claire. "If you're lucky, the housing will be adequate—that means there's a roof on the building and hopefully a toilet on the *inside* of that building."

"It can't be that bad."

"Oh, no? Come on Miss Pollyanna, would I lie to you? On some reserves it comes close." She shook her head. "You're unbelievable. Where are they sending you?"

"Red Star. It's a little town on Cold Creek Reserve. Red Star has the only clinic on the whole reservation."

"Aw, hell." Julie threw herself back onto the sofa. "That's one of the poorest reserves in the country." She buried her face in her hands, then looked up. "Do you know what happened to the last doctor they had there?"

"No."

"Well, neither does anyone else. He walked out of the clinic one day, and no one's seen him since."

"You mean he completely disappeared?"

"Yeah. Poof. No trace of him anywhere. The tribal police said he must have gotten lost up in the hills. His car was gone, but everything was still in his house. It had been messed up, like there'd been a fight. The FBI showed up, and they couldn't even find him. Everyone thinks he was murdered."

"You can't scare me off with wild stories."

"I won't have to. Cold Creek will do that . . . and more."

Neither spoke for a few moments, and the sounds in the ER seeped into Claire's office.

Julie looked away. "When do you go?"

"Next week." She glanced at Julie, noting the pout on her friend's lips. "Please, can't you be happy for me? I'm really looking forward to this."

"Harrumph," Julie snorted. "Just remember, life isn't like that Forrest Gump guy said. It isn't a box of chocolates. It's more like a jar of jalapeños. What you do today just might burn your ass tomorrow." She snorted again. "Don't expect a send-off party."

Claire watched Julie, regretting that she'd upset her. Her marriage to Keith had broken more than a bone or two, and she was still putting herself back together. Making this life-altering decision was just another step in that process. Perhaps it was best to let this topic drop for a while; besides, there was another matter she needed to talk to Julie about, a question she needed to ask. "You've told me that your mom came from the Rosebud Reservation. Do you speak Lakota?"

Julie looked at Claire, her eyes wide with surprise. "What?" She quickly stood. "I don't believe this." She paced back and forth in front of Claire's desk. "You want me to teach you to speak enough Lakota so you can be an idiot and trek off to Cold Creek?" She shook her head. "Oh, no. No way. Even if I could . . . I wouldn't."

"No, no," Claire protested. "This doesn't have anything to do with that. It's something else."

Julie's eyes narrowed as if she were trying to see into Claire's mind. "I understand enough Lakota to get by when we're with my mom's family, but don't ask if I understand anything said by the Polish Jankowski side. So, what do you want to know?"

How far should she go? Should she tell Julie about the dream, about the dogs and Dane, about Dane's sister and, about the one single word that always accompanied the dream? "I'm not sure if this is even a Lakota word, but it sounds Indian. It's been stuck in my head for days; I've been trying to figure out what it means."

"Okay, let's hear it." Julie sat down again.

"*Iktomi.*"

"*Iktomi?*"

Claire nodded. "Did I say it correctly?"

"Yeah, you came pretty close. *Iktomi* is a legendary character from Lakota stories. He's known as the trickster. He's always doing what you don't expect, sometimes changing his shape, pretending to be something he isn't, things like that. The stories are like . . . morality stories." Julie frowned. "Where'd you come up with his name? Not too many non-Indians are familiar with the stories about him."

Claire caught her bottom lip between her teeth. Would Julie think she was insane if she told her the truth about the odd dream? *Probably, but what the hell.* "I know this sounds ridiculous, but I've heard it in a drea—"

A sharp rap resounded on the office door an instant before it flew open. "Dr. Colby."

Claire quickly stood. "What is it, John?"

"We just got a call from Wakefield Penitentiary. We've got a prisoner coming in on LifeLine. It's a stabbing. They couldn't stabilize him in their clinic and are sending him here."

"What's the ETA?"

"The chopper is about ten minutes out," the paramedic replied. "We're prepping treatment bay twelve for him now."

Claire quickly moved toward the door. "Alert Security, and I want the bays on either side of twelve to be cleared of patients." Stepping out into the ER, she glanced at the unit secretary. "Kathy, call Radiology and make sure we've got a portable machine and a tech down here. Page Dan Rasch, I think he's the surgical resident on call, and make sure there's an available OR upstairs." She turned and looked at Julie. "Come on, Jankowski, it's show time."

6

✍

"DR. COLBY," THE UNIT SECRETARY CALLED TO CLAIRE, "it's Dr. Rasch." She held up the telephone receiver. "He wants to talk with you."

Claire glanced at the automatic doors as they swung open and the LifeLine team wheeled the stabbed prisoner into the ER. Two armed guards flanked the stretcher, and she could see that the prisoner had been handcuffed to the rails.

"Go ahead, talk to Rasch," Julie said. She gave a quick nod toward the treatment bay. "We'll get things started."

Claire took the phone from the secretary and spent what felt like an eternity instilling in Dan Rasch that he was definitely needed in the ER, stat, and that the successful completion of his residency depended on it. She dropped the receiver back into the cradle. "Residents. Egomaniacal jerks," she muttered.

"Amen," the unit secretary added.

Turning on her heel, Claire headed toward her new patient at a fast jog. Until she knew the extent of his injuries, she had to gauge treatment time within the magic hour, and delays were unforgiving.

A quick glance assured Claire that her staff was right on course. She could hear the LifeLine doctor giving the victim's stats to Julie as the heart monitor electrodes were being placed on the patient's chest and legs. Another ER nurse rolled the EKG machine into the bay, and the X-ray team had arrived with the portable unit.

"Patient is a thirty-four-year-old, alert Indian male with three stab wounds," the flight doctor reported. "The left chest wall has been punctured, the femoral artery in the left thigh has been nicked, and there's a single deep stab wound in the left shoulder. The majority of the blood loss has been from the patient's leg wound. His pressure is seventy over forty, and he's on a saline drip."

Before Claire could step into the treatment bay, Julie caught her by the arm, drawing her aside. "Hon, wait a minute."

"What's the matter?" Claire looked down, surprised to find her arm still in Julie's firm grip.

"You need to know something before you go in there."

"What? What's wrong?" Claire tried to move closer to the gurney, but Julie blocked her way.

"Wait!" Julie's fingers tightened on Claire's arm. "Listen to me." She moved closer to Claire and whispered in her ear, "It's . . . Dane White Eagle."

The floor seemed to dip beneath Claire's feet, and she felt her entire body going numb. A wild sense of déjà vu washed over her, shaking her to her core. Memories of a snowy December night flashed in rapid vignettes in her mind before her well-trained internal voice had the chance to caution her, had the chance to let its mantra calm her rapidly beating heart. *Objectivity. Keep your objectivity. No matter who it is . . . or what he's done, he's a patient first. Focus, focus . . . a patient first.*

She sucked in a bolstering breath, squared her shoulders,

pulled on a pair of surgical gloves, then stepped up to the left side of the gurney. "Okay people, how are we doing?"

"Chest tube and Pleurovac are in place, and we have good reinflation of the lung," Julie replied. "He's on thirty-five percent oxygen, and his breathing is stabilizing."

Determined not to make eye contact with Dane White Eagle until she absolutely had to, Claire looked down to make her own assessment of his wounds and almost lost her damned precious objectivity.

Completely stripped with only a small towel across his groin, the bronze shade of Dane White Eagle's smooth skin played in dark contrast to the white sheet and electrode patches. More muscular than she had imagined, the sight of his well-toned body drew a soft gasp from her lips. *Objectivity. My God, Claire, you're a doctor, you see naked men almost every day. Dane White Eagle is just another ER patient. Believe it . . . objectivity.*

Quickly building an emotional and professional buttress, Claire continued her examination, lightly probing the depth of the wound on Dane's shoulder. It pleased her to find only a slight amount of bleeding. X rays would confirm the actual depth of the wound. She turned to one of the guards. "How did this happen?"

"You mean that particular wound?" the guard asked, a puzzled look on his face.

"No," Claire replied, gritting her teeth. "All of these wounds. How did the patient get stabbed?"

"Yard fight." The guard shrugged. "These guys will fight over anything."

"Aren't there any guards in the yard to stop these fights?"

"Sure, but they happen quick." He chuckled. "It's a prison, not a social club."

Claire didn't care for the man's cavalier attitude. "Where's the weapon?"

"Back at Wakefield, I guess."

"You guess." She nodded. "Do you know if the blade was intact after Mr. White Eagle was stabbed?"

The guard laughed, gesturing toward Dane with a quick jerk of his thumb. "Lady, these guys can make a knife outta cottage cheese. There's no telling what this one looked like, how much went in, or what came out."

"So, no one found the knife that wounded this man?"

The guard heaved an exasperated grunt. "Look, I didn't see the stabbing, I didn't see who did it, and I didn't see the knife." He scratched his jaw. "What's this got to do with sewing him up so we can take him back to Wakefield?"

"Nothing, absolutely nothing, Mr."—she peered at his name badge— "Scruggs." Claire dabbed some disinfectant on the wound on Dane's shoulder and covered it with a sterile gauze. "And Mr. Scruggs, I doubt that your prisoner will be going back to Wakefield for a few days." Claire dropped the subject. If the blade tip had broken off and was still in the wound, the X ray would give her that information.

She knew Dane White Eagle was watching her. She'd felt his gaze touch her the moment she'd stepped close to the gurney. Her determination grew. She refused to look in his face. Not yet. She wasn't ready. Instead, she continued her examination.

She slowly moved her hands from Dane's shoulder wound down to the puncture site in his left side. Satisfied with the job the LifeLine team had done inserting the chest tube, she lightly trailed her fingers across his chest, hesitating long enough to feel the strength of his breathing. As her hand traveled lower over his stomach, his muscles tightened beneath her touch. Startled, she hesitated, then lifted her hand. The mantra began again. *Objectivity. Focus. Stay focused.*

Julie leaned closer. "You okay?"

Claire bristled, embarrassed to be caught off guard. "Of course I am. Why wouldn't I be?"

Julie's left brow quickly lifted into a high arc. "Just checking."

Resolute to remain detached and block any personal feelings, Claire moved her hand lower. As her fingers grazed the point of his right hip, she discovered a fresh bruise and a slight abrasion. The wound wasn't serious, but without proper care it could become infected.

Her attention slowly traveled lower, across the small towel that covered his groin to the wound on his thigh. She glanced up at the flight doc, who was keeping manual compression on the wound. "How long have you been applying pressure, Frank?"

"About twelve minutes," he replied. He pointed to the LifeLine nurse with a slight lift of his chin. "Linda did about fifteen on the flight in. Compression isn't going to close it, Claire. It needs suturing."

Claire nodded, then checked the pedal pulse in Dane's left leg and then his right. Although the left was weaker, she could still easily find it. "Julie, move in here and take over compression." She looked up at Julie. "How much blood has he lost?"

"From his pressure," Julie replied, "I'd say he's down at least a pint."

Claire glanced over her shoulder as Dan Rasch finally showed up. "Glad you could make it, Doctor. We didn't disturb your sleep, did we?" Without waiting for his answer to her cut, she continued, "Take care of the nicked femoral in the left thigh." Turning to one of her team nurses, she gave another order. "Get his blood type and match, and we'll start transfusing with one unit."

Trying to ignore the handcuffs, Claire examined Dane's right hand and found nothing: no cuts, no scrapes, no bruises. When she leaned over him to look at his left hand, she felt the heat of his body as her stomach touched his. The muscle along the edge of her jaw tightened, and she tried to swallow the soft gasp that rose in her throat. She had been so aware of this man during his trial; he had stayed in her thoughts for months, and now this. Why? What was the attraction? What was the connection? *Come*

*on Claire, focus, damn it. You're a doctor, not a hormone-
riddled teenager.*

She pushed the disquieting sensation and questions
from her mind and opened the fingers of his left hand. No
cuts or scrapes marred this hand, either.

The icy reality of what had happened in the prison yard
hit hard. There had been no fight. There were no defense
wounds on his hands or arms. Dane White Eagle had been
attacked from behind by a left-handed assailant. He'd had
no chance to defend himself.

The thought shocked her, and all of her defenses tumbled into emotional dust. Her gaze flew to his face, and she
found Dane White Eagle staring up at her.

"Well, look who we have here." The raspy, breathless
sound of Dane's voice exposed his pain. "Dr. Colby, what a
coincidence." His full mouth curved into a slight smile,
then dropped into a tight line. "I was just in the neighborhood and thought I'd stop by."

Claire quickly stepped back from the gurney. "Mr.
White Eagle, from the looks of these wounds, I'd say that
you were in the wrong neighborhood."

"You ought to know, Doctor. You helped put me there."

So, there it was. The accusation. It hadn't taken as long
as she had thought it would. "I'd say that your own actions
played a much more important role than mine."

She turned away, pulled the bloodied surgical gloves
from her trembling hands, and tossed them in the trash.
"Dr. Rasch, I'm sure you can continue here." Without a
backward glance, she left the treatment bay and walked
back to her office, praying with each step that her trembling legs would hold her upright until she got there.

"LOOKS LIKE YOU took a hell of a hit," Jack Gaines said,
moving closer to the bed and peering down at the bandages
on Dane's bare chest.

"Yeah, they tell me I'm not a full-blood Lakota anymore," Dane replied. "I got a pint of crazy white man's blood in me now. No telling what kind of stupid things I'll do."

"You do look a little pale," Gil Pardue chuckled.

"How about taking these off?" Dane pulled against the handcuffs that secured him to the bed rail. "With stitches holding my artery together, I'm not going anywhere for awhile."

Jack Gaines sat down on the edge of the bed. "Sorry, can't do it. We've got to play the game a little longer." He jerked his thumb toward the closed door. "As long as you've got guards outside, you're a prisoner in here."

"How's a man supposed to scratch an itch with his hand locked down?" Dane pulled on the cuffs again.

"Sounds like a personal problem, man. Maybe if you use the call button and get one of those cutesy-pie nurses in here, she'll scratch it real good for you."

"Yeah, right." Dane chuckled. "Only one problem with that. Every time I push the button I get Nurse Godzilla."

"Quit your whining. Do you wanna scratch or do you wanna—"

"Shut up, Gaines. What I want is to get out of here."

Gil Pardue sank into the chair beside the bed. "Well, you're almost there. We've got Bobby Big Elk in solitary. No one can get to him, no visitors, especially Leland." He laughed. "Brother Leland is probably going crazy trying to figure out what to do. It's just where we want him . . . off balance and looking for someone to buddy up with." He pointed at Dane. "I guess that's gonna be you, buddy."

"What in the hell did you say to Bobby that pissed him off enough to cut you?" Gaines asked.

"I told you, it wasn't Bobby." Dane shifted, trying to find a comfortable spot. He was getting bored with having to stay in bed.

"You don't think he had it ordered?"

Dane shook his head. "No, I don't. I don't think it had anything at all to do with Bobby, so let's drop it. It happened, and it's over. Let's just use it to our advantage."

Gaines shrugged. "That's what we're doing." He stood and poured himself a cup of water from the pitcher on the nightstand. Drinking it down in two gulps, he turned and faced Dane. "We filed your appeal yesterday, and with a push or two from the powers that be in the right direction, it should go through in the next couple of weeks. Illegal search and seizure . . . oops." He chortled. "Who'd have thought those cops would forget to get a warrant before they searched your truck and apartment? Tsk, tsk, tsk. Why, that's just plain sloppy police work." He winked. "Funny thing, eh? It never came up in your trial, either. I guess sometimes folks just assume everything's done by the book." He plopped back down on the side of Dane's bed. "Not. But it's a great Get Out of Jail card."

"I feel kinda sorry for poor Dickie Buford," Dane said. "You've got to give the guy credit, though. He kept trying."

"He's probably gone back to ambulance chasing and is making more money than the three of us put together." Gaines tossed the empty paper cup into the wastebasket.

"I hear Claire Colby was working the night they brought you in," Pardue said with a teasing grin on his face.

Dane didn't like the quick skip his heart made when he heard her name. Damn it all, the woman meant nothing to him. "Yeah, so?"

Pardue shrugged. "Just thought it was a funny coincidence, that's all . . . you know, with her bein' the one when you brought Kylee in, her testifying at your trial, and all." He cocked his left brow. "So, is she the one who fixed you up?"

"What the hell is this, an interrogation?"

"Hey man, I'm just making idle bedside conversation," Pardue replied, holding up his hands as if to ward off an attack. "Don't get so hostile."

"Well, go make some conversation with the judge and

get me out of here. The food here is as bad as Wakefield's." Dane pulled against the handcuffs again. "And while you're at it, get these damned bracelets off me."

Jack Gaines shook his head and glanced at Pardue. "Speaking of hostile, this Injun sure is kinda testy, ain't he?"

CLAIRE STOOD IN the shadows of the room, Dane White Eagle's chart in her hands. She'd come up to his room three nights in a row, running the gauntlet of the floor nurses and guards and risking Dan Rasch learning that she was checking on his patient. *I was the admitting physician, after all.*

At two in the morning the floor was quiet except for the usual night sounds: soft snoring, the whoosh and bleeps of some of the patients' monitors. She'd had a close call or two as nurses peeked in to check on Dane, but by sheer luck her nightly visits had gone undetected.

Dane wasn't her patient anymore, but she couldn't stay away. Not only because she was curious about his care, but snippets of the recurring dreams of him, a pack of dogs, and a voice that softly repeated the name *Iktomi* kept teasing her.

A shaft of soft light from the hallway eased through the partially open door and into the room, just a pale glow, yet bright enough that she could watch him sleep. She smiled. They had removed the handcuff from his left wrist after she'd told Rasch that Dane needed to be able to move the arm and keep his shoulder from getting stiff. Using her penlight, she scanned Dane's chart. His oxygen had been stopped, and his breathing was returning to normal rhythm and volume, a sure sign that his lung was almost healed. His pain medications had been reduced, and he'd been up walking for about ten minutes that afternoon. The news pleased her and yet disappointed her, as well. She was glad he was getting better. It meant his wounds were healing nicely, but it also meant he'd be going back to Wakefield soon.

"You going to hide in the corner and stare at me all night again, or are you going to sit down and talk?"

Startled, Claire gasped and almost dropped the chart and her penlight.

"Things must be pretty quiet down in the ER if you're up here sneaking around and looking at half-naked men while they sleep. I bet folks would be pretty shocked to find out you've got some kind of voyeurism fetish."

7

"MY INTEREST IN YOU IS PURELY PROFESSIONAL," Claire replied, finally finding her voice. She stepped out of the shadows and moved closer to the bed, clasping Dane's chart to her chest. "I follow up on all of my patients who have been admitted." The lie almost stuck in her throat.

"Really?" He pushed the control button and raised the head of the bed, causing the sheet that covered him to drop halfway down his bare chest. "And here I thought I was the only patient whose room you sneaked into late at night." A grin, marvelous in every way, lifted the corners of his mouth. "Should I be jealous?"

"Jealous? Hah!" She almost choked. "That's preposterous. You're a patient—I'm the doctor. There is absolutely nothing personal between us."

"Of course there is . . . Claire. You just haven't figured it out yet."

Her pulse leapt. "There is nothing to figure out, Mr. White Eagle. Our only connection outside of this hospital involved your trial. I would hardly call that personal."

Dane shrugged, causing the bed sheet to slide farther down his body to his waist. "You sound disappointed. Perhaps *you'd* like there to be something personal between us?"

His soft chuckle lightly caressed her senses and tipped her emotional balance. Claire didn't have to see her cheeks to know that the hot flush she felt had turned them a bright red. Thank God there was little light in the room, and what light there was, was at her back. The last thing she wanted was to let Dane White Eagle know he had ruffled her feathers. This kind of teasing was an unexpected part of his nature, too. She found it oddly disconcerting. Her internal voice returned. *Objectivity. Use your professional objectivity. Don't involve your emotions.* "I think you should stop wasting your time making wild assumptions or claims."

Struggling to regain her composure, Claire shoved thoughts of his smooth skin and tautly muscled chest out of her mind and flipped open his chart. Using her penlight, she pretended to study the notes on each page. She hoped it would make her visit look more official, and she hoped it would keep her gaze from wandering over his bare chest. Unfortunately, she couldn't read the chart, couldn't make out a single word. Her eyes wouldn't focus on the page. "Well, you seem to be doing quite well," she said, pretending to read. "You should be released very soon."

"Released. Ah, now there's a word that's music to an inmate's ears."

Claire closed his chart with a loud snap and lifted her chin, determined to give herself a more commanding appearance. "I think the only music you'll be listening to, Mr. White Eagle, is a chorus or two of 'Jailhouse Rock.'"

"Ouch," Dane replied, a grin lifting the corners of his mouth. "You hit hard, don't you?"

"Apparently not as hard, as someone hit you," she said. Forgetting that she hadn't turned it off, Claire pointed the penlight at his left thigh. She missed her aim, and the bright beam hit him between his legs. For a moment that seemed to stretch into an eternity, she stood frozen with embarrassment, the penlight still casting its bright ray. Finally regaining her senses, she fumbled with the switch. "I'm so sorry," she mumbled, finally turning off the light. "Obviously I'm a poor shot."

Dane's laughter filled the room, and she was hit hard by the urge to join him. It felt so right that it frightened her.

"Dr. Colby?"

Startled, Claire jumped and turned at the sound of a woman's voice. The door swung open, allowing a wider shaft of light from the hallway. The night duty nurse stepped into the room, the guard a few steps behind her. Claire groaned. How had this simple middle-of-the-night foray gone so very wrong? "Good evening, Miss Snyder. I'm just checking on Mr. White Eagle. He seems to be doing very well, don't you think?" She abruptly handed Dane's chart to the nurse and stepped toward the door, hoping to make her exit as quickly as possible.

The sound of Dane's voice followed her out into the hall. "Good night, Dr. Colby. Sweet dreams."

Her step faltered, and she grasped the edge of the doorframe. Were Dane's words a coincidence? Why would he mention dreams? *Oh, come on, Claire, get a grip on yourself. The man is just being facetious. It's an expression: sweet dreams, sleep tight, don't let the bedbugs bite. There's absolutely no way he could know.* Without invitation, the word *Iktomi* slipped through her mind. *There's no way.*

Out in the hallway she leaned back against the wall and drew one deep breath after another, trying to gain her senses. She held her right hand out in front of her and watched it shake like a leaf on a tree in the wind. Closing her eyes, she rested her head against the wall, and her inner voice, the one that always reminded her about objectivity, had a brand-new message: *Going into Dane White Eagle's room was a damned stupid thing to do.* Claire shook her head. *No, it was a damned stupid thing to get caught.*

"Dr. Colby?"

Claire's eyes popped open to find the guard back at his station outside of Dane's door and Patty Snyder standing in front of her, still holding Dane's chart.

"You look pale. Are you all right? Would you like some water? Do you need me to get you anything?"

Yeah, a new brain. "No, I'm fine thank you, Patty. Just a little tired, that's all. It's been a long shift."

"Boy, I know how those go. I've had a few myself." She nodded her head toward Dane's room and pressed her hand over her heart. "He's something else, isn't he? Wow! Women dream about men like him," Patty added with a breathless sound to her voice.

"Or have nightmares about them," Claire replied, glad to hear that her own voice had found its strong edge again. "Aren't you forgetting why there's a guard outside his door or why he's been handcuffed to his bed rail?"

"Oh, Dr. Colby," Patty Snyder giggled. "Everybody knows he's innocent and will get an appeal. He didn't do that terrible thing. He didn't kill his sister. He couldn't have. Look at him. He's gorgeous." She sighed. "No one who's that handsome could kill anybody."

Claire's left brow climbed upward in disbelief. "Really? Have you ever seen any photos of Ted Bundy?"

THE RAPPING SOUND roused Connie White Eagle from her sleep. She sat for a few minutes hoping that whoever was at her door would go away. The hard knock came again, resounding in her head like a hammer.

She pushed herself up from the rocking chair and shuffled to the door, sidestepping the magazines and papers that littered the floor. The moment she placed her hand on the doorknob, the knock came again, much louder, more determined.

"Connie. I know you're in there."

Clement. She expelled a deep sigh, wishing the old man would go away and leave her alone. He'd developed an annoying schedule, stopping by at least two times a week. This was his third visit this week. If this kept up, she'd definitely have to figure out how to keep him away. The old man was pushy, and lately she just didn't want to be pushed.

She drove her fingers through her tangled hair, then pulled her housecoat around her and tied the belt. Grasping the collar together just beneath her chin, she took a deep breath, opened the door only a few inches, and peered out at Clement. "You back so soon?"

"Hello to you, too," Clement Runs After replied, pushing against the door, opening it wider and making her step back.

Connie watched his gaze travel down to her bare toes and then up to her uncombed hair. She bristled at his silent appraisal. So what if she hadn't gotten dressed. So what if she wanted to sit around the house in her pajamas and watch TV. So what if she didn't feel like cooking or keeping the place neat and tidy.

"It's after three in the afternoon. You not feeling good?"

She settled her mouth in a hard, straight line. "I'm fine. I just didn't think I'd have company again . . . so soon. You got nothin' better to do?"

Clement apparently chose to ignore her comment and, squeezing between her and the doorframe, stepped into the living room. She watched him look around at the clutter, the dirty dishes on the table and countertop, half-empty glasses of milk that had soured and congealed, and the piles of dirty laundry.

"This place is a mess."

She moved back to the rocker and sat, folding her arms across her breasts. "If you're gonna insult my housekeepin', you can leave. If you can be polite, you might as well sit down . . . if you think you can find a clean place."

Clement settled into his favorite chair, rested his elbows on the arms, and leaned forward, propping his chin on his steepled fingers. "You heard?"

"'Bout what? The price of onions? The war in God

knows where? Elvis is alive and working with Custer at Wal-Mart? What?"

Clement apparently chose to ignore these comments, too. "I didn't know if you'd heard it on the news." He tilted his chin at the television. "If you hadn't, I thought you'd like to know, you bein' his mother and all."

Clement paused as if waiting for her to demand he tell her everything. *Damned if I'll give him the satisfaction.* She tightened her arms as if that would protect her from anything Clement Runs After had to tell her. "I ain't heard nothin' 'bout nothin'."

"Your boy's in the hospital."

Her heart leapt in her chest with fear and worry, but Connie pushed the feelings down deep into her gut, denying their existence and refusing to let them show on her face. "So? Ain't no worry of mine." She rocked for a few moments, determined not to ask the question and finally unable to keep from knowing the answer. "He sick or something?"

"He got stabbed. It was bad. They flew him from Wakefield into the city in one of them fancy helicopters with doctors and nurses on it."

The twist in her gut gave a hard yank. She fought to ignore it and began fiddling with the belt on her housecoat, running the ends through her fingers over and over again. Glancing up at Clement, she shrugged. "Ain't no business of mine. Sometimes folks get what they deserve." Her gaze dropped back down to her lap as she continued to twine the belt around her fingers.

"I'll take you into the city if you wanna go see him."

"It don't matter if he's in the hospital or in jail, I ain't got no use to go." She stood and made her way to the kitchen. "You want some coffee?"

"I want you to go talk to Dane."

"If you think he needs company so bad, you go." Connie filled two mugs, carried them back to the living room, and gave one to Clement.

"They won't let me see him. You gotta be related, and them white guys don't know nothin' 'bout Indian relations."

Connie stared at the reheated, two-day-old coffee in her cup, then took a long sip. The next question rose to her lips and was asked before she could stop herself. "How bad is he?"

"From what I hear, he lost lots of blood. Almost died. They say he's doin' good now and going back to Wakefield tomorrow or the day after."

She nodded, feeling a sense of unexpected relief wash over her. "So, he ain't bad off now, then. Ain't no need to even talk about going." She straightened her shoulders as if she could forget the dread that had touched her, as if she had nothing to worry about anymore. But the ache in her heart remained, as strong and persistent as it had been since a snowy night in December.

FOOTSTEPS ECHOED IN the long corridor, and Dane sat on his bunk, listening to each one, counting them off as they neared his cell; fifty-three from the guard station to his cell. Each footfall brought him closer to walking out the front gate of Wakefield, brought him closer to freedom.

Since returning, he'd been kept in protective custody, away from the other inmates, but he didn't doubt for a minute that the grapevine had carried the news of his return and then his acquittal. He'd seen some of the TV news and newspapers reporting on his release. Some had called it a huge miscarriage of justice, a travesty—releasing a convicted child killer back into society all because of a simple error made by the police. Others had ridiculed the cops for their sloppy work. Either way, the fact that the cops didn't have a warrant when they'd searched his truck and apartment for evidence had led to the charge of illegal search and seizure. It was his ticket out of Wakefield . . . just as Gaines and Pardue had planned.

With Bobby Big Elk in solitary, word was that poor Leland was getting nervous and needed somebody to hold his hand. Dane's job would now be to step in and play Leland's new best pal. Chances were this would get the FBI the information they'd been wanting for almost six months. Maybe there'd finally be an end to this case after all.

The first thing Dane wanted to do when he got home was to go into the sweat lodge and cleanse his spirit and body, ridding himself of all the poisons spending six months in prison had put inside him. He needed to feel like himself again, and that was a good place to start. Maybe it would be a good place to talk to the old man about his dreams, too. Clement would understand better than anyone else. In the three weeks that he'd been back at Wakefield, the dream of Kylee, Claire Colby, and the pack of rez dogs had repeated itself at least four or five times. There was only one way to find out what it meant. *I need to talk with Clement when I get home. And then I want to go to Kylee's grave.*

Without being in the general population, he'd also had time to think about his future . . . the future after his involvement in this case was over. His number one priority was to find Kylee's killer. His determination burned deeper and deeper each day. And then there would be changes: where he lived, maybe what he did for a living, what he wanted in his life. But before any changes could be made, he had a lot of fences to mend. Maybe there was one to build, too: Claire Colby.

The footsteps stopped.

"You ready, Chief?" The rotund guard stood in front of Dane's cell, his hand resting at his waist on the butt of his gun. "Ya know, it's a fuckin' joke. I oughta be taking you to death row." He sucked loudly on his teeth and nodded. "You oughta be rottin' in hell instead of getting out." He gave a quick hand signal and called over his shoulder. "Open fourteen."

The hallway resounded with a hard clank as the latch holding the cell door was electronically released. The metallic screech the barred panel made as it moved along the track was a sound Dane would never forget. He'd listened to it at least four times a day for the last six months, the squeal of metal sliding against metal, the finality of the latch as it locked. It was the loneliest sound in the world.

"Grab your stuff and let's go."

Dane stepped out into the corridor empty-handed. There was nothing in the cell that he wanted to take with him, nothing that he wanted to remind him of the lost part of his life.

It felt odd not having handcuffs or the chain around his waist; it felt even more unusual to be wearing his own clothes again, his boots, his jeans, and a navy blue shirt. He swore to himself that he'd never wear anything that reminded him of prison uniform beige again.

The guard walked behind him, and when they reached the door at the end of the hallway, a loud buzzer sounded when the lock was released. Dane opened the door and stepped through, finding Jack Gaines and Gil Pardue on the other side.

"Well, look what we got here," Gaines laughed, reaching out his hand. "Looks like a free man to me."

Dane shook Gaines's hand. "Just get me processed and let me out of here."

"You're all clear to go," Pardue said. "All the papers have been signed, everything's been taken care of."

"That's all it took?"

"Yup . . . when you're let out on a technicality they wanna get rid of ya . . . fast."

Pardue stepped forward and handed Dane a slip of paper. "This will get your truck out of impound without a fee."

Dane reached for the paper, then hesitated, the weight

of grief almost too much to bear. He dropped his hand. "I don't think I can touch it . . . my sister . . ."

"Don't worry, Dane," Pardue said, placing his hand on Dane's arm. "Everything's been taken care of. The Bureau had your truck replaced with an identical one. The ignition and locks were switched and so were the plates. Nobody will know the difference." He patted Dane's arm. "All your belongings are in there but, sorry man, we couldn't match the rust spot on the rocker panel."

Dane smiled at Pardue's attempt to lighten the moment, but inside he felt numb. *Get hold of yourself. You knew this wasn't going to be easy.*

Gaines handed Dane a cell phone. "This is yours to use, it's in your name, but the bill will go to a blind Bureau post office box in town. If you need to get in touch with either Pardue or me, just hit three on the speed dial. The phone's also equipped with GPS. If you leave it turned on, we can find you . . . anywhere."

Dane studied the phone in his hand. "This is an expensive little unit. Thanks, guys. Unlimited long distance, I hope."

"Smart-ass," Pardue responded. "Keep it handy; you never know when you'll need a lifeline."

Dane nodded and clipped the phone to his belt. "Where are you guys taking me, back to the city or to Cold Creek?"

"We ain't takin' you anywhere," Pardue replied, heading down the corridor to the reception area. "It seems you've already got a ride waiting outside that'll take ya wherever you want to go."

Dane's hopes rose. "My mom?"

Gaines shook his head and shot a sheepish glance at Dane. "No, sorry, pal." He placed his hand on Dane's shoulder. "Leland Big Elk."

8

FREEDOM. HOW COULD SEVEN LETTERS STRUNG together into one single word pull so damned much emotion out of a man? Tears burned in Dane's eyes, and a lump rose thick and heavy in his throat, making it difficult to swallow. He scrubbed his eyes with the heels of his hands and tightened his emotional reins. *For God's sake, White Eagle, keep it together.*

His thoughts went again to that word. *Freedom.* Wasn't that the word that Mel Gibson had cried out at the end of the movie *Braveheart*? *Freedom! Yeah, that was it.*

Dane tipped his head back and gazed up at the blue July sky. *Funny, it never looked this blue in the prison yard.* He drew a deep breath. The air out here even had a different, sweeter scent. He could taste its delectable flavor, and it even felt clean and fresh against his skin.

He heard the prison door close behind him and fought the impulse to turn around. And then the reality of it all took hold. Although the job wasn't done, and although he would have to spend at least another month or two undercover, the sound of the closing door, the electronic click of the lock, the blue sky, and the pure smell of the air meant one thing and one thing only: freedom.

Maybe freedom would also mean a healing of spirit with the people he loved and respected. He'd have the chance to make peace with his mother, with Clement, with his Lakota people . . . and with Kylee.

It wasn't going to be easy, he'd known that going into this scam, but he'd never imagined the pain-filled weight of it all. It compared to walking a tightrope without a net. The balancing act was physically dangerous no matter which way the rope swung, but he hadn't expected the emotional danger. He thought he'd done a good job handling it until Gaines and Pardue had told him someone was going to pick him up when he got out. He could have kicked himself for the hope-filled question he'd asked. He hadn't wanted them to see his weakness. Besides, it didn't take an Einstein to figure out that if his mother still believed he was guilty of Kylee's murder, she'd be the last person who'd be waiting for him on the outside with open arms. It made him all the more worried about the kind of reception he'd get when he got back to Cold Creek.

Another thought tumbled into his mind. Maybe freedom meant being able to follow other things that piqued his interest. And a lady doctor with a wayward penlight certainly piqued his interest. *Good God, White Eagle. You're a fool if you even give her a second thought. Every time you'd look at her you'd remember.* He slowly shook his head. *And every time you looked at her you'd want her.* In spite of his denial, her name slipped in a whisper over his lips. "Claire Colby."

"Hey, *kola,* you plannin' on standin' there all day, or do ya wanna go home?"

Cruelly yanked from his thoughts, Dane looked across the wide, well-manicured lawn that surrounded Wakefield's administration building to find Leland Big Elk in the parking lot, leaning against the front left fender of a brand-new bright red Dodge Ram. Dane knew at a glance that he'd never seen so much chrome and fancy paint on a pickup truck in his life.

Hitching the thumb of his right hand in his pocket, he ambled toward the parking lot. As he walked closer, his gaze traveled over Leland Big Elk. He guessed the man to be close to fifty, maybe a little older. His features were classic Lakota. His hair had begun to gray at the temples, and he wore it in long wrapped braids like some of the younger men, but he was beginning to show the easy life and frybread around his waist. His clothes were expensive, a custom-made suede jacket and a silk shirt, Lucchese boots, and tailored jeans. Somehow it all looked out of place on him; the clothes had more class than the man. *What in the hell does my mother see in this jackass?* "Hey Elk, what did you do, buy that new set of wheels just to pick me up?"

Leland laughed, then touched the fender of the truck as though he were caressing a beautiful woman. "She's a beauty, eh *kola?* Best pony on the rez. Hell, probably the best damned pony in the state." He patted the truck again. "Business has been real good."

Especially good if you've been pocketing a little bit of brother Bobby's share. Business would be very good for Leland Big Elk until brother Bobby walked out of Wakefield's doors, down this sidewalk, and asked for his money.

"With you gettin' out, we're gonna rock the rez," Leland said. "I bet you could even use a better cut of the profits; then you could get yourself one of these." He laughed again. "I'll see what I can do."

Another cut from Bobby Big Elk's split of the take? It sure won't come out of Leland's.

Leland pushed away from the truck and stepped up on the curb. "Come on, man." He draped his arm over Dane's shoulders. "Let's get you outta here." Leland glanced back over his shoulder. "This place gives me the creeps." Giving Dane a hearty hug, he asked, "Where you wanna go, back to the rez or to your place in the city?"

"What are you, the local limo service?" It wasn't hard to figure out that there'd be a price for Leland's generosity. The Big Elk brothers always wanted something in return for a favor. With Bobby tucked away in solitary and unavailable to tell Leland how to run the business, big brother Leland was getting nervous. It was clear to Dane that Leland was setting him up to pump him for information about Bobby. He glanced at Leland again. No, Leland wasn't nervous, he was scared. *That's okay; I can pump right back and find out what's happening in Red Star . . . on Cold Creek . . . what's going on with my mother.*

From the beginning of this sting, Dane had wanted to go to work on Leland first. Leland liked being a big shot, liked impressing people. Shooting off his mouth would make him feel important. Dane believed the FBI would have a better chance finding out where the Big Elk brothers were making their E from Leland. But Pardue and Gaines believed they'd get what they wanted from Bobby. If Dane was in Wakefield, what did it matter what secrets Bobby told him if he wouldn't be out for twenty-five years? And it was even more probable if the person you told was a homeboy and somebody already on your payroll. Their plan sounded good in theory at the time, but when they'd talked him into it, he'd been too numb to think it through clearly.

Their plan didn't work, and Dane couldn't help but resent the fact that he'd spent six months in prison for a scam that had failed.

"So, what's it gonna be? The city or the rez?" Leland asked again. "Your apartment or your mom's place?"

The two choices didn't leave Dane any leeway. His apartment rent had been kept up, but there was no way he wanted Leland Big Elk to know that, and he knew the welcome mat wasn't going to be out for him at his mother's house. Dane laughed. "Hell man, I haven't paid rent since I got arrested. I don't have a place in the city anymore, but

I've got to get my truck out of the police impound lot in the city. Can you do that?"

Leland's laughter joined Dane's, and he smacked him on the shoulder again. "You mean the truck the cops searched without a warrant?" He shook his head. "Man, you really lucked out on that one." He jogged around the front of the truck and slid behind the steering wheel. "Yeah, no problem, *kola,* I'll take ya to the lot. No problem at all. You got enough money on ya to bail it out? If not, I can take care of it." He patted his pocket. "Like I said, business has been good."

Dane shook his head. "Thanks for the offer, but my new lawyers are tough." He was glad that Gaines and Pardue played their attorney roles well. "I've got a paper that says I don't have to pay anything. The cops impounded the truck without just cause."

"I love legal talk, don't you? Lawyers can think of twenty different ways to say one thing and have you over the barrel in all of 'em."

Dane settled into the passenger seat and breathed in the scent of the new vehicle. It should have smelled delicious, should have made him a little envious because his truck had been three years old with a rust spot on the left rocker panel. Most men would have been enthralled by the leather seats, the dashboard full of expensive gauges, and the state-of-the-art sound system, but all he could think of was the cost. Not the dollars and cents that the truck dealer had charged Leland Big Elk, not the money that had kept rolling in from addicts and the teenagers, but the cost in the lives of the kids who had died taking the bright pink *waskuyeca wakan.*

If the FBI had wanted to insure that he'd stay on the case, they couldn't have picked a better way to persuade him than to have Leland Big Elk pick him up in his damned new shiny truck.

The first few miles were made in silence, and Dane

could almost smell the smoke from Leland's brain as the man tried to figure out what to say. Finally the fire was lit.

"I hear ya got pig stuck real bad in there," Leland said, turning out onto the interstate.

Here it comes. The topic of conversation Leland had chosen came as no surprise to Dane.

"Any idea who done it?"

"Yeah, I know exactly who it was," Dane replied. There was no doubt about it. Leland was scared that Bobby had wielded the knife. "It was some Cree guy named Primeaux. You know him?"

"Lucien Primeaux?" The sound of relief in Leland's voice was unmistakable. "Yeah. Sure. Well, I don't know him, but I've heard of him." Leland glanced over at Dane. "Bobby talked about him some. He'd met Primeaux a few years ago at a powwow somewhere up in Montana." He looked back at the road. "Funny they'd meet up in Wake-field again, but hey, they move prisoners around in the sys-tem all the time." Leland punched a few buttons on the sound system and a Toby Keith CD began to play. "They buddied around a bit inside Wakefield. What'd Primeaux have against you?"

"Damned if I know." Dane shrugged. "Maybe he got upset because one of Bobby's homeboys showed up and crowded him out."

Leland nodded. "Yeah, I could see that." He glanced at Dane again. "I thought maybe they put Bobby in the hole because . . . well, because . . . he'd done it to you." He turned his attention back to the road.

"What the hell would he want to do that for?"

Leland's laugh had a nervous shake to it. "Yeah, you're right. Besides, it sure wouldn't stand too good with your mom, either, with me bein' Bobby's brother, and all."

At the mention of his mother, Dane shot a quick look at Leland. God, he wanted to ask him about her. He wanted to know if she was okay and what she'd been doing for six months. He wanted to know if she ever talked about him.

Just keep focused. Now isn't the time. Focus, damn it. "You thought Bobby cut me?"

"Well, yeah, 'cause they put him in the hole. Not that I'd believe it for a minute, *kola*. You're one of ours." He put his turn signal on and pulled over into the right lane.

"Primeaux would've got me good, would have finished the job, if it hadn't been for Bobby." Dane unconsciously rubbed his leg, feeling the slight rise of the scar beneath his jeans. "He pulled the son of a bitch off me."

"Then why the hell did they stick him in solitary?" Leland's voice held a slight whine. "That don't make no sense if he saved ya. And it sure don't make things easy for me out here. Man, I'm tryin' to take care of business, and without Bobby to . . . well, we're in it together, and he's been runnin' the show, makin' the decisions." Leland cranked the air conditioner up another notch. "I ain't got the business savvy like Bobby."

Yeah, you're scared shitless that you're going to goof up and get yourself in trouble. Too late, you've hit the jackpot. "You know your brother, Elk. He got a few licks of his own in on Primeaux and then fought the guard who tried to pull him off. Bobby saved my life, but he got himself some cold storage for a while."

"Like I said, him bein' in there has sure put a snag in business, but it's a damned good thing you're out and can work with me." He paused for a moment, the silence stretching and becoming uncomfortable. "You're gonna stick with me, ain'tcha?"

Dane laughed. "Hey man, don't worry. The money's too easy to give it up."

For a mile or two only the sound of Toby Keith singing about his favorite bar filled the cab of the truck. Dane had almost nodded off when Leland began to talk again.

"You worried 'bout the cops maybe keepin' on your tail? Word is they're pissed that you got off 'cause of their lousy mistake."

Dane moved his shoulders in a slight shrug. "It might be

a little touchy in the city for me for a while, but they're the ones who need to be careful. If the cops get too pushy, they know my lawyers will scream harassment."

"You'd do that? Wow." Leland laughed. "What about your job at Bronson?"

"What job? Hell, man, they canned my ass the minute I was arrested. I don't want to work for those assholes anyway." *White Eagle, you should get a damned Academy Award for your acting.* "I'm in with you and Bobby and plan on staying tight."

"All right!" Leland hit the steering wheel with the heel of his hand, his relief mixed with excitement. "I got an idea, *kola,* I've been thinking about something ever since I heard you was gettin' out. My brother-in-law Raymond and cousin Calvin Iron Cloud are big shots on the tribal council. It's the council who hire and fire the tribal cops. Maybe I can get you on. You got experience . . . well, your security job counts, eh? And you should be able to get your gun permit back. Hell, if you're on the rez and one of our cops, I bet that's all the permit you need." Leland drew a cigarette out of the pack in his shirt pocket and put it in his mouth. Touching the tip with the dash lighter, he took a long drag, then allowed a stream of smoke to slip between his lips. "It sure would help us to have a cop on the inside, and it'd give you a great cover." He laughed, releasing another puff of smoke. "Calvin Iron Cloud is the chief of police, and he might be family, but he's too damned straight to get interested in Bobby's business."

Dane thought he'd choke trying to keep his laugh under check. His life for the past six months would make a hell of a plot for a movie. But there was one problem. Nobody in their right mind would believe it. It didn't make sense to him, either. "You'd do that for me? You'd get me on the force?"

"Hell man, I gotta take care of my girlfriend's boy." He slapped Dane on the shoulder again. "We're almost family."

• • •

"DR. COLBY, WELCOME to Cold Creek." Jerome Rabbit shook Claire's hand with an exuberance that crushed her fingers. "It's been a long time since we've had our own doctor at the clinic." He tugged at the long chain attached to the belt loop on his pants and pulled a bundle of keys out of his pocket. Fumbling, he finally selected one and slid it into the lock.

Claire stood back and studied the small house. She'd thought it might be situated closer to the clinic, but the little bungalow was on a piece of rough, unattractive land about three miles away. There wasn't an inch on the surface of the house that didn't need a repair or repainting. Two of the shutters hung askew, and the hinges on the screen door had been tied together with twine. An innovative repair but certainly not practical. She hated to think what else needed to be fixed in places she couldn't see.

"Ain't nobody been living here since Dr. Butz," Jerome said. "Well now, that's not quite so, we had some squatters—one of Mattie Old Horn's boys and his wife—moved in, but we kicked 'em out 'fore ya came." He pushed the front door wide open, ignoring the loud screech of the hinges. "I'll get that oiled for ya." He moved aside as she stepped into the house. "When's your stuff comin'?"

"Next Saturday," Claire said, trying not to wince from the musty, rodent smell that permeated the small house. "Was this the way the house was when Dr. Butz and his wife left?"

Jerome Rabbit nervously cleared his throat. "Dr. Butz weren't married and, well, he didn't really leave. He just kinda . . . disappeared."

Claire shot Jerome Rabbit a quick glance. So Julie hadn't been kidding when she'd said no one knew where the last Cold Creek Clinic doctor had gone. "Disappeared?"

"Yup." Jerome Rabbit ducked his head. "Just gone one night . . . poof. He put in a full day at the clinic, went home for the evening, and him and his old Chevy were both gone in the morning. Nobody ever seen him again."

"Wasn't anyone concerned? Didn't anyone look for him?"

Jerome Rabbit shrugged. "Sometimes on the rez people just come and go. Doc Butz wasn't from here, so we just figured he'd decided to go home."

"Without taking his clothes, his things?"

Jerome shrugged. "Calvin Iron Cloud, the tribal police chief, had his men looked around, but they didn't find nothin'." Rabbit cleared his throat. "You wanna see the rest of the place?" He lightly took her elbow and led her into the kitchen.

Two gaping holes opened up between the cabinets on one side of the room. "Damn. The stove and refrigerator are gone." He nervously chuckled. "I'll make sure you got 'em when you move in. Might not be new, but they'll work."

An uneasy feeling settled over Claire. "You mean that someone came in here and stole them?"

Jerome rattled the handle on the back door and stepped back as the door swung open. "No tellin', but kinda looks that way. Looks like they took 'em out through here." He glanced over his shoulder at her. "I'll get this fixed for you, too." He turned back to Claire, an ingratiating smile on his full lips. "We had a little trouble keeping some folks from living here. Like I said before, Mattie Old Horn's youngest son and his new wife moved in without the council knowin' anything 'bout it."

Claire crossed her arms over her breasts and slowly looked around, inspecting the room. Its filthy walls and floor made her cringe. How had anyone lived here? Graffiti covered the cheap wood cabinets, and shards of glass from the broken window over the sink glittered on the counter-top. "There is a lot of work to be done to make this house livable, Mr. Rabbit." She tentatively lifted her foot from the sticky floor. "I wasn't expecting anything fancy, but I certainly didn't think I'd find something as bad as this."

"Dr. Colby, I'm sorry. I'll get some of the women in here tonight to start cleaning up. If I can run down Jackie Old Horn I'll have him and his wife come and work on the place, too. Most of this mess is theirs." He lifted his chin and pointed at the graffiti with his pursed lips. "I'll get Mattie to come over, and I bet Connie White Eagle will help, too."

Claire quickly looked at Jerome Rabbit, every nerve in her body suddenly alert and zinging. Connie White Eagle? Was she related to Dane? Did he have another sister, or was Connie White Eagle his mother? She tried to settle her nerves. *I'd forgotten that Dane was from Cold Creek . . . or had I?* Would anyone remember she had testified against him? Would it make a difference to the patients who came into the clinic? Surely if anyone remembered, it would have come up during her interview. She drew a deep breath and tried to settle her nerves. *First things first. Take care of where you're going to live . . . and pray it won't look like this, and then worry about any repercussions from the trial.*

She took another disapproving glance around the room, then wandered down the hall and peered into the small bathroom. It wasn't any better than the kitchen. The floor tiles were lifting around the sink, and the seat was missing from the toilet. A crack stretched from one corner of the mirror to the other, the shower nozzle hung askew, and the dirt in the tub made her shiver. She closed her eyes, hoping she was in the middle of a bad dream. Opening them again, she found reality almost too hard to bear.

Two bedrooms remained for her inspection, and she was almost afraid to expect anything better than what she'd already found. The first door she opened proved to her that things could always get worse.

A dirt-encrusted mattress lay on the floor, and cat feces

littered its surface. A flash of white and gray fur disappearing through the opening in the broken window proved that the cat still lived in the house. She pulled the door closed, moved to the last room down the hallway, and with a silent prayer, pushed open the door.

Sunshine pressed its way through the filthy windows and highlighted the ghastly purple paint on the walls. A stained, well-worn lime-green carpet covered most of the floor. Someone had taken the door off the closet, and there was a hole about the size of a basketball in the wall beneath the window.

"It's a good place, Dr. Colby," Jerome Rabbit said, leaning against the wall beside her. "It just needs a little . . . cleaning . . . that's all."

Jerome Rabbit's optimism was admirable, but Claire wondered if burning the place to the ground would be the only way to clean it up. She hated to think of how many barrels of disinfectant it would take to make the house livable. She glanced up at Jerome. "Mr. Rabbit, I don't mean to be difficult, but I'm afraid this house isn't acceptable. Surely there's another place . . ." Her words trailed away as she watched him slowly shake his head.

"Nope. This is the house for the clinic doctor. Don't you worry. Mattie and Connie'll get it all cleaned up for ya." He slowly walked around the room. "Why, this ain't so bad, eh? Just needs some window cleaning and curtains." He pointed at the large hole in the wall. "And a little plaster board to patch this up."

Claire squared her shoulders. When she'd interviewed for the position at the clinic, she should have checked out the housing. She should have remembered that Dane White Eagle had come from Cold Creek, and she should have figured he'd still have family here. She had no one to blame for her predicament but herself. *This is the kind of job I've wanted for a long, long time, and I'll be damned if I'll back out because of something that can be fixed with some el-*

bow grease and friendship. "I'd appreciate the help you've offered, Mr. Rabbit. I'll be moving in the first of the month, next Saturday, and begin seeing patients at the clinic on Monday morning."

She watched Jerome Rabbit breathe a sigh of relief. He'd never know how close the clinic came to having another doctor disappear.

9

DANE TURNED OFF THE HIGHWAY AND DROVE ONTO reservation land. The last time he'd made this trip was the cold, snowy day in December . . . the cold, snowy day when he'd last picked up Kylee and took her to the city . . . the cold, snowy day he took her to her death.

An excruciating pain filled his chest, every bit as realistic as if bands of steel were being twisted around his ribs and his heart. Guilt. God, didn't it ever go away? Maybe someday, but not today.

He drew a deep breath, as deep as the steel bands would allow, and fought to settle his emotions. He'd waited a long time to make this drive, but it wasn't a celebration. That would come the day he locked handcuffs on Kylee's killer and put him away. Today was nothing more than a returning to his roots, a returning to finish a job.

He took his gaze off the road and looked out at Cold Creek as though he were seeing it for the first time. The land swept back from the road with few trees to break the view of scrub brush and buffalo grass. There wasn't anything pretty in a citified or manicured way about the reserve. No prim hedges lined people's driveways; hell, finding a real driveway would even be a problem. Only the occasional house had flower beds, though most had an old junk car or two or a pile of kids' bikes and other clutter. A few Cold Creek homes had a well-tended, neat look about them, but only a few. Even the houses in towns like Red Star had an untended look about them.

Had he expected that some kind of miracle would have happened in the six months since he'd been gone? Maybe. In fact, little had changed. A sighing breath escaped Dane's lips. Everything had changed for him, but Cold Creek was still the same. It was still home.

A huge motor home hogging most of the road and towing a small car passed him, heading back to civilization. "Tourists," Dane muttered, giving his head a slight shake. They came every summer, driving up from their motels to spend a few hours experiencing the rez, to see how the noble red man lived under the tender care of the U.S. government. They'd poke around town, hand out candy to the kids, stroll through the cemeteries, disturbing the little gifts that folks left on the graves, and then have their picture taken with old Willard Red Bull for five dollars. Before they left, they'd stop and buy beaded key chains, ridiculous gaudy dream catchers or mandalas, and tax-free cigarettes at the Blue Moon Smoke Shop. They'd be appalled by the poverty, not realizing that if they wanted to see white picket fences, pretty little houses, and shiny cars, they needed to go to one of the casino reservations where money flowed like the free booze.

Some of the tourists who came were do-gooders bringing boxes of clothing, some old, some new, to the tribal office or the church. They'd expect to see rapt expressions of gratitude on everyone's face, but would be disappointed to see embarrassment—which they'd mistake for hostility. Others came, the wannabes, looking for that total Indian encounter, seeking a spirituality they assumed was missing in their own lives. They believed the Indian people had

what they wanted. These were the suckers who'd pay anything to experience what they were told were the old ceremonies, the old ways. They'd gladly hand over a wad of
bills to some enterprising Indian who'd promise them a
real vision quest or an unforgettable experience in a sweat
lodge or at a sun dance.

And then there were those who came searching for their
ancestry because they felt that in their hearts they were already Indian. The litany was always the same. "My great
grandmother was an Indian princess. . . . My family never
talked about their Indian relatives. . . . I'm searching for
my roots." Hell, the Cherokee didn't corner the market on
these people, the Lakota had their fair share, too.

Dane snorted. *Whack nuts. Tourists.* Didn't these folks
realize that if the Indians had all the wisdom, all the spirituality, and all the answers, reservations wouldn't exist?
Did the idiots really believe that alcoholism, poverty, suicide, and diabetes didn't exist on the rez? Did they care
that there were kids so desperate to forget the way they
lived that they'd wig out on ecstasy, that they'd be willing
to risk dying by taking *waskuyeca wakan?*

Surprised and annoyed by the anger that had boiled out
of him, Dane needed a breath of fresh air. He turned off the
AC and rolled down the window. Hot summer air rushed
into the truck and in an instant negated everything the air
conditioner had accomplished in the past hour. He lifted
his foot off the gas and downshifted, slowing as he took the
corner in front of Jerome Rabbit's house. Ellie Rabbit and
her kids were sitting in the front yard. He honked the horn
and waved, glad to get an exuberant wave in return. If
everything was so normal, why did he feel so lost?

Following the two-lane, he passed the Baptist church,
the Red Bulls' house, and the health clinic. He glanced at
the full parking lot at the clinic. "Whoa, that's a surprise,"
he muttered. *They must have found a new doctor since I've
been gone, or maybe nosy old Butz turned up.*

Dane smiled, remembering the man who'd tenderly

cared for Kylee until he'd vanished. Martin Butz had been the doctor on Cold Creek for almost twenty years. A Johns Hopkins graduate, he'd dedicated his life to Indian health care, and at the Sweetgrass Powwow ten or fifteen years ago, he'd been taken in by the Rabbit family, given an Indian name, *Omawasté,* Makes Me Feel Good, and had become a member of the tribe. Martin Butz saw patients seven days a week, knew everybody's business, and ran a free after-hours clinic for anyone who had a drug problem and wanted help. His disappearance a little over a year ago had shocked everyone. Mattie Old Horn swore that aliens had taken him. Maybe she was right.

Forty-five minutes later, after being sworn in and being issued his badge and gun, Dane was back on the road. He flipped on his turn signal and took the next road to the right. A fresh coat of oil had been sprayed on the dirt road to keep the dust down, and the smell of the black goo rode heavy and unpleasant on the hot afternoon air. Small government-built houses lined both sides of the road on half-acre lots, one identical to the other. Looking five houses down the row on his right, Dane picked out the small bungalow where he'd spent his childhood. Slowing down, he stopped his truck and sat looking at the house. He gripped the steering wheel, let go of it, then turned his hands over and looked at them. When had his palms begun to sweat? *The moment you started out for home, White Eagle.*

He studied the house again. The sparkle the little house once had was gone. Road dust coated and dulled the windows, and the pile of trash on the side yard looked as though it had been growing for months. His mother's car was gone, but Clement Runs After's ancient truck, its once-black paint faded to a dull slate gray, was parked just off the road. The old man sat on the stoop, elbows on his knees, and stared back at Dane. *I guess there's no hiding from the sharp eyes of an old warrior.*

Resigned, Dane put his truck in gear and moved up behind Clement's Ford. Getting out, he slowly walked toward the house.

"She ain't home, so you don't have to walk all hang-tailed, boy." Clement stood, removed his old cowboy hat, and took Dane into his arthritic embrace, patting him heartily on the back.

"How is she?" Dane's question came at a great cost to him. Did Clement know his mother had never contacted him the whole time he'd been gone?

"She's got herself a job at the health clinic." He nodded. "She had it rough for a long time."

"And now?"

Clement gave his shoulder a slight lift. "Things are getting better." He nodded again. "They ain't back to what they should be, but the job helps. It helps with keeping her busy, and it helps pay her bills." His hug tightened. "It's good to see ya, boy. It's real good to see ya."

Dane absorbed what Clement had told him but wanted to know more. *Slow down,* he admonished himself. *You'll get your questions answered in good time. Don't push.* "It's great to see you, too, *Tuŋkasila*. Thanks for taking care of things around here for me."

The old man nodded. "I didn't do much. Just checked in on yer mom once in a while."

"Are you waiting for her to get home from work?"

"Naw. She don't get home till after five. I been waiting on you."

"Me?" Dane couldn't keep the sound of surprise from his voice. "I've been out a little over a week. How'd you know when I'd come?"

Clement shrugged. "I figured you'd be comin' this way sooner or later, so I just been waitin'."

"You've been sitting here every day?"

"Yup. Figured if I looked up that road long enough, I'd see ya comin'. Took ya a long time, but here y'are." Clement chuckled, then slowly settled himself back on the stoop and patted the concrete beside him, a silent request to have Dane join him.

Dane took off his cowboy hat and sat down beside Clement. "You look like an old tired yard dog sitting here."

Clement's chuckle grew into a full laugh. "I see them guys in Wakefield didn't take any of the orneriness outta ya. Could be they gave ya a bit more." He settled his old stained and skewed Stetson back on his head, tugged it low to shade his eyes, and let a moment or two pass before he spoke again. "You better now? All healed up and okay?"

"Yeah," Dane replied. "I'm doing fine. I've just got a few battle scars."

Clement leaned forward and propped his elbows on his knees again. He looked sideways up at Dane, his eyes sharp and watchful. "Good how things worked out for ya . . . eh? Who'da thought you'd be so lucky and get out 'cause someone goofed up. Who'da thought?"

Dane suddenly felt as though every word Clement Runs After was saying had another meaning entirely. "Who'da thought."

"So, whatcha gonna do? Got a job?"

"Yeah, as a matter of fact, I do." Dane reached in his pocket and withdrew a shiny hunk of silver and handed it to Clement. "I was just sworn in."

The old man slowly ran his finger over the carved and raised lettering and emblem on the silver badge. "Tribal police. Hmm." Clement fell silent but continued to run his gnarled finger back and forth over the lettering. "They got no problem with . . . what ya just gone through and where ya been?"

Dane shook his head. "No. There's no record. I was acquitted."

Clement looked up at Dane and slowly nodded. "Well, I guess I'd better watch how fast I drive from now on." He handed the badge back to Dane.

Dane didn't know why, but Clement's reaction wasn't at

all what he'd expected. Maybe he read too much into his offhanded response, or maybe there wasn't enough approval in the old man's voice. Whatever was wrong, it set Dane on edge and made him wonder if Clement Runs After knew more about certain things around Cold Creek than he let on.

Clement slowly stood and seemed to wait a moment while his legs steadied beneath him. He looked down, then laid his hand on Dane's head as though he were delivering a benediction. "You listen to me, boy. If things don't work out good here"—he pointed with his pursed lips toward Connie White Eagle's house—"you come on up to the hills. I got room for ya up at the cabin with me." He glanced off toward the north. "Maybe it's time you felt the wind on your face again and heard the old songs sung the way they're supposed to sound. Maybe it's time you remembered where you come from and the old people whose blood still runs in your veins." He stopped and seemed to study Dane for a moment. "And maybe I'll tell ya some of them old *Iktomi* stories . . . like I used to."

Every muscle in Dane's body tightened, burned by the rush of adrenaline as it ran like a flash fire through his veins. *Why the hell had Clement mentioned* Iktomi? *What the hell is going on? Don't be an idiot, it's nothing . . . it's nothing. Yeah, you've heard the word* Iktomi *in your dreams. So what? It's a coincidence, nothing more. It's just the old man trying to give me back some of my roots . . . my heritage. Maybe.* Dane looked up and found Clement's dark eyes watching him as though he were appraising his reaction. *No. This is ridiculous . . . coincidence, nothing more.*

"Well, you remember that. You gotta place up there with me," Clement said, pointing toward the north again with a quick lift of his chin. He then placed the palm of his hand against Dane's heart. "It's a good place to get healed, especially . . . here."

Dane stood, set his black Stetson back on his head, then

burrowed his hands deep in his pockets. Struggling to push his uneasiness aside, he followed Clement's gaze to the hills. "I appreciate that, *Tuŋkasila*. Thank you, Grandfather."

Clement nodded, a sly, slight grin on his face. *"Wasté."* He moved down the two steps to the dirt walkway, then turned and looked back up at Dane. "Go see your mama now. Don't wait. Start the healin' as soon as you can." He shuffled off toward his truck, then stopped about halfway across the yard, turned again, and added, "Leland Big Elk is a dangerous man, and your mama can't see it. I'm hoping that somebody's gonna come along and get him outta her life." He headed for his truck once again and without turning around a third time, lifted his hand and waved good-bye.

The bite of adrenaline still gnawed Dane's gut, keeping a sharp edge on his disquiet. *Iktomi. It's a damned coincidence, an old man and his stories, nothing more. Nothing more.* Dane watched Clement drive off. The old man had been driving the same Ford truck for as long as Dane could remember. It still bucked and rattled. It still coughed and creaked. And it still spewed a glut of smoke out of the tailpipe. Nothing changed. *Yeah, nothing's changed except the burning in my gut.*

Getting in his own truck, Dane headed back up the road toward the clinic. He turned out onto the paved two-lane and drove less than a hundred feet when movement to his left caught his eye. The blast of adrenaline returned, scrambling through his veins again and leaving him gasping for breath. His dream, the one that repeated itself over and over, seemed to have become reality.

Ears flapping in the breeze and with their tongues lolling out the sides of their mouths making them look like they were grinning, a dozen or so rez dogs broke from the scrub brush and loped along the road beside him.

"PHEW," CLAIRE BREATHED, sliding into the chair behind her desk. "We've been going full blast since nine this morning." She reached for the bottle of cola on her desk, her fingers slipping in the icy cold condensation.

"You've got about twenty minutes till the next patient shows up," Connie White Eagle said, checking the appointment book she held in her hand. "Mattie Old Horn. She's complainin' 'bout her belly again."

Claire nodded. Mattie had been a regular patient since the clinic had reopened, coming at least once a week with one complaint or another. "I think her belly problem is nothing more than loneliness."

"How do you figure that? She's got family around her all the time."

Claire shook her head. "No, she's got her grandkids around her all the time. Her daughter drops the kids off for days at a time." Claire glanced up at Connie. "Don't get me wrong. I know Mattie loves those babies dearly, but I think she misses talking to another adult."

Connie snorted. "Ain't nothin' new, lots of Indian grandmas raise their grandbabies. Besides, she's not alone like me. She's got herself a husband. Why don't she talk to him?"

Claire shrugged. "Maybe he doesn't talk back." She stood and stretched, seeking some easement for her aching back. "I left the clinic mail in my car this morning. I'm going out to get it." She hesitated at the office door and looked back at Connie. "A pack of wild dogs were in the field across the road when I came in this morning." She dropped her stethoscope into her pocket. "I hope they're gone."

"Could be coyotes," Connie replied. "If they are, they won't bother ya. Just make a lotta noise and that'll spook 'em." She laughed. "That's something you gotta get used to around here."

Slowly walking through the clinic, Claire couldn't stop the smile that lifted the corners of her mouth. She loved her new job, loved caring for people she'd see time and time again. A few folks weren't too sure about having a woman doctor—a white woman doctor—but soon the number of patients had begun increasing each day. In just the short time she'd been here, some of the faces were becoming familiar, and the names were becoming easier to remember, too. She nodded and smiled at an elderly couple in the waiting room, pulled open the front door, and stepped outside.

The midday sunlight blinded her for a moment, and squinting didn't help at all. Claire raised her hand to shield her eyes and with her next step bumped into the solid wall of a tall man. The impact knocked the breath from her body in a loud whoosh. As she teetered, fighting to keep her balance, strong hands firmly grasped her arms and steadied her.

The familiar timbre of the man's laugh stopped her cold and triggered an almost paralyzing panic. Claire's hands flew into the air to push away from him. Her left hand felt something hard at his waist. *Oh, my God! A gun!*

Her pulse quickened, racing with an insane speed, and her instinct to run kicked in. Quickly stepping back, her ankle twisted, and she began to stumble again. Once more, strong hands gripped her arms and caught her. Still holding on to her, he turned her around until the sun was no longer in her eyes. In that moment Claire found herself looking up at a man she had never expected to see again. Dane White Eagle.

"What . . . what are you doing here?" Her voice quavered. "You're supposed to be in prison." She glanced down at the gun and then back up. "Please . . . I don't want any trouble here. Go . . . go away." She tried to back away. "I won't call the police. Just leave. Please."

"Whoa, whoa, slow down, take a breath," Dane interrupted. "Apparently you don't get much news out here."

"Please . . . I don't know what you want, go away—"

"Shh." He placed his index finger against her mouth and tried to ignore how soft her lips felt. The safest way to do that was to take his finger away; he didn't hesitate another second. "Don't worry, I didn't escape, they let me out—all nice and legal—on a technicality. The gun's legal, too." He flashed a wide grin and his badge at her. "And I came to see my mother.

Claire drew a long, shuddering breath. "But I thought that—"

"Yeah, I know. You thought I'd come to steal your penlight."

10

〜

DANE WHITE EAGLE LOOKED NOTHING AT ALL LIKE AN escaped convict. His jeans, though faded and worn in a few interesting places, fit like a second skin over his narrow hips and long legs. Boot-cut Wranglers were definitely not prison issue. Neither was the large oval silver belt buckle that accented his flat stomach. A navy blue western-style shirt skimmed over his chest and hinted at the broad shoulders and muscles beneath. Claire didn't need a hint; she clearly remembered what he'd looked like naked.

His near-black hair fell almost to his waist in thick, shiny braids that were wrapped and tied at the ends with thin white buckskin thongs. A black cowboy hat, set low on his forehead, shaded his eyes and added the perfect final touch. At six foot three, he towered over Claire, and she knew she'd never seen a man as breathtaking as Dane White Eagle. The reality had come to her the first time she'd seen him, and now she was even more convinced it was true.

"Now that you've studied me from head to toe," Dane said, interrupting her thoughts, "do I look like a convict, or do I look like a free man who's just been released from prison?" He cocked his brow at an impudent angle.

His question startled her, interrupting her ill-timed appraisal. How could she allow herself to be so distracted? How could she forget who and what he was? And then it struck her what he had said. *Released.* "What do you mean, released? I don't understand." Her nervous glance moved to the holstered gun at his waist. "It's impossible. You're guilty." She raised her gaze back up to his face and peered at him as if trying to find a clue of innocence or guilt in his expression.

Dane shrugged. "Am I?"

She watched him fold his arms across his chest, and then he had the audacity to smile at her. Her temper flared. Tangling with suspicion, it was soon joined by the unbidden crazy pounding of her heart. "Yes. You are. A court of law . . . the jury found you guilty. You were sentenced to twenty-five years." She mirrored his stance, crossing her arms over her breasts, and then glanced again at the gun. "What do you intend to do with that?"

"Nothing . . . at the moment."

Claire took another backward step. Adrenaline tumbled like an avalanche through her body. *Keep calm. Breathe. Steady, now. Don't panic.* "If you were released from Wakefield, the tribal police should know about it . . . right?"

"Oh, I bet they do."

Claire watched his infuriating smile broaden into a grin. She raised her chin, putting it at a defiant angle. "Maybe I should call them and find out."

"Oh, you could, but I don't think that's necessary."

Dane's hand moved toward the gun at his waist, and she gasped. *Have I pushed him too far? My God, he really wouldn't shoot me . . . would he? You ninny, if he'd kill his own sister of course he'd . . .* Her hand flew to her face and covered her mouth. "Please," she croaked. "Just go away. I won't tell anyone you were here . . . Please, go."

She loathed the weak tone she heard in her voice. She hadn't heard it in a long, long time—not since she'd left Keith. The thought immediately triggered new and untried determination. Too many months of hard work and counseling had taken place since her divorce for her to toss it all away. *No, I won't allow myself to be the victim again. It may be very foolish and very risky, but I'm not going to let Dane White Eagle bully me.*

She shot a quick glance over her shoulder at the clinic door, then turned and met his gaze, hoping against hope that he'd fall for her bluff. She drew a fortifying breath and began, "There are a lot of people inside who know you, people who will recognize you. You can't shoot us all. If you hurt me or any of them, I promise, you will go back to prison, and this time you will find yourself on death row. Think about it very carefully before you do something you'll regret and can't undo." For some reason she felt that if she kept talking, she'd be safe, he wouldn't do anything. He wouldn't pull the gun out of the holster. He wouldn't shoot her. Mesmerized, she watched his fingers touch the flap on the holster. *My God, I'm wrong. He would do it!* Her resolve shattered. "Oh, please. Stop, please stop. Help! Hel—" She choked on the word before it was completely out of her mouth, and suddenly she felt very foolish.

Wide-eyed, her gaze followed Dane White Eagle's hand as it passed the holster and slowly dipped into his jeans pocket.

He withdrew his hand and held it out to her, palm up. Sunlight careened off the object that lay in his hand, and she shut her eyes against its glare.

"Officer White Eagle of the Cold Creek Tribal Police at your service, ma'am."

Stunned, Claire opened her eyes. A badge, a tribal police badge, filled his palm. She didn't know what to say, what to do . . . what to think. When her words came, their cadence was uneven. "I . . . I don't understand. How . . . cou-could you be a . . ."

"A cop?" Dane finished the sentence for her.

"Yes," she choked. "How?"

"I must have answered all the questions on the application right." He chuckled as he slid the badge back into his pocket. "I needed a job, met the qualifications, and got hired."

"That's ridiculous. You were convicted of a . . . a felony. How can you carry a gun? How can you be a cop?"

Dane watched her face change expressions, going from fear to confusion. "Claire, my conviction was overturned. There is no felony record. Poof." He snapped his fingers. "Gone."

"No." She shook her head. "It's wrong. Don't you remember? I was in the ER that night . . ." Her voice softened. "I know what you told me. . . . I was at your trial when—"

"I remember," Dane interrupted. "How could I forget?" He could see she was uncomfortable bringing up the night Kylee died. "The Rapid City cops didn't have a search warrant. Their search of my truck and apartment was illegal. I've been acquitted on all charges."

"That doesn't make you innocent." She stepped farther away from him.

"In a court of law it does." Dane stepped closer. "Look, you're just going to have to trust me on this, okay?"

She looked down at the gun again, then back up, meeting his gaze. She didn't know what to think. She didn't know whether she believed him or not. "Under the circumstances, I think you're asking for a lot."

"Yeah, I suppose I am. But, at this point, I don't have a choice." He shrugged. "I'm just trying to get some of my life back."

"I know how that feels."

Claire Colby had spoken the words so softly, Dane wasn't sure that she'd really said them. What had happened to make her leave her job at Pennington General and come to Cold Creek? He pushed her for an answer. "Maybe I should ask you what *you're* doing here. There aren't too many white girls moving to the rez these days." Claire Colby's smoky blue eyes widened with a little spark of what . . . irritation? Indignance?

"It would seem that we're both working on some lifestyle changes," she replied. "Some more deserved than others."

A bright flush colored Claire's cheeks, and she took a step forward and placed her hands on her hips.

"And how dare you lead me on, making me think you were going to pull your gun out of the holster. You did that on purpose. Well, I hope you enjoyed your silly little game."

Dane watched her lift her chin in a snooty little tilt. Her courage had quickly returned, and it brought a smile to his lips. He hadn't realized there was this wonderful feisty side to her. Claire Colby had a few thorns, and if he didn't watch himself, he just might get pricked.

"For your information, I moved to Cold Creek for my new job. I no longer work at Pennington."

"Got fired, did you?"

She gasped. "I most certainly did not. How dare you imply something so ridiculous. I decided it was time for a career change and took—"

His laugh stopped her explanation cold. "You call that a career change?" He pointed at the clinic. "What kind of a career can you have on Cold Creek? This isn't exactly the job capital of the world. There's a lot more money and prestige working at a McDonald's."

She drove her hands into the pockets of her white lab coat. "In case you've forgotten, Mr. White Eagle," Claire continued, "I'm a doctor, and this was a health clinic in need of a doctor." She turned and pointed at the sign over the door, at herself, and then back at the sign. "Clinic . . . doctor . . . clinic. I'm sure that even you can grasp the concept."

Dane's gaze wandered down Claire's body, from the

crown of thick and shiny brunette hair, her blue eyes, her flushed cheeks and inviting full lips, to the sensible shoes she wore on her feet. He approved of every sweet curve he found. There was more than the concept of clinic and doctor that he'd like to grasp. It still surprised him that he was so attracted to Claire Colby. He knew it was more than her beauty that intrigued him, but what? What was it about Claire Anne Colby that made his pulse race and made him think of soft lips and softer breasts, the sweet scent of vanilla and of slender, gentle hands? *Maybe if I can get to know her better, maybe . . .*

"I wondered when you'd show up."

The familiar voice burned into his thoughts, and its icy tone froze whatever pleasant thoughts and hope he'd harbored. Dane turned and found his mother standing in the open door of the clinic. He stepped toward her.

Connie White Eagle's face twisted with contempt. She jerked her arm up and pointed at him, her hand becoming a warning, a barricade. "Don't you dare come near me." Her pointing finger jabbed in the air at him. "Damn you . . . stay away from me." Filled to the brim with the sound of anger and loathing, her voice quavered. "I don't know you. Go away." She dropped her arm to her side and pressed her fisted hand against her thigh.

"Ina, please." The steel bands around Dane's heart suddenly returned, twice as vicious as before. "We have to talk."

"I ain't no *ina* to you. I got nothin' to say to you. I don't talk to murderers. So, don't be comin' around. You wanna talk to somebody, go find old Clement. He's so lonely he'll talk to anything. You're dead to me." Her mouth fell into a hard, flat line.

Dane watched his mother's gaze travel over him, stopping at his thigh, his left side, and his shoulder where he'd been stabbed. Her eyes settled once again on his face. Had he seen a softening in her expression, or had it just been a trick of shadow and light in the afternoon sun?

"I got better things to do than stand out here and waste my time. I got work to do." She turned to Claire. "I'd send this trash on its way if I were you, Dr. Claire." Connie abruptly turned and disappeared into the clinic.

He couldn't move. Every nerve in his body and every thought in his head told him to follow her, but he couldn't move. *God, the pain . . .* He closed his eyes for a moment, waiting for it to pass. It didn't, and he knew it wouldn't for a long, long time.

The touch on his arm was light and tentative. He looked down at Claire's small hand, pale and delicate against his dark shirt.

"I'm so sorry."

He glanced at her and tried to pull off an indifferent shrug but knew immediately when he recognized pity in her gaze that he'd failed. Her soft touch added another steel band of pain in his chest. Dane pulled away. *I don't need pity. I don't need anybody's damned pity.*

"Dane, I . . ."

He turned away from Claire and, without a backward glance, walked toward his truck. "You'd better get back to your clinic, Dr. Claire, no need for you to get involved in Connie White Eagle's embarrassing family problems."

Leaving Claire Colby standing in the afternoon sunlight was one of the hardest things he'd ever done in his life.

THE DIRT ROAD to the tribal cemetery hadn't been graded in years. Ruts and potholes pocked its surface, and rocks kicked up by the tires pinged against the undercarriage of his truck. Dane slid the Black Lodge tape, Kylee's favorite, into the player and cranked up the volume. It continued to play as he parked the truck and stepped out. Standing just outside the cemetery, he glanced around at the roughly cut buffalo grass that grew throughout the graveyard. He had no idea where Kylee had been buried and knew he'd have to walk up and down every row until he found her grave.

Maybe that was okay. He'd see the names of old friends and elders he'd respected and know Kylee wasn't alone.

Dane slid the cell phone from the holder on his belt, turned it off, and then put it back. The outside world had no place here, not now.

He pushed open one side of the rusted iron gate and stepped through. Once inside, he stopped and slowly glanced around. Cold Creek Cemetery was a typical reservation burial ground. Little red flannel tobacco ties decorated a few bushes, and an interesting collection of gifts placed by family and friends rested at the bases of their loved ones' gravestones. A pack of a favorite brand of cigarettes, a favorite CD, a pretty ribbon or two, some family photographs, a can of a favorite drink, or maybe a bit of their favorite food . . . all could be found at one grave or another. To outsiders the cemetery might have an unkempt look about it, but this was the way that Indian people honored and remembered those they'd lost.

Dane stopped and looked around, searching for Kylee. At first his gaze traveled past it and then, as though someone had called his name, he looked back, and there it was. His heart thudded against his ribs, and he couldn't breathe. The ground sloped away, rising upward, and there on top of the hill was a lone cottonwood tree. *Funny, I don't remember ever noticing that before.* And then Dane knew where he'd find his sweet *Taŋski.*

He began walking toward the hill, and with each step his pace quickened until he was running, his breath rasping, his heart racing. The pall of déjà vu settled over him, and once more the dream had become real.

A large, pink granite headstone stood beneath the tree, Kylee's name deeply engraved in its surface. Feathers and carvings that were supposed to look like beadwork had been cut into the stone in a gaudy design. Dane knew that Kylee would hate it. A Snickers bar, a photo of Connie and Clement, a small box wrapped in Christmas paper, and her beaded cane lay at the base of the stone, but it was what was beside the marker that sent him to his knees, that made him weep.

Standing in the shade of the cottonwood, the little lilac bush patiently waited for spring so it could burst forth again with its fragrant purple blooms.

Dane settled himself on the ground and laid his hand over Kylee's grave. He spent over an hour softly talking, telling her everything that was in his heart and watching the evening arrive.

When he rose to leave, he laid his hand on the top of the headstone. "I love you, *Taηski*. I won't forget my promise. I'll find the bastard who stole you from us, and I'll send him to hell."

As he turned to leave, movement in the cemetery at the bottom of the hill caught his eye. Scattered throughout the graveyard, the pack of rez dogs moved at a slow trot through the rows of headstones. As though drawn by a command, they gathered together at the bottom of the hill and looked up at him. Kylee's pup stood in the midst of the pack.

"Pirate," Dane whispered, shocked to find the pup running wild. He knew he would have recognized the dog anywhere. The black patch around the dog's right eye that had given it its name, made it easy to recognize.

Dane slowly moved down the hill and, speaking softly, stepped as close to the dogs as he dared. *This is a damned foolish thing to do. These damn dogs are wild and could tear me apart in minutes.* But it was worth the risk if he could catch the yearling pup and take it up to Clement's. It didn't seem right that Kylee's dog was with the pack. Why had his mother turned the pup out to fend for itself?

Every dog in the pack watched him, a few growled and bared their teeth, but none backed away.

He held out his hand and crouched low, talking to the young dog in a singsong voice. "Come on, Pirate. Here boy. Come here."

The dog lifted its ears, tilted its head, and listened to Dane's voice. Its tail began to move in a timid wag.

"Come here, Pirate. Good dog, good dog." Dane took his eyes off Pirate for a moment and nervously glanced at the rest of the pack. They'd shifted and moved in a circle around both Dane and Pirate.

And then, as if it remembered him, the pup began to move out of the pack, its tail beating an enthusiastic rhythm as it crept closer. Stretching its neck as far as it could, Pirate sniffed at Dane's hand. Dane held his breath. If he grabbed the dog, how would he hold him? Would the dog remember a human touch enough to let him pet him?

Dane hunkered down lower. "Hey Pirate, how you doing? Remember me? I'm the guy that got rid of that nasty coyote for you." Inching forward, Dane finally was able to touch the pup's nose. Encouraged by the tentative lick of Pirate's tongue, he slowly moved his hand, stroking the pup's head and then down its neck.

As Dane scratched the black and white dog behind its ear, the loud crack of a rifle shot splintered the quiet early evening.

Instinctively, Dane dropped, pressed his body flat against the ground, and tried to tell where the shot had come from. A second shot kicked up dirt less than ten feet away. The dogs scattered. Racing off, they disappeared into the tall buffalo grass.

"Hey, *kola*. You okay, man? I didn't mean to spook ya."

Damn. What the hell was Leland doing here? Dane stood and watched Leland Big Elk walk through the cemetery, casually carrying a rifle in his hand. "You didn't spook me, you damn near killed me." Dane fisted his hands and knew he'd have to hold a tight rein on his temper, or else one of his fists was going to make Leland's face hurt . . . a lot.

Leland laughed and held up the rifle. "I got a scope on this thing that's so powerful, I could shoot a flea off a dog's ass."

"Is that what you were aiming at? Fleas?" Dane lifted

his chin and pointed with pursed lips to the spot where the dogs had vanished.

"Hell, no, *kola.*" Leland sounded as though his feelings had been deeply hurt. "Them wild dogs was all around ya. I thought you were in trouble. They're worse'n coyotes. Hell, I've heard that they can take a buffalo down and eat it whole in ten minutes." He gave Dane's shoulder a light punch. "Hell, you're smaller'n a buffalo, besides, I sure couldn't have anything happen to the tribe's newest cop."

"Yeah? Well, I could run you in for shooting at that new cop." Dane brushed dirt and bits of grass off his jeans.

"If I'd wanted to shoot ya, you wouldn't be standing here talking to me." Leland stared at Dane, clearly pushing his point. Turning away, he looked at the nearby graves and began to laugh. "Well, at least ya can't get me for disturbin' the peace." He glanced up the hill toward Kylee's grave. "So, what d'ya think of the headstone I bought her? Pretty fancy, eh? Your mom didn't have the money, and I knew she wanted one. It cost a big bundle, but it made your momma happy. When she's happy, I'm happy." With a sweep of his arm he pointed to the other graves in the cemetery. "Most expensive stone in here. Nicest one, too."

Dane fisted his hands again, forced himself to swallow the anger that had filled him like bitter bile, and made himself another promise. He'd be damned if Leland Big Elk's garish headstone would mark *Taŋski*'s grave much longer. As soon as he could, he'd have it replaced.

"What are you doing up here?" Dane asked, moving away from the hill.

"I came lookin' for you. Ellie Rabbit said she saw ya earlier, and I figured you'd be here, first chance you got, and all." Leland shuffled along beside Dane, holding the rifle on his shoulder as though he were playing soldier. "We need to make a delivery to the city. It's a good buy, and I can't pass it up." He glanced up at Dane. "I got the stuff in my truck. You gotta make the drop by eight tonight. The guy will meet ya at the Shoney's on I-90. It's a five thousand dollar deal, so make sure you get the right amount of cash. I don't like bein' shortchanged."

"What's in it for me? I'm the one taking all the chances."

"Don't worry, *kola*. I'll take good care of ya. How's five hundred sound?"

Dane shook his head. "I can't hear you; that's a pretty low sound."

"Okay, okay. I'll make it a grand, but don't expect that much every time. It'll be a welcome home present." Leland punched Dane on the shoulder again. "It's good to have ya with me, *kola*. Where are ya stayin'?"

"I don't have any plans yet."

"Well, how in the hell am I goin' to find ya? I can't be driving all over the rez every time I need ya."

"Quit whining, Elk. I'm one of those modern Injuns." He pointed to his right side. "I got a cell phone."

"Yer a smart-ass Injun. Does your cell phone have a number?"

Dane quickly jotted the number on a piece of paper and traded it for the package that Leland held out to him.

"The customer's name is Stedman," Leland said.

Dane took the package and stowed it under the driver's seat in his truck. He smiled to himself. Stedman was the code name that Gaines and Pardue used. The FBI was buying some more ecstasy.

11

AN EARLY EVENING RAIN HAD BEGUN TO FALL, AND the reflection of the streetlights glistened on the wet pavement. Dane sat at an isolated table next to the window and watched Jack Gaines park his car in the Shoney's lot, then dash through the downpour and into the restaurant.

"Coffee, sir?" The waitress stood at Dane's elbow.

"Thanks. Make it two. I'm expecting someone."

She returned and placed two mugs and a carafe of fresh coffee on the table just as Gaines arrived.

"Do you gentlemen want anything else?" The waitress whipped her pad out of her pocket. "We've got some fresh lemon meringue pie and a great strawberry pie."

"No, we're okay," Dane replied without waiting for Gaines's response. "Thanks."

Gaines waited until the waitress left before he settled into the chair across the table from Dane. "Hey, pal, the idea of you having a cell phone is so we can get ahold of you. I hate having to call Leland and act like some drugged-out addict. It's too dangerous. And now the Bureau's got to make another buy. My budget is shot all to hell. I hate putting more money in Leland's pocket." He shook the raindrops from his jacket, then draped it over the chair next to him. "You weren't out of the mainstream long enough to forget what cell phones are used for, were ya?"

"Did you want to meet just to chew my ass or did you have some important reason?"

"Funny you should ask." Gaines glanced around, hesitating for a moment at each filled table. Apparently satisfied that no one would be able to hear their conversation, he leaned forward and began. "What do you know about Martin Butz, Dr. Martin Butz?"

Dane suddenly felt on edge. Where had this come from? What did Martin Butz have to do with the Big Elk sting he was working on? He shrugged, still unsure what Jack Gaines was looking for, and answered the question. "I knew him. Hell, everyone on Cold Creek knew him. I didn't know him that well, though. A kid didn't get too close to the guy who gave him flu and tetanus shots every year. I can tell you that he took good care of my sister." He studied Gaines's face, looking for a clue to the man's interest. "Is this about his disappearance?"

"Yeah, it sure is."

Puzzled, Dane frowned. "That was, what, almost two years ago? Why the interest now? Isn't it ancient history?"

"A cold case, maybe, but certainly not ancient history."

Dane nodded. "So, you're telling me the Bureau is looking into Butz's case again?"

"Let's just say we never stopped." Gaines picked up the carafe, filled his mug, and took a sip. "Did you know Claire Colby is now running the clinic?"

"Yeah, I do. As a matter of fact, I talked to her today . . . at the clinic," Dane replied. Trying to fit all the pieces of the puzzle together was beginning to frustrate him. "What's this about, Gaines? The tribal police and you guys never came up with anything on Butz. No blood, no body, no missing car, nothing. What's this got to do with Claire?"

Gaines grinned and waggled his eyebrows. "So we're on a first-name basis now, are we?"

Damn it, Gaines didn't miss a thing. "Hell, the woman's seen me naked two or three times. On the rez that means we're almost engaged."

"Okay, okay." Gaines laughed. "Then you probably won't have any trouble asking her for a favor."

"Depends," Dane answered. The edgy feeling gave him another hard poke. "Suppose you tell me what's going on and if it puts my cover in jeopardy."

"If you play it cool, it won't blow your cover, especially now that you're a gen-u-ine tribal cop."

Dane shook his head. "News travels fast. Calvin Iron Cloud didn't swear me in until this morning."

"You think you're the only contact we got?"

"Probably not," Dane replied, his voice a little sharp even to his own ears.

Gaines paused and appeared to study Dane's mood. Apparently satisfied, he continued. "When Butz disappeared, we went through the usual investigation: searched his house, the clinic, lifted fingerprints, interviewed coworkers, neighbors, and family. We put out an APB on his car and posted his photograph around the country."

"Of course you had all the right paperwork put together for *his* search warrant. Right?" Dane hoped his joke would ease the tension he felt.

Gaines chuckled. "Oh yeah, we're real careful about those kinda things. Once in a while you goof up, but only when it matters."

"Thank God for goofs."

Gaines grinned. "We knew you'd like it."

"So, what's the deal about Martin Butz? Why are you throwing his disappearance into the mix now?"

"When we searched Butz's clinic records, we found that some of the files were missing. Checking a little deeper, we were able to tag those files to some of the Big Elk boys' customers."

Dane leaned forward, his mind racing ahead of Gaines's accounting. He didn't like where this conversation was headed. He asked the question again. "What does this have to do with Claire Colby?"

Gaines lifted his coffee mug to his lips, took another sip, and watched Dane over the rim. "We think the Big Elks were involved in Martin Butz's disappearance. We think that he was getting suspicious when he started having too many patients show up at the clinic who were having a bad ride on E." Gaines shrugged. "Sometimes when a guy is close to dying, he'll get loose lipped with the man who can save him. He'll spill his guts. We believe Butz was hearing some very interesting stories." He put his mug down on the table. "And we think Bobby and Leland took him for a one-way ride."

Dane's stomach twisted and burned as adrenaline raced through his body. "This had to have gone down a short while before Bobby was arrested and sent to Wakefield."

"Yeah, he must have figured it was a whole lot better to take an eight-year sentence for possession of a controlled substance with the intent to sell than going down for murder one."

Was my mother seeing Leland then? Dane racked his brain trying to remember when she'd started dating Leland. *Yeah, probably. Son of a bitch! Why didn't I do something? Why didn't I tell her the truth and get rid of him when he first started coming around?* It made him sick to think that his mother's boyfriend was a murderer. Another horrible thought elbowed itself into his head and twisted his gut. It wasn't a new thought. It was one he'd had before. *Aside from the kids who'd died from the bad batches of E, was Butz their only victim? Did Leland and Bobby Big Elk have anything to do with Kylee's death?*

The question was never answered; it only left him with another question. What reason would the Big Elks have to kill a thirteen-year-old girl who was already dying of cancer?

Dane pushed the idea and the questions aside. They didn't go easily, but he knew they'd be there waiting for him when the time was right. He focused his attention back on Gaines. "So, what did getting rid of Martin Butz do to cover up the Big Elks' dirty business?"

"We don't think they went after Butz in the beginning. We figure they broke into the clinic and were looking for patient charts so they could steal and destroy them, so there'd be no records of their customers. Maybe there was something in Butz's notes, or maybe Butz caught 'em in the act, but once he'd found them out, they had to get rid of him."

Dane already knew the answer, but he still had to hear Gaines put it into words, to say it out loud. "Cut the damned runaround. Get to how this involves Claire."

Gaines nodded. "Okay, here it is. She's probably going to start getting those same kinds of patients, too. Even with Bobby locked up in Wakefield, they're gonna worry about what she finds out and what she's gonna do about it. If it looks like she's going to the cops . . . well, let's just say that old Leland isn't gonna let that happen."

Dane tried to ignore the cold wave of fear that washed over him. Could he juggle working undercover being one of Leland's boys, and still keep Claire safe? He'd damn well have to. "What's the favor?"

Gaines stared at Dane for a moment or two and then continued. "We want you to ask her if she's had anyone show up with a drug problem that can be attributed to ec-stasy. We want you to keep on it, check with her every few days. Pass it off as a case you're working on with the tribal force. She should buy that."

"What about her safety? She lives alone out there. She's easy game if Leland finds out—"

"If Leland finds out, you're just keepin' an eye on things for him, for the business. Hell, tell him you've been as-signed to check into things by Iron Cloud, your boss in the tribal office. You'll handle it. He'll buy it. I'm not worried."

"What about patient confidentiality? That lady's got strong ethics. I can guarantee she won't do anything to jeopardize her patients."

"You're not asking for names, just information on the number of substance abuse cases she sees, especially those she suspects used E," Gaines replied. "Shouldn't be any trouble getting that. Besides"—Gaines began to laugh—"maybe if she saw you naked again, it'd entice her to give out any information you want."

"Leave my sex life out of this."

"I didn't know you had one, White Eagle."

"Better than yours," Dane quipped, challenging Jack Gaines with a laugh, hoping to ease the dread he felt.

Gaines pointed to himself and grinned as if he figured he had Dane beat. "You've forgotten, I'm a married man."

"Yeah, that's exactly what I mean, which means my sex life's better than yours. I don't have to put up with headaches and PMS."

"Ouch," Gaines cackled and placed his hand over his heart. "You're speaking about the woman I love."

"You're damned lucky she'll have you."

"And it takes a ton of Godiva chocolates and jewelry from QVC to keep me that lucky."

Dane laughed, then checked his watch. He'd been talking with Gaines for over half an hour. He glanced out the window. "We'd better wrap this up in case I'm being watched." He put the package Leland had given him on the table. "I wouldn't put it past Leland to follow me or send one of his other boys to do the deed. Slide me the money."

Gaines nodded and handed Dane an envelope. "Okay, but keep in touch. Be careful, and remember, Pardue and I are just a phone call away." He stood, picked up the package, and left.

Dane waited another ten minutes, slowly drinking the cup of coffee he'd poured for himself. Gaines had thrown him another curveball. He'd wanted to stay as far away from Claire Colby as Cold Creek Reservation would allow, but, from the looks of things, the Bureau had another plan in mind. *I'm getting damned tired of all this.* He looked out the window at the falling rain. *When do I get my life back?* An ache swelled in his chest. *Sometimes I don't even remember who the hell I am.*

Dane picked his hat up off the seat beside him. He set it on his head, then tugged the brim until the hat sat in its usual position, low on his forehead. Leaving a generous tip for the waitress, he paid the bill and left.

The rain had let up, and he breathed the clean, fresh air as he walked to his truck. He'd bunk in with Clement until he found somewhere else to live. At least the old man would welcome him with open arms and wouldn't ask him for anything but friendship.

CLAIRE PULLED THE window shade down to the sill. She knew it was ridiculous to feel so uneasy, but the night noises on Cold Creek were like nothing she'd ever heard before. Branches on the tree outside of her bedroom window tapped with an eerie cadence on the panes as they moved in the wind, and last night she'd heard what she thought were coyotes howling nearby. "Or those darned wild dogs I keep seeing," she muttered, closing the living room curtains.

"I need to get a dog. A big dog with a loud bark." She checked the lock on the front door for the third time. "A great big, mean, loyal dog with a loud bark."

Turning to face the living room, she found herself still amazed by the transformation. Connie White Eagle, Mattie Old Horn, and Jerome Rabbit's wife Ellie had worked hard for almost a week, scrubbing and polishing, painting and vacuuming. The tribal council had put in a new stove and refrigerator, the old carpet in the living room and bedrooms had been torn up and new put down. The kitchen and bathroom tile had been repaired, and the ghastly purple walls in her bedroom were now a pretty dusty rose. Some

of the neighborhood ladies had made the curtains, and
Jerome and his two sons spent one afternoon carting away
trash from the yard. The council promised that the outside
of the small house would get a new coat of paint, too.

Claire liked the little house, its cozy rooms and the big
yard, but the darned noises at night were enough to drive
her back to the city.

I'll get used to them, she promised herself, knowing that
she'd probably just told herself a lie.

Bone tired, she leaned back against the front door and
closed her eyes. The ten-hour days at the clinic were piling
up. *I need help, someone I don't have to train. I need Julie.*
Claire slowly shook her head. No chance of that happening. Julie wouldn't set foot on Cold Creek. She'd already
made that clear before Claire had left Pennington General.

Claire stepped away from the door. "Bedtime," she muttered as her fingers touched the switch on the table lamp.
Before she could turn off the light, a loud knock rattled the
front door. Startled, she gasped and quickly drew her hand
away from the lamp, almost knocking it over. As she fumbled to keep the lamp from falling off the table, Julie's
warning rang clear in her head. *If someone comes to the
door after dark, never, and I'll repeat that, never open the
door. You never know what you're gonna find.*

The knock came again.

Taking one tentative step after another, Claire moved
toward the door.

Another knock broke the silence.

"Go away," Claire croaked. "I've got a big dog, I've
called the police, and I've got a gun." Was that a laugh she
heard?

"You don't have a dog, you haven't called the police,
and I'll bet my gun's bigger than yours."

She knew that deep, rich voice. "Dane? White Eagle?"
Claire didn't know whether she felt relieved or ridiculous.
Should she open the door? The image of him sitting in the

courtroom, the news of the verdict and the TV pictures of him being handcuffed and taken to Wakefield filled her mind. *Surely the tribal council wouldn't have hired him if . . .* "Just a minute." She reached out but hesitated before her fingers touched the lock. Indecision. "Now what?" she breathed, torn between what she knew she should do and what she wanted to do.

"Claire?"

"Okay, okay." She flipped the deadbolt, unlocked and opened the door.

He stood in the soft beam of the porch light, his feet slightly apart. There was a sense of integrity and nobility about him that defied everything he'd been accused of, but doubt and distrust still remained in Claire's mind. There was another side to her dilemma, too. She'd never found a man so . . . so intriguing in her life.

His dark eyes were shaded by the brim of his hat; she could almost feel their touch, and the grin on his lips was indescribably delicious. Oh yeah, Julie had been so right. *Never open the door. You never know what you're gonna find.*

"Don't you think a simple 'Who's there' would've been a whole lot easier? And a lot friendlier."

"What do you want?" Still a little shaken, Claire knew she sounded unfriendly. Maybe that was for the best. Nothing in her life had prepared her for a man like Dane White Eagle.

He looked up at the sky and then back at her. "It's raining out here. You going to ask me in where it's dry?" The grin broadened.

Claire hesitated longer than was polite and then gave in. She moved to the right as he stepped inside. "I want to go to bed. I hope whatever you want won't take long." The moment she said the words she regretted them, especially when his left brow lifted in a teasing arch.

"That's kind of rushing things isn't it, Doc?" Dane

replied, his teasing expression still in place. "I like to take it slow and easy, get to know you better, but if that's what you want."

Claire suddenly felt like a giddy teenager experiencing her first serious romantic encounter. She folded her arms across her breasts and put her mental armor in place. "What do you want, Mr. White Eagle?"

"Dr. Colby," Dane responded, his tone mimicking hers. "I'm here on official business and need to ask a favor of you."

Dane watched her step back and saw her puzzled expression. He hadn't intended on coming to her so soon with Gaines's request, but when he'd driven by and saw her lights still on, he figured now was as good a time as any; besides, he didn't want anyone at the clinic overhearing his request. He'd expected the cool reception, the look of distrust in her eyes, but he hadn't expected the tousled hair, the blush on her cheeks, or the intriguing way her jeans hugged her hips and bottom. He knew he'd never see an Indianapolis Colts football jersey again and be able to think of football, either.

"Would you like something to drink? A Coke, some coffee?"

As though he'd suddenly been pulled out of a trance, it took a few seconds for him to respond. "Uh, no, thank you." He whipped the hat off his head and wiped the dampness from the brim with the palm of his hand. "This won't take long."

She pointed to the chair near the door. "Sit, please. You said something about a favor?"

It took Dane fifteen minutes to spin the half-truths. He hated setting her up like this, but there was no other way to get the job done. With each word he also became more and more aware of the danger she faced. When he'd finished, he waited anxiously for her response.

She thoughtfully nodded. "Unfortunately, I'm very aware of the problem. I had a few cases show up in the ER at Pennington." She glanced down at her hands in her lap. "I lost a couple of kids. Couldn't do a thing to help them." She looked up at Dane. "Why have you come to me? There are laws, you know. I can't give you information about any of my patients."

"I'm not asking for names. I need you to tell me if you suspect any ecstasy use. We need to get an idea about how much is getting into Cold Creek." He paused, expecting her to ask him more questions. When she didn't, he continued. "Out here the kids call it *waskuyeca wakan,* strong candy. If you hear these words, they're talking about E. There are other names that you might hear, as well. Beans, X, baby slits, love potion number nine, love trip, or X-ing. These are just a few. The kids talk about wiggin' when they're on it or getting wigged out. Sometimes they get together for wild parties called raves to take this stuff. It's all about ecstasy. And sometimes, it's all about dying."

Dane watched a frown crease Claire's brow, and her expression didn't set him at ease; in fact it made him very edgy.

"For someone who just started with the police," she began, "you seem to be very knowledgeable about all this. I find that surprising."

He felt her scrutiny and knew he'd better be careful what he said and how he said it. Claire Colby wasn't going to be easily fooled. He shrugged. "I guess you could say I'm a quick study. Besides, you learn a lot about street stuff when you're in the penitentiary." He feigned a slight smile. "So, will you consider helping me?"

She looked at him without speaking for a few minutes. A soft furrow creased her brow, and he knew she was struggling to make up her mind.

"No names?" she asked again.

Dane nodded. "No names."

"I'll think about it and give you my answer . . . tomorrow."

"That's fair. I didn't want to push you into an answer tonight." He stood and moved to the door. "I'm sorry for keeping you up. I should have waited until morning to talk with you about this." He lightly touched her arm, feeling the warmth of her beneath the Colts jersey. "Good night. Sleep well."

Her smile was faint, and she spoke softly. "Good night."

Dane stepped out into the night, feeling the rain on his face. He settled into his truck and looked back at the house, surprised by the loneliness that filled him. She stood silhouetted in the open doorway.

He didn't want to leave. He didn't want to be out in the rain or go sleep in an old man's cabin in the hills. He wanted to stay, to take her back into the house. He wanted to spend a few hours feeling like a normal man in a normal world with normal needs and appetites. But he knew you rarely got what you wanted on Cold Creek.

12

∽

" 'BOUT TIME YOU GOT HERE," CLEMENT QUIPPED AS
Dane stepped out of his truck. "It's late. I'd almost given
up on ya. Thought maybe ya'd had a better offer."

Dane sidestepped the two wet dogs that greeted him
with wagging tails and muddied paws and took his duffel
bag out of the backseat. "No better offer anywhere,
Tuŋkasila. You've got the best hotel in town. Sorry I kept
you waiting. I had a few things to take care of." He drew
back and studied Clement as the old Lakota walked toward
him. For the first time Dane noticed how crippled he'd become with arthritis. "You're not taking care of yourself."

"Don't worry none 'bout this old buffalo," Clement
replied, holding his hand out and catching some of the rain
on his palm. "Old *tatanka* bones just don't like rain." He
chuckled. "Old bones don't like snow, they don't like long
walks, and they don't like gettin' outta bed too early in the
morning." He shuffled the last few steps to Dane's side.
"I'm thinkin' maybe I should go see that new doctor at the
clinic." He glanced up at Dane. "Heard tell she's quite a
looker. I'm gonna go check her out for myself." The

chuckle returned. "A good-lookin' woman can make a man feel real healthy."

Dane tried to ignore Clement's comments about Claire, but the old man didn't fool him for a moment. Clement knew that Claire Colby was the doctor who had testified at his trial. And, whether he wanted to or not, Dane had to agree. To put it in the old man's terms, the woman was quite a looker. There was much, much more to her, though: her integrity, her kindness, her feisty spark that made him admire her strength, and her courage to come to a place like Cold Creek. Dane also knew that under his current circumstances, until the Big Elk case was done and no one was in danger, he had no choice. He had to continue denying the attraction he felt for her.

And after?

He didn't know. He didn't want to hope. Would she ever believe he was innocent? And when all the truths were known, would she be able to forgive his charade?

The image of tousled coffee-colored hair, smoky blue eyes, and an Indianapolis Colts jersey falling over soft, lovely curves filled his mind and touched his heart, but Dane gently pushed it aside, saving it for another time.

Clement pointed to his cabin with pursed lips. "I got your bed ready for ya. Ain't nothin' fancy like the Holiday Inn or the Moonlight by-the-hour Motel in town, but it's dry and warm, and there's a pot of hot venison soup on the stove."

"That sounds better than any Holiday Inn I've ever stayed at." Dane put his arm around Clement's shoulders and the two men slowly walked to the small house.

"You look tired, Grandson," Clement said after a quick glance up at Dane.

"It's been a hard day."

Clement nodded. *"Hau,* sometimes they're like that."

Dane stepped into the cabin and stopped, breathing in the scent of the old man's home. The wonderful crisp fragrance of cedar and sage—the herbs used in so many ceremonies—blended with woodsmoke and the delicious smell of hot soup. A smile moved Dane's lips as he looked around the familiar small room. Two well-used chairs and a small table filled one corner. The oil lamp on the table provided a warm glow. An old chrome kitchen table with two chairs and another oil lamp crowded another corner near the stove. On the opposite wall a folding bed had been made up with a nice Indian-patterned blanket. The blanket looked new, and Dane figured it had probably been something Clement had received in a giveaway at a recent pow-wow. One of the kitchen chairs had been placed beside the bed, a makeshift nightstand, and a wind-up alarm clock stood on its seat. Clement had covered the small patch of floor beside the cot with a tattered red, white, and blue rag rug—a place for warm feet on a cold morning. Just like the old man, the décor was simple and plain, the kind that made you feel comfortable and welcome.

"It look okay?" Clement pointed toward the bed in the corner with a quick lift of his chin. "You need somethin' else?"

Knowing it wasn't the traditional way and would embarrass Clement if he acted too enthusiastic, Dane gave a simple nod. "It's good."

"Put your things down and come eat 'fore this soup boils away to nothin'." Clement glanced at the pot on the woodstove. "I ain't no Emeril Lu-gassy, but I cook good deer."

Looking around the kitchen, Dane spied the grease-stained paper bag on the counter. Frybread. He'd bet his shiny new badge it was from his mother's kitchen. Connie White Eagle was known to make some of the best frybread on Cold Creek. She kept Clement well supplied each time he came to visit, and in the summer she always turned her talent into good extra money with her frybread booth at a couple of local powwows.

"Ya look like a starvin' wolf," Clement cackled. "Set your haunches down so I can feed ya."

Dane hadn't realized how hungry he was. He hadn't had a bite since early that morning before he left the city. He was due for a good meal. Following Clement's directions, he dropped his duffel bag on the floor and settled himself at the table on one of the old rickety chairs. His gaze followed Clement as the old man trundled to the stove and ladled up a large bowl of soup. Clement then dipped his hand into the paper bag and pulled out two pieces of frybread.

"Bet ya didn't get any of this good food in that prison, eh?" Clement said. "You must've got real hungry for your mama's cookin'."

Dane nodded his agreement between mouthfuls. *Not just for her cooking . . . for so much more.*

For the next hour their conversation was punctuated with two refillings of Dane's soup bowl, the sound of the soft clinks of his spoon on the side of the dish, and the rattle of the paper sack as Clement got him more frybread. For the first time in almost a year, Dane felt at home. He felt at ease with himself. He felt Lakota.

"When you start your new job?"

"I guess I'm official now," Dane replied with a slight shrug. "I'm supposed to check in at headquarters in two days. They wanted to give me a little time to get settled."

"Good idea," Clement said as he slowly rose from his seat, took Dane's empty bowl and spoon, and carried them to the counter. He turned and faced Dane. "Just so you know, we got somethin' to do in the mornin'." He refilled their glasses of iced tea and set them on the table. "I been collectin' firewood and found some nice fresh cedar up the creek. I checked out the old sweat lodge the day before yesterday, made sure everything was okay, and got some new good strong rocks for the fire pit. We gonna sweat tomorrow morning. I wanna take care of you, boy. I wanna get rid of all that bad stuff, that grief and that prison poison that's holdin' your spirit down."

A mixture of surprise and gratitude filled Dane. "How did you know I wanted to sweat?"

Clement grinned. "You're Lakota, ain't cha?"

"Yeah," Dane lowered his head and said quietly. "By tomorrow afternoon I will be."

Clement clapped Dane on the back. "Welcome home, boy. Things ain't been good around here without you." He dropped into the chair across the table. "The council did a good thing hiring you for the force. Some of those guys are real stupid, they think they got the right to tell everybody what to do, but they did okay by hiring you on. You gonna be working on anythin' in particular?"

Dane knew the old man was looking at him. He glanced up, meeting Clement's dark eyes. "Nothing specific that I know of." He shrugged. "They'll probably start me off on simple things for awhile, speeders, parking tickets, stuff like that."

Clement furrowed his brow and pursed his lips. "I thought maybe you'd be checkin' a few things that nobody's been able to take care of 'round here."

"Such as?" Dane closely watched the old man's expression.

Clement shrugged. "Depends how far back ya wanna go. Ain't nobody found out nothin' 'bout Martin Butz. He'd been with us a long time and then just up and gone one night." He leaned forward as though he were about to tell a secret. "I don't think he's livin'. I think someone sent him on his long journey." Clement nodded and then continued. "Then there's the trouble Ellie Rabbit had in town with that tourist guy who paid counterfeit dollars for the beadwork he'd bought from her. Ronald Red Horse had his car broken into and his radio and new boots stole." Clement paused and seemed to be carefully pulling his words together before he spoke again.

Dane began to bolster himself. He knew what was coming next. He knew without a doubt that Clement was going to ask him about Kylee's case. And he knew that the best way to save himself from the agony of being asked, and save Clement the unease of asking, was to bring the topic

up first. "I won't be working on finding *Taŋski*'s killer.
That's the FBI's job. Besides, it happened off the rez, so
the Rapid City police are involved, too."

"Maybe they won't let ya help 'cause of the trial thing."

"No, it's just out of Cold Creek's jurisdiction," Dane re-
stated. "That's all." He wanted to drop the subject. Picking
up the glass of iced tea that Clement had set in front of
him, he quickly drained it. The cold liquid felt good going
down his throat.

Clement thoughtfully nodded but didn't reply for a few
moments. When he did, his words triggered an odd chill
throughout Dane's body.

"Then maybe you can look into some of the strange
stuff I got goin' on once in a while up here," Clement said,
his voice soft against the light fall of rain on the roof. "The
weird stuff started happenin' over a year or so ago. Every
now and then Buffalo Creek comin' outta the hills gets a
stinky smell to it. I don't know if it's 'cause of the dead fish
or there's somethin' in the water. Good thing I get my water somewhere else." Clement screwed his face up as
though he'd tasted something bitter. "I walked up there
about a month ago when it happened again and found a lot
of dead critters. There was dead fish floatin' and frogs lying dead on the banks all puffed and rottin'. I found a couple of deer and then in another place there was a whole
family of raccoons. Funny thing is they weren't near the
creek, but I think it had something to do with that stinky
water. Animals just don't up and die all at once." He shook
his head slowly. "Damned peculiar."

Clement lifted his glass of iced tea and took a long
draught. He slowly put the glass down on the table. "Every
now and then I hear strange noises in the middle of the
night, voices, horses callin' out, and the like. One time the
wind was blowin' just right and there was somethin' that
sounded like a car with a bad muffler." He lifted his glass
of tea, swirled it a few times, and downed it all in a couple
of swallows. Putting the empty glass on the table, he

looked up at Dane. "And, every once in a while, I seen ghost riders goin' across the ridge at night."

A sense of foreboding slid its icy fingers up Dane's spine, causing him to shiver. He studied the old man's expression, waiting for the wide grin that would tell him it was all a silly story. The grin didn't materialize. "What do you mean, ghost riders?"

"You know, like black figures, just shapes against the sky. Like they was *wanagi* of the old ones ridin' in the night."

"Maybe you were just dreaming."

Clement snorted. "Maybe *you* forget there's truth in dreams."

Dreams. The icy chill persisted. Dreams of rez dogs, Kylee and Claire, and the name of *Iktomi*. "No, I haven't forgotten. Tell me what you heard and saw."

"Ah, so you're the big tribal cop now, questioning the witness." Clement's chuckle relieved some of the uneasiness, and his dark eyes twinkled with humor.

"You brought the strange stuff up, *Tuŋkasila*," Dane charged. "I'm just being polite—a good guest—and asking."

Clement nodded. "Okay. I'll tell ya, and if it don't get you wonderin' and askin' more questions 'bout what's goin' on, the council better be gettin' themselves a new cop."

CLAIRE PARKED IN front of the clinic. The early morning sun crested the low hill across the road and painted a rosy glow on the sandstone bricks on the front of the building. Connie White Eagle's old blue Ford was already parked in the space at the far end of the row.

"The woman certainly isn't afraid of hard work," Claire murmured, stepping out of her car.

Connie White Eagle had been a godsend, first with her hard work in getting the little doctor's house in livable shape and then at the clinic. Over the few weeks since Con-

nie White Eagle had come looking for a job and Claire had
hired her, it had almost become routine for Connie to get to
the clinic first in the morning. When Claire arrived, the examining rooms would be spotless, supplies would be re-
stocked, and a list of appointments for the day would be
waiting on Claire's desk. They worked well together.

Connie had also been a great help by reassuring everyone on Cold Creek that Dr. Colby was a good doctor and
that they shouldn't be afraid to come to the clinic. When
Connie had car trouble, Claire never minded picking her
up, and they frequently ate lunch together at the picnic
table behind the clinic. But, in all that time, never once had
Connie White Eagle mentioned her son. It was as though
the woman considered Dane to be dead. But then, wasn't
that what Connie had said to him the day before?

Claire had seen the pain that had flashed in Dane's dark
eyes, and she had felt so helpless to do anything about it.
There were some things she didn't know how to heal.

Claire pushed open the clinic door and stepped inside.
"Good morning, Connie. You're here bright and early."

"I like gettin' here before the stampede starts." She
smiled. "It gives me time to get everythin' ready for ya."
She pointed at the pile of patient files. "We've got a full
day, but it don't matter how busy I get, I like workin' here."

"So do I," Claire replied. "So do I." The realization hit
as she said the words. She'd never felt as content with her
life as she had since coming to Red Star, to the Cold Creek
Clinic. She'd made the right decision in taking this job.

Connie glanced down at the floor, then shifted her gaze
and looked out the window. "'Bout yesterday afternoon,
Dr. Claire," she said, her voice quiet. "I'm real sorry
about that. . . . Well, I'm real sorry about him comin' here
like that." She looked at Claire. "I told him to stay away. I
told him there weren't nobody here for him. You heard
me tell him."

Claire felt uneasy now that Connie White Eagle had begun talking about Dane, and it surprised her to find that she wanted to come to his defense. She tried to ignore the impulse. *How can I defend him when my own mind about his guilt or innocence hasn't been settled yet?* She chose her words carefully. "Connie, it isn't any of my business, and I'm not asking for any explanations, but Dane *was* released from jail. His lawyers won the appeal for his release, and he was acquitted. That means there is no record of his jail time or his guilty verdict. Decisions like that aren't made lightly."

"That don't make him innocent." Connie fell silent for a moment and then continued. "I know you was questioned at his trial. I want you to know I don't hold that against you." Her silence returned, and when she spoke her voice softened and trembled with emotion. "I never said it, but I'm thankful yours was the last hands that my *Taηski* felt." She shook her head. "No, I don't blame you for nothin'." Connie abruptly turned away, stiffened her stance as if steeling herself against any emotion she might feel, and began to pick up the stack of patient files from her desk. "Just 'cause some folks say he's innocent, that don't make it so."

"No, it doesn't," Claire replied. "But I can't have any problems at the clinic if, or when, Dane comes in again." She moved closer and placed her hand on Connie's arm. "If you don't want to talk to him, you don't have to. It's as simple as that." Claire took the stack of files for the day's patients from Connie. "You've probably heard by now that he's working for the tribal police."

"Yeah, I heard," Connie replied.

"The night before last Dane asked me to help him get some information. This means he *will* be coming here from time to time."

Connie shot Claire a sidelong glance. "What kinda information? Can I ask that?"

"Of course you can. He wants to know about how many patients we might see who have been taking drugs . . . illegal drugs. When I was in the city we had some sad cases where the kids get together at parties they call raves. They use a fairly new drug called ecstasy, and some have died. I think he's afraid something like that might happen or be happening here on Cold Creek."

Connie shrugged. "It's happened some already. Over a year ago after the Cold Creek Powwow, Ellie Rabbit's two nephews were found dead. They'd been at the 49 and took some of that ecstasy stuff, well, that's what they called it in the newspapers and on TV."

"The 49?"

Connie grinned. "Yeah, it's like a party some folks have after a powwow dance. They sing round-dance songs with crazy English words like 'My sweetie has chicken legs but I love her just the same.'" Connie's grin bloomed into a full-blown laugh. "There's a lotta snaggin' goin' on, too . . . hookin' up." Her mood sobered. "Anyway, my friend Leland Big Elk found them boys the next morning. They was already dead. Hit him hard, too." She nodded. "The kids here on the rez call it *waskuyeca wakan.*"

"Waskeya . . . ?" Claire tried to say the words but couldn't get her tongue around them.

Connie smiled at Claire's aborted attempt to say the words. "It means *strong candy.* It's strong, all right; it killed them boys."

"That's what Dane told me."

"Well, it ain't no concern of mine what he wants, and like I said yesterday, I got no son. As long as you respect that, we're okay." Connie began to leave the room but then stopped and turned to face Claire. "Bein' white I don't 'spect you to understand, but it's an old Lakota way, and you gotta honor that if you're gonna stay here and live on the rez with us."

Connie's words had a bite to them, but Claire didn't take offense. "I've got so much to learn," she replied, her heart aching for both Dane and his mother. She didn't believe for one moment that Connie White Eagle had stopped loving her son, and she certainly didn't believe that Dane didn't love his mother and was going through hell wanting to be . . . what? Forgiven?

Yes, there definitely was still a question in her own mind whether he was responsible for his sister's death or not, and it wasn't something that could be resolved by an acquittal based on nothing more than a mix-up over a search warrant. "I'm hoping you'll be willing to teach me all the Lakota ways that you can."

Connie nodded. *"Wasté. Han,* yes. You helped me, and I'll help you. That's the way, too."

The ringing telephone interrupted their conversation, and Connie picked up the receiver.

"Cold Creek Clinic." Connie listened to the caller then glanced up at Claire and covered the mouthpiece with her hand. "Mattie Old Horn is comin' in again. She says she got a really, really bad bellyache." Connie screwed up her face and snorted. "Course it don't have anything to do with all them fried potatoes with onions, hot chili, and jalapeño peppers she eats. Bah, that woman'd eat a horse if it were walkin' real slow."

Claire smiled. "Put her on the schedule. We've got a good supply of antacids." She glanced out the window into the field that butted up to the clinic property. "I'd better go tell Jerome Rabbit that Mattie's coming and that he'd better get his horses out of the pasture and put them in the barn where they'll be safe."

Connie hooted with laughter as she lifted the phone to answer the other line.

Two hours later there wasn't an empty chair in the clinic waiting room. The three examination rooms were filled, and the new nurse from Health Services was doing her best to keep up. As Claire escorted Mattie Old Horn out of the examining room, the clinic door opened. The chatter in the waiting room immediately stopped, and the only sound

was the soft whir of the overhead fan until Mattie Old Horn
opened her mouth.

"Eyee, lookit you, eh guy? Well I'll be real damned,
ain't you got the big nerve comin' in here?"

13

"HEY, MRS. OLD HORN, IT'S REAL GOOD TO SEE YOU, TOO,"
Dane said, smiling at the old woman. "Your belly acting up
again from those jalapeño peppers?"

Claire's breath caught in her throat as she looked up and
saw Dane.

He turned to Claire and ignored the laughter that had
suddenly filled the room. "Hi. I stopped by to get your answer." He spoke softly, as though there wasn't another soul
for miles.

Claire glanced at Mattie then back at Dane. Without
hesitating another moment, she steered Mattie Old Horn
to Connie's desk. "Connie, please give Mrs. Old Horn
some antacid samples and schedule another appointment
for her for—"

"Eyee, next week," Mattie pronounced, a slight whine in
her voice. "I'm gonna come back next week."

"For next week," Claire quickly concurred, knowing
that this time it was better to agree with the old woman
than argue with her. When she turned to face Dane, he

stepped closer. Oh no, she certainly hadn't been wrong the first time he'd come to the clinic.

The man filled a pair of blue jeans better than anyone she'd ever seen before. A colorful, intricately beaded buckle had replaced the oval silver one, and he'd clipped his tribal police badge to the left side of his belt, his gun and holster to the right. The red shirt he wore, open at the collar, covered his chest and shoulders as though it had been tailor made just for him. It provided a striking contrast with his near black braids and bronze-hued skin.

His eyes were shaded by the brim of his black cowboy hat and hidden behind mirrored aviator sunglasses. Claire could see her own reflection in the silver lenses. But most infuriating of all, that darned gorgeous grin curved his lips again and offered a glimpse of his straight white teeth. She forgot about the full waiting room, about the patients in three examination rooms, and about Mattie Old Horn who reeked of jalapeño peppers.

The waiting room chatter began to return to its normal pace and volume, and a few of the men came forward to talk to Dane.

"Hey, Dane. How ya doing, *kola?*"

"Good to see ya, Dane. You back for good?"

"Glad you beat that bum rap, Brother."

"Hey *kola,* good ta have ya home. You gonna play hockey with the Ice Dogs this season, blood?"

"Nah, bro, Dane ain't gonna hit the ice with those *wintkes,* he's got a rep to hold up."

"Got a job on the tribal force, eh? Eyee, man, can ya fix my speedin' ticket?"

Claire lightly touched Dane's arm to get his attention. "Why don't you come into my office?" She indicated the direction with a slight tilt of her head. "We can talk there."

She led him down the hallway. As they passed Connie White Eagle's desk, Claire saw Connie look up at her son with love and concern, then harden her expression and turn away. A lot of healing needed to take place between these two, and Claire knew that nothing she'd ever learned in medical school would help.

Dane stepped into the small office behind Claire and dropped into the chair beside her desk as she shut the door. "I hope you've decided to help me," he said without waiting for her to initiate the conversation.

Claire turned away from the door and stopped in her tracks. When had the room become so small? No matter which way she moved to get to her desk, she would come in contact with him. Her leg would touch his. Her hand would touch his arm. Her breath would meet his somewhere in the air. She steeled herself against all of the possibilities. Drawing a fortifying breath and with the light enticing graze of her thigh against his elbow, she finally reached the chair behind her desk. Her rapid pulse reminded her that it had not been an easy task. When she sat, she folded her hands on the edge of her desk, closing one over the other.

Dane removed his hat; the mirrored sunglasses followed. Claire looked up. Her pulse tripped, then settled into a higher speed. Her mind spun away from the true reason for Dane's visit and into the realm of her own thoughts, thoughts she hadn't had in a long, long time. After her divorce from Keith, she had refused to date. Her marriage had brought her enough pain to last a lifetime, and she'd denied herself any romance. But now, for the first time in three years, she wanted to change her decision. She wanted to take the gamble and discover again what it felt like to be held by a man. She wanted to discover how it felt to be kissed, to be loved, and she wanted to find delicious ecstasy with a man. She wanted not just any man. To her amazement, she wanted this man . . . this man who was accused of murder . . . this man who made her blood race and her heart hum with the promise of delicious ecstasy.

"Ecstasy has become quite an epidemic both in the city and on the rez," Dane stated.

The sound of his voice yanked Claire away from her

thoughts. He had said one word that startled her more than any other. *Ecstasy? How did he know what I've been thinking? Ecstasy? An epidemic? What an odd thing to say.* Then the realization struck, causing her cheeks to burn with what she knew was a bright blush as she remembered why he had come to see her. *Of course he doesn't know what I've been thinking, he's talking about something else entirely. How could I be so foolish? He's talking about—*

"We've had reports of two deaths in the last month on the Pine Ridge and another on the Rosebud before that," Dane added, interrupting her thoughts. "Over the last few years we've had our fair share here, too, and I know you've seen them in the city at Pennington." He leaned forward. "The drug use isn't only dangerous, it leads to other crimes in the community. The kids have to pay for their addiction somehow." He paused for a moment as if hoping to read her mind and find his answer. "Can I count on your help? I need you, Claire."

There were a hundred ways she wanted to answer, but only one was appropriate. "Yes. I'll do what I can." She paused and watched his wonderful smile return. "I don't know what help I can be, though. You say there were ecstasy cases here, but when I went through the clinic files last evening, I couldn't find a single one. There wasn't anything. Isn't that odd?" When Dane didn't reply, she continued, "So, I don't know what helpful past information I can give you." Unclenching her hands, she picked up a ballpoint pen from her desk and nervously toyed with it. "I'll only be able to report on new patients or those regular ones that I suspect might be using the drug." She dropped the pen into the pencil cup beside her calendar. "I'm afraid that's the best I can do."

Dane nodded. "That's great. Thanks. I appreciate any help you can give, Claire." He stood, reached into his breast pocket, and withdrew a small folded piece of paper. He leaned over the desk and handed it to her. "This is my cell phone number. Keep it with you at all times, I've always got my phone with me, and I want you to call me immediately if anything happens that . . . anything that doesn't feel right to you. Or, if you need help of any kind. Anytime, day or night."

She hesitantly took the paper from him, feeling its warmth from being in his pocket. His fingers grazed against hers, creating another kind of heat—the kind that made her draw a quick breath. The moment stretched into seconds before she was able to sweep a few intriguing thoughts from her mind. "I . . . ah . . . I don't understand. Why would I need to call you?" Puzzled, Claire studied Dane's face and found his expression serious, almost stern. "If I have any kind of trouble, can't I call the tribal police dispatcher?"

"Claire, please, just do as I ask. Okay?" His tone softened. "They'll just send me anyway, so you might as well call me first."

She slipped the paper into her desk drawer.

"No," Dane said more forcefully. "Put it in your pocket or keep it in your wallet, but damn it, Claire, keep it with you at all times."

The urgency in his voice triggered a rush of adrenaline and sent it blasting through her body. She looked up, noting the hard line of his mouth. Her pulse began another wild race. What was really happening on Cold Creek?

Dane settled back into his chair and watched her slip the piece of paper with his cell phone number into her purse. He liked how her slender hands moved with an elegant grace. What would they feel like enveloped by his own hand, her fingers entwined with his? What would they feel like touching his skin, touching him? Only one word came to mind: *wonderful.*

He studied her face, the dusky blue eyes under long, dark lashes and gracefully arched brows, and a nose that slightly turned up in an appealing tilt. Her ivory complexion was almost flawless, marred only by a delightful sprinkling of pale freckles across the bridge of her nose. But it was her mouth that interested him most. Its full shape and soft pink color invited kissing, a lot of kissing.

Dr. Claire Colby was a beautiful woman, but he'd met beautiful women before. What was it about this woman, this white woman, that captivated him so much? It had absolutely nothing to do with the ridiculous notion of forbidden love so often found in the Indian warrior–captive white woman novels. That idea was ludicrous and had never been an issue for him; he'd dated both Indian and white women, but none had come to him in his dreams night after night.

She wore the same dusty rose blouse she'd worn the day she had testified against him in court and a tailored pair of soft pink slacks covered her legs. The color suited her, complementing her skin and dark hair. Her white lab coat and the black and chrome tails of a stethoscope sticking out of her pocket added a professional touch. He liked the way she dressed, no nonsense, no fluff or frills, but still letting the world know she was all woman. There certainly wasn't a doubt in his mind, or his body, that she was all woman.

Perhaps more than anything else, it was her caring nature, her honesty, and her courage that attracted him. There was no vanity and certainly no pretense in her nature.

Dane shoved his emotional barriers into place. This certainly wasn't the right time for any of these kinds of thoughts or the feelings that went along with them. Maybe the time would never be right, but he'd already put her in jeopardy, and he'd damned well better keep his wits and objectivity about him if he intended to keep her safe. It stood to reason that if the Big Elks had been worried about any information Martin Butz had learned, they'd be just as worried about Claire.

It didn't matter that he was captivated by Claire Colby or that he wanted to get to know her much, much better; his first obligation was supposed to be to the FBI and the case he'd been working on for over a year. His head reminded him but to hell with that; his heart had another message.

Keeping Claire Colby safe was definitely his number one priority.

"Are you satisfied now?" Claire asked. "Your phone number is in my purse. You'll be the first person I call when my water pump goes out or the lawn needs mowing or maybe when those wild dogs harass me again."

Every nerve in Dane's body suddenly went on alert. "What wild dogs?"

Claire laughed. "Don't look so shocked. They're just a pack of wild dogs that seem to show up at my house and here. At least I think they're the same pack, a few of them look familiar. I've heard them at night, and the other morning they were in the field across the road here at the clinic."

What the hell is going on with these damned rez dogs? This is getting too bizarre. "Just be careful. Okay? Don't go thinking they're pets. They're not. Every one of them has gone wild, some were born wild, but they're all dangerous. Most are part coyote and will chase down and kill anything they think might make a good meal, pretty lady doctors included."

"Warning taken," Claire replied with a shy smile.

A light blush colored her cheeks, and Dane found himself fascinated that his simple comment would embarrass her.

"There is an awfully cute white and black one running with them, though," Claire continued. "He has a large black spot around his eye. He looks as though he's been someone's pet."

The air seemed to vanish from the small office, and Dane quickly stood, trying to ease the pain that had suddenly gripped his soul. Reaching the door and with his hand on the doorknob, he turned and looked at Claire. "That's Pirate. My sister's dog." His voice sounded tight and hollow to his own ears, and he watched the expression on Claire's face change, shock and then embarrassment replacing her smile. *I've got to get out of here . . . now. I can't breathe.*

Without another word he opened the door, left Claire's office, and walked down the short hallway. Ignoring his mother, the people he knew in the waiting room, and Claire who had called to him, Dane stepped outside. He tipped his head back, drew a deep draught of air into his lungs, and slipped his sunglasses back on. *I'm tired of this damned hellish game of cat and mouse. I'm tired of not having my own life.*

As he settled his hat back on his head, a quick movement across the road caught his eye. "Damned rez dogs." He slowly moved down the three steps to the walkway below, never taking his eyes off the pack of dogs playing in the tall buffalo grass on the other side of the road. "Clement," he whispered, "you're going to have to tell me what this is all about. I'm a modern Lakota and don't have all the old answers to these old dreams and odd coincidences."

"Dane?"

At the sound of Claire's voice he turned. She stood just outside the clinic door, the morning sun touching her hair with golden highlights.

"Did I say something wrong?" She took hesitant steps down the stairs. "If I did, I'm sorry."

He shook his head. "No, you didn't say anything wrong. I'm the one who owes you an apology. I saw the pack the other day at the cemetery, and it just surprised me to find my sister's pup among them."

Her blush vanished and she blanched. "I'm sorry, I didn't know. . . . I just thought it was a cute dog."

"Yeah, I know," Dane replied, beginning to feel like a heel for making her uncomfortable. As he took a step toward her, three blasts of a horn shattered the quiet morning. Dane quickly glanced over his shoulder just in time to watch Leland Big Elk speed by in his fancy bright red Dodge Ram.

"That's Leland Big Elk, isn't it?" Claire asked.

Surprised, Dane turned to face her. "You know him?"

Claire shrugged. "No, not really. He stopped by when I

first opened the clinic and has brought your mother to work a couple of times. He was very nice, welcomed me to Cold Creek and offered to help me get settled. I think he and Connie . . . uh, your mother are—"

"Dating," Dane said, finishing her sentence and almost choking on the word.

"I was going to say 'good friends,' " Claire replied.

"That, too."

Claire glanced back at the clinic and then at Dane once more. "I've got to go. I've got patients stacked knee deep this morning, and I'm already behind." She hesitated and almost shyly said, "Bye."

Dane watched the slight sway of her hips as she turned and climbed the steps to the clinic door. His eyes traveled across the enticing curve of her bottom and wandered lower down her long legs to her trim ankles. He smiled. She wore the same sensible shoes she'd worn at Pennington the night he'd caught her in his room. "Thanks for agreeing to help me out," he said. "I'll be in touch."

With nothing more than a nod and the smile that he liked to watch take shape on her full mouth, she opened the clinic door and disappeared inside. Turning back toward the parking lot and his truck, his gaze wandered across the road toward the patch of buffalo grass. The dogs were gone. They'd disappeared as though every one of them had been a figment of his imagination.

14

DANE STOPPED HIS TRUCK AT THE INTERSECTION, then turned out onto the main road. He breathed deeply, enjoying the smell of sweetgrass that grew wild on Cold Creek. He'd always kept a couple of braids of it in his old truck. Sweetgrass was better than any store-bought air freshener, and the smell of it always reminded him of home. The Bureau had done a great job replacing everything that was in his old truck, but just like his own life, some things had gotten lost in the shuffle.

He'd gone only two or three miles when Leland Big Elk's truck appeared in his rearview mirror. The Dodge Ram sped by. About thirty yards ahead the back end of the red pickup began to fishtail as Leland jammed on the brakes and pulled onto the shoulder of the road. He motioned for Dane to stop behind him.

A hot breeze whipped across the low hills and offered little relief from the heat of the day as Dane stepped out of his truck and walked toward Leland.

"Hey, *kola,* I saw ya at the clinic. You makin' a play for the new lady doc?" Leland grinned and removed a well-chewed toothpick from his mouth. "Goin' a little outta your league, ain'tcha, Bro?" He gave Dane a light punch on the shoulder.

Dane stepped back out of range in case Leland decided that another good-old-boy punch was called for. "Just doing business, man. I got orders from Iron Cloud to check up on some things."

Leland's eyes narrowed. "Yeah? Like what?" He stuck the toothpick back in his mouth and rolled it from one side to the other as he waited for the answer.

Dane gave what he hoped looked like a casual shrug and then a broad counterfeit grin. "You know, man. *Waskuyeca wakan.*"

The toothpick stopped moving. *"Hoka hey!* You're kiddin', right?"

"Nope. I guess the chief thinks there might be some drug trouble on the rez." He forced a laugh.

"What'd give him that idea?"

Dane heard the hint of panic in Leland's voice. "Maybe it had something to do with the pink pills they found being passed around at the 49 after the powwow last weekend. Or maybe it had something to do with the kids who have been dying from E." He could swear he saw Leland blanch.

"Hey, they can't pin nothin' like that on me." Leland shook his head and backed away. "I ain't the only one sellin' E. Besides, who's to say how much those kids dropped at one time? When they get rollin' they can't keep track." He suddenly stopped backpedaling, stepped closer, and began to jab Dane in the chest with his index finger. "Why the hell'd he pick you? You didn't let something slip to anybody, did ya?"

Dane grabbed Leland's hand and pushed it aside. "Do I look like an idiot to you? Do you really think I'm going to shoot my mouth off to anyone, especially the cops, about my private business?" He spun around on his heel and with a quick lift of his chin, pointed back in the direction of the clinic where he'd just left his mother. "Hell, my own

mother doesn't even know I hang with you." He turned
back and faced Leland. "Besides, man, why would I choke
off the great flow of tax-free cash?"

Leland looked contrite. "Hey, *kola*, I was just makin'
sure you was bein' straight with me. With Bobby in solitary
and me not bein' able to talk to him, I've been kinda left
hangin' on my own. I gotta be careful, cover my ass, ya
know."

"Just so *you* know, Bobby's already heard about the kids
dying."

Leland's body jerked, and his eyes grew wide with surprise. He nervously shuffled from one foot to the other and
ignored the thin trail of sweat that trickled down his cheek.
"Who told him? You?"

"I didn't have to. The prison internet told him."

"What'd he say?" Leland peered uneasily at Dane and
clenched the toothpick between his teeth.

"What do you think he said?" Dane took his sunglasses
off, cleaned the dust off the lenses, then slipped them back
on. "He's not stupid. He knows you've messed with the
recipe by sliding PMA into the mix. And he's mad as hell."

Leland began to squirm. "Why didn't you say somethin'
'bout this before now?" The whine had returned to Leland's voice.

"Maybe I thought you'd realize what your new recipe
was doing and would dump the stuff before anyone else
died. What in the hell were you thinking, messing with
PMA?"

"The only reason I did it was to beat out the competi-
tion. If the kids get a better buzz on our stuff, they ain't
gonna buy anything else." Leland lifted his chin and
smirked. "Hell, it's nothin' but smart business."

Bastard! Dane curled his fingers into tight fists and
fought the urge to drive them right into the middle of Leland's smirk. "Killing your customers is not smart business. They stop buying when they're dead."

Leland shrugged. "There's always others waitin' to get high."

Dane had expected Leland to show some remorse, hopefully some regret for the lives he'd taken. He certainly hadn't expected his arrogance. The Big Elk brothers had known some of these kids since they'd been born. Their families had lived on Cold Creek for generations. How could the son of a bitch live with himself?

Disgust filled Dane every time he thought of Leland Big Elk with his mother. Connie White Eagle had no idea how Leland got his money; she didn't know that the new television set or Kylee's grave marker had been bought with drugs and death. Ever since he'd begun working this case, he'd carried a heavy weight of guilt. His job with the FBI wouldn't allow him to tell her what he knew about Leland Big Elk. But what made him gut sick with shame was worse. It was worse because for the last six months he'd been dogging Leland and Bobby and not putting every waking moment into finding Kylee's killer. He knew he'd get his chance when this job was done, but as far as he was concerned, it couldn't come soon enough.

Now, every impulse screamed at him to push Leland facedown on the hood of his truck, slap the cuffs on the bastard, and haul his ass off to jail. He drew a few deep breaths, hoping they'd help cool him down. They didn't. *Easy, easy, easy.* Dane took another breath or two. *You've invested too much of your life in this case to throw it all away now. You're getting too close to the prize. Play it smart. . . . Play the game just a little longer.*

"If you don't get rid of the E with PMA, I'm pulling out, and you're on your own," Dane said, the bite of his anger unmistakable in his voice.

"Ain't you actin' like some kinda big shot? You ain't got no say in Big Elk business," Leland said, swaggering over to the front of his truck and leaning against the fender. "Ain't you forgettin' that if Bobby and me go down, you're fallin' with us?" He sniggered. "Maybe I'll just put the whole damn thing on you, tell 'em that you made the bad mix."

"Yeah? And how are you going to explain that I don't even know where the stuff is made?"

"You think the cops are gonna worry about that? They'd figure if you killed your own sister, you wouldn't give a damn about kids you don't know."

Rage intermingled with pain and guilt blasted through Dane's body, almost shattering his hard-won self-control and goading him to strike out. *They're just words, White Eagle, and words don't hurt. The hell they don't. Act cool. Show the bastard he can't rattle you.*

He stepped as close to Leland as he could, forcing Leland Big Elk to flatten his body against the fender of the truck. Standing toe-to-toe with him, Dane leaned closer, getting into Leland's face. He drew a deep, hissing breath, and when he spoke, his voice dripped with cold venom. "Don't push your luck, Leland. Taking you Big Elks down would be as easy as burping a baby. I don't think you want to tempt me." He chuckled, making the sound as unnerving as he could. "You wouldn't like it."

Leland slithered to one side, escaping Dane. "You . . . you're the one who'd damn well better watch hisself. All I gotta do is tell Bobby that you—"

"Shut up, Leland. How are you going to tell Bobby anything? Wakefield has him in solitary. Remember?" Dane turned away and took a few steps toward his own truck. As though it was an afterthought, he stopped, turned, and glanced back at Leland. "You're in a tight spot, *kola.* I'd say you need all the help you can get, and with Bobby in lockdown, I'm the best damn help you got. If you want me out, all you've got to do is say so." Dane left Leland and walked to his pickup.

"No, no, *kola.*" Leland followed on Dane's heels. "We're a good team. Bobby even said so before he got sent up to Wakefield."

God, it's like leading a puppy around on a string. Dane turned and leaned back on his truck. "I spent a lot of time with Bobby in Wakefield, and he told me that if I got out before him that he wanted me to work close with you, keep the business going, and keep the E clean ... even work with you in the lab." *Will Leland take the bait? Will I finally get to find out where they're making the damned stuff? Crank it up a little more.* Dane popped Leland on the shoulder with a good-old-boy punch of his own. "Besides, who else have you got keeping you one step ahead of the law?"

"I don't know, man. Bobby always said that nobody was to know where we made the stuff, that it was just for family." Leland began to slowly pace back and forth. "But if Bobby trusted you, then maybe it's okay. Just let me think 'bout it a day or two."

Well, that's a lot closer to finding the place than I was five minutes ago.

Leland lifted his ball cap and wiped the sweat from his face with his sleeve. "You can't blame me for protectin' myself ... and the business. And of course, Bobby," he stammered, a contrite expression settling on his face.

"You know damned well, Leland, that if Iron Cloud gets to poking around and comes up with anything, he's going to call in the FBI."

"We sure don't need no FBI snoopin' around. See, I told ya gettin' ya on the tribal force was a great idea." Leland nervously giggled. "Hey, ya know I was just blowin' off my mouth before, eh, *kola?* No offense, eh? I wouldn't set ya up or rat on ya. Hell, you're my girlfriend's son. Eyee, we're like family."

"Just don't expect me to call you Daddy," Dane muttered.

"And I wanna know what info ya get from the clinic, too." Leland paused for a moment and shook his head. "Ya know ya can't just go in and grab it. Bobby and I tried when Butz was here. It took a little personal persuasion, but we finally got what we wanted."

Dane thought every nerve in his body would explode, and he struggled to stay straight-faced. He'd suspected all along that Leland and Bobby had something to do with Martin Butz's disappearance. Was Leland just going to blurt it out? Was he going to say what he and Bobby had done? Was he going to tell where the old doctor was? *Push him a little; it might be all he needs to spill his guts.* "What are you talking about? You got some stuff from the clinic before?"

He glanced at Leland and immediately knew what folks meant when they talked about someone having a "Bambi-in-the-headlights" look on their face. Leland Big Elk certainly had that look.

"I shouldn't have said nothin', and I ain't talkin' 'bout nothin'." Leland spat out the toothpick and paced a few steps back and forth in front of Dane. He gave Dane a shifty sidelong glance. "Ain't nothin' you need to worry about. It's none of your damn business." He came back and stood in front of Dane. "If you get anything from the clinic, I wanna know what it is." There was an uncertain and uneasy sound to Leland's voice. "You're gonna tell me, right?"

Leland was getting careless, and he was getting panicky. It was right where Dane wanted him to be. As long as he wasn't able to talk to his brother Bobby, Leland Big Elk had few friends he could rely on, and Dane knew he had to be one of those friends. But Dane also knew he was walking a fine line. He had to keep Leland's trust, and he had to make damned sure that Claire was safe. If Gaines was right, if the Big Elk boys were responsible for Martin Butz's disappearance, Claire was in jeopardy, too.

Dane laid his hand on Leland's shoulder. "That's okay, man. I understand how some of these things work. You do what you've got to do to protect your own interests." He shrugged. "No skin off my nose. But you'd better be careful what you let slip, *kola.*"

Leland stared at him for a moment. "I'm sorry, man. I'm just gun-shy, that's all."

He had to keep Leland mollified. Stroking his ego was the best way. "Well, I've got to hand it to you, you were right on. Bobby would be proud. Getting me on the tribal force *was* the damned best idea ever. Keeping ahead of the law makes more sense than running scared."

Leland's expression hardened. "Big Elks don't run scared." He almost spat the words, then struck himself on the chest over his heart. "Big Elks are strong warriors. Don't you damn well forget it."

Dane was beginning to tire of Leland's whining and posturing. "Well, having inside information makes you even stronger." He began to head back to his truck. "I'd better get back to work."

"So, did the lady doc have anything to tell ya?" Leland called to him. "She had any wigged-out kids show up?"

Dane stopped, turned, and hooked the thumb of his right hand in his pocket. "Nope. Not a one."

Leland nodded. "*Wasté yelo.* It's good." He walked toward Dane, broadly smiled, and waggled his eyebrows up and down. "She's a damned fine looking *winyan*. Maybe you oughta move in on her . . . get real close. Couldn't hurt." He snickered. "Might feel kinda good."

"That an order, boss man?"

Leland's harsh laugh split the quiet prairie morning. "You'd damn well better believe it is, *kola.* You probably ain't gonna get one any better."

That's the smartest thing you've ever said, asshole. "I ain't looking for a *wasicu*," Dane replied with a disparaging tone to his voice. He had to keep Leland as far away as possible from Claire Colby, and just hearing him talk about her made him nervous, especially now that his suspicions about Bobby and Leland's involvement in Butz's disappearance had been all but confirmed. "White women aren't my style."

"I hear paleface women dream of takin' a chance on an Indian blanket with a big, strong warrior. White women are easier to find in the dark, too, *kola*." Leland grinned. "The old ones used to take 'em all the time." He slapped his leg with glee. "Hell, the only reason they killed all those white guys in the wagon trains was just to get their glow-in-the-dark women."

The sound of Leland's laughter chilled Dane to the bone. He couldn't let Leland suspect for a moment that his interest in Claire was anything more than the information she could give him. "The old ones only wanted them to carry wood so their own red women weren't too tired at night. I told you, I'm not interested, besides, I don't have a fireplace. I don't need any firewood." He turned away from the rolling dust cloud kicked up as Jerome Rabbit sped by in his yellow van, a couple of short blasts on the horn and the rattle of a loose fender drowning out the sound of Leland's laughter. "I'm not interested in getting run over in the middle of the road by some crazy Indian driver, either."

"You oughta arrest Rabbit for that ugly van. That yellow paint hurts my eyes. That's a helluva ugly color for a reservation pony." Leland began walking toward his truck. "I could use a cool brew, how 'bout you, Bro. The Broken Arrow's open. I'm buyin'. They got good burgers and fries, too."

Dane hesitated, checked his watch, then nodded. "It's just about lunchtime. No beer, I'm on duty, but I'll take you up on a Coke and a burger." He headed back to his truck. "I'll meet you there."

Two hours later, Dane walked out of the Broken Arrow, an ice-cold can of Coke in his hand. It would be hours before Leland would leave the bar. He'd found a couple of suckers who were willing to drink the beer he bought and part with all their money over a couple of hustled games of pool. Dane knew if he stuck around he'd also see Leland dealing a few tabs of E.

He slipped his cell phone from his belt and, using his thumb, punched in the speed dial for Gaines and Pardue.

After a few rings, Jack Gaines answered. "Where in the hell have you been, White Eagle? It would be real nice if you'd report in once in a while."

"If you'd quit your whining, I'll give you a damned report," Dane said. "I'd say that in the next day or so we'll know where the stuff is being mixed. Leland's just about ready to take me on a little excursion."

"Now, that's the kind of report I like to hear," Gaines replied. "Just be careful, Dane, and keep the phone with you, so if you need us, we can track you."

"I've talked with Claire Colby, and she hasn't had any new cases but promised to let me know if any come in." He paused for a moment and knew he had to tell Gaines the rest. "Leland saw me talking to her. I told him I wanted to keep an eye on her so we'd know if she got suspicious if too many patients started showing up with E problems."

"Hmm," Gaines purred. "Keepin' an eye on Claire Colby sounds real good to me. I wouldn't mind the job, myself."

"How's Becky and the kids?" Dane teased.

"Good talkin' with ya, White Eagle. I gotta go."

Dane heard Jack Gaines laugh, and then the line went dead.

Five minutes later, Dane parked in the back row of the parking lot at the police station and headed inside. The cold, air-conditioned air hit him like a hammer of ice when he walked inside. Debbie Old Horn, Mattie's daughter, sat behind the receptionist's desk, fanning herself with a sheaf of papers.

"Man it's cold," he said, rubbing his arms. "I wouldn't be surprised if it started to snow in here." He pointed to the thermostat on the wall. "Why don't you turn the conditioner down?"

Debbie grinned. Leaving her chair, she stood next to

Dane. "'Cause I'm hot, and I ain't got conditionin' at home. I might as well keep myself all cool when somebody else is payin'." She grabbed the Coke can from Dane's hand, pressed it against the side of her face, and then took a long drink, ignoring the dribble of cola that slipped down her chin. "How's it goin', good-lookin'? Caught any big, bad crooks yet?" She pressed her body against Dane's and began to rub her hand up and down his arm.

The icy room, Debbie's flushed face, her thirst, and her compulsive need to touch him raised Dane's suspicions, but one look at Debbie Old Horn's eyes told Dane everything he needed to know. She was high.

"Did ya see Leland Big Elk this morning?" Debbie asked. "He was in here lookin' for ya." She giggled, lifted her index finger to her lips, then continued in a hushed singsong voice, "Leland's my candy man."

If he'd had any doubts before, there were absolutely none now. Mattie Old Horn had more problems than a bellyache from her addiction to jalapeño peppers. Her daughter was an addict. She was one of Leland Big Elk's customers, and she wasn't shy about using her *waskuyeca wakan* on the job.

"Ya want some?" Debbie reached into her pocket, withdrew a plastic bag, and dangled it in front of Dane. She pushed her hips against him. "I share . . . everything."

She jumped away, stuffed the bag back into her pocket, and quickly sat back in her chair as the door behind her opened.

"Hey, Dane." Peter Rabbit clapped him on the shoulder. "It's good to have you on the force. You getting around okay?"

"Sure am," Dane replied. Peter had a flat, twisted nose, the product of too many fights to defend his name. Dane had always thought the broken nose should have gone to his parents who'd named him in the first place. "I came in to check the roster and find out when Debbie's got me scheduled for training." He looked over his shoulder at

Debbie. She just shrugged her shoulders and grinned back at him.

"I gotta be honest with ya, I was real worried about you comin' back here," Peter said, pouring himself a cup of coffee. "A lot of people still think—"

"Yeah, I know," Dane said, not wanting to hear the words Peter was going to say. "It'll just take time." He looked over at Debbie. She'd left her desk and moved to the air conditioner and now stood right in front of it. A light coating of sweat covered her face.

"I been on duty since midnight. I'm ready for some shut-eye. See ya later, Bro," Peter said, heading for the locker room in the back of the building.

Dane grabbed Debbie's arm and drew her back to her chair. "How much did you take?" He gave her a shake when she didn't answer. "I said, how much?"

"Relax, handsome. I just took a half a tab. Eyee, you think I wanna lose my job, eh?"

"If you don't get straight, you're going to lose more than your job. You know damned well that kids have died using E."

"Ain't no concern of yours. You ain't so innocent yourself, are ya?"

"Grow up, Debbie." Disgusted, Dane turned and headed for the door. "Get clean. Go home and raise your own kids. Your mother's already raised hers." He opened the door, and before he shut it, heard one last angry salvo from Debbie Old Horn.

"At least I ain't no sister killer."

15
~

THE DAY HAD STARTED OUT WELL, BUT SOMETIME
about an hour ago, everything had made a turn for the
worse.

Every Wednesday while Martin Butz was in charge, he
had closed the clinic for the day. Every Wednesday, Dr.
Butz had made house calls to the folks who didn't have any
way to come to the clinic or to those who were too sick to
make the trip. Claire had decided to start the program
again.

At first she'd been nervous about making the trips
alone. Some of the patients lived quite far from the clinic,
and some she'd never met before. Connie had been a big
help, spreading the news that there was a new doctor at the
clinic. With Connie's encouragement and a map she'd
drawn, Claire had looked forward to her day. She loved her
work at Cold Creek, but her trip today was turning into an
experience she would rather have avoided.

Claire spread Connie's handwritten map out on her lap.
*This will teach me to keep my mind on what I'm doing and
off of Dane White Eagle.* With her thoughts occupied by

his clinic visit a few days before, she'd obviously missed a turn or two somewhere. She glanced around. Nothing looked as it did on the map. She traced her finger down the penciled line until it forked and went off in another direction. Each of her three destinations was marked with a small *x* and she was looking for the patient who was closest, Margaret Makes Plenty. Putting her car into gear, Claire slowly turned around and drove back three miles and found where she'd taken the wrong road.

After turning right, following the arrow that Connie had drawn on the map, Claire twisted the dial on the car radio and settled for a static-free station from Rapid City. Tim McGraw was singing about being an Indian outlaw, and once more her mind was filled with thoughts of Dane White Eagle. *Oh no. Stop it. Thinking about him can get you in a whole lot of trouble.*

Claire quickly changed stations. She found a rock station and heard the DJ talking about the Rolling Stones. Hoping that some Stones would help erase any lingering thoughts of tight jeans, black cowboy hats, and mirrored sunglasses, she stayed on the station. In the next instant Mick's voice screamed out the lyrics: "I can't get no . . . satisfaction . . ." "Aw, hell!" Claire flipped off the radio with a sharp twist of the knob.

The first time the car shuddered, she thought she'd hit a pothole. The second and third time it happened, she checked the gas gauge. Almost full. By the fourth and fifth time, when the engine coughed, she knew she was in trouble.

A quick glance around heightened her concern. There wasn't a building in sight. There wasn't anything but rolling miles of prairie grass and low hills. The motor coughed again, and Claire pressed the gas pedal, hoping that would help. It didn't. The next time the car bucked, the engine stopped, and she wrestled with the steering wheel until her black Mustang came to a halt on the side of the road.

"Now what?" she muttered, turning the ignition key. The engine sputtered, whined, and then died. Three more times she tried to start the car and then gave up. With each attempt the motor had sounded less and less enthusiastic. *No point running the battery down.*

Claire pulled the hood release, opened the door, and got out. The afternoon heat felt like a blast furnace on her skin, and she wished she'd remembered to bring a hat. *If I get out of this mess alive, I'll make sure to keep one in the car all the time.* Lifting the hood, she peered down at the intricate trails of wires and hoses and metal. "What am I doing? This is ridiculous," she muttered. She stepped back and pushed the hood back into place. "Why am I even looking? I don't know the first thing about motors."

She looked to her right and then her left. Which way was the closest way to help? Reaching in the car, she retrieved the map and studied it. If she was where she thought she was, there wasn't a house for at least two or three miles.

Claire leaned against the car. "Now what, city girl?" She quickly glanced up at the sun and then back down the long, narrow dirt road. "You're going for a walk, that's what."

Reaching into the car, she retrieved her medical bag, her car keys, and her purse and headed off, up the road to her right. She hoped she'd find someone who would be able to help her start her car or drive her back to the clinic.

After walking for almost twenty minutes, she found a rare shady spot under a tree and stopped for a short rest. Her medical bag seemed to be getting heavier and heavier. If it weren't for the small supply for narcotics she'd brought with her, she would have left the bag in her car. After sitting beneath the tree for about five minutes, Claire picked up her bag and purse and began to walk again.

Maybe it was the loud sound of the locusts and heat bugs singing in the grass beside the road, or maybe it was her own loud humming of a senseless tune, but whatever the reason, she didn't notice the other noise.

As she took another step, a truck horn beeped behind her. Startled, she stumbled. Her foot came down on a loose rock, her ankle twisted, and in the next instant Claire found herself sitting in the middle of the road and looking up at the dust-covered chromed grill of a pickup truck.

"My God, Claire. Are you all right?" Dane leapt out of his truck and in three strides was at her side.

"I'm okay . . . I guess." She tentatively touched her legs and moved her feet. "No broken bones." She looked up at Dane. "Just a bad case of bruised dignity."

Anger overrode his concern. "Are you insane? Has the sun fried your brains? What in the hell are you doing out here by yourself?"

She pushed her hair out of her eyes with an angry swipe of her hand. "Dane White Eagle, you scared me to death! It's your fault I'm sitting in the dirt. Before you fire any more questions at me and treat me like a five-year-old, do you suppose you could help me up?"

Relieved that she was okay, Dane couldn't resist teasing her a little. "A little testy, aren't you?"

"Testy? You think I'm testy?" Her voice was full of angry steam. "Wouldn't you be, too, if some big galoot in a truck sneaked up on you and blasted his horn?" She looked at his pickup.

"Galoot?" He chuckled. "What the hell is a galoot?"

"It's a . . ." She glanced up at him, squinting against the bright sunlight. "It's a big imbecile who goes sneaking around scaring people half out of their wits."

Dane shook his head and chuckled. "Hmm, you're a lot more irritable than I thought. By the way, I didn't sneak up on you." He looked back at his pickup and pointed at it with a quick jerk of this thumb. "This is a big truck with a big motor and a hole in the muffler." He placed his hand over his heart. "Trust me, it doesn't sneak anywhere."

"You . . . you could have hit me," she sniped.

"Yeah, I suppose I could have." He pursed his lips and shrugged. "I saw you strolling down the middle of the road from a half mile back. Taking aim would've been easy, but if I'd hit you, you'd have messed up my shiny front bumper."

"I wasn't . . . strolling and you, your *big* truck, and shiny bumper can go—" She stopped short and breathed an exasperated sigh. "Oh for Pete's sake, never mind. Just help me up." She stuck her hand up in the air and wiggled her fingers.

Dane ignored her hand, folded his arms across his chest, looked off into the distance, and waited.

She shot him a questioning look and received his reprimand. "Dr. Colby, remember your manners."

"*My* manners? Are you kidding? It's *your* fault that I'm down here." She wiggled her fingers again. Dane didn't move. "Oh, all right." She made a slight growling noise deep in her throat. "*Please.*"

"Now, that's much better."

"Galoot," she muttered.

Dane smiled at her barb. *Cheeky little brat!* Getting to know Claire Colby was proving to be a very interesting affair. He bent over, took her hand, and was immediately amazed to discover how delicate and how perfect her hand felt in his. Dane wrapped his fingers around hers, tucked his other hand under her elbow, and helped her to her feet. Although she could stand without his help, he didn't let go of her hand; instead, he began tracing her soft, warm palm with his thumb.

He didn't know if he continued to hold on because he believed she still needed his help or because he couldn't bring himself to let go. *Hell, it's probably the latter. But what difference does it make, especially now . . . or later when she finds out who and what I really am?*

The top of her head came to just below his chin, and in that instant he knew that if he put his arm around her and drew her against him, she would be snuggled perfectly against his shoulder. She looked up at him, a slight questioning look on her face. He studied her upturned face, awestruck by her eyes. Deep blue, they reminded him of the sky at the halfway time between late afternoon and early evening. The lush sweep of her dark lashes provided an intriguing and dramatic contrast to the color.

His attention traveled down the slope of her nose to the sweet bow of her mouth. Wide-eyed she stared back at him, and as he watched, her lips parted slightly. A breath caught in his throat, and he heard a similar slight gasp escape her lips. The moment lengthened, stretched, time slowed, and in that instant everything else in the world lost its importance.

The fascinating flutter of her pulse just above her collarbone drew his gaze. If he lightly touched that intriguing spot with the tip of his tongue, would she taste like sweet vanilla? She'd worn the fragrance in court, and he'd carried that memory with him for a long time. Her skin held the light scent of vanilla now. Another question slipped into his mind, boldly daring him to seek the answer. What would that tender portion of flesh feel like beneath his lips?

Dane's attention moved back again to her mouth, and a soft groan slid from his throat as the tip of her tongue slowly swept across her upper lip. God, he wanted to taste that, too. His body agreed, proving that men weren't designed to withstand such hunger, such temptation.

And then, as though she had awakened from a trance, Claire suddenly pulled her hand away. "Thank you," she whispered, "for helping me up."

"My pleasure," he replied, his answer spoken as softly as hers.

She stepped away and began to efficiently wipe the dust and road dirt off her slacks as though the last few minutes had never happened, as though she hadn't been as caught up in the moment as he had. Only the telltale slight shake of her hand and her uneven breath gave her away.

Delighted that her reaction to the moment was as per-
plexing as his own, Dane watched her settle her nerves
and gather her courage. The task completed, she stiffened
her stance, then glanced up at him and raised her left brow
in an impudent arch. "Now, what was your idiotic question? Something ridiculous about sun-fried brains and my
sanity?"

*Ah, so she's a little porcupine again, okay, I'll play
along.* "I asked you what in the hell you're doing out here
by yourself." Once again his concern took priority and out-
weighed his humor. "Good God, Claire, don't you know
any better than to wander around the reservation alone?"

"I live here now. Are you saying I'm not safe where I
live?"

Her naïveté surprised him. No, more than that. It frightened him. "Claire, you do know where you live, don't you?
This is an Indian reservation. You're white. For the most
part the folks here are great people, but the old hostilities
remain strong for some." He paused and tried to decide if
his words were making an impression. Unsure, he added to
his argument. "They'll come to you with their health problems and let you treat them. They'll bring you vegetables
from their gardens, invite you into their camps and feed
you, and call your name in a giveaway at a powwow. But in
spite of all that, you will always be an outsider. And outsiders are treated differently."

"Oh, I see, and that's why you're treating me differently? That's why you're treating me like a child?" She settled her hands on her hips and glared at him.

The woman is too stubborn for her own good. "I'm trying to tell you how things are on a reservation." He pulled
his sunglasses off, slipped them into his shirt pocket, and
stepped closer to her as his frustration grew. She stood her
ground. "Damn it, Claire. Cold Creek isn't a city park
where you can go for an afternoon stroll. There are some
dangerous animals out here . . . four-legged . . . and two-
legged."

She lifted her chin, challenging him. "Is that so. And what makes you think there aren't dangerous animals like that in a city park . . . four-legged *and* two-legged?" She glanced down and vigorously brushed at another dirt stain on her slacks. When she looked up, her anger clearly showed in the tight expression on her face. "I'm a big girl. I've been on my own for quite a while. I can take care of myself, thank you very much."

"Not out here, you can't." He retrieved her purse and medical bag from the side of the road and tried to calm down. "I saw your dead pony a couple of miles back. What's wrong with it?"

"Pony? Oh, you mean my car, my Mustang. How would I know? I'm a brain-fried, white, city doctor roaming in the hostile wilderness all by myself. I'm not a mechanic." She drove her fingers through her hair and pushed it away from her face. In the next moment the angry arch to her brow fell and, lowering her head, she released a deep sigh. "Oh Dane, I'm so sorry. It's not like me to act so immaturely, but then, this hasn't been one of my better days." The breeze blew another few strands of her hair across her face, and they stuck to the light sheen of perspiration on her brow. She wiped them away and tucked them behind her ear. "The motor started coughing, and it wouldn't take gas. Then it quit." She shrugged. "I tried starting it a few times, but it wouldn't turn over. I stopped trying because I didn't want to run the battery down." She looked up at him, her expression hopeful. "What do you think is wrong with it?"

Dane shrugged and allowed a grin to curve his lips. "What do I know? I'm a big galoot Indian cop who sneaks up on unsuspecting doctors. I'm not a mechanic, either." He enjoyed the sound of the laugh she gave him, open and honest, no pretense at all. It was the sexiest laugh he'd ever heard. He reluctantly shoved the thought aside, knowing that thoughts like that about Claire Colby would only be trouble, would only lead him down a dead-end road.

"Sounds like maybe you've got a clogged fuel line or

fuel pump problems," Dane said. "I'll call Denny Old Horn
and get him to tow the car back for you. Denny's reliable.
He's a good mechanic." Dane looked over his shoulder in
the direction of Claire's car. "Out here a dead pony on the
side of the road is as good as roadkill . . . fair game for the
picking." He reached for his cell phone. "I'll take you
home."

"Thank you, but no. I'm not going home. I'm going on
house rounds." She grabbed her purse and medical bag out
of his hands and lifted her chin in a defiant tilt. "Dr. Butz
used to do it, and I'm continuing his practice. I've got three
patients who need me to visit today."

He studied her for a moment. Dedication to her patients
was an admirable trait, but not if it put her in danger. And if
she didn't get out of the sun soon, she'd end up as somebody else's patient with sunstroke or a nasty sunburn. He'd
also wager that she had no idea where she was or where
she was going. Once you'd left Red Star, the back roads of
Cold Creek had few signs to guide outsiders. "What are
you going to do? Walk?"

"If I have to." She squared her shoulders and tried to
stand taller. "I have patients who need me."

Dane's laugh was harsh. "Claire, you don't even know
where the hell you are."

"I've got a map." She waved the crumpled piece of paper in his face. "See?"

He grabbed the paper out of her hand and spread it open
on the front fender of his truck. "You don't have a map,
you've got a grocery list."

Her defiance returned. She stepped closer to Dane,
peered at the piece of paper, and then tried to take it away
from him. "The map is on the other side."

Moving out of her reach, Dane flipped the paper over
and laughed again. "You still don't have a map. Whoever
drew this forgot to put in a couple of roads, a couple of
very important roads."

"Your mother drew the map, and I'm sure it was an honest oversight." Claire pulled a pen from her purse. "If you'd kindly draw in the missing roads and write down their names . . . or numbers, I'll be on my way."

He shook his head. "Claire, I guess you haven't noticed. There aren't any road signs out here. Hell, there aren't even stop signs. They either get used for target practice and shot all to hell or the kids practice steer roping off the back of a pickup truck and pull them down." His finger traced the three names at the bottom of the page: Jimmy Long Bull, Paul Young Horse, Margaret Makes Plenty. He took Claire's arm. "Come on, Margaret's place is closest. I'll be your guide and taxi."

Her jaw dropped with surprise, and he grinned. He enjoyed keeping Claire Colby a little off balance, and this day was turning out a whole lot more interesting than he'd first thought it would be. He tugged her arm again. "Come on, Claire. Get in the truck."

She hesitated, looking first at him and then at his truck. "I don't know." She looked up at him again. "I'm not sure if it's such a good idea. I'm not sure if I should."

"Any reason in particular, or are you still trying to figure out whether or not I should still be in prison?"

Her eyes popped wide, and a bright pink blush colored her cheeks. "No . . . that's not what I was thinking. Of course not. I . . . uh . . . aren't you on duty?" Her hands settled on her hips once again. "Shouldn't you be out arresting speeders or . . ."

Dane decided to let her off the hook. "Look, you're in the middle of nowhere, the sun is going to burn you to a crisp, and you're setting yourself up to become a coyote snack, maybe worse. Come on, Claire, just accept my offer with a nice thank-you and get in the truck."

She took a step toward the pickup, then hesitated again. "You've got to trust me a little."

"No, I don't." She wiped a trickle of sweat from her brow.

"The truck's air-conditioned."

"You're offering to drive me on *all* my rounds today?"

"Yup."

"Air-conditioned?"

"Yup."

"Okay, I accept."

"Good. Wise choice." He helped her into the cab of the pickup, shook his head, and laughed. "I don't believe it. No roses, no chocolates, no fancy dinners, no promises of fantastic vacations, and no gifts of diamonds to get you into my truck? Just an air conditioner? Who'd have thought that line would work? I'll have to remember it for future conquests."

"I see what you mean about dangerous two-leggeds." She grinned and then added, "Women are more likely to call you a dog."

"Ouch." Dane laughed. "Don't worry, Dr. Colby. While you're sitting in *my* truck, enjoying *my* air conditioner, letting *me* drive you on your rounds, don't worry, this dog won't bite."

"Too bad," she quipped back. "I was hoping to put my rabies shots to the test."

DANE DROVE THE truck up to Margaret Makes Plenty's door. Claire had to admit she never would have found the old woman's cabin on her own, and she certainly wouldn't have found it before nightfall. Margaret Makes Plenty lived at least five switchback miles from where Dane had found her.

"Margaret's probably out at the barn." He pointed to a small, dilapidated shed behind the house. "She collects animals."

"Collects animals?" Claire had never heard the expression before and didn't know what Dane was talking about.

"Some folks have a gift. You'll see. Come on."

Behind the small cabin was a sight that Claire would never forget. White-tailed deer were everywhere. A few bolted when they spied the two of them, but most of the deer stayed, their large brown eyes watching Margaret's two visitors with a great deal of interest.

Margaret Makes Plenty sat on an overturned bucket in the middle of the herd, and a small fawn lay in her lap. Her gnarled fingers held a baby bottle, and the fawn was eating its meal with noisy enthusiasm.

"Grandmother," Dane called. "You've got company."

The old woman turned and greeted them with a friendly nod and a toothless grin.

Claire leaned close to him and whispered, "Why didn't you tell me that she's your grandmother?"

Dane laughed. "I can see I'm going to have to give you a lesson in Indian relationships. We're all related because we're a tribe. The words *mitakuye oyasin*, all my relatives, are said in our prayers because we're all family. *Tiospaye.*"

"But you're not all blood related. Are you?"

"No." Dane smiled. He paused and seemed to put some more thought to his answer. "Okay, to put it in terms that an educated white city girl can understand, it's like the Three Musketeers."

"What? What are you talking about?"

"All for one, one for all."

"Stereotyping doesn't become you, Mr. White Eagle. This educated white city girl understood what you meant until you brought the musketeers into the mix."

"Point taken," he replied with a grin. "The relationship is through our common bond in the tribe and, because she's a respected elder, she's called Grandmother. Not just by me, but by a lot of other folks." He shrugged. "Some that call her that are even older than she is."

Margaret Makes Plenty gently placed the spindly legged fawn on the ground, and it bounded across the small corral to join two other whitetail orphans about the same size. She eased her bent body up from the bucket. "Eyee, Dane. Is good you come to visit. You bring me more milk like I asked? These babies think I'm a wealthy woman."

"I sure did, *Uηci*. It's in the truck."

"*Wasté, wasté.*" She vigorously nodded, then narrowed her eyes and peered in Claire's direction. "Who you got there?"

Dane drew Claire closer to the old woman. "*Uηci,* this is the new doctor from the health clinic. Her name is Claire Colby. She wanted to come and meet you." He gave Margaret a hug. "She's a good doctor, *Uηci.* Be kind to her, let her doctor you, or I won't dance the two-step with you at the next powwow."

"Eyee, *Takoja,* maybe I snag you at the 49 instead, eh? Snaggin's more fun than dancin'." Margaret laughed, her belly shaking, as she looked up at Claire. "Welcome to my place, Dr. Claire. If this young warrior says you okay person, you are welcome. Is good we have doctor again." She nodded. "My sugar's been missin' that old guy, Dr. Butz."

Dane leaned close to Claire's ear. "Diabetes."

Claire nodded.

"You gonna take care of my sugar?"

"I'd be very pleased to be your doctor," Claire replied.

Margaret stopped and peered at Claire through eyes that had begun to cloud with cataracts. "Eyee. Ain't there no Indian doctors?" The old woman cackled with glee, obviously enjoying the chance to tease her visitors. "Come sit on my porch, and we'll talk. I got some sun tea. We'll drink a little and get to know each other better."

Their visits to Jimmy Long Bull and Paul Young Horse went just as well. Claire cleaned and changed the dressings on Jimmy's ulcerated foot, and after examining Paul Young Horse, she left some medicine with Paul's mother to treat his bronchitis. With appointments set up to visit them both the next week, she felt good about her day. As tired as she was, for the first time in a very long time she was truly satisfied with her profession.

Dane had been wonderful. He'd driven her mile after mile through the back roads of Cold Creek. He'd introduced her to each of the families, and she knew they wouldn't have trusted her without him. He'd helped her encourage Margaret Makes Plenty to stay on her diet, test her sugar level twice a day, and take her insulin. He had even promised the old woman to bring the groceries she needed.

Dane had lifted Jimmy Long Bull from his bed so Claire could soak and clean his foot, and he'd patiently waited, never rushing her, as she gently talked to little Paul Young Horse, who was afraid of getting his antibiotic shot. When she thought of the mess she would have been in if Dane hadn't come along, if he hadn't helped her, she shuddered.

She watched Dane as he drove her home. His right hand casually rested on the steering wheel, his left arm on the window ledge. He was a very handsome man. *No, more than that.* She altered her opinion. *Dane White Eagle is a beautiful man.* She smiled. Some people might think the word *beautiful* was too feminine to describe a man, but it was a perfect fit for Dane White Eagle. There was no denying his heritage, his bronze skin spoke of it, his dark eyes, sculpted lips, and long near-black hair showed it, and there was an unpretentious nobility, a characteristic that she'd seen in so many of the Lakota she'd met. Being six foot three would make him stand out in a crowd, but he had the long and lean muscle that perfectly complemented his height. He moved with a lithe gait when he walked, every movement pleasurable to watch. Yes, Dane White Eagle was beautiful.

There was also what appeared to be a relaxed ease about him, but Claire knew it was a lie. Dane White Eagle was aware of everything that went on around him, and there was a tension that lay beneath the calm facade. Memories of his trial came bubbling to the surface. She had seen it then, too, the casual posture, the look of boredom, and eyes that missed nothing.

The trial. Questions still swirled in her head about his trial. Guilty or innocent? She didn't know the answer. She knew what she wanted it to be, but wanting wouldn't make it so. If he was innocent, why hadn't he fought harder to prove it? Why had he never taken the stand in his own defense? Why had he assumed the charade of indifference? None of it made any sense, because there was absolutely nothing indifferent about Dane White Eagle.

Late evening had fallen by the time Dane turned off the road and stopped his truck in front of her little house. He didn't turn off the motor, and the headlights continued to shine on the weathered front door.

Neither spoke for a moment, and then Dane broke the silence.

"You're a very good doctor, Claire."

His softly spoken compliment pulled her away from her thoughts and came as a great surprise. She doubted that compliments came easy to Dane White Eagle. "Thank you, that's nice of you to say."

"I watched you today; you have what the old ones call a healing power. It's a quiet manner and a gentle touch. It heals and soothes at the same time." He chuckled. "I should introduce you to my friend Clement. He's a healer, too, but his methods and his patients' needs are a little different than yours. He treats the heart of a person, their spirit. His technique is . . . unique. He pushes and wheedles."

"He sounds like a good friend, especially if he wheedles. Wheedling 101 is the first class of the second semester of med school."

Dane chuckled, the sound wonderfully deep and resonant. "Clement Runs After wheedles well enough to teach the graduate level course."

"Thank you for all of your help. I admit I was in quite a predicament."

Dane nodded. "You're very welcome."

Silence stretched out between them again, and Claire began to feel uncomfortable. It hadn't taken them long to run out of conversation. Was he waiting for her to get out and go inside? It was obviously time to say good night.

She glanced at the dark house. *It's going to be lonely inside.* The odd thought startled her with its blatant candor, and her next words came without hesitation. "Would you like to come in? You must be hungry. I am." She gathered her purse and medical bag. "I've got a couple of thick steaks, and I know how to make a great salad." She looked at him and tried to guess what his reply would be. "Consider a home-cooked meal my way of thanking you for today."

A moment or two passed before he answered, and when he did, the sound of regret filled his voice. "Claire, you must be tired. . . . Besides, I don't think that's a good idea."

She tossed his words back at him, words he'd used earlier in the day. "You've got to trust me a little."

16

THERE WAS NO PROBLEM TRUSTING CLAIRE; IT WAS
being able to trust himself that worried Dane. Letting his
guard down wasn't an option. Until this case was over, he
couldn't afford to allow anything into his life that would
distract him, would make him vulnerable. He was beginning to enjoy Claire's company too much, and it put them
both in danger. Besides, when it came time to walk
away . . . well, caring for someone wasn't in his plans, either. Claire Colby certainly hadn't been in his plans . . . but
damn it, here she was, and he didn't want her to go away.
*What the hell, White Eagle. If you can't trust yourself for
an hour to have dinner with her, you're pretty damned
hopeless.* He turned and looked at Claire. "Are you a good
cook?"

"I've never killed anyone . . . yet."

"Yet?"

"Relax." She laughed. "I'll leave the arsenic out of the
salad."

"It's the cyanide in the iced tea that worries me."

"Don't worry," Claire replied, her voice still light with laughter, "I promise it will be a fast and painless death."

As he grinned and shook his head, movement in the tall grass in the field off to the left of his truck caught Dane's attention. With the headlights aimed at the house, it was difficult to tell what he'd seen. He cut the engine, flipped off the headlights, and lowered the driver's side window for a better look. Whatever was in the grass moved again, shifting about ten feet to the left.

"Come on inside for your poison." Claire opened the door, and the courtesy light flickered overhead. "I'm hungry enough to eat a whole cow, arsenic and all." She began to step out of the pickup.

"No, wait!" Dane quickly reached across the console and grabbed her arm. "Claire, stay in the truck and close your door."

"What?" Her eyes widened with alarm. "What's wrong?"

"Shh. Just sit still for a moment. I need to check on something." He let go of her arm and, opening the lid of the console, retrieved a flashlight. Turning it on, he shone the light out into the dark field. Eight pairs of eyes stared back, glowing red in the flashlight beam.

He heard Claire gasp, then felt her hand on his arm.

"Oh my God, Dane! What . . . are . . . are they?" she whispered. "There are so many." She pulled away.

"Coyotes or rez dogs," Dane replied quietly. As he watched, two of the night visitors moved out into the open. They stood as still as statues, boldly staring into the light, their heads lowered and lips curled back from their long teeth. Dane moved the beam of light first to one dog and then the other. Both had been with the pack at the cemetery. Then, as if some unseen command had been given, they sniffed the air, turned away, and disappeared back into the tall grass.

"Dogs," Dane said, his voice hushed. "It's the same

pack that have been hanging around the clinic and Red Star. Damnedest thing I've ever seen."

"Dane, this is so . . . peculiar," Claire whispered. "You're not going to believe this, but I've been having the weirdest recurring dreams for the past few months . . . about a pack of dogs." He heard her draw a slow breath. "Since I moved here I've seen these dogs . . . everywhere." She paused for a moment, looked away from him, and added, "Your . . . sister is in the dream, too." She glanced back at Dane. "There's also a word that I hear. I can hear it but . . . there isn't anyone in the dream who says it, and . . . it really isn't a voice, it's like a . . . vibration. I know that sounds ridiculous, but I don't know how else to describe it."

Dane wasn't sure if he wanted an answer to his question, but he had to ask it. "What does the voice say?" Dane watched her throat constrict with a nervous swallow. He knew exactly how she felt.

"It says . . . *Iktomi.*"

Once again, she placed her hand on his arm for a fleeting moment, and he could feel her trembling. Adrenaline burned like an avalanche of Arctic ice as it blasted through Dane's body and sent a frosty chill up his spine. He shot a hard look at Claire and studied her face. *The dogs? Iktomi? My God, she's telling the truth! Even Clement mentioned the damned old trickster. What in the hell is going on?*

The dogs had returned to his dreams, too. They had returned the first night he'd stayed with Clement. It was disturbing enough when they ran through his own sleep, but to learn they were mirrored in Claire's dreams made them more bizarre, more disquieting in every sense of the word.

Clement had told him stories about shared dreams, but he'd always thought they were just old myths or legends that were passed down and told around the campfires.

What in the hell is going on? Should I say anything about my dreams? The expression on Claire's face gave him the answer. No. It would frighten her. *Hell, it frightens me.*

No, he wouldn't say anything to Claire, not now, but he would have a long talk with Clement, a hell of a long talk, and he'd have it soon.

Dane turned away and slowly opened the truck door.

"What are you doing? Dane, where are you going?" Claire's grip on his arm tightened.

"Don't worry, I'm just going to scare them off, that's all. You don't want them hanging around." He glanced at her and laid his hand over hers for a moment, then turned away. "Stay in the truck."

"But . . ."

"Claire, please." He looked back at her. "Don't argue. Stay in the truck."

Dane slid out of the driver's seat and silently closed the door. His steps slow and cautious, he moved toward the pack. With a slight movement of his hand, the flashlight beam swept across the field and finally found the dogs. Bunched together in a tight pack, they milled around, hiding just inside the field behind a stand of scrub brush and buffalo grass. Usually they took off like a shot when anyone got near them, but tonight they held their ground, almost challenging him for the space.

"What in the hell is going on?" he breathed. "I've never seen them act like this. Never."

"Dane? Please . . . be careful."

One dog moved away from the pack and stood at the edge of the field. Its white and black coat gleamed in the full beam of Dane's flashlight.

"Pirate."

The flashlight flickered, dimmed, and went black.

"Damn!" Dane shook the light. The bulb lit for a second or two and then went dark again. Now only the pale cast of moonlight illuminated the yard, but he could still see the black and white pup standing apart from the others. Dane eased closer, dropped to one knee, and held out his hand. "Hey Pirate, how're you doing, buddy? Remember me? Come here, boy. Come on, pup."

Seeing Kylee's dog in the pack still bothered him and made Dane all the more determined to catch him and take him up to Clement.

The dog took a few tentative steps, stretched its neck, and sniffed at Dane's hand. As it took another step, the pup glanced back over its shoulder at its comrades as though asking for permission. A sharp bark answered the pup's silent question. Tightly tucking its tail between its legs, the little black and white dog slunk back into the tall grass.

Once more the pack regrouped. Drawing together, they moved as one body and bolted out of the field. They raced by so close that Dane felt the slight graze of furred bodies and the disturbance they left behind in the air. Dazed, he drew a sharp breath, then turned and watched the pack cross the road and disappear into the night, defying anyone to prove they'd been there at all.

He heard the truck door open and close and listened to Claire's tentative footsteps as she crossed the grass. She stopped and quietly stood beside him. He'd never smell the scent of vanilla again without thinking of Claire Colby.

"Your mom says she's never seen wild dogs come so close to people before," she said, her voice filled with quiet awe.

Dane glanced down at her, then back to the open field across the road. "I haven't either. There are wild dogs on most reserves but they usually stay out in the hills." He chuckled. "When I was a kid my friends and I used to chase them. We pretended we were great warriors and the dogs were wild horses."

"Did you ever catch them?"

Dane looked back at Claire and shook his head. "No. None of us were fast enough. We probably would have been badly bitten if we had." He stepped closer. "Claire, you've got to promise me. Don't try to get near them. If they come back here or show up at the clinic, stay inside until someone gets rid of them for you. You've got my cell phone number. Use it."

Without thinking about what he was doing, Dane lifted his hand and lightly traced down the edge of her jaw with the tips of his fingers. He watched her eyes widen with surprise, and a delightful warmth spread through his body. As quickly as his enchantment came, it was doused by the return of the warning voice in his head. *What in the hell are you doing, White Eagle? Are you crazy? What's wrong with you?*

He quickly withdrew his hand and pushed it deep into the pocket of his jeans. Maybe if it were in his pocket, he wouldn't be able to touch her again without consciously thinking about it. "Don't forget for a moment that the dogs are wild. They hunt in packs . . . just like wolves, and when they're hungry, even a human could be on the menu. You'd make a very tender lunch." He studied her face for a moment. "They aren't pets . . . well, at least some haven't been for a while."

He watched, fascinated, as Claire reached up and touched the side of her face in the same place where his fingers had been only seconds before. A shy smile curved her mouth.

"That white and black one . . . was Pirate, your sister's dog, wasn't it?" She spoke softly, as if she knew her words could possibly cause him pain.

"Yeah," Dane answered, speaking in little more than a whisper, watching her fingers lightly move along her jaw. "Yeah, it was her pup." He didn't miss the tears that welled up in her eyes or the single tear that broke free from the barrier of her lashes and slowly slid down her cheek. He began to lift his hand out of his pocket, intending to gently brush the tear away. *No, don't be a fool.* The words echoed in his mind, and he buried his hand back into the safe depth of his pocket.

Claire shyly smiled. "Sorry." She brushed that tear and the others that followed off her cheek.

Dane tried to swallow. How in the hell was he going to keep his distance from this woman? How was he going to deny that he was attracted to Claire Colby, not just by her beauty but by every facet of her? Their lives had been strangely and intimately entwined since the night Kylee died, and now her admission about her dreams bound them together even tighter. None of it made any sense. Absolutely none of it.

Dane stepped back. He knew he had to move away from her. If he didn't, he'd lose his mind and pull her into his arms.

He took his time walking back to his truck, time to cool down, time to regain his senses. He stowed the flashlight in the console and, unable to postpone the moment any longer, left the truck and followed Claire into the small house.

"Would you like something cold to drink?"

He followed Claire through the house as she flipped on the living room light and then the light in the kitchen. "I've got some cola and some beer."

"A Coke sounds good," Dane replied, looking around the room. The house was identical to his mother's. In fact, most of the government-built houses on Cold Creek had the identical floor plan. "You've done a nice job fixing this place up."

Claire laughed. "You should have seen it before your mother and Ellie Rabbit went to work on it. I couldn't have moved in without their help and hard work." She handed him his drink. "There's a lot that still needs to be done outside, some work on the roof, some painting and repairs to the gutters. I love gardening and want to put in some flower beds and maybe a small vegetable garden."

"You can't do all that by yourself. You'll need some help."

"Jerome Rabbit told me that he and his son would do the roof and the painting. I want to do the garden myself, though."

Dane took a long drink and closed his eyes as the cold

liquid eased his parched throat. "If you're out there by yourself, just remember what I told you about the dogs."

After he helped her set the small dinette table, he watched her work in the kitchen. He liked the way she moved, efficient yet graceful. He liked the way her hair, thick and dark, stirred when she turned her head.

Although her cheeks were pink from being exposed to the wind and sun, her complexion was flawless, and he knew her skin would be silken to touch. She used very little makeup, perhaps just a pale lipstick, but with her coloring, her dark lashes and ivory skin, she didn't even need that.

Dane's gaze moved from her face and traveled down over the curves of her body, completely enjoying the journey. Her clothes skimmed her figure, following the tempting lift of her breasts, accenting her small waist, her hips, and proving that a pleasing womanly softness lay beneath. There wasn't any pretense to Claire Colby. She was as honest outside as she was inside.

In that moment Dane knew without a doubt that no amount of denial was going to work. He forced himself to look away, to look at the wall, to look at the ceiling, to look anywhere but at her, anywhere it was safe. But he knew that even if he fought his growing feelings for Claire Colby, even if he told himself that what he felt was just physical and nothing more, and even if he told himself that he could walk away and forget her, it would be the biggest lie of his life. No place and no excuse was safe. And how could he deny the other connections they shared? How could he ignore the shared dreams with the images of Kylee, the whispered word *Iktomi,* as though they didn't exist?

"Ranch, French, or balsamic vinegar?"

Dane looked up. "Uh . . ."

"Ranch, balsamic, or French dressing?" She pointed to the bottles on the kitchen counter. "For your salad?"

Caught off guard, it took Dane a few seconds to reply. He tried to make light of his distraction. "Surprise me."

"Here's your poison. Please excuse the bottle." She handed him the balsamic dressing. "Set it on the table, please." Moving back to the counter, she put a couple of potatoes in the microwave.

Dane turned toward the table, stopped, and stared down. The attractive grouping of lit candles, the delicate wineglasses, and the soft music playing on the radio all created the illusion of something more than a friendly, casual dinner.

He stared at the candles. Claire Colby in bright sunlight was tempting enough, but Claire Colby in candlelight would push his resolve to keep their relationship purely professional to the limit.

"Rare, medium, or well done?"

Claire's words interrupted his thoughts again, and he looked up at her just in time to see her unwrap a stick of butter and set it in a small dish. He drew a sharp breath, then stopped breathing as she slowly sucked a small dollop of butter from her finger.

"Your steak," she repeated, her tongue taking one more small lick on her fingertip. "Rare, medium, or well done?"

"Uh . . . medium is fine," Dane replied, finally finding his voice, although his eyes were still riveted on her butter-coated lips. His hunger for food immediately disappeared, and an undeniable urge to satisfy his hunger for Claire Colby took its place.

Damn it, White Eagle, you're in deep, deep trouble. "Yeah, medium would be great," he replied, trying to keep his mind on track. And then his trouble deepened. *Ah, hell.* The view as she bent over and slid the steaks under the broiler in the oven seemed to make his problem bigger and yet definitely worthwhile. He cleared his throat, hoping to get through the moment unscathed. "Is there anything else I can do to help?"

Claire stepped back from the stove. "No, thanks. I think everything's just about ready." The beep of the microwave interrupted, and she turned away.

In moments the mouthwatering smell of broiling steaks filled the small kitchen, but somewhere in the back of his mind, Dane could still smell the alluring scent of vanilla.

CLAIRE TOOK THE potatoes out of the microwave, set them on the dinner plates, then quickly glanced at Dane. How odd. She mentally shook her head. No, perhaps not odd, but possibly very unwise. A little over six months ago she had testified against Dane White Eagle in a murder trial, and today she had spent the whole day with him. And now, now they were alone together in her house.

"There's a bottle of burgundy in the refrigerator," she said, trying to put her uncomfortable thoughts aside. "Would you open it, please?" Turning away, she opened the oven and retrieved the steaks from the broiler. Glancing over her shoulder, she found him watching her.

"Got an opener?"

"Oh. Yes. Of course." She pointed at the drawer where she kept the corkscrew and watched him efficiently open the bottle. *I don't believe this. Julie would skin me alive and hang me out to dry. This is totally surreal. I'm alone in my house, I've spent the day, and I'm about to sit down to dinner with a man whom I helped send to prison for killing his own sister. Was I wrong? Oh God, I don't know. How can I be sure?* The argument swirling in her head was beginning to give her a headache.

She carried the plates to the table. "Did I miss anything?" She looked around the kitchen.

"Frybread."

"Excuse me?" she replied.

Dane laughed. "If you're going to live on a reservation, you're going to have to learn how to make frybread. It's the backbone of Indian life." He buttered his potato. "Ask my mother to show you how it's done. Everyone at the pow-wows lines up for a piece of Connie White Eagle's frybread."

His conversation had a light sound to it, but Claire saw the pain in his eyes every time he talked about his mother. The same pain was in Connie's eyes when she thought that no one saw her looking at Dane. If his own mother believed he was guilty . . .

"Claire, I didn't do it."

She felt her heart tumble and drum wildly in her chest. "I didn't say—"

"You didn't have to." Regret filled his voice. "I've quickly learned to recognize the look on people's faces."

Claire placed her fork on her plate. "Dane, I'm sorry if I've made you uncomfortable, I certainly didn't intend to."

"I know, and I apologize for bringing it up, but I wanted to clear the air between us." He paused, the moment lengthening, as his dark eyes seemed to watch for her response. "Friends should trust each other."

Her heart wildly hammered again. Friends. *Is that what we are or where we're heading?* An odd sense of disappointment washed over her and left her wondering why it mattered, why it made any difference at all. She lowered her gaze, then looked up, finding him still watching her. *How do I respond? Can I trust him? Can I believe he's telling the truth?* Once more the memory of the night he'd brought Kylee into the emergency room at Pennington filled her mind. The answers were there. Nothing he'd done or said that night were the actions of a guilty man. She remembered panic, and she remembered fear, but nothing that gave the slightest hint of guilt. Nothing, except that he'd said it had been his fault. Was it possible that he believed it was his fault because he hadn't been able to stop it, that it was his gun that had been used, that it had been his carelessness that had put the gun in the killer's hands?

He reached his hand across the table. "Friends?"

"Yes . . . of course." Claire smiled and took his hand. "Friends."

Dane grinned and nodded. "Good." He gently shook her hand, then released it. "Now, please pass the salad, I'm beginning to really like the taste of arsenic."

The pleasant warmth of Dane's touch remained on Claire's skin, and the sensation left her unsure how to interpret what she was feeling. Her marriage to Keith had left her guarded and unwilling to allow herself the vulnerability that came with ... with what? Friendship? Romance? Love? *Friendship, I'll allow friendship.*

Her mind settled, easy conversation accompanied the rest of their meal.

"Your mother told me that there is a herd of buffalo on Cold Creek. Are they dangerous?"

"They can be. They're wild and only like people in small doses."

"Do they belong to the ... uh ..."

"Tribe," Dane said.

She felt the heat of a blush touch her cheeks.

"It's the right word to use, Claire. We're a tribe of people, members of the great Sioux nation." He stabbed a piece of steak with his fork. "The buffalo belong to the tribe. We were given a bull and ten or twelve cows thirty years ago, and since then the herd has almost tripled in size."

"Are they used for food? Wouldn't cattle be easier to raise?"

"They aren't specifically for food, they're for ... pride. Buffalo have been part of our culture for many, many generations. At one time our ancestors depended on the buffalo for almost everything—for food, clothing, housing, tools, blankets—everything." He paused for a moment, then added, "And then white hunters almost wiped out all the herds."

"They aren't going to show up in my front yard like those dogs, are they?"

Dane laughed. "Probably not. You don't have enough

grass to tempt them. Would you like to see them up close?"

"That would be wonderful. Could I?"

"Sure. They hide out in some pretty rough country. The only way in and out is on horseback. Clement has a couple of horses. We could ride out some afternoon and see if we can find the herd."

The pure Hollywood image of Dane White Eagle—his bronze chest bare, his long hair blowing in the wind while riding a galloping horse across the prairie—filled her mind. "Oh yes, I think I'd like that very much . . . uh . . . going to see the herd."

"Do you ride?"

"Yes. I used to have my own horse, but when I got married—" Seeing the surprised look on his face, she paused and then quickly added, "I've been very happily divorced for a couple of years."

Dane nodded. "Then I guess it's a date. Clement's old Indian ponies know all the trails in the back hills."

When the last glass of wine had been drunk and when the last piece of chocolate cake had been eaten, Dane helped her clear the table. They moved back and forth in the small kitchen until all of the dishes were in the sink, accidentally brushing lightly against each other and offering a softly spoken "Excuse me."

"I'll wash, you dry," Dane offered.

"No," Claire replied. "Tonight you're my guest, and guests don't do cleanup work. Next time you can wash."

She watched his left brow take a quick climb.

"So I'll be invited again? There'll be a next time?"

Why did I say that? Her answer was noncommittal and safe. "Maybe."

Dane replied with a full-bodied laugh. "Aw, quit teasing me, Claire. This was the first good home-cooked meal I've had since I've been home."

"I thought you were staying with your friend . . . Clement. Doesn't he cook?"

"Oh yeah, he cooks, but the word 'good' doesn't have anything to do with his cooking."

"It can't be that bad." It felt good to laugh.

"I'll have him invite you to dinner sometime. Just remember to bring your medical bag."

Dane blew out the candles, and Claire recognized a sad sense of finality to the deed. Their day together was coming to an end.

"I'd better go."

He had spoken the words softly. Claire thought she might have heard a hint of regret in his voice. *Or am I just hoping it was there?* She followed him to the door and watched him pull it open. "Dane, thank you again for helping me today." She looked up at him and was suddenly filled with the urge to reach out and touch him, to follow the arch of his eyebrows, to trace the edge of his jaw, to touch his hair and allow the length of it to slowly slip through her fingers. She leaned closer to him and began to lift her hand.

"What time should I pick you up in the morning?"

His question came out of the blue and surprised her. Realizing that she'd almost done a foolish thing, she dropped her hand to her side. "What? What do you mean?"

His smile was slow, his lips lazily lifting at the corners. "Until you get your car back from Denny, you're going to need a ride." His grin widened. "Unless you intend to walk to the clinic and back and fight wild dogs along the way."

Her gaze settled on his mouth. She couldn't look away. "Seven-thirty or eight. Is that too early?" Her voice sounded soft, slightly slurred. Had the air in the room thickened? Why couldn't she catch her breath?

"Eight is fine. Clement rises with the sun each morning. Being quiet isn't one of his talents. He can sure ruin a good dream."

And then she felt his touch. His index finger gently lifted her chin, and when she looked up she found an exciting intensity in his eyes. She stopped breathing. Gaze upon gaze, skin upon skin, the air between them became electric.

"Claire."

He'd whispered her name, the sound like a lover's caress. A slight gasp fled her throat. *Lover.* Why had that word come to her mind? She drew a slow breath as he moved his hand upward and cradled the side of her face. She pressed her cheek into his palm, closed her eyes, and embraced the essence of the moment. Everything around them disappeared, and the only sound in Claire's ears was the rapid thrumming of her own heart.

She looked up and watched, mesmerized, as Dane leaned closer and lowered his head until his lips brushed against her ear. Excitement rose with the heat from his touch, and once again her heart tumbled beneath her breast. He moved his hand upward, his fingers delving into her hair. He pulled her close, shaping her body against his.

"Kiss me," he whispered. "Kiss me, Claire. If you don't, I'm going to die."

Time slowed, her anticipation increased and finally found fulfillment the moment his lips touched hers. Claire closed her eyes, fell into his arms, and Dane White Eagle fell into her heart.

He teased her, lightly touching the edge of her mouth with the tip of his tongue, seeking her response, coaxing her to open up to him, rewarding her with a soft moan when she did. The pressure of his lips on hers increased, becoming more insistent, more needful. When she responded, his hand slowly left her cheek, traced a tantalizing trail down the side of her neck, across her collarbone to the swell of her breast. Lifting her arms, Claire twined them around his neck and surrendered, surrendered to everything she had ever dreamed of, surrendered to what she had always wanted to find in the arms of a man. In that moment, in the breathless excitement of his kiss, she knew she was where she wanted to be.

She felt him shift against her. She breathed a soft sigh,

and then the cool evening air touched her hot skin. In an instant, her arms were empty.

Startled, Claire quickly opened her eyes to find Dane standing outside on the stoop. What had happened? Why had he pulled away? She stepped forward, hungry to reclaim the bliss. There was only confusion when he shook his head and raised his hand to stop her.

"Good night, Claire. I'll . . . uh . . . pick you up at eight." Dane abruptly turned away and stepped out into the night.

He took no more than ten or twelve steps and paused. Facing her once again, he hesitated. She could see him searching for the right words to say.

"That shouldn't have happened," he finally said. "I'm sorry."

In the next moment he was gone. As long-forgotten feelings awoke and began to flourish and bloom deep inside of her, Claire watched Dane's truck disappear down the road.

Leaning back against the doorjamb, she lifted her hand to her mouth and lightly touched her lips where the sensation of his kiss remained. "I'm not," she whispered. "I'm not sorry."

17

DANE STRUCK THE STEERING WHEEL WITH HIS HAND. "You're a damned fool, White Eagle." Reaching up, he whipped off his cowboy hat and tossed it onto the seat beside him. With a few quick tugs, he pulled off the leather thong at the nape of his neck and loosened his hair. Lowering the driver's window, he allowed the wind to whip the strands of hair away from his face, and then chided himself once again. "You're the biggest damned idiot I know."

He had scolded himself, muttering from the time he'd left Claire's house, all the way to the turnoff that led into the hills and up to Clement's cabin. "You should've stuck like a burr to Leland today. How the hell do you think you're going to find out where the Big Elks' damned E lab is if you don't tag the son of a bitch twenty-four/seven?" Frustrated, he slapped the steering wheel again, then drove his fingers through his hair. "What were you thinking, playing tourist guide and running around all day with her? So what if she's been married. What damned difference does it make? It has nothing, absolutely nothing to do with you." But if that were true, why had he been so surprised?

Why was he feeling jealous like a schoolboy? "And while I'm whipping myself, what was that kiss all about? That wasn't just dumb, it was dangerous, dangerous as hell!"

Dane cranked the steering wheel to the right, and the truck veered off the main road and onto the long, narrow dirt lane that led to Clement's cabin. The rear end of the truck fishtailed in the potholes and loose dirt, spewing rocks into the tall grass on either side of the road. He spun the wheel, correcting the slide before the truck ended up in the ditch. "No point killing myself. Somebody will probably do that for me if I don't start paying better attention to what I'm supposed to be doing."

The truck crested the rise where Clement had built his small house, years before. The old Lakota preferred his cabin in the back hills of Cold Creek to the government-built houses in town.

The cabin was dark; not even a candle glimmered in the windows. "Maybe he's visiting in Red Star," Dane mumbled.

As he pulled up to the front of the house, he saw Clement's old truck parked in the dark shadows. *The old tatanka must be in bed. Sounds like a good place for me to be . . . alone.*

Dane got out of the truck and quietly closed the door. Walking softly, he headed for the porch. *No point waking the old man.*

Midway to the cabin, Dane stopped and looked up at the clear night sky. The stars, bright and gemlike, looked close enough to pluck like berries from a bush. God, how he loved this place. He loved this land. He loved the dirt, the buffalo grass, the rolling hills, and the starry night skies that weren't dimmed by city lights. He drew a deep breath. He loved the air, too. Pure and crisp, it tasted sweet and clean as it rode over his tongue. No matter where he went, no matter what he did, Cold Creek would always be home.

One of Clement's old yellow dogs brushed up against him, greeting him with a slight whimper and a wagging tail. Dane bent to scratch the dog's head and pat its furred side. "Go lay down, Chewy, it's bedtime." The dog ambled off into the night, and Dane headed for the cabin. He stepped up on the porch, put his hand on the latch, and began to open the door.

"You not goin' to say hello?"

The sound of Clement's deep voice came from the dark corner of the porch, and Dane almost jumped out of his skin. "You old *tatanka,* you scared me half to death!"

"Eyee," Clement cackled. "You're such a big strong warrior, eh? It sure don't take much to scare ya. Just one pitiful, tired, and weak old man." He rubbed his chin and stared thoughtfully at Dane for a moment. "Hmm, I'm thinkin' maybe you ain't really Lakota. Maybe you're just one of them wannabes that come up here in the summer lookin' for a feather and an Indian name."

Dane ignored Clement's teasing. The old man was a pro at it, and encouraging him by falling prey to his game only prolonged the agony. "What are you doing sitting out here in the dark?" he asked, perching on an old wooden crate beside Clement's rickety chair. "It's chilly."

"It ain't that bad. Just a little damp, but that dew makes the sweetgrass smell good." Clement took a big whiff of air, then pulled his handkerchief out of the pocket of his red plaid flannel shirt and blew his nose. He folded it with meticulous care, then stuffed it back into his pocket. "I been wonderin' where you were . . . when you were comin' home. You're getting in kinda late from work, ain't ya?"

Dane shot the old man a hard look. "I didn't know I had to follow a curfew while I'm staying with you." He immediately regretted his words and the sharp edge to his voice, but damn, he'd already done a good job of chewing his own ass all the way from Claire's house; he didn't need any more help. "If you had a phone, *Uŋci,* I could call and let you know if I'm going to be late."

"I don't want a phone. If ya got a phone, only bill collectors call ya."

"You don't have any bills," Dane argued.

"Then I don't need a phone. Without bills, ain't nobody gonna call me."

The old man could always make Dane laugh, but tonight the laughs weren't coming easily. He watched Clement's two spotted horses dozing by the sagging fence. *That's what I need to do . . . get some sleep.*

"You hungry? I got some frybread, commodity cheese, and Spam."

Dane glanced at Clement and drew a deep, calming breath. "Sounds like a gourmet meal, but no thanks. I've . . . already eaten." He saw a hint of disappointment in the old man's expression. "Is that why you stayed up waiting for me . . . to make sure I got something to eat?"

Clement shrugged. "I was just wantin' to talk with ya before I went in for bed." He leaned over and peered closely at Dane. "*Takoja* . . . Grandson, you look like a man with a big problem."

"Is there anything you don't know?"

"Yup," Clement said, easing back in his chair.

"Yeah? Like what?"

"Like what time you was comin' home."

This time Dane's laugh came effortlessly. The old man was something else. The Great Spirit, *Tuŋkasila*, had made Clement Runs After out of everything Lakota and good, and then had tossed the mold and the recipe away. Clement was one of a kind. "What do you want to talk about?"

A silent moment or two ticked by, the air grew thick with anticipation, and then the old man began to speak. "I seen that rider again tonight." He pointed toward the ridge behind his cabin with a quick jerk of his thumb.

Dane sat up, every nerve in his body suddenly alert. "What rider? What are you talking about?"

Clement snorted. "Don't play that dumb cop stuff with me. That Columbo guy on TV does that when he's tryin' to make somebody spill his guts." He curled his lip and shook his head. "It's sneaky."

"You've never had a television. How do you know what Columbo does?"

"I got ways of knowin' these things. Besides"—a grin broke on Clement's face—"you definitely ain't no dumb cop, so quit trying to be . . . sneaky."

What the hell is this all about? Dane shifted uneasily on the wooden crate. "Okay, Grandfather, tell it your way."

"Good. *Wasté.*" Clement leaned forward, set his elbows on his knees, and clasped his hands out in front of him. "About nine o'clock, I think it was nine 'cause that pow-wow singin' show was on the radio, I come out here to sit. Ten minutes later those two old spotted ponies of mine began hollerin' and runnin' up and down along the fence. I knew there were horses somewhere nearby. Them ponies only kick up when they see 'em, hear 'em, or smell 'em." He pointed down at the two yellow dogs at his feet and then lifted his chin toward the back shed. "These two stood out there and was growlin' their fool heads off."

"How many riders were there?"

"Just one."

"Where was he? Which way was he going? Show me." Dane began to stand up.

"Sit down, Grandson. I'll show ya when I'm done talkin'."

Dane settled back on the crate. Clement Runs After was on the low end of eighty; maybe the old man was seeing things or getting his dreams mixed up with reality. He studied Clement's age-creased face for a moment. *No, there isn't a clouded thought in his head. Clement's as sharp as the proverbial tack.* "The other day you called the riders you'd seen . . . *wanagi.* Maybe this rider was a ghost, too?"

"Naw, them guys I told you 'bout seein' last summer weren't really *wanagi,* either. They was just movin' slow and quiet like they was ghosts. Them guys had an extra horse with 'em, too. They was leadin' him like a pack-horse." Clement leaned over and picked up a mug of coffee from the porch floor by his feet. "I'm no old fool. I believe in those old ghosts. I been 'round long enough to know the difference between a live man and a *wanagi*." He lifted the mug to his lips and took a sip. "I've seen 'em out there, them *wanagi*." He glanced out at the hills to his right, then back at Dane. "I've seen 'em walking the hills and the old battlegrounds." He slowly shook his head. "But this weren't one of 'em. This rider weren't no ghost."

Dane nodded. "Okay, if he wasn't a ghost, he was probably just some kid sneaking out at night to meet up with his girl." He thought for a moment. "Don't Carla and Duane Standing Crow live out this way? They've got a boy about fifteen or sixteen. Maybe he—"

Clement shook his head. "No, it weren't no kid out for a night ride, either. Kids run the hell out of their horses. They push 'em as if they were four-legged hot rods. That Standing Crow boy's the worst of 'em." He jerked his thumb toward the ridge behind his house again. "Whoever was out there was ridin' slow 'cause he wanted to be quiet, but he weren't smart enough to fool a couple of old spotted Indian ponies and two toothless yellow dogs."

"If you'll let me take one of the horses, I'll go out in the morning and see if I can follow the tracks."

"You can ride my horses any time you want, but going lookin' for tracks won't do no good. I tried when I first saw them riders." He shook his head. "I bet this horse was barefoot like most ponies around here, and I bet there were somethin' tied over its hooves to hide the tracks." He looked over at Dane. "It's an old Indian trick, but they ain't gonna trick this old Indian for long. I'm gonna find out who it is and what they is doing botherin' my dogs and ponies."

Dane didn't like that idea at all, and he didn't like the next idea that eased into his mind, either. Bobby Big Elk had been sent to Wakefield at the end of October, but he would still have been on Cold Creek about the time Clement first saw the two night riders. Was it possible? Were the riders Bobby and Leland Big Elk? If it was them, what were they doing out in the hills late at night? If it was them, where were they going?

The answer, the only reasonable answer to those two questions, slid into Dane's mind. *The lab. They were going to the lab.* Excitement zipped through his body. *The lab . . . right here under Clement's nose.*

He turned to Clement. "You're not going out looking for anybody. You're going to let me take care of it. If I find out who it is, where they're going, what they're doing, and if what they're doing is legal, that's okay. If it's not legal"— he tapped the tribal police badge pinned to his belt—"this will take care of them. But you keep your nose out of it."

Clement shrugged, then set his mug back down on the floor. The silence grew between them, and then Clement looked up and nodded. "Okay, Grandson. You do what you've got to do." Silence stretched between them again, but this time when Clement spoke, his words came hushed, yet steady. "Lately I've found out there's a lot of strange stuff goin' on 'round here. Folks you've known all their lives sometimes ain't at all what you think." He paused for a moment, then leaned toward Dane. "Ain't that so?"

Dane jerked his gaze away from the two yellow dogs asleep on the floor and stared at Clement. He shivered. When had his blood turned ice cold? When had it become so hard to breathe? What the hell was the old man up to?

Clement settled back in his chair, sighed, and stared up at the star-littered sky. He looked relaxed, as though there wasn't a thing on his mind but easy conversation, but the adrenaline racing through Dane's veins proved that theory was dead wrong.

"You know, in the old days our people would sit around a fire on a night like tonight, and the old ones would tell stories to the children," Clement continued, his voice sounding wistful with memories. "Those were good times. Them stories have meanings; they're lessons so our children can learn how to be Lakota. Them stories never change. For hundreds of years they've been told the same way." He leaned over and laid his gnarled hand on Dane's knee. "I bet you remember when your mom would bring you up here. You weren't much more than six or seven. I'd have a fire goin', and we'd sit out there for hours while I told you them stories. Later she brought *Taŋski*, too." He sat back, rested his elbows on the arms of the chair, and propped his chin on his steepled fingers. "Your favorites was the stories about *Iktomi* the Trickster and his pal Coyote." He began to chuckle, but his eyes, steady and guarded, never left Dane. "Sneaky guy, that *Iktomi*. He would make folks think he was somethin' he weren't." Still closely watching Dane, Clement thoughtfully rubbed his chin again. "Yup, just like someone I know."

Dane's gut tightened and wrenched into a painful knot. Every nerve in his body burned with alarm. Claire had mentioned *Iktomi;* the trickster had even been in his dreams. *And now Clement is talking about* Iktomi? *What the hell is going on? Coincidence? Damn, I don't know.* He looked at Clement and tried to read his expression. *What do you know,* Uŋci? *What the hell do you think you know?* Dane rubbed the palms of his hands on the knees of his jeans. *Did I screw up somewhere? Did I say something . . . do something that set him off? What did I let slip?*

"I done a bit of detective work a while back, just like that TV guy," Clement said, as though he'd heard Dane's silent questions. "Maybe I oughta go get myself one of those messy lookin' brown coats." He paused, picked up his coffee mug, drained its contents, and set it back on the floor. "Ya never know what yer gonna find when ya go detectin'. Some of it's a shocker . . . but then when ya think 'bout it . . . some of it ain't." He crossed his arms over his chest, his steady gaze still resting on Dane.

Get on with it you old tatanka. *Quit yanking me around. Tell me what you know.*

A slow smile moved on Clement's mouth and lifted the corners of his lips. "Here's somethin' that might interest you. It seems that some guy named Dane White Eagle didn't tell nobody that he got himself graduated from the University of Virginia . . . got himself a law degree. How 'bout that, eh? Don'tcha wonder why he did that?" He chuckled. "And would you believe that same guy passed the . . . uh . . . what do they call it?" Clement scratched his head, overdoing his playacting.

"The bar," Dane offered, trying to stay calm, his wildly beating heart making that impossible. *There's no point in trying to deny the truth, but how had Clement been able to track down the information about my years at U of V?* Clement didn't have a telephone, but he'd sure found one to call the university. *Has he told anyone else? My mother?* He thought about his question for a moment. The answer was quick in coming. *No. I don't think so. If Clement had told Mom, she would have told Leland, and that son of a bitch would have come gunning for me already. But what else did Clement's snooping uncover?* Dane's gut gave another hard yank. The two things he definitely didn't want to hear Clement Runs After say were Quantico and FBI. And then there was Claire Colby. How did she fit into all of this? He shifted his shoulders and tried to ease the tense muscles in his body. It didn't help.

"Yeah. That guy passed that bar and ended up a real lawyer. Ain't that somethin'? Then you know what?"

Damn, here it comes. "Hurry up, old man, get it over with. Get to your point."

"Like I said, that *Iktomi* ain't the only trickster I know, is he?" He leaned forward again, a severe expression on his face. "You gonna tell me what all this trickin' is about, or you gonna make *me* tell *you?*"

Dane slowly stood and looked up at the clear night sky. He knew if he pressed Clement to tell everything he'd found out, or how he'd gotten the information, it would just make Clement more suspicious, and he might start poking deeper. *Just take it easy. Stay cool.* He looked down at Clement and tried to gauge what was going on in the old *tatanka*'s head. He'd planned to talk to Clement about the dreams, the dreams he'd been sharing with Claire. *I need answers. I need to know what's going on, why my life is unraveling. But damn it, now that he's mentioned* Iktomi, *tonight definitely isn't the right time.*

Clement pushed again. "So, you gonna tell me what's goin' on with you?"

Dane moved to the edge of the porch and stood staring out at the bare, moonlit hills of Cold Creek before he answered. "I'll tell you when I can, *Tuŋkasila*. Until then *you* don't know anything. You're not Columbo, so quit acting like you are."

"And why should I do that, Grandson?"

Dane turned, crossed the porch, and opened the cabin door. "Because it's the only thing that might keep you alive."

He left the old man sitting alone on the porch, but Dane was the one who felt painfully lonely.

THE SOUND, A steady thrumming, woke Dane. It took him a few moments to recognize what it was. Rain. Not just a light rain, it was a hard downpour. He swung his legs off the narrow cot and walked, naked and barefoot, to the window. Staring out at the ridge that ran a little over a half mile away from the back of Clement's cabin, he knew there was no point looking for any horse tracks now. What little trail that might have been left by the night rider would certainly have been washed away by the rain.

He'd tossed and turned all night long, wondering how he could keep Clement from doing any more snooping and worrying how he was going to be able to keep the old man safe. If it was so damned easy for Clement to find out about his university records, who else would look? Who else would be as successful?

Thoughts of Claire had kept him awake, too. God how he wished the time was different, the place was different, and everything about how they'd first met . . . was differ-

ent. It seemed so cliché to say that he'd never felt this way
about any other woman he'd known, but it was true. God, it
was so true. How did you stop falling in love when you
were halfway there already?

When sleep had finally come, so had the dream, more
vivid, more insistent than usual. But there had been subtle
changes in it, changes that when he awoke left him unsure
of his own sanity and positive, now more than ever, that
Clement had abilities that defied explanation.

The dream had started in the same way with the pack of
rez dogs running across the hills of buffalo grass, and he
was among them, running with them, his dream legs pump-
ing with great speed. He had felt the ground shake beneath
his feet, had heard the dogs panting, but above it all there
was a new sound, a voice. Not the voice that had softly
spoken before in the dream, but it was his own voice. Deep
and distinct, he spoke only one word: *"Iktomi!"*

"You goin' down to Red Star this morning?"

Yanked from his thoughts, Dane felt his heart leap in his
chest. He turned and found Clement standing a few feet
away. How in the hell did the arthritic old man walk so quietly? "Yeah, I've got to check in at the station. No telling
what kind of duty I'll pull today in this rain." There was no
reason to tell Clement that before he went to the station,
he'd give Claire Colby a ride to the clinic and then check
with Denny Old Horn about her car. The nosy old man
would run on and on about Dane finding a good woman to
settle down with, and that was the last thing Dane wanted
to deal with this morning. He was having enough trouble
with it, himself.

"Bein' the new guy leaves ya kinda in a tough spot. Low
man on the totem pole always carries the biggest, heaviest
load." Clement lit the kindling and paper in the woodstove.
"A cup of coffee will take the rough edges off a morning
like this." Clement pointed at Dane with a lift of his chin.
"You get a new uniform?" He cackled.

Dane suddenly remembered he was butt naked. "Sorry, I uh . . ."

"Kinda hard to pin yer badge on, ain't it?" Clement's laughter grew and shook his whole body. "No worry. Ain't the first time I seen ya without your britches." Clement dumped a couple of scoops of coffee into the pot. "That's quite a rain out there." He glanced up at the ceiling. "I hope my patch on the roof holds."

Dane watched the old Lakota put water in the pot and set it on the stove. It was obvious that their conversation was going to completely skirt the discussion they'd had the night before. He'd still wanted to ask Clement to tell him about shared dreams. He wanted to know what forces were at work, tying him to Claire Colby. And he wanted to know if it was Clement who was tying those knots, but the old man had taken their discussion in another direction. Many on Cold Creek called Clement Runs After a *wicasa wakan,* a holy man, and the stories Dane had heard about him while growing up did nothing to discourage the rumor.

Dane glanced at his watch. Any talk about the dreams would have to wait. He'd promised to be at Claire's by eight, and that left less than an hour to get there. He grabbed his towel from the back of the chair beside his bed. "I'm going outside for a shower. Have you got a bar of soap?"

"Ain't you gonna put on any clothes?"

"To have a shower?"

Clement scratched his head, then tossed the soap to Dane. "What if someone comes callin' and you're standing out there like that. It ain't decent."

"Don't worry, I won't let your horses see me like this."

"Ain't the horses I'm worried about," Clement muttered, as he poked at the fire in the stove. "I don't want you scarin' my dogs."

Dane stepped outside, stood on the edge of the porch, and breathed the fresh morning air. The scent of sweet-

grass and the musky, full-bodied smell of wet earth filled
his nostrils. The city never smelled this good. He glanced
up. From the dull gray clouds that filled the sky, it was a
safe bet that it would probably rain most of the day.

Dropping the towel in Clement's chair, Dane took the
bar of soap and stepped off the porch. A steady rush of
rainwater ran off the corner eave, and he moved under the
makeshift shower. The cold water hit the top of his head,
soaked his hair, and then poured over him, raising goose-
flesh all over his body. Mud oozed between his toes. *This is
exactly what I needed last night, a cold shower. . . . The
muddy feet would've helped, too.*

For the next five minutes he lathered his body with the
pine-scented soap and, as though he were showering in the
privacy of his apartment, he sang one powwow 49 song after another.

> *When the dance is over, sweetheart,*
> *I will take you home in my one-eyed Ford,*
> *Eh ya hey, ya hey yo, hiya.*
> *Eh ya hey, eh ya hey.*
> *When the dance is over, sweetheart . . .*

Sweetheart. Claire Colby immediately slipped into his
mind, and to offset the thought, to push it aside, he began
another song.

> *Cheyenne girls, Cheyenne girls*
> *How I love those Cheyenne girls*
> *Eh ya hey, eh ya hey, ya hey.*

Dane worked the soap into his hair, then slid his lathered hands down over his body. He slowed their travel as
his fingers found the raised scars on his shoulder, his side,
and then the one on his leg. They were still tender to touch,
and he winced a little. But these weren't the only scars he'd
carry for the rest of his life. The Cheyenne girls song had

been Kylee's favorite 49 song. The scars on the outside would fade with time, but the ones on the inside would stay fresh and painful forever.

He tossed the soap onto the porch and, closing his eyes, stood directly under the heaviest flow of water and let the rain rinse away all of the soapsuds. It wasn't a grand hot and steamy shower by any stretch of the imagination. There weren't any shiny walls or a variable spray nozzle, and he didn't particularly care for the brand of soap, either, but Dane knew it was the best damned shower he'd ever had.

After a few minutes, he stepped back from the eaves and began to finger comb and squeeze the excess water from his hair.

It was Chewy, barking and running back and forth, who warned him that company was coming up the road.

18

THE RED DODGE PICKUP CRESTED THE HILL AND, after a quick over-the-shoulder glower, Chewy voiced his displeasure with a low growl and slunk away toward the back shed.

"Wish I could go with you," Dane grouched. He grabbed his towel off the porch, wrapped it around his waist, then turned and greeted Leland Big Elk with a counterfeit smile.

"You goin' native, *kola?*" Leland laughed and pointed at the towel around Dane's waist.

Dane ignored the jab, just like he'd like to ignore Leland. "What are you doing way out here? It's too early in the day for you, isn't it?" Dane adjusted the towel. "I was heading into Red Star, to the station, in about an hour. You didn't have to come all the way out. You could have met me there."

Leland snorted. "Yeah, sure, like I'm going to do business in the cop shop." He tossed a clear plastic pouch at Dane. "You've got a delivery."

The bright pink tablets sounded like maracas when the

bag landed in Dane's hand. Just from the weight, he figured there were about five hundred pills in the bag. "Aren't you forgetting? I've got a job."

"Yeah?" Leland snorted again. "Aren't you forgettin' who got you the job? Aren't you forgettin' you work for me?" Leland brushed the raindrops from his shirt as he stepped up onto the porch. He scanned the yard, the outbuildings, and the small house, then looked down at Dane and shook his head. "Man, how the hell do you stand it, livin' up here with this old man? His O is out back." He pointed to the outhouse out near the shed. "He don't even have a shower. Hell, you gotta wait till it rains to get clean . . . just like a damned hog."

Dane lightly bounced the plastic bag of E tablets in his palm. If he didn't keep his hands busy, he knew he'd close them into fists and rearrange Leland's attitude. He held up the bag. "Where does the stuff go?"

"You're gonna meet the guy in Rapid City at the Bright Flash gas station just off the first I-90 exit. He'll be there at noon in a black Corvette." Leland scraped the mud off the bottom of his fancy cowboy boots on the edge of the porch. "I told him three bucks a pill, fifteen hundred for the bag. He'll try to give you less. Don't let him. No samples, either."

"You got a name for this guy?"

Leland cocked his left brow. "You don't need nothin' more than what I've already told you. Like I said, he's drivin' a black 'Vette, he'll be at the Flash at noon, and he's supposed to give you fifteen hundred. That's it. A no-brainer."

Dane shot an arched-brow look right back at Leland. "I've got to stop by the station and take care of some other business first."

Leland sniggered. "Yeah, I been seein' how yer takin' care of business. You've been keeping busy with that hot new doc, that Claire Colby. Gettin' a little chummy with her, ain't ya? I hear you were drivin' her all over the rez yesterday." He slowly rubbed his belly. "Don't tell yer mom, but I wouldn't mind getting some of that kinda doctorin' for myself."

Dane didn't know if the shiver that wracked his body was because of the cold rain or the blast of rage that surged through his body. *When this is over, I'd better get a chance to flatten this son of a bitch.* He forced himself to move with a nonchalant swagger. "Hey, weren't you the one who told me I should keep track of her and see if she's had any of this stuff come through the clinic?" He tossed the bag of bright pink tablets up into the air, caught it, and tossed it again. "I'll make your delivery, but I'm keeping the money." The small bag landed back in his hand.

Leland stepped off the porch and pressed close to Dane. "The hell you are. You ain't keepin' nothin', *kola.*"

Dane flipped the bag and caught it, letting it rest in the palm of his hand. "You haven't paid me for the last delivery I made. If you don't keep the help happy, Leland, you end up all alone. You owe me."

"Oh yeah?" Leland scowled and took a step forward. A surprised look moved on his face when Dane didn't back away. "I don't need you. I can get another delivery boy." He spat the last two words and then laughed.

"You going to stiff him, too?" Standing a foot taller than Leland, Dane took advantage of his height. Moving closer, he leaned over Leland. Wide-eyed, Leland gave up ground and stepped back. Dane took another menacing step forward, tightening the gap between them. "You don't want to make any enemies, Leland. You've already got more trouble than you want. Maybe even more than you can handle."

"Bobby told me to—"

"Bobby didn't tell you shit," Dane snorted. "He's still in lockdown."

Leland turned away, taking mincing steps through the mud until he reached his truck. When he finally spoke, his voice sounded weak and squeaky. "Just make the damned delivery. Noon. No later."

"And the money?" Dane taunted.

"You can shove the money in your—"

"Pocket," Dane finished Leland's sentence and laughed.

"Yeah, whatever." Leland turned and pointed his finger at Dane. "You and me gonna have a talk, boy. I don't like your damned attitude."

"Ditto," Dane muttered. Stepping up on the porch, he moved to the edge, stuck his foot out under the fall of water from the eaves, and rinsed off the mud. Without saying another word to Leland, he went inside the cabin and closed the door. A moment later he heard the Dodge start up and the tires slip and spin in the mud as Leland headed out to the main road. Chewy delivered one last insult, chasing Leland down the lane and barking until the truck was out of sight.

"You've got bad taste in friends."

Dane spun around. "Damn it, old man. You're going to give me a heart attack. You've got to quit sneaking up on me."

Clement delivered one of his famous cackles. "Good warriors learn to sneak up, just like our sneak-up dance at the powwows. Maybe you need to be doin' some practicing, too. Ya never know when it's gonna be handy." He sobered, and his expression grew taut. "I don't like the friend you got. I don't like him for your momma, and I don't like him for you. There'd better be a damned good reason why you're messin' 'round with Leland Big Elk."

"There is," Dane said, pulling a clean pair of socks and jeans from his duffel bag.

"Yeah?" Clement's gaze dropped to the small plastic bag Dane had pitched onto the bed, and he pointed at it with a quick lift of his chin. "You wanna tell me what that stuff is?"

"Not particularly. Like I told you last night, I'll tell you all I can, when I can. This is something I've got to do my own way and in my own time."

Clement shrugged. Turning away, he opened the cabin

door and stepped out onto the porch. "We've all got secrets. Just make 'em worthwhile keepin'." He closed the door, leaving Dane alone.

THE RAIN HAD stopped by the time Dane pulled out onto the main road. Unclipping the cell phone from his belt, he hit number three on the speed dial and waited for either Gaines or Pardue to answer.

He heard a soft click on the line, and then Gaines began barking in his ear. "Where the hell have you been, White Eagle? Damn it, I've told you to keep your phone turned on. How're we supposed to keep track of you . . . and where the hell were you yesterday? You're supposed to check in with us daily."

I hate caller ID. It takes all the fun out of calling anybody. "Take a breath and cool your jets, Gaines. If I called you every day, you'd just start taking me for granted. I've got my pride, you know."

"Damn it, White Eagle, are all Indians as aggravating as you?"

"Why don't you ask Custer?"

Gaines chuckled. "Okay, cut the smart-ass history lesson. What've you got for me?"

"I've got a delivery to make in the city at noon, and you guys had better be there to take the buyer down. I'm bringing five hundred E tabs, and I don't want this crap to hit the streets."

"Where's the drop?"

"At the Bright Flash just off I-90."

"I know the place," Gaines replied. "Who's the buyer?"

"Black Corvette. I'm sure it's DiMaio."

"Well, I'll be damned. Cootch DiMaio," Gaines hissed. "We've been after that son of a bitch for a long time. He's always bought out of state before, bringing it in over the state line, which puts him right in the FBI and ATF's jurisdiction. Any idea why he's buying local?"

"Could be that he's got something big in the works and needs a fast supply."

"We hit one of his rave parties last night, but someone must have tipped him we were coming. We missed Di-Maio, but we got his stock."

"Well, if you don't screw up . . . you've got him today. When you take him in, just make sure he can't get any messages back to Leland, through his lawyer or anybody. Wait till I make the switch before you guys grab him. I'll drop the money and take off like a jackrabbit."

"You telling me how to do my job?"

Dane mentally counted a slow ten before he answered. "No, Gaines, I'm telling you how to keep me safe, undercover, and in the field. I don't need Leland waiting for me with a bullet when I get back to Cold Creek."

Dane pulled into the driveway in front of Claire's small house. "You guys hold onto the money. DiMaio won't get suspicious if it looks like I've bolted to save my own skin. I've already told Leland I'm keeping the cash, so he won't be expecting me to bring it back."

"What about the lab? You got anything yet?"

Dane began to get out of the truck to go to Claire's door. "Yeah, maybe." He looked up and saw Claire step out of the house, close and lock the door, and then, dodging puddles, run toward his truck.

"Where? Where is it?" Gaines asked.

"I'll talk to you later."

"What have you found out?"

"Later," Dane said and hit the Power Off button on his cell phone. He turned toward Claire, and his breath caught in his throat. A morning softness shaded her complexion. Her hair fell tousled around her face, and dark smudges lay under her eyes. *She didn't sleep too well last night, either.*

"Good morning," she said with a professional edge to her voice. "Thank you for driving me to work."

So that's how it's going to be. He didn't blame her. Keeping a safe distance between them was a good idea.

Yeah, such a good idea that I should have remembered it last night. "Good morning," Dane replied, wishing he could kiss her instead of just mouthing the polite greeting. He opened the passenger door and helped her into the truck.

Settling himself into the driver's seat, Dane slid the keys into the ignition and started the motor. He risked a quick glance and found himself staring at her mouth, the soft mouth he'd kissed the night before. He remembered how she had tasted, the hint of red wine, the flavor of sweetness that was hers alone, and the trace of yearning. A moment passed before he found his voice. "Sorry I'm late."

"You're not late," Claire replied. "It's just eight. Besides, I'm not expecting many patients today, so I'm not in a rush to get to the clinic. Commodity Thursdays are usually quiet."

Dane smiled. "You're picking up the jargon around here pretty well."

She returned his smile, and with that simple act the tension between them eased. "My second week here I thought my career was doomed when hardly anyone kept their appointment on Thursday. Your mother consoled me just before she asked to take the afternoon off. She explained that on the second Thursday of the month, everyone went to pick up their commodities."

"I've got to warn you to be very careful," Dane said, an ominous tone to his words.

"What? What do I have to be careful of?" Claire's eyes widened with concern.

"Just be careful. When your patients start trying to trade off their commodity cheese for their medications, don't hesitate for a moment. Say no as fast as you can. If you don't, you'll end up with three tons of hard cheese sitting in the middle of the clinic and not enough time in your life to eat it."

"Oh, Dane." Her smile turned into a laugh. "You really had me worried. Don't scare me like that."

Dane watched her touch the tip of her tongue to her top lip, and for the second time this morning his breath caught in his throat. *So, this is how a circus juggler feels with too many balls in the air. Just catch the ones you can, White Eagle. Keep your distance, and don't add to your problems.*

Putting the truck in reverse, he backed away from her small house, headed toward the clinic, and was finally able to draw a deep breath. "I talked with Denny Old Horn this morning. Your car won't be ready until tomorrow afternoon. He has to go to the city for a part."

"That long?"

"Don't worry, I'm a good taxi, reliable and friendly."

She nodded. "Yes, you are definitely that, but I can't keep imposing on you."

Oh, yes you can. "Don't worry. I wouldn't have offered if I didn't want to do it." He tried to keep his response casual, noncommittal yet affable. "I've got to make my rounds anyway." He turned the truck into the clinic parking lot, pulling to a stop at the front door. "What time should I be back to pick you up?"

"You really don't have to. I could probably get your mother to give me a lift home. It's not even that long a walk, and I could use the exercise."

Dane ignored her. "I'll be here about five. Is that okay?"

A slight smile curved Claire's lips. "That would be . . . okay." She looked up at him. "See you at five?" A moment passed before she added, "Thanks again for the lift. I really appreciate it."

In the next instant she was gone. Dane watched until she was safe inside the clinic before he put the truck in gear and began to pull out of the parking lot. "What are you going to do about this, White Eagle?" he muttered. "You've got to come to a decision before you go crazy." A harsh, cynical laugh fled his lips. "Nothing. That's what you're going to do. That's all you can do. Absolutely nothing."

•   •   •

DANE GRINNED AS he drove back onto Cold Creek. He'd
grinned the entire trip back from the city. Cootch DiMaio
was in federal custody, five hundred ecstasy pills were
never going to make it to the street, and the summer sun
had come out in full force, drying up the puddles and mud.
He checked his watch. Three-twenty. He'd been gone
longer than he'd planned, but there was still time to run patrol on the west end of the reservation before he picked up
Claire.

He'd driven about three miles when his cell phone rang.
"White Eagle."

"Hey Dane, Chief Iron Cloud here."

"Hi Calvin. What can I do for you?"

"Where are you, close to the station?"

"I'm in the west quad, up by Margaret Makes Plenty's
place. What's up?"

"You seen Debbie anywhere today?"

"Debbie Old Horn?"

"Yeah. She didn't show up for work this morning. Usually she calls if she's not coming in. I talked with Mattie.
She doesn't know where she is either. She said Debbie had
gone to a party last night, but didn't know where."

Dane didn't like the thought that immediately came to
mind. *She's probably off somewhere wigged out on E.*
"Have you been out looking for her?"

"Pete Rabbit, Arvin, and me went out earlier. We
didn't find nothin'. Nobody's checked out the west quad,
so keep your eyes peeled and lemme know if you . . .
see . . . anything."

Two miles up the road, Dane found Debbie Old Horn.

19

❧

DEBBIE OLD HORN LAY SPRAWLED IN THE DITCH, MUD and rainwater covering most of her body. If it hadn't been for her bright pink T-shirt, Dane wouldn't have seen her in the tall buffalo grass. Mud and leaves matted her hair, and her left arm lay at an odd angle over her head. He'd known Debbie almost all of her life, and now he was the first to know her in her death.

Overhead, buzzards circled, riding the air currents high over the rolling hills and floating with their wings outspread. He'd scattered them when he'd first found Debbie, and he now stood guard, keeping them away from Mattie Old Horn's daughter.

Almost an hour had passed since he'd called the station and talked to Calvin Iron Cloud. *What's taking him so damned long to get out here?*

Dane glanced at Debbie's body, wishing he could move her, take her out of the water, cover her with a blanket from his truck, and give her some little dignity in her death. There was absolutely nothing he could do. He'd have to wait for Iron Cloud; besides, if he even stepped near her, he'd contaminate the scene.

He turned away, trying to harden his feelings, trying to be the objective lawman he'd been trained to be, but it was damned difficult. Debbie Old Horn had grown up in Red Star in the small government-built house next door. He'd known her as a little girl. He'd watched her grow into a young woman. He'd survived her teenage crush on him when she'd ask him to be her two-step partner at every pow-wow. And he'd watched her belly swell with her first baby.

Dane removed his aviator sunglasses. From what he could see standing at the edge of the ditch, there didn't seem to be any signs of violence. The only footprints in the mud were Debbie's. He could see where she'd stumbled, tried to regain her balance, and then fell. There wasn't any blood on her body, on the ground, or in the ditch water. He couldn't see any bruising or signs of a struggle, but there was absolutely no doubt in his mind. Debbie Old Horn had been murdered. Not murdered outright from a bullet or a knife, not beaten or strangled. As he scanned her body, her words from the day before replayed in his head like a tape recording: *"Leland's my candy man."*

Dane knew he could bet his paycheck without worrying about losing a single penny. Leland Big Elk's deadly ec-stasy recipe had claimed another victim.

How did she get here? He hunkered down and studied the tire tracks left on the muddy road. *There are too many to single out any, but whoever had driven down this road was going to have muddied tires. I'm positive that someone had brought her out here. There's no way she could have walked out this far. But who? Who could have brought her out here and left her?*

Getting the answer wasn't going to be easy. Knowing Debbie, it could have been anybody.

It was difficult feeling sorry for her; she'd set herself up for trouble. Debbie Old Horn had earned herself the repu-tation of being a good snag at a 49. She liked to party hard, she liked pot and booze, didn't mind sharing her bed, and she'd obviously developed a taste for E. All that added up to someone who'd chosen to live wild and loose. But no one deserved to die alone in a ditch.

Dane slid his glasses back in place and heard Calvin Iron Cloud's truck before it crested the hill. Calvin sped down the road and braked to a stop behind Dane's Ford. Two vehicles followed Iron Cloud's; Dane recognized Pete Rabbit's truck. Arvin Runs Buffalo rode with him. It took only the flash of a second to recognize the third car, a black sedan, a Bureau car.

Dane pushed away from the right fender of his truck where he'd been leaning while waiting for the chief. *What in the hell are Gaines and Pardue doing here? Why didn't the Bureau send somebody else?* His pulse quickened, but it jumped and took off at a wild pace when he saw who was with Calvin Iron Cloud.

Claire stepped out of Calvin's 4×4. Retrieving her medical bag from the truck, she turned and stared at Debbie Old Horn. Dane watched the play of emotions on her face.

When she looked up at him, he tried to encourage her with a slight smile and a nod of his head. He wished it could be more. A touch, a squeeze of her hand . . . something. Ignoring Gaines and Pardue, who had joined them, Dane followed her to the edge of the ditch.

"Not a pretty sight, is it?" He spoke softly.

"No, it isn't," Claire replied. "Sometimes death isn't pretty at all."

He shot a glance at her. "You're saying that sometimes it is?"

She nodded and quietly replied, "When it comes gently. When it comes quickly, or comes after great suffering . . . it can be."

Stunned, Dane didn't know how to respond. Dr. Claire Colby had probably seen more death, useless and ugly death, as an ER doc than he'd see in ten years with the Bureau, and yet she could still find good in it.

Calvin stepped up beside them and pointed at Pardue and Gaines with a quick jerk of his thumb. "It don't take long for the Feds to push in, does it?"

"Just like the buzzards," Dane replied, turning his back on the two FBI agents. "How'd they find out about . . ." He glanced across the ditch at Debbie.

"I . . . uh . . . had to call 'em. You know it's the law, Dane."

"Yeah, I know," Dane replied. "I don't like it, but I know." He suddenly felt like a Judas. Straddling the fence—being Indian and FBI—sometimes was a damned hard place to be. When this undercover case was all over, it was quite possible that his own people wouldn't accept him anymore.

Calvin interrupted Dane's thoughts. "I sure weren't expecting anything like this when she didn't show up for work this mornin'." Calvin sniffled, then pulled his handkerchief out of his pocket and wiped his nose. "I didn't call Mattie yet. No sense her coming out here and seeing her baby girl like this. Lots of times Debbie never made it home, so Mattie ain't really missin' her yet." He shook his head. "It's a sad thing. She's got two kids." He glanced at Dane. "Did you . . . you know . . . look around?"

"No," Dane replied. "I figured it would have to wait till they got here." He jerked his thumb at Gaines and Pardue.

Calvin nodded. "Well, let's get to it." He pointed at Claire with a quick lift of his chin. "You two know each other, eh? Dr. Colby is here to examine . . . the bod . . . Debbie."

"This your new guy, Calvin?" Gaines stepped forward, butting in.

"Yeah," Calvin replied, his tone cold and unfriendly. "Dane White Eagle, Special Agent Jack Gaines . . . FBI. The other one is Gil Pardue."

Dane forced a sarcastic chuckle, keeping the deception going. "Doesn't take you guys long to start shoving us around, does it?" He looked across the ditch at Debbie Old

Horn's body. "You could at least respect our ways and give us time to take care of our own . . . in our own way."

"Easy," Calvin said, placing his hand on Dane's arm. "You know there ain't nothing we can do about it. It's their jurisdiction now. Suspicious death on the rez always brings 'em out like . . . like . . ."

"Flies on shit," Dane said, completing Calvin's sentence.

"Can we cut the insults and get busy here?" Pardue stepped closer. "I don't know about you, but standing around and jacking jaws while there's a crime scene to process isn't my idea of a pleasant afternoon."

With the FBI on the scene, the tribal police were no longer in charge of the site. Dane moved out of the way, back to his truck, and leaned against the front fender again. "Okay," he said, broadly gesturing with his hand. "It's all yours. Do your thing."

Jack Gaines stepped in front of him. "We've got jurisdiction, White Eagle." He looked over his shoulder at Claire. "Dr. Colby is here to examine the body and issue a death certificate before we move it to the morgue for autopsy."

Pardue stepped up to the edge of the ditch with his camera and shot a number of pictures of the ground around Debbie Old Horn. He took close-ups of the footprints she'd left in the mud and of her shoes. "Okay," he said, turning to Claire, "you can examine her now."

With the élan of a gentleman, Calvin Iron Cloud helped Claire step over the ditch. Pardue followed with his camera, cussing with a loud hiss as his shoes sank in the mud.

A surprising touch of pride filled Dane as he watched Claire ignore the dirt, the water, and the mud and kneel down beside Debbie's body. Her hands moved slowly, gentle and deliberate, as she began her examination.

"Any signs of foul play?" Gaines asked, stepping closer to the ditch.

"None that are readily visible," Claire quietly replied, lifting Debbie's hair, examining her scalp, then moving her attention down to her face. "There are no signs of injuries except for a few scratches on her arms that she could have gotten when she fell in the ditch."

"How long do you think she's been . . . like this?" Calvin asked, peering over Claire's shoulder.

"Rigor is still present, which means she's been dead at least ten to twelve hours." She lifted the pink T-shirt, exposing Debbie's stomach and side. "There's almost full lividity, but without a core body temperature, I can only make a guess." She pulled her hand out of the way when Pardue stepped in to take another photo, a close-up of the discolored skin she'd just exposed. "My guess is that she died between midnight and two A.M., but that's purely a guess. The death certificate will have the time I examined her, though. That's procedure." She glanced at Pardue. "I don't have any forms with me. Do you?"

"Yeah, I've got some in the car."

"Thank you," Claire replied, returning to her examination.

Calvin looked up and watched the persistent buzzards still circling overhead. "How soon before we can take her home?"

"Calvin," Pardue answered, changing the roll of film in his camera. "We'll have to take her to the city morgue first for autopsy so cause of death can be determined. The morgue van should arrive any minute."

"This might help you with your findings. It was in her left hand." Claire held up a small clear plastic bag with five bright pink wedge-shaped tablets inside. She handed the bag to Pardue, then looked over at Gaines. Her eyes widened. She quickly looked back at Pardue and then at Gaines again.

In that moment Dane knew that Claire had recognized Jack Gaines and Gil Pardue. Her frown told him she couldn't remember where she'd seen them before, but he realized it wouldn't be long before she remembered the two men who had taken him into her office on a snowy December night, two men who had held him against the wall and arrested him.

"Agent Gaines," Claire said, the frown still creasing her brow, "have we met before? Both you and Agent Pardue look very familiar to me."

Gaines reached into his pocket for his sunglasses and settled them on his nose, a ploy to hide his face. "I don't think so, Dr. Colby. I'm sure I would have remembered if we had."

"Here's the van," Pardue said, turning away from the body and from Claire, relief evident in the tone of his voice. The black van from the morgue topped the hill and came to a stop beside Dane's truck, blocking the road.

Gaines passed close to Dane as he headed for the van and spoke in a hoarse whisper, "Get her out of here before she remembers where she's seen us. If she puts two and two together, you're fried possum."

In less than fifteen minutes, Debbie Old Horn was taking her last trip off of Cold Creek.

Dane lightly touched Claire's arm. "If you're ready, I'll take you back to the clinic." He looked down at her mud-stained slacks and spattered white lab coat. "Or would you like to go home and change first?"

"I'm sure that Chief Iron Cloud will drive me back." She glanced over at Calvin, then back at Dane. "I've closed the clinic for the day." A slight smile lifted the corners of her mouth. "Remember? It's commodity Thursday, not many patients to cancel. I'd better wait for Chief Iron Cloud."

"This isn't like the junior prom," Dane teased. "You don't have to go home with the guy that brought you." He looked up at Iron Cloud. "I'll tell Calvin you've got a ride home, and I'll get you out of here."

After talking with Calvin, Dane helped Claire into his truck. Turning the pickup around, he drove away from the ditch where Debbie Old Horn had died.

"Dane, who is going to tell Mattie?"

He took his eyes off the road for a moment and glanced over at Claire. "Mattie and Calvin go back a long way. He'll do it. He'll take his wife, Cora, with him. Cora will stay with Mattie and contact the other women. When Debbie comes home, Cora and the others will help Mattie get Debbie ready for her wake. They'll help Mattie wash and dress her." He paused, not sure how much he should tell Claire, how much she'd understand. "Some of the other women will cook and feed all the mourners, everyone who comes. They'll stay with Debbie . . . all day and all night . . . until she's buried. It's the Indian way."

Claire nodded. "I've a lot to learn, don't I?"

"You'll catch on. It won't be hard. Half the learning is in admitting what you don't know."

"That must be a Clementism."

Dane laughed, a full-bodied laugh that felt exhilarating and cleansing. "Oh yeah, that's one of Clement's." He braked the truck to a stop at the main road. "Do you want to go to the clinic or go home? Left or right?"

"Left. Home. Remember? I closed the clinic for the rest of the day." She glanced down at her dirty clothes. "I need to clean up."

"I have an idea how to end this day with a good memory, one that will stay with you all your life."

"How? What are you talking about?"

"Dr. Claire, let's get you into a pair of blue jeans and boots. You're going on an Indian buffalo hunt this afternoon."

CLAIRE WASN'T SURE if going riding in the back hills of Cold Creek with Dane White Eagle was the right thing to do. She chewed nervously on her bottom lip. *Stop it,* she chided herself, trying to push her uncertainties aside, but as much as she wanted to dismiss it, the question of his guilt or innocence still weighed heavily on her mind.

"It looks like you've got a welcoming committee waiting for you," Dane said, stopping the truck in front of Clement Runs After's cabin.

Claire looked up to see an old Lakota, bent with age and arthritis. The stained and battered cowboy hat sitting on his head looked as though it was as old as the man who wore it. Two nondescript yellow dogs sat on the porch beside him, tongues lolling from their mouths, tails thumping on the wood planks in a mismatched rhythm. The man's aged skin resembled dark cherry wood that had been carefully carved in deep, intricate patterns. White hair, tinged with memories of the black hue it once had, fell in two thin braids over his shoulders. Barrel-chested and bowlegged, the old Lakota couldn't be any taller than five foot six or eight. But it was the old man's dark eyes that impressed her the most. Bright and alert, they were eyes that didn't miss anything. Sharp and watchful, they held her mesmerized.

"He's straight out of a Hollywood movie, isn't he?" Dane laughed. "Don't let him fool you, though. He's an old softy who has a tender spot for a pretty *winyan*."

Dane helped Claire out of the truck, and they walked toward the cabin.

A wide grin spread on Clement's face. "Eyee, *wasté*, Grandson. It's good. You caught a woman to cook and clean and carry firewood for us." He leaned closer to Claire and narrowed his eyes. "Hmm, she don't look Pawnee or Crow. Ain't got much muscle, either. Where'd you find this scrawny woman?"

"Behave, you old *tatanka*," Dane laughed. "That's no way to greet your guest." He took Claire's hand and drew her close. "Claire, this old rascal is Clement Runs After. Whether you like it or not, he'll be the best friend you'll ever have."

Claire held out her hand, amazed by the large size and vital strength of the gnarled one that enveloped hers. "I'm very pleased to meet you, Mr. Runs After." She glanced at

Dane, then back at Clement. "I've heard a great deal about you."

"Don't believe nothin' that pitiful one tells you." He pointed at Dane with pursed lips. "I'm a wonderful fellow. And you, Dr. Colby, are always welcome in my home."

She laughed. "Please, call me Claire."

"Then you must call me Clement."

Claire watched Clement's dark eyes appraise her once again, then felt Dane take her hand and begin to lead her toward the two Pinto horses dozing in the sag-fenced corral. Clement followed, his bowed legs keeping pace.

"I promised to show Claire the tribe's herd of buffalo. You know where they've been seen lately?"

Clement lifted his chin, pointing toward the north. "I hear they've been up by Stone Bluff. There's some pretty babies in the herd this year. No white one yet, though."

Claire looked at Dane, then Clement. "White one? Is that special?"

"You bet it is," Clement answered. "When the white buffalo calf comes, everything will be returned to the people: our lands, our warriors, our old ways." He nodded his head. "The promise goes back to the time of White Buffalo Calf Woman when she came and brought us the seven sacred ceremonies and the sacred bundle. It's a good thing, a very good thing." Clement turned to Dane. "The saddles are in the back shed. They're a little dusty." He paused and glanced at the pintos in the corral. "You take Maza Cante and let Claire ride Wanbli."

Claire lightly touched Dane's arm. "What are their names? How do I pronounce them?"

Dane grinned. "The old man is just being fancy. He's saying that the horses' names are Iron Heart and Eagle, but I know they'll answer to anything." Dane looked over his shoulder at Clement then back at Claire. "Most of the time he just calls them Spot. Spot One and Spot Two."

In twenty minutes Dane had saddled and bridled the horses. After helping Claire climb onto Spot Two, they headed out, away from Clement's cabin, on a trail that headed north.

"Did you tell him?" Claire asked, breaking the silence. "About Debbie?"

"Yes."

Dane nodded. "He wasn't surprised. Sad, but not surprised. He'll go down and sit with her when they bring her home."

They crossed the ridge behind Clement's cabin and descended the steep grade on the other side. At the bottom of the hill, emptiness spread out all around them. Claire had never seen anything like it in her life. The wide expanse of land, undisturbed by buildings or anything touched by man, left her breathless. The wind, blowing across the prairie, set the tall grass into a strange, undulating movement, creating ripples like waves on the ocean.

"Look." Dane stopped his horse and pointed toward the sky. "Eagles."

Reining her horse to a stop beside him, Claire looked up. High overhead, two large birds rode the currents, gliding with their wings outspread, swirling around one another in an aerial ballet. As though bored with the graceful dance, the eagles broke free and climbed higher and higher. In an instant they turned, plunged toward one another, and seemed to collide in midair. Locked together, talon to talon, the birds plummeted toward the ground.

Claire gasped, watching in awe as mere moments before crashing into the ground, the birds separated and climbed high into the sky and began their dangerous aerobatics once again.

"Why . . . why do they do that?" she asked, her voice breathless with wonder. "That is . . . unbelievable."

"They're a mating pair," Dane replied. "Eagles mate for life. It's quite a sight, isn't it?"

"Oh, yes. But why do they hold onto each other until they almost hit the ground?"

He removed his sunglasses and looked at her. "Trust.

It's all about trust. Loving someone, wanting to be with that someone for a lifetime, and staying with that someone . . . it's all about trust."

Caught in his gaze, she couldn't turn away, not even when she heard the shrill call of the eagles as they soared overhead. Finally, she found her voice but could only whisper her answer. "Yes, it is . . . all about trust."

The air around them seemed to be charged with electricity as they stared at one another. Neither spoke, neither moved. The only sounds were the calls of the pair of eagles in the sky. It was Dane who broke the moment.

"We've got a ways to go," he said, his words as soft as the breeze that carried them to her. "We'd better get going."

He led her over hill after hill, and she followed willingly, mindless of the heat that pressed around them.

The late afternoon sun beat down, making Claire grateful for the ball cap that Clement had loaned her. To keep as cool as she could, she'd gathered her hair up off of her neck and pulled it through the hole in the back of the cap. The bill shaded her eyes, and she was able to watch Dane as he followed a broad trail of hoofprints.

He pointed to the swath trampled in the tall grass. "Buffalo. They've come this way in the past couple of hours."

He dropped his horse's reins across the swells of the saddle and rolled up his shirtsleeves. Claire stared at his forearms, awestruck by the beautiful play of the muscles under his smooth, bronze skin.

Dane White Eagle was quite a sight. Although his clothes were modern, his hat and boots all cowboy, Dane White Eagle on a horse was magnificent. He looked as though in a blink of an eye, time could suddenly reverse and years would fall away: twenty, forty, sixty, a hundred, a hundred thirty. And in those many years past, his body would be naked except for buckskin leggings, his hair would be unbound and blowing free in the wind, and he would be breathtaking. Dane White Eagle belonged in this wild place; he was the essence of this place.

Claire grabbed onto the saddle horn and closed her eyes, hoping to erase the image that filled her head and tempted her heart. The touch on her arm was light and tentative.

"Claire, are you okay?"

She opened her eyes to find Dane peering at her. A hot blush touched her cheeks. "Yes . . . I'm fine."

"You're sure?"

"Yes, of course."

"We can stop for a while if you need to rest."

"No, I'm fine, I was . . . uh . . . just trying to imagine this place a hundred or so years ago."

A slow smile that seemed to tease her played on his mouth. "I don't think it was much different. Just a whole lot of nothing."

He reached out and gently touched her face with the tips of his fingers. He followed the curve of her cheek, lightly rimmed the edge of her lower lip, and then his touch was gone. Once again she found herself caught in his gaze. And in that instant she knew it was a wonderful place to be.

Dane pulled away and reined his horse around, taking the lead back to the trail. He knew if he rode behind Claire, he wouldn't be able to keep his mind on anything but the saucy swing of her ponytail hanging out the back of her ball cap and the enticing sway of her hips in the saddle. Oh yeah, riding out front was the best place to be.

Ten minutes later, still following the tracks the buffalo had left in the grass, they crested the top of the broad hill.

"There they are," Dane whispered as he stopped his horse on the top of the hill. He pointed across the wide field to the herd of buffalo. "Aren't they magnificent?" The sight of the buffalo always thrilled him, no matter how many times he saw them.

"I've never seen anything like it," Claire replied, her voice filled the wonder.

"We'd better stay up here. We don't want to spook them, and we certainly don't want to upset the old bull. A charging buffalo can be deadly . . . for both horse and rider."

In a single, easy movement, Dane swung out of the saddle, then helped Claire to the ground. "Come on. We can sit on the edge of the hill and watch them for a while." He held out his hand.

Before they sat down, he quietly began to point out the various individuals in the herd. "There's the bull. Clement calls him Old Romeo because he's got all these pretty ladies to keep happy. The young bulls are there, off to the right. None have had the nerve to challenge Old Romeo . . . yet." He scanned the herd. "This group are the young cows, and look, over there. Look at the babies," he said, pointing to the far side of the field. "They're napping with their mamas."

"Where? Where are you looking?"

Dane stepped close behind her and bent over slightly so that their line of vision was the same. Placing his right hand against her cheek, he moved her head slightly to the left until her face touched his. With his left arm pointing over her shoulder, he directed her to the small group of cows and their calves beneath a few of the only trees in sight.

Close . . . you're too close, White Eagle. What in the hell are you doing? He ignored the unrelenting voice of his conscience. "Can you see them now?" He felt her nod and felt the light touch of her breath on his bare arm.

"They're adorable. I never imagined they'd have so much soft hair. Can't we move a little closer?"

She quickly turned her head to look up at him. With a hungry moan that lifted from the center of his being, Dane knew he'd lost the struggle. She trembled, and without a moment's hesitation, he drew her into his arms and tilted her chin up with a light touch of his finger.

"Kiss me," she whispered, her words echoing his of the night before. "Kiss me, Dane. If you don't, I'm going to die."

20

DANE SWEPT THE BALL CAP OFF OF CLAIRE'S HEAD AND tossed it aside. Gently laying the palm of his hand against her cheek, he searched her eyes for . . . what? Approval? Acceptance? This was the biggest gamble he could take, but damn it, it was more than worthwhile putting in all his chips.

He drove his hand deep into her hair, threading and weaving it between his fingers. It became hopelessly ensnared in his grip, which was exactly what he wanted. Curving his hand around the back of her head, he pulled her to him. With his mouth just above hers, feeling the heat of her on his lips, he had to have the answers to a few questions. "You're sure this is what you want? No worries? No doubts?"

Claire's hands encircled his bare forearms, her fingers clutching him, her nails pressing into his flesh. Remembering what he'd told her about the eagles, she held on as if she would fall to the ground if she let go. "There are always worries," she whispered against his mouth. "There are still doubts . . . but not about this. Yes, this is what I want." She pressed her body against his and slid her hands up his arms. "Oh yes . . . this is what I want."

"You're the doctor," Dane breathed. Slowly moving his hands lower across her cheeks, he lifted her chin with the gentle pressure of his thumbs. Exposing her throat, he brushed his lips against the vulnerable curve of her neck. The rush of her pulse throbbed beneath his mouth. Lightly nipping with his teeth, he traveled the silken column of her throat, soothing each nip with a light lick with his tongue. Then, gazing down and watching the play of expressions on her face, he leisurely traced the full shape of her mouth with the tip of his fingers. Claire slightly parted her lips in response, her invitation clear.

Dane lowered his head, watched her eyelids slowly close, and covered her mouth with his. He tilted his head, adjusting the angle until the fit of their lips was perfect. And a moment before he completely lost himself in the scent and the taste of her, one fleeting question crossed his mind: *What in the hell am I doing?* And one resolute answer followed: *You're falling in love, and it's the most dangerous thing you could do at this time.*

She fit perfectly against him, curve filling hollow, angles aligning one to another, soft meeting hard. Pushing all caution and all reason aside, he sank his tongue into the heat of her mouth and completely lost his heart.

The sound began as nothing more than an annoying intrusion, like the buzzing of a fly. It grew and grew, boring into his mind, tugging at him, pulling him away from the paradise he'd found in Claire's arms. He felt the vibration begin, growing until the ground shook beneath his feet.

Quickly stepping away from Claire, he immediately felt the loss of her touch.

"Dane?"

"Come on, sweetheart. We've got to go." He tried to keep the urgency out of his voice. He failed.

"What? What's wrong?"

Without another word, he pointed down the hill. "Something's got the buffalo spooked." He watched the herd mill about, watched Old Romeo push the cows and their babies into a tight group, and watched the young bulls scatter. Movement at the north end of the field grabbed his attention. "I think I've found the culprits. Damn it to hell!"

"Who?"

"Not who . . . what." He pointed to the stand of trees where minutes ago the cows and their calves had been resting.

Nearly concealed in the grass, their exact numbers were hidden. They moved in a tight pack, but one or two broke from the ranks and charged a few feet forward, harassing the buffalo, aggravating Old Romeo before returning to the group. "The damned rez dogs."

"You're kidding me." Claire stepped closer to the lip of the hill and looked to the north. "How did they find us?"

Her question surprised him, her words hitting him like a ten-pound sledgehammer. Why hadn't he thought of it before? Why hadn't he put all the clues together? Yes . . . it was too much of a coincidence that the dogs kept showing up, following them, finding both of them. He didn't know what it was all about, and he sure as hell didn't like it, but there had to be an answer. *And if I can corner him long enough, Clement's going to tell me what it is.*

"Now what do we do?" Claire asked, clutching his arm. "I'm afraid."

Dane glanced down at the woman who moments ago had been in his arms and who had rocked his world. "Come on, before they get Old Romeo and the herd riled up into a full stampede, and before the horses get scared and hightail it back to Clement's without us . . . we're getting out of here." He lightly touched her cheek with the back of his knuckles. "Don't worry. It's going to be okay."

After gathering her horse's reins, Claire turned back to Dane. "I don't remember." Her voice trembled. "Is this Spot One or Spot Two?"

"I forget, but I don't think it really matters." He chuckled. Her attempt to make light of their touchy situation was obvious. He bent down, picked up her ball cap, and settled it on her head. Speaking in little more than a whisper, he added, "But I'll never forget this . . . and it really matters." Without hesitating, without arguing the pros or cons of his feelings for Claire Anne Colby, Dane kissed her again. He plundered her mouth, determined to brand her with a hunger as great as his own.

The intrusion came again, the sound almost silent yet loud with stealth as it bored its way into his head. An icy finger of disquiet rode the ridge of his spine, setting off an internal alarm that he couldn't ignore, no matter how wonderful her lips felt beneath his. Slowly stepping out of Claire's arms, Dane turned toward the hill, knowing what he'd find.

The rez dogs were no longer in the gully below. Lined up in rank and file, as if under regimental orders, they sat on the rim of the hill no more than forty feet away.

Dane put himself between Claire and the dogs. "Claire, get on your horse now." He spoke quietly and didn't look back at her. "Go slow and easy. No sudden movements." He took a tentative step away from her. "Don't wait for me, don't look back, just walk your horse on out of here. I'll catch up."

THE DOGS FOLLOWED them for almost two miles, staying in a tight pack and trailing far enough behind that occasionally Dane lost sight of them. Kylee's black and white pup was still among them, bounding along beside the large black leader of the pack. Seeing that the dog had grown, losing its puppy look to adult muscle, sent a wave of sadness over Dane. Pirate no longer was the pup that Kylee had left behind.

After leading Claire down into a shallow gully, Dane looked back over his shoulder. Once more the dogs had lined up on the rim of a rise, like birds on a wire, but this time they didn't follow. For the next mile, he kept checking, looking back, searching for the dogs, but they had disappeared.

"Can you see them anymore?"

He glanced at Claire as she nervously chewed her bottom lip. "No. They've either headed off in another direction or have stopped for a rabbit or a nap."

Claire looked away from the far hill where they'd last seen the dogs and shifted her gaze to Dane. "Why doesn't the tribal council get rid of them or . . . I don't know, maybe . . . catch them . . . and . . ."

"And then what?" Dane slowed his horse until he rode beside her. "They're wild. Most of them have been born wild. They'll never be pets. They're as close to wolves as you can get. You can't fence them in, and they're dangerous." He wanted to scare her, wanted to know she wouldn't get all kindhearted and try to make friends with the dogs. "They'd think nothing of biting the hand that fed them. Bite it? Hell, they'd chew it off as an appetizer." He slowly shook his head. "Besides, no one on Cold Creek has the time, inclination, or the money to even think about taking them in or feeding them."

"What about old Margaret Makes Plenty? You said she had a gift with animals."

"These dogs would eat every one of Margaret's deer, chew on her rabbits for snacks, and probably have Margaret for dessert. All in less than a week."

Moving at a slow jog, the horses followed the narrow trail for another five miles. Every once in a while Dane checked behind them for the dogs but never saw anything but a few rabbits, a deer or two, and one lonely porcupine. Climbing the slope of one more hill, they stopped on the top of the ridge and looked down on Clement's cabin and corral.

"His pickup's gone," Dane said. "He must be in town, maybe down with Mattie and her family."

"Do you want to go?"

Dane shook his head. "No. I doubt if I'd be welcome." He looked up at the early evening sky. "Things aren't quite back the way they used to be around here . . . yet. I'll go to the funeral."

"Dane! Oh, my God! Look. The dogs . . . they're down there!" Her hand shook as she pointed toward Clement's cabin. "How did they get here first?"

Dane looked down the hill at the two dogs ambling about Clement's yard. He swallowed the chuckle that filled his throat. There was no way he wanted to tease her about being afraid of the rez dogs. "No. It's okay, Claire. That's Chewy and What's His Name. Those are Clement's two flea buses."

"I thought they . . . I thought . . ." Claire sheepishly dropped her head.

"Yeah, after today I would have believed they were, too."

She glanced up, then back down at Clement's two dogs. "Is that dog's name really What's His Name?"

"It sure is, but what do you expect? The man named his horses Spot One and Spot Two." His horse, anxious to get home, stomped its hooves and tossed its head. Dane glanced at Claire. "Come on, cowgirl, let's call it a day."

By the time the horses had been unsaddled, brushed down, watered, and fed, the sun had completely set behind the western hills, and the stars were bright in the clear night sky. A half-moon provided all the light they needed to walk across Clement's yard to Dane's truck.

"Thank you," Claire said as Dane helped her into the pickup. "Thank you for the wonderful end to a . . . difficult day."

"I'm glad you enjoyed it, even if we did have to cut it short." He slid behind the steering wheel, turned the key in the ignition, and steered the truck down the rocky, pothole-filled lane to the main road. "Maybe when things calm down a little, we'll go out again and get to spend a little more time."

"With or without the rez dogs?"

Dane glanced over at her. "Without would be best. I'm sure the buffalo would think so, too." He turned his attention back to the road.

"I saw your sister's dog in the pack." Claire's words came softly. "The others might be hopeless, but have you thought about trying to . . . catch him and . . . take him home?"

Dane's breath caught and burned in his throat. "Yeah, I've thought about it, but I guess that first I'd have to have a home to take him to."

Claire nodded. "Maybe your mom would take him."

Anger, which had burned in his soul since he'd first seen the black and white pup running with the pack, rose up again and added fire to his words. "Who in the hell do you think turned him loose?"

"But why? I don't understand. He belonged to her daughter, there was a connection—"

"The *connection* was that the pup was a birthday present. The *connection* was that I gave Pirate to *Taŋski.*" He didn't have to say anything more; Claire had seen his mother's icy welcome the first day he'd gone to the clinic.

"If you caught him . . . you could bring him to me."

Surprised by her offer, he quickly glanced at her. "Why? Why would you want him?"

"Because he means something special to you and because seeing him running with the pack of wild dogs hurts you more than you'd ever admit."

He clenched his teeth, tightening the muscle along the edge of his jaw, fighting the harsh ache of Kylee's loss that had suddenly returned. Struggling to hide his pain from Claire, the sharp edge remained in his voice. "Maybe you shouldn't worry yourself about this."

"Maybe it's too late to tell me that, Dane. Maybe it's much too late."

Did Claire know what she was saying? Maybe he was reading more into her words than was really there. The argument between his head and his heart began to rage again, but the fix was in. There was no way that his head was going to win.

Turning into the lane beside Claire's small house, the beam of his headlights hit the red Mustang parked under the small cottonwood tree. "It looks like Denny got your car fixed. I told you he'd take care of you," Dane said, thankful to have something to talk about other than Kylee's dog. "He said he'd leave the bill on the dashboard."

"Great, but I don't have an extra set of keys. He wouldn't leave the keys in the ignition or in the car, would he?" She turned toward Dane. "Anyone could come along and steal it if—"

"No," Dane interrupted. "I told him to leave them on the kitchen window ledge." He opened the door. "Come on, I'll get them for you."

Halfway to the house, Claire grabbed his arm. "Dane, look. Over there by the bushes. I don't understand . . . How is it possible? I don't believe this."

Once again Dane knew what he'd find before he even turned to see what Claire was pointing at. He knew there'd be a pack of wild dogs, and among them would be the white and black pup, Pirate. What surprised him was that they looked no more vicious than family pets dozing on the lawn. Only a few of the dogs lifted their heads, only a few stood and continued to watch them, but he wasn't going to take any chances. "Get in the house. Don't run, just keep walking and get in the house."

"What are you going to do?"

"Hell, I'm coming with you."

HER HAND STILL shaking, Claire flipped on the lamp in the small living room. Warm light filled every corner of the room, helping to ease the fear that had filled her only moments before. She looked up to find Dane still standing by the door, his hand on the knob. "You look as though you're ready to bolt." She kicked off her boots. "Come into the kitchen and keep me company while I fix us something to eat."

"I should go," he insisted, yet not moving to open the door. "You've had a rough day and should get some sleep."

"You can't go out there now. What if the dogs are still in the yard?"

Dane touched the gun at his waist. "One round and they'll scatter."

"Good. Then while I'm putting a salad together, you can get my car keys. Please."

"God but you're a hard woman. You want to send me out to the wolves? I don't think so." Dane laughed, then brushed by her and headed for the kitchen. He leaned over the sink, lifted the window, and retrieved the car keys from the outside sill. Turning around, he held up his hand and dangled the keys in the air.

"Thank you." Claire reached for the keys and laughed as Dane raised his arm, lifting the car keys higher than she could reach. "This time I did say please and thank you." *Good grief, I'm acting like a giddy schoolgirl.* "You didn't have to remind me of my manners."

Dane's grin was ridiculously boyish as it spread wide across his face. "I can't give them to you until we decide on my reward."

Claire stepped back. "You expect a reward?" She was enjoying his teasing game. It had been a very long time since she'd allowed herself to enjoy a man's company, since she'd played courting games, since she'd . . . wanted. *And I want Dane White Eagle. I want him more than I've ever wanted anything in my life. I'd forgotten how wonderful it feels. No, how can you forget something you've never felt before?* She stood her ground until the voice in her head spoke again. *If you want this so much, if you want to stop being afraid of life . . . of love . . . you have to be the one to . . . start the game.*

"Well? What do you think would be a good reward?" He

jiggled the keys, causing them to softly clink against each other. "If you can't decide, I suppose I could come up with a few." He jiggled the car keys again. "In fact, I already have a few suggestions."

"Oh, you have, have you?" Claire set her hands on her hips. "I think I have one or two ideas of my own, thank you very much."

His grin broadened, and a devilish sparkle lit up his dark eyes. "Do I have to guess, or are you going to tell me what they are?" He rattled the keys again, trying to tempt her.

His ploy wasn't going to work. She'd already made up her mind, she'd already collected her courage, she'd already promised herself—his reward was going to be her reward, too. Claire dropped her hands off her hips and slowly moved forward until she stopped mere inches from him. "Now, why should I tell you or make you guess when it would be so much more fun to . . . show you?" Mimicking a flirty expression that she'd seen Julie use a hundred times before, she traced the line of buttons down the front of his shirt with her finger.

The look of surprise that quickly touched his face delighted her. She'd never toyed like this with a man before. She'd never imagined that it would feel so wonderful. *Can I go through with this?* She hesitated for only a millisecond. *Hell, yes! Julie would be so proud of me.* She drew a fortifying breath and began to give Dane White Eagle his reward.

Gazing into his eyes, Claire slowly reached up and removed his black Stetson and tossed it onto the kitchen table. She took his braids, one in each hand, and let them slip through her fingers, all the way down to the leather thong wraps at the tips. It took only a slight tug to pull off the wraps, but it took every ounce of her willpower to battle the temptation to loosen his braids. *Do it now. You want to do it now. No. Wait. Later. There'll be more than enough time . . . later.*

She placed her hands, palms flat, against his stomach,

and the heat from his body immediately warmed her skin. The sensation kicked her pulse up a notch and deepened her breath. Her eyes never wavered from his, not even when he gave her a wicked wink, not even when his mouth lifted in a wicked quirk.

Lowering his hand to his side, Dane leaned close and whispered in her ear with an exciting husky quality to his voice. "I'm really enjoying my reward. Need any help?" His breath scorched her skin.

"Shut up," she whispered, determined to keep control of the moment.

"Yes, ma'am," he replied with a deep chuckle.

Not hesitating another moment, because to do so would give her the time to change her mind, time to back away, Claire spread her fingers and slowly began to move her hands upward over Dane's stomach. His muscles tightened under her caress, and with an unhurried touch she traced their hard definition. If she gave it any thought, she could identify every muscle, but now, in this moment, she was not Claire Colby the doctor, she was Claire Colby the woman.

Her hands continued their leisurely upward push, savoring each inch, delighting in Dane's response to her touch. As her fingers passed over his nipples, she heard him draw a ragged breath, saw him close his eyes, and watched, fascinated, as the tip of his tongue slowly licked his top lip from corner to corner.

Reluctantly dragging her thoughts away from his mouth, she looked down at her hands, took a moment and tried to settle her racing pulse. It didn't happen.

"Don't stop now."

Startled, she looked up. His dark eyes held her captive once again, boring into her soul, creating a fire deep within her belly. Liquid flames flowed through her veins, feeding her courage, firing her craving. "Don't worry," she replied in a voice she barely recognized. "I'm just beginning."

Her hands moved again, continuing their ascent, her fin-

gers grazing over his shirt collar and finally settling on his
hot bare skin. The sensation of her skin against his was incredible, a prize, a reward of her own. Moving higher up
the strong column of his neck, the pads of her fingers
lightly traveled over the ridge of his jaw, then explored the
full, soft shape of his mouth. She hesitated for a moment,
and in that moment Dane caught her fingers between his
teeth and lightly licked them with the tip of his tongue.

Her sharp gasp exposed her surprise, and she quickly
withdrew her hand, stepped back, and tried to ignore the
delightful thrill that raced throughout her body. "Not fair.
We're playing by my rules, remember? You don't want me
to stop, do you?"

Dane lifted the keys, dangled them in front of her, and
gave them a little shake, causing a chorus of soft, cheeky
clinks. The broad grin on his face was every bit as cheeky.
"I apologize for . . . breaking *your* rules. Please, by all
means, continue."

"Smart decision," Claire replied, unable to stop looking
at his mouth. "Now, where was I?" She thoughtfully
chewed on one of her fingers that only moments before had
been caressed by Dane's tongue. "Ah yes." She raised her
hands and cupped his face. "I was right here. . . ."

Lifting her gaze to meet his, she knew from the intensity in his eyes that there would be no turning back. Not
now. Not ever. She slowly drew his head down as her
heart flipped and raced beneath her breasts, beating
against her ribs in a rhythm that made her dizzy. How
could she breathe? Then there it was . . . the delicious
warm touch of his mouth on hers. What did it matter if
she could or couldn't breathe? She sighed, the sound
hushed by their kiss.

With just the tips of her fingers, she touched their lips,
touched where his mouth met hers, touched where they had
become one.

When his tongue went searching inside her mouth, she
welcomed it. She dropped her hands, clutched his shoul-

ders, and pressed herself against his body, luxuriating in the heat and wanting that she'd created. Dane's kiss deepened, consumed her and robbed her sanity.

She heard the clink of her car keys as they hit the floor, and then Dane's hands were on her. His arms slid around her waist, hers around his neck. He drew her body tightly against his, and where hers was bowed, his arched to meet it.

As he kissed her, his hand moved to the front of her jeans. He fumbled with the belt and then the button and zipper until all were undone. He tugged at her T-shirt, pulling it free, and without hesitating, lifted it higher, his knuckles grazing over the tips of her breasts. The touch stole a gasp from her lips, and she stepped back. *Who in the hell am I? I've never wanted or acted or felt this way before. Never.* Looking up at him, her gaze locked with his. But now was different, so very different. She silently begged for more.

As though he'd read her mind, Dane drew her T-shirt up and over her head and tossed it onto the kitchen table. It landed on his hat.

He laid a line of kisses down from her mouth, across her jaw to her neck, triggering a delicious shiver and a crop of goose bumps across the field of her skin. Tipping her head back, Claire gladly gave him full access to her throat, and Dane accepted her invitation.

The moment he slid her bra straps off her shoulders, the moment he cupped her breast in his hand and stroked his thumb across the excited peak of her nipple, the moment he replaced his thumb with his mouth, his tongue, Claire knew she had lost control.

"I want you naked." Dane growled his words against her skin. "I want you naked in a bed, and I want you naked in a bed now."

Claire pulled his shirt free and worked feverishly to open the buttons. She shoved the fabric from his body, and her hands splayed over his bare skin, riding over the hard ridges and planes of his chest. He bent to lift her. She pushed against his shoulder. "Don't you dare try to pick me up and carry me like some Rhett Butler wannabe."

"Shut up, Scarlett," he growled again. Ignoring her protest, he scooped her up in his arms.

She laid her head in the hollow of his neck and kissed his bare skin, tasting its salty tang. "Okay, Rhett, down the hall, last door on your right."

21

HE LAID HER GENTLY ON THE BED, AND SHE ARCHED her back as he bent over her, his hot breath igniting her skin wherever it touched her.

"Why you? Why now?" he rasped, allowing her to unbraid and loosen his hair.

"Why not?"

"Damn it, Claire. You don't know a thing about me. . . . You don't know me . . . the real me."

She shifted to accommodate him, and the intimacy of his body pressed hard against her stole her breath away. "Maybe someday you'll tell me . . . all about you," she said quietly, hoping he hadn't heard the slight tremor in her voice. She kissed his shoulder, nipped at him with her teeth, and kissed her way up to his lips. "Right now, I know all I need to know."

"The hell you do."

He slid his hand between them and then, his actions impatient, he pulled away from her and stripped her jeans and panties from her hips. He shoved them down her legs, re-

warding her with a deep, sexy laugh when she impatiently
kicked them away.

"Your turn," Claire whispered, sounding bolder than she
felt as she unhooked his large beaded buckle, unsnapped
the top button of his jeans, and began to lower his zipper.

Dane rolled off the bed.

"Where are you going? What's wrong?" She sat up.

He pointed down to his feet. "There's nothing erotic
about seeing a man bouncing around on a bed, trying to get
out of his pants with a pair of cowboy boots on his feet."

"Oh, I don't know. I guess it depends on the man." She
laughed. "It could be very exciting."

His snort was sarcastic, through and through.

"Oh, okay." She grinned, beginning to really enjoy the
game. "But hurry." Unhooking her bra, she finished the job
that Dane had started earlier, and fought off the shy impulse to cover her naked breasts.

He leaned over, kissed her mouth, and lightly rubbed
her nipples with his knuckles. "Trust me, I'll make sure it's
worth the wait."

"It's your reward. Take your time." She leaned back,
amazed by her own counterfeit boldness. Adjusting the pil-
low behind her head, she watched him kick off his boots.
"I'm just along for the ride."

Dane's full-bodied laugh filled the small bedroom. "The
hell you are."

He straightened up, dropped his jeans to the floor, and
stood naked before her, his hair loose around him, all Indian, all man, all ready to satisfy his blatant hunger for her.
The man was nothing short of magnificent—from head to
toe and all the interesting places in between. Claire's
breath caught in her throat, her heart leapt up and joined it,
and her blood coursed hot and wild through her veins. *I'm
lost. I am so lost.* She made her confession out loud,
"You're right, the hell I am . . . just along for the ride."

Dane joined her on the bed again, and she welcomed
him back by raising her arms and drawing him into her em-

brace. His hair fell around them like a dark curtain, and she twined her fingers in its silken length, wondering if she could bind him to her forever. *Maybe not forever, but if not forever, will tonight be enough?* Her head responded. *Yes, yes, if it has to be, yes.* But her heart disagreed. *Liar. There will never, ever be enough.*

Dane's mouth claimed hers again, sucking lightly on her bottom lip, then kissing her long and hard. While they shared each other's breath, he slid his hand down her belly, making her tremble when his journey ended between her legs. His fingers gently parted her, and she sighed, the sound filled with her need. His boldness, his impatience, was a powerful aphrodisiac, setting off tiny explosions deep within her. Greedy, she wanted more. Tilting her hips up into his hand, she filled his palm and gasped again when his fingers began to slowly stroke her.

His kiss deepened, his tongue courting hers, eliciting her response and gifting her with a throaty moan when she gave it. And then he moved on, laying a line of kisses down her neck, across her collarbone, and over her breast until he captured her nipple between his lips. Drawing the tightened bud into his mouth, he teased it with his tongue and then moved on to worship her other breast, her other nipple. Amid it all, the pressure of his hand and the slide of his fingers increased, each stroke driving her wild with need.

"Claire," he breathed, moving between her legs. "Can I have my reward now?"

Claire reached up and cupped his cheek. Touching the tip of her tongue to his, she plundered his mouth with another kiss, and then replied, "Only if I can share."

One smooth and sure stroke planted him solidly inside her, completely filling her. She drew a sharp breath, the pressure, the pleasure almost painful in its intensity. They clung together as though their very existence depended on never letting go of each other until the time was right. In that instant she understood what he'd told her about the eagles.

It was impossible to say who moved first. Perhaps they began the delicious parry and retreat at the same time. It didn't matter because however the rhythm began, it was sweet and hot perfection. There was breathless delight in their total possession of each other.

Dane began to delve deeper, grinding against her, pressing against her most sensitive places. Extending himself, he lifted her leg against his hip to accommodate his possession, to create a bliss-filled friction, and to reach the very center of her soul.

As the cascade of ecstasy began, Claire flung her head back, trusting him to fly with her. And then he followed. He had no choice in the matter.

After reaching the highest heights and floating there for unmeasured time, still clinging, one to the other, they began the delicious downward spiral. They lay pressed together, the dark of night enveloping them, their limbs entwined, light skin against dark, one's breath echoing the other's.

Dane awoke with a start. *How long have I been asleep?* He didn't know, but it took only a moment for him to remember where he was. Claire lay on her right side, snuggled against him, her head on his shoulder. His arm was caught under her.

The corner of the blanket hid her hip and covered his leg that was casually draped over hers. With his left hand, he pushed her hair back from her face and kissed her, his tongue following the tight curl of her ear. Her vanilla scent teased him, and he wanted to taste more. Touching her with nothing more than the back of his hand, he traced a slow caress down her arm. Then, lifting her hand, he kissed her palm and closed her fingers around the kiss. "For safekeeping," he whispered, branding the moment forever in his heart.

She stirred and woke, stretching, pushing her body against his, and then looked up at him. Her smile did him in all over again.

"I was afraid that I'd only dreamed of you," she said, an early morning husky quality to her voice. "I had to wake up all through the night just to make sure you were really here."

"Claire, I need to ask you—"

She touched her finger to his lips. "Shh. Nothing needs to be said, we're both adults."

"You have no idea what I was going to say."

"I can guess."

"Well, you guessed wrong." He pushed his hair behind his ear. "Sweetheart, what I need to tell you is that I have to move my arm. It's numb."

She chuckled, allowing him to pull his arm out from under her head. "Thank you."

"For what?"

"For holding me all night long." Covering a yawn with her hand, she stretched, arching her body against his again.

"If you don't lay still, I'm going to be doing more than holding you."

"And you have a problem with that?"

"Oh no, not at all." Dane gathered her in his arms and quickly rolled onto his back, taking her with him. He nuzzled her neck and tugged at her earlobe with his lips. "And I don't think you do, either." He pulled her head down and kissed her hard. "Open your legs for me," he breathed into her mouth.

Without hesitation she did as he asked, and he heard and felt her draw a ragged breath as he slowly pushed himself deep inside her. His labored breath blew on her breasts, and when her nipples pearled in response, he made love to them with his mouth.

Holding her hips, he pulled her farther onto him as he rocked against her, increasing the rhythm and breathing her name with each thrust. She tightened around him, and when her release began, her body trembled. Rolling her onto her back, he pressed into her, and then they soared . . . together.

They dozed in each other's arms without separating until the shrill screech of Claire's alarm clock rudely intruded.

"What time is it?" Dane nuzzled her neck.

"Seven. I have to be at the clinic by eight-thirty."

"Do we shower separately or together?"

"It's your call."

Dane grabbed her hand and pulled her off the bed. "Come on, Scarlet. I'm going to get you all wet."

An hour later, Dane backed his truck out of Claire's driveway and headed south to the police station in Red Star. Claire drove her Mustang out onto the main road and headed north toward the clinic.

CLAIRE WONDERED HOW she was going to make it through her day at the clinic without waltzing around the reception room or telling everyone who came in that she was in love. They'd made no plans to see each other after the clinic closed, but she didn't doubt that Dane would come over and they'd be together.

There was also no denying that she now knew in her head what her heart had known all along: She loved Dane White Eagle. She'd finally been able to put her doubts about him aside. The man she'd gotten to know, the man she'd fallen in love with, the man whose arms had held her, the man who had made love to her throughout the night wasn't a man who had killed his sister. She'd seen his pain. She'd heard the grief in his voice, and she'd seen the love and respect he had for his people and for his traditions. Dane White Eagle was a man of honor, not a murderer, and she loved him with all of her heart.

"Eyee, you look like you won the lottery or the big slots at the casino," Connie said, bursting through the clinic front door ten minutes late. "Sorry I'm late. I suppose you can dock me my pay if you want. I sat up with Mattie Old Horn all night and didn't get much sleep."

"Don't worry about your pay, Connie. Of course I'm not going to dock you." Claire slipped into her white lab coat. "How is Mattie? How is she doing?"

Connie shrugged. "How does a mother do when she loses her baby?" She flipped on the lamp on her desk. "What is it you doctors say? Doin' as well as can be expected under the circumstances." Dropping into the chair behind her desk, Connie glared up at Claire. "I hope they find the bastard who done it to Mattie's girl."

"What are you talking about?"

"I hope they find the bastard who killed her."

"You think someone . . . killed her?"

Connie shrugged again, crossed her arms over her chest, and looked up at Claire. "That's the talk."

"Nothing was said about anything like that yesterday. Has something happened? Have the police or FBI found something that makes them think—"

"Yeah, maybe. Something like somebody must've taken her out there and left her. Something like nobody knowin' where Dane was the night before last when she died. He got back to Clement's real late."

"No." Claire shook her head and slammed her fist down on Connie's desk. "No. I won't let you blame Dane. I won't let you even think he might have done it. Your son was with me until quite late, and then he went back to Clement's. I know that Clement will tell you when he got there, and if you want to know, I'll tell you when he left my place."

Connie looked up, her eyes wide with surprise, and then her expression changed. Her face returned to the hard, emotionless mask she wore each time she mentioned Dane. "I have no son."

"Oh yes you do. You have a son. He's a wonderful, kind, thoughtful, loving man, and you should be proud of him."

"He killed—"

"No, he didn't." Claire threw caution aside and, not caring that the woman was Dane's mother, she stood up to

Connie White Eagle. "He said he didn't do it, he didn't kill Kylee, and, unlike you, I believe him."

Connie raised her left brow, and her mouth twisted with a smirk. "Ah . . . so that's how it is." She snorted.

"Yes," Claire challenged. "That's definitely how it is."

"You two gonna get to wrasslin' on the floor pretty soon, or are you gonna talk to me?"

Startled by the sound of the deep voice, both women turned to find Clement Runs After standing in the middle of the clinic's reception room.

"Damn you, you old *tatanka*," Connie barked. "You gonna give me a heart attack."

"Good. It might be the only way I can get your attention." He pointed at Claire with a quick lift of his chin and a pursing of his lips. "Good thing there's a doc nearby."

Claire buried her hands deep in the pockets of her lab coat and tried to figure out why Clement had come calling. She didn't believe for one minute that it was a social call.

"You have a good time seein' the buffalo yesterday?"

"It was wonderful," she replied, deciding to play along and see where the old Lakota was going. "Thank you for letting me ride your horse."

Clement shrugged, glanced at Connie, and then back at Claire. "Can we talk private? I gotta question 'bout what you found in Mattie's daughter's hand yesterday."

Ah, so the fishing expedition begins. No preamble, just right to it. Another thought shoved its way into her head. *Who told him that I found anything? Dane? Calvin? Who?* She led Clement down the hall to her office, offered him a seat, and closed the door. "Maybe we should begin by you first answering a question of mine." She settled herself in the chair behind her desk.

Clement nodded. "Seems fair." He looked around. "Only 'cause we're at your place."

"Who told you I found anything?"

His dark eyes steady, watching her like a hawk, he

replied, "Pete Rabbit. He's got a big mouth. All them Rabbits do."

"I don't know about all of them, but I'd say that you're right about Deputy Rabbit." Claire realized she was now in a bind. How much could she tell Clement? How much *should* she tell him? *Careful, be very careful. Debbie wasn't my patient, but there are still police confidentiality issues.* "Have you asked Calvin Iron Cloud or Special Agents Gaines or Pardue what was found?"

"Nope," Clement replied, taking off his old Stetson and threading the brim through his fingers, turning the hat around and around. "I came to you 'cause I didn't want to get a runaround." He turned up the charm. "I'll tell you what I know if you'll tell me what you . . . can. Deal?"

"Let's see what you know, first."

"Ah, a poker player, eh?" Clement smiled. "Okay." He leaned forward in the chair. "I know you found a little plastic bag in that girl's hand, and I know there was pink pills in that bag. Am I right so far?"

Make up your mind, Colby. What are you going to tell him? "Yes, there were pills in the bag."

"Was they pills she got from you or another doctor?"

Claire shook her head. "No, she didn't get them from me. I can't reply to the rest of your question."

"Fair 'nuff." Clement's fingers stopped toying with his hat. "Was them pills . . . illegal drugs?"

"Clement, I don't know. Special Agent Pardue took the pills, and I'd imagine they're going to have them analyzed to find out exactly what they are."

"But you've got an idea, right?"

"I've seen pills like them before."

"Here . . . on Cold Creek?"

She nodded. "Yes, and in the city." She tried to settle her conscience.

"And what was they . . . the ones ya've seen before?"

Claire stood. "Clement, there's a problem, here on the

reservation, on all of the reserves, and in the city, with a
new drug that the kids are taking. It's called a designer
drug because it can be made anywhere by anyone with the
recipe. Each maker can give it their own unique look and
their own unique mix of chemicals. The drug is called ecstasy . . . E . . . MDMA. There are a lot of other names that
the users have for it, too." She moved to the window and
looked out at the horses in the field behind the clinic. "Re-
cently, a new chemical has been added to the recipe, PMA.
It's very dangerous, and some of the kids taking the
pills . . . have died. I had a couple that were brought into
the emergency room when I was at Pennington, and I've
heard that there have been some deaths here and on a couple of the other reserves. If the pills that I found in Debbie
Old Horn's hand are ecstasy and they have PMA in
them . . . then I wouldn't be surprised if that is how she
died."

Clement's brow furrowed. "Is it always in small bags
or . . . what?"

Claire shook her head. "No. It can be bought or carried
in any quantity. It's sold by the pill. It can be bought one at
a time or hundreds at a time."

Clement looked down between his legs at the floor and
spoke quietly. "How do the kids get this stuff?"

"There are scum who make it in secret labs, there are
scum who carry it and supply the dealers, and there are
scum who stand on street corners or go to parties and sell it
to the kids."

"And how do we get rid of these . . . scum?"

Claire's reply was filled with cynicism. "That's an on-
going problem that the police are having very little success
in solving."

Clement nodded and, using his gnarled hands to push
himself out of the chair, stood. "Thank you for the information. I gotta go."

Clement stood on the stoop of the clinic and looked up
at the blue summer sky. He didn't think he'd ever feel joy

or happiness again. He knew he'd never trust his heart again. It was a hard lesson to learn so late in life.

"Yeah, *Iktomi* is quite the trickster." He pulled his handkerchief out of his back pocket and muffled the sniffle that struck with a tightness in his chest. "He sure tricked me."

22

DANE STOPPED HIS TRUCK IN FRONT OF CLEMENT'S cabin and got out. Chewy and What's His Name greeted him with wildly wagging tails as though they were starved for human companionship, and he was their very best friend. Dane wasn't fooled, especially when Chewy turned and ran onto the porch, picked up his food bowl in his teeth, and returned, dumping it on the ground in front of Dane. The dogs were just starved for breakfast. "Okay, okay. I'll feed you guys."

The spot at the side of the cabin where Clement always parked his truck was empty. *Maybe the old man stayed in Red Star all night with Mattie and her family. Good. The last thing I need is that old* tatanka *playing den mother again and wanting to know where the hell I've been.*

Leaving Claire earlier had been one of the hardest . . . and the best . . . things he'd ever done in his life. The hardest because being with her made him feel complete. The best because they both needed some cooling-off time, time to sort things out, time to decide where they'd go from here.

Married. That one had been a surprise. He didn't know why, but until she'd mentioned it, he hadn't given any thought to the possibility. She hadn't elaborated, in fact had been quite closed about it, but she had said "happily divorced." At least that sounded encouraging.

After pulling out of her driveway, he'd slowed down and watched her in his rearview mirror. She'd backed out onto the road and headed off to the clinic in the opposite direction. The morning sun glittered off the chrome on her little red Mustang. "Oh yeah." He laughed. A little cooling-off time was a good idea, but as far as he was concerned, cooling off was going to take forever. At least for the rest of his life. The woman definitely made him hot and set him on fire.

The corners of his mouth quirked up into a smile that just kept growing. Although he was tied up in knots with everything else going on right now in his life, it was still going to take a Mack truck to haul the grin off his face and cool him down.

He glanced at his watch. Eight-thirty. *Damn, I'd better get going.* There was just enough time to fill the dogs' food bowls, change his clothes, and get to the station by nine for roll call.

In ten minutes Dane was back in his truck and on the road to Red Star. "Time to get your ass in gear, White Eagle," he muttered. "This whole damn case is taking too long; it's got to end." Frustrated, he hit the steering wheel with the side of his fist. "You've got to take out Leland and his lab, and you've got to do it now."

He was tired of the charade. The sooner he could wrap up the case and put his life back together again, the sooner he could track down Kylee's killer, the sooner he could figure out how an Indian Health Care doctor and an FBI undercover agent could work things out . . . the sooner he'd feel alive again.

"Leland is going down, and he's going down hard." The steering wheel took another hit.

Dane pulled into the parking lot behind the police station, surprised to see Leland's Dodge Ram parked in the handicapped space. *I ought to give the son of a bitch a ticket.*

"Hey, *kola.* I've been waiting to talk to ya," Leland Big Elk said, swinging out of his truck as Dane walked by. "Bad news about Debbie Old Horn. You found her, eh?" He took a sip from the Styrofoam cup of coffee he held in his hand and began to whine again. "I heard when the FBI showed up they found something in her hand. So, what'd they find? They figure out what happened, how she died?" Beads of sweat glistened on Leland's upper lip, and he shuffled nervously from one foot to the other while waiting for Dane's answers.

Alarm bells rang in Dane's head, alarm bells he'd heard the day before when he'd found Debbie. Leland Big Elk was definitely acting like a man who knew more than he should about Debbie Old Horn's death. He was acting like a man who was scared that somebody else might know more. For Dane, that added up to one strong possibility: Leland Big Elk was probably the last person Debbie Old Horn saw before she died.

Take it easy. Don't spook him. Play it cool, and you'll get what you want. "Leland, get out of here. I'll catch up with you later." As Dane began to walk away, Leland grabbed his arm.

"Answer my questions, damn it."

Dane swung around and pointed back at the police station with a jerk of his thumb. "I'm not going to stand in the parking lot outside of the cop shop and give you inside info on the case."

"Yeah, but you were there, you found her, eh? You saw what they found." The whine in his voice now shook with panic.

Easy, easy. String him on. Keep him on the hook. "I don't know any more than I did yesterday when the FBI took her back to the city." Dane pulled his arm out of Leland's grip. "Give me an hour to see what I can find out, and I'll meet you at the Broken Arrow." He pointed at Leland's truck. "While you're waiting for me, get your truck washed. It looks like shit with all that mud on it."

Leland stepped close to Dane and poked him repeatedly in the chest with his index finger. His courage had apparently returned. "You'd damn well better show up. We got things to talk about, you and me. I got some news yesterday I didn't like, and you've got some explaining to do, *kola.*" He gave Dane a couple more hard jabs. "And it better be good."

"Do you want to give me a hint what I'm going to be explaining, or is it a surprise?"

"You'll find out soon enough. Just be at the Arrow." Turning on his heel, Leland climbed into his truck, backed out of the handicapped spot, and sped away.

"Asshole," Dane hissed. Halfway through the station door he stopped. "Damn," he hissed. "The mud!" He turned and ran back out to the parking lot. The red Dodge Ram had disappeared. "You're a lousy cop, White Eagle," he muttered. "There's mud all over Leland's truck, just like the mud you got on your truck yesterday out where you found Debbie, and you just told the sorry son of a bitch to go get it washed."

"Hey, White Eagle." Arvin Runs Buffalo stood in the station doorway. "Iron Cloud says to get your ass in here."

Roll call took only ten minutes. Jerome Rabbit's oldest daughter had been partying with her boyfriend and had run over the only stop sign in town. Somebody had tipped over the soda machine at Denny Old Horn's gas station and swiped all the money and all the Cokes, leaving two Dr Peppers, a diet cream soda, and five empty pop cans. Obviously robbing a soda machine made you thirsty. The last bit of news . . . was no news. The FBI hadn't sent any information from Rapid City yet on Debbie Old Horn's death.

No word on when she'd be autopsied or when she'd come home to Cold Creek. It was just another day on the rez. Not quite.

With roll call over, Dane stepped back outside. He'd pulled patrol duty again. He didn't mind. At least he wasn't tied to a desk job. Besides, driving patrol gave him the time he needed to deal with Leland and look for the lab.

Leland was already at the Broken Arrow when Dane pulled into the lot and parked beside the red Dodge. Relief washed over him. Mud still coated the rocker panels, fenders, and tires of the Dodge. *Maybe forensics can run a match.*

Rummaging around his truck's console, he found a plastic fuse box. "Perfect." Dumping the fuses into the ashtray, he hunkered down between his truck and Leland's and filled the fuse box with mud. He closed the lid, dropped the box into the console, and headed into the Arrow.

"'Bout time you got here, *kola.*"

"Get off my ass, Leland. I'm ten minutes early." He glanced up at the waitress, who'd just wandered over to the table. "Coffee and . . ." He quickly scanned the menu. "I'll have the number two breakfast, eggs over easy." He slid the menu back into the holder on the table.

"Juice?" the waitress asked.

"Yeah, orange. Thanks."

Leland watched her walk back to the kitchen with Dane's order. "She's Cheyenne. Moved here a couple of months ago and is livin' with Arvin. Nice butt, eh?" He cupped both of his hands and held them out in front of him, palms up. "I like a good handful." He sniggered and began to sing, "Cheyenne girls, Cheyenne girls, how I love them Cheyenne girls, eh ya hey, eh ya hey. . . ." Leland sobered. "Hey, don't get me wrong, *kola,* no woman's as good as your mama, though. Ain't none any better, but a man likes a little variety. Right? Hell, a man's *gotta* have variety." Leland winked his left eye, laughed, and then added, "Did yer mama tell ya I wanna marry her?"

"Yeah, she told me," Dane answered, struggling to keep the sound of disgust out of his voice. "She said she told you no, too."

"Hey, not because she don't want to . . . only because of your sister. I told her I'd be a good daddy to Kylee"—Leland shrugged—"but she said she wouldn't till after Kylee died." He shrugged again. "Now that the kid's dead . . . I'm still waitin' 'cause your mama's still mourning." He tapped his finger on the tabletop. "I am gonna marry her. I'm gonna, 'cause that's what I want. You'll see, it'll happen."

"Cut the romantic talk, Leland." His stomach lurched in a nauseous roll. Just to hear Leland say Kylee's name was enough to make him sick, but he also had to ask himself the question he'd asked a thousand times before: *What in the hell does my mother see in this bastard?*

Dane knew he had to end this conversation, and he had to do it as soon as possible before he lost control, before he showed Leland his opinion on the matter. He glanced at his watch. "What did you want to talk about? I've got a busy day going here."

Leland scrunched into the corner of the booth and stretched his arm across the back of the seat. "Tell me, *kola,* do you believe in coincidences?"

"Depends." Dane nodded his thanks to the waitress and took a sip of the orange juice she'd brought him. "What kind of coincidences?"

Leland retrieved a cigarette from his pocket, stuck it in the corner of his mouth, and lit it. He took a long, slow drag, taking even longer to exhale a cloud of smoke. He wasn't fooling Dane with his stalling. If it was a ploy to try to make him nervous, Leland's plan wasn't working.

"Well," Leland finally began. "I'm beginning to wonder about you. You're just ass deep in coincidences, ain't ya, *kola?*" His upper lip moved in a disdainful lift. "The strangest things happen when you make a delivery or when you're makin' E sales on your own." He took another drag on the cigarette. "Why didn't you tell me Cootch DiMaio got nailed by the cops when you were making your delivery to him? A lot of your drops seem to get themselves picked up by the cops."

Adrenaline began to flow through Dane's body. *Okay, Leland, you've got my attention. Get to the damned point so I can see where you're going.*

"Remember the three that got nabbed just before you went to Wakefield?" Leland dropped his cigarette in the ashtray and leaned forward, placing his forearms on the table. "Coincidence?" He shook his head. "Word is that when the cops nailed Cootch and you, you dropped the money and hightailed it outta there, before the cops got you." He snorted. "Another coincidence? Ain't it funny that you never mentioned it to me?" He stared at Dane. "And ain't it funny that the cops didn't seem to try too hard to catch ya?" Leland snorted again. "You're getting to be a liability, *kola*. You got me feelin' real suspicious. I'm suspicious about who you are and . . . where your loyalties are."

Think, White Eagle. Think, damn it. You've got to calm the bastard down, convince him you're as loyal as a Labrador retriever. "You know damn well who I am. I've been with you and Bobby a long time." He leaned forward. "Where do you get off asking me about loyalties? Bobby saved my life, so where do you think my loyalties are?"

Dane paused as the waitress set the plate with his breakfast down in front of him. His appetite immediately disappeared. Sitting across the table from Leland Big Elk and a plate in front of you with eggs floating in brown grease were enough to make anyone swear off eating.

Leland stole an overcooked strip of bacon off of Dane's plate and loudly gnawed on it. "Words are easy. You gotta be able to back 'em up. Can ya?"

"What are you talking about?"

Leland sat back and draped his arm over the back of the booth again. "I'm talkin' about you and me doin' a little job here on the rez."

"What kind of a job?" Alarm bells jangled again.

"Just be patient, *kola*. I'll get to that." Leland began to chuckle. "You were a naughty boy last night, weren't you? I hear your truck was parked all night at the lady doc's house. Lemme guess where *you* were parked. . . ." He lewdly jerked his hips, sniggered, reached over the table, and punched Dane on the shoulder. "Hey, *kola*, ain't it the doctor who's supposed to make house calls?" He finished off the bacon and slowly licked the grease off his fingers, wrapping his tongue around his knuckles and making vulgar little groaning noises. His snigger returned. "So, how was she, eh? Good? Tight and juicy? Did you make her scream and holler when she came? Oh, yeah, I like it when they do that."

Dane fisted his hands under the table and pressed them into his left thigh. He pushed them against the scar left by his knife wound, hoping that the pain would help clear his head and keep him from going over the table and driving his fists into Leland's face. His gut twisted with rage, but he put on his well-trained charade face, forced himself to look relaxed, and moved his lips into what he hoped looked like a friendly smile and not a scowl. "A gentleman never tells tales on a lady."

"Bullshit," Leland snorted. "I tell on 'em all the time." He picked up a piece of toast from Dane's plate, slathered some jelly on it, and stuffed it in his mouth. "I hope you weren't plannin' on going back for seconds tonight. You and me is gonna be a little busy."

"Doing what?"

"You're gonna show *me* what a good and loyal pal you are. *We're* gonna break into your sweetie's clinic tonight and get ourselves a nice supply of syringes and narcotics. Street value on needles and Demerol and maybe a little morphine is pretty good. If she's got any Ritalin . . . the kids are doing that now, too."

Another icy blast of adrenaline shot through Dane's body, making it difficult for him to keep his breathing steady. He didn't have a choice, damn it, he didn't have a choice. "We go in late. I don't want to chance that anyone would be there." He pointed his finger at Leland. "Nobody gets hurt, got it? Nobody."

"Yeah, sure, of course." Leland flipped his hand, waving off the idea as ridiculous. "What do you take me for, a bad guy? Even good old Doc Butz liked me." Leland slid out of the booth. "I'll meet you back here at ten tonight. Your little sweetie should be home safe and sound in bed . . . alone . . . by then." He pursed his lips into a bogus pout and laughed. "You can always go nail her again when we're done."

After Leland left, Dane sat in his truck. He looked down at his shaking hands. He drew a deep breath, unclipped the cell phone from his belt, and pressed number three.

"Well, I see you're getting better at checking in."

"Do you ever answer the phone and just say 'Hello,' Gaines?"

"What are you so damned testy about, White Eagle? You mean this isn't a social call?"

After telling Gaines about Leland's plan, there was a long pause on Gaines's end of the line.

"I've got to go through with it," Dane continued. "If I don't, I've thrown away almost a year of my life. Besides, if I bail out now, we've blown our shot at getting the lab."

"What do you want us to do? You want us to come out and—"

"And what? You know damned well that if you guys step one foot on Cold Creek, the whole rez will know it in about ten seconds." He mulled things over for a moment. "Just stay close to the phone. Stay handy. If I need you for any reason, I'll call." He took the phone away from his ear for a moment, looked at the keypad, and then put the phone back to his ear. "This thing's got GPS, right? You can track me . . . find me by the phone signal?"

"Hey, of course. Just askin' me that, you're hurting my feelings. You're real lucky. You've got the best James Bond telephone money can buy at Wal-Mart." Gaines laughed, but his laugh sounded taut and forced. "I'm going to rally the forces. We'll be just off the rez. If you need us, we'll be there in a flash."

"Anything on Debbie Old Horn yet? Was it Big Elk's ecstasy?"

"Yeah, you're right. She had more in her pocket, all of it loaded with PMA. Autopsy was early this morning. Here's an unbelievable thing about PMA. Her core body temperature was still up in the nineties and it was what, almost forty-eight hours after she'd died. Oh, and she'd had sex before she died. We're running DNA, and if nothin' comes up off the computer files, at least we've still got it for suspect comparison. That and the fact she didn't get out there on her own . . . we're calling it a homicide."

Dane reached into the console and retrieved the small plastic box with the mud from Leland's truck. "I've got something else for you. Maybe the lab can pin down the exact location where some mud I scraped off of Leland's truck came from. It won't tell us if he did it, but it could possibly put him in the neighborhood."

FOR THE REST of the day Dane drove patrol all over Cold Creek. He passed the clinic at least eight times, and eight times kept going without stopping. *Should I warn her about tonight? No. If I do, I'll have to either tell her the truth or tell her lies, and that will make me look twice as guilty.*

Unclipping the phone again from his belt, he pressed the number for the clinic and felt a harsh ache when he heard his mother's voice.

"Cold Creek Clinic."

"Hi, Mom. How are you?"

Silence, cold hard silence.

"I need to talk with Claire."

More silence greeted his request, and for a moment he

thought maybe she was going to hang up on him.

"Hello, this is Dr. Colby."

Relief touched his heart. He closed his eyes and imagined her on the other end of the line. "Hey," he said, his voice almost a whisper. "I've been thinking about you . . . about us . . . all day long. Claire, I don't know what to say other than that what happened was . . . special, very special. I want you to know that I'm not backing away. I think that what we've started is worth . . . exploring further."

"I think so, too," Claire replied without hesitation, her voice soft and breathy.

"Can I see you later?"

Only a moment or two passed before she replied, her single word filled with more emotion than he'd ever heard: "Yes."

He was about to tell her a lie, another lie. "One of the guys is out sick, and we're splitting his late shift. I won't be able to get to your place until ten-thirty or eleven. Is that okay?"

"Yes. I'll be waiting."

23

CLEMENT WAS SITTING ON THE PORCH WHEN DANE drove up to the house. The old man didn't move. There wasn't a smile. There wasn't a wave or any kind of a greeting. Instead, there was a sadness. His shoulders were hunched, and his body seemed to have sunk in on itself.

Dane climbed the two rickety steps onto the porch. "You okay, *Tuŋkasila*? You not feeling good?"

Excited to see him, Chewy and What's His Name jumped onto the porch to greet Dane with wagging tails and wet licks, but Clement immediately shooed them away. "Git, you dirty flea buses! Git! You gotta learn to choose your friends better." He ignored Dane and looked off toward the far hills.

Dane couldn't have felt more shocked if a barrel of ice water had been dumped on him. He settled beside Clement on the wood crate that had become his usual porch chair. "What's going on, old man? You've obviously got something on your mind. Why don't you take it out on me rather than your dogs?"

Clement slowly turned toward Dane. Little emotion

showed on his dark face, his eyes had lost their spark, and for the first time Dane was aware of just how old Clement Runs After really was.

"You want to know what's goin' on? There's lots on my mind and none of it good." He looked away, back out toward the hills. "It's bad enough when our people are betrayed by outsiders, but when it's our own . . ."

"What in the hell are you talking about?" Dane took his hat off and dropped it on the porch. Leaning forward, he looked up at Clement. "What's happened? Who's betraying who?"

"You're good. You oughta win one of them actin' awards. Sure had me fooled . . . and a lot of other folks around here, too." Clement shook his head and then looked down at the rain-warped boards beneath his feet. When he spoke, his words came slowly, and his voice cracked with emotion. "Here I've been fightin' for ya for months, tellin' your mama she was wrong, that her son was a good man, a good Lakota man." He glanced up at Dane, then back at the floor. "You done a good job of trickin' everybody. Sure had me fooled . . . *Iktomi.*"

At the sound of the trickster's name, Dane's blood ran ice cold. "I don't understand. What's going on?" He reached out to touch Clement, only to have the old man draw away from him. "Damn it, Clement. Talk to me!"

Clement Runs After slowly eased himself out of his chair, stood up, and walked to the edge of the porch and stared out across the yard. He jerked his thumb back toward the cabin door, toward a pile of clothing on the floor. "That's all yer stuff. Get it and you outta here." He yanked his handkerchief out of his back pocket and rubbed it across his face and then his nose. "Get off my place. You're lucky I ain't callin' Iron Cloud to come get ya."

Stunned, Dane couldn't move; the pain was too great. "What in the hell is going on? What in the hell—"

Clement quickly turned to face him. "What's goin' on is that I don't want no murderer, no filthy drug dealer in my house . . . in my family . . . in my life." He took a step closer to Dane. "I found out what was in that plastic bag you got from Leland. I know what those pills are. I also found out what was in Mattie's daughter's hand when you found her. Same stuff." He paused, and his body shuddered as he drew a deep breath. "How many have died from it, now? Kids, our kids . . . and I hear some city kids, too." He turned away and stared out at the yard again. "Get off my place so I can cleanse it, so I can pray."

For the first time since he'd sat down, Dane noticed Clement's cedar bag, the bundle of sage, the eagle feather, and the large abalone half shell on the low table beside his chair. He knew then that he had no choice. Whatever risk it created for him, he had to tell Clement the truth. He had to tell the old man everything. There was no way he could go through with Leland's plan knowing that Clement felt this way. If it hadn't been for the old man's support, Dane knew he wouldn't have been able to hang on as long as he had.

He got up and moved to Clement's side. "You asked me the other night what was going on. I told you that you'd know when the time was right." He slowly shook his head. "I'm putting my life in your hands, *Tuηkasila*, but because of what you've found out, because of what you think . . . I've got to take a chance and tell you now."

Clement didn't turn around, but his posture stiffened as though he was bracing himself for a blow.

"Grandfather, please. Sit down so we can talk." He touched the old man's shoulder, encouraged that this time Clement didn't pull away.

Clement shuffled across the porch and slowly eased himself back into his chair. "Just 'cause I'm listenin' don't mean I'm believin' ya. You got a lotta talkin' to do to get me back to that place, so ya better start flapping yer lips."

It took Dane almost twenty minutes to tell Clement the truth . . . the truth about his years at university and his law degree, the truth about his training at Quantico, and the truth about the undercover case he'd been working on as a

special agent with the FBI for over a year. He told
Clement about Leland's plans to break into the clinic at
ten that night, and then he went to his truck and retrieved
his FBI identification from under the liner in the bed of
the truck. "Now you know about as much as I do,
Tuŋkasila. There are still some things I've got to do. Leland and everyone else have to believe the lies a little
longer." He watched Clement's face, hoping to be able to
read the old man's expression, hoping to find out what
Clement was thinking.

The silence seemed to stretch out between them. Even
the night sounds seemed to grow louder and louder as
Dane waited for Clement to speak.

Tears came first, and once again Clement stood up and
drew his handkerchief out of his back pocket. "It felt like
you'd died, Grandson." His voice trembled, and he cleared
his throat. He held Dane's FBI identification in his hand
and looked at it once again. "With this I can believe you
about the drugs and going undercover, but I gotta know
about the other . . ."

"About *Taŋski.*" Dane watched Clement slowly nod his
head. "I didn't kill her. Even with the cancer there was always hope. Sometimes miracles happen." He fought the
painful tightening in his throat, looked away, and watched
the two horses dozing in the corral. He drew a deep breath,
hoping to ease the pain. It didn't help. "The Bureau came
up with the plan to make it seem as though I'd done it so I
could go into Wakefield and try to get the information we
needed from Bobby Big Elk. They just couldn't put me in
there, because too many people would know it was a scam.
It had to be a big news story, too, splashed all over the papers and TV, so people would believe I was guilty."

"But what about the *waglula,* the worm who killed her?
Why did he do it?"

"I don't know, *Tuŋkasila,* but I promise you and my
mom this: I'm going to find the bastard who killed *Taŋski* . . . and they will pay the maximum."

Clement sniffled. *"Wasté, wasté."* He continued to nod his head. "Good."

"I need to know, *Tuŋkasila*, do you believe me? Please, let me hear you say the words."

In the next moment he was engulfed in the old man's arms, the strength of Clement's embrace defying his age. As Clement clung to him, guilt punched Dane in the gut. He could feel the old man's body shake.

"Well," Clement said, stepping away, swiping his face with his handkerchief again. "I guess you got things to do tonight." He straightened the old hat on his head, then pointed to the pile of Dane's clothes near the front door. "I'll . . . uh . . . put 'em back inside for ya."

Dane watched Clement trundle toward the door. *"Tuŋkasila*, wait. There's something else I need to talk with you about." Where should he begin? "I think it's about things the old ones knew, but I'm not sure."

Clement turned and came back to where Dane was standing. He stared into Dane's face for a moment and then moved toward his chair and sat. He pointed to the wood packing crate. "Sit. We'll talk. 'Bout time you start askin' about these things."

The expression on Clement's face changed many times as Dane told him about the rez dogs and how they seemed to follow him around. Surprise lit up Clement's face when Dane told him that they were doing the same to Claire.

"And then there are the shared dreams."

Clement immediately sat forward. "Shared dreams?"

"Yeah. We've both been having the same dream . . . well, they're not really identical because—"

"She sees them from her eyes and you see yours from your eyes?"

"Yeah, something like that." Dane dropped his gaze to the floor. "Claire doesn't know anything about . . . our Lakota stories or traditions, but she's told me that she'd heard a Lakota word in her dream and has seen . . . *Taŋski*."

Clement nodded. "Has *Taŋski* also been in your dream?"

Tears welled up in Dane's eyes. "Yeah, all of them."

"And the word that Claire hears . . . you gonna tell me what it is or am I gonna have to guess."

"*Iktomi.*"

A smile, almost smug in its shape, lifted Clement's mouth. "I ain't a bit surprised."

"So, what do you think it all means?"

Clement looked at Dane; the spark had returned to his eyes. "Point is, what do *you* think it means?"

Dane slapped his knee. "Damn it all, Clement. You sound like one of those hundred dollar an hour psychiatrists."

He leaned out of his chair and laid his hand over Dane's. "Grandson, I've lived a long time, but in that time I haven't learned everything. I can only tell ya what some of the old people told me when I was a kid." Withdrawing his hand, he sat back and shrugged. "Maybe it used to be part of our beliefs, I don't know, but if you believe it's possible, then I guess it's . . . a belief.

"Our people believe lots of things come to us in dreams, things that change everything in our lives. Ceremonies like the *Yuwipi* and the *Lowanpi* have been said to come to our people like that. You and your doctor lady have been dreamin' the same dreams, seein' each other in those dreams, and I think that means there's a special connection between you. Somethin' as simple as destiny or fate." Clement paused, his brow furrowed with deep thought. "I'd say maybe the Creator has got a say in you two bein' together, and that's His way of showin' it."

Stunned, Dane didn't know what to think of Clement's explanation, but there was still a problem. "What about the rez dogs?"

"Is *Taηski*'s little black and white dog still runnin' with 'em?"

"Yeah, he is. He's runnin' up front with the pack leader all the time."

Clement began to laugh. "That one's easy."

"It is?"

"Yup." He slapped his knee and continued to laugh. "Just work on it. You'll figure it out."

Frustrated by Clement's nonanswer, Dane stood and paced back and forth on the small porch. "You know, old man, one time . . . just one time I'd like an answer that's an answer . . . not some goofy, quasi-spiritual esoteric stuff you old guys always give the tourists."

"All I'm saying, Grandson, is that the answer has been with you from the start. Be patient. Open yourself to it. Accept." Clement looked up at the night sky. "It's gettin' late. Ain't it almost time for you to go meet up with Leland?"

Clement stood, and picking up the little bag from the table, he drew out some of the dried cedar and placed it in the shell. He pulled a book of matches out of his pocket and touched the flame to the cedar and to the end of the sage bundle. The soothing scent of cedar and sage smoke filled the night air, its fragrance reaching Dane's soul.

Lifting the eagle feather and the shell in his hand, Clement began to pray, the Lakota words flowing smoothly from his tongue. Then, slowly moving around Dane, Clement used the feather to lift the smoke and pat it on Dane's chest, over his heart, his arms and shoulders, and his head. Dane lifted his hands and washed himself with the smoke, drawing it up to his face, breathing in the pungent, soothing fragrance.

Clement prayed for Dane's safety, and he prayed for his courage and for wisdom. With a final touch of the feather to Dane's heart, Clement stepped back. He looked into Dane's eyes. *"Wasté.* It's okay for you to go now. The old ones will be with you." He tapped his gnarled fingers over his heart.

"Thank you, Grandfather." Dane gripped Clement's shoulder and gave it a squeeze, then stepped off the porch.

"Grandson," Clement called to him, "thank you for telling me. Your secrets are safe with me." A smile appeared on the old man's lips. "I think I know someone else who believes you're innocent." He moved to the edge of the porch. "You're a very lucky man to have a good woman love you that much."

Surprised by Clement's words, Dane quickly looked up at the old Lakota. "Don't go playin' matchmaker, old man."

Clement shrugged. "Why should I? The match is already made."

DANE PARKED HIS truck off to the side of the Broken Arrow. The restaurant was closed, and there wasn't another vehicle in the parking lot. Leland hadn't shown up yet. *Maybe this whole damn thing is just a test to see if I'd even show up.*

Dane tipped his head and closed his eyes. If he thought he'd get a few minutes' sleep, he was wrong. Images and thoughts floated through his mind, warming him, firing his pulse. Claire. Claire, her hands gently touching *Taŋski*, touching Debbie Old Horn with the same compassion, and touching him while making love. Claire, sunlight putting dancing highlights in her hair. Claire, candlelight touching her skin like a caress, deepening the blue of her eyes, highlighting the blush of her lips. Claire, the healer, the temptress, the aggressor, the wanton woman, the child. *God help me . . . no, God help* her, *I love her.*

A pair of headlights arced into the lot and sliced into Dane's thoughts. They hit Dane's truck and then were turned off. A dark Chevy, a typical Indian car, at least fifteen years old, beat up and rusty, pulled to a stop beside Dane.

The driver's window on the Chevy lowered. "I didn't think you'd show up, *kola.* Come on, get in. No sense taking both rides. Hey, if you've gotta flashlight, bring it with ya."

After locking his truck, Dane turned toward the old Chevy. Something about the dark sedan seemed familiar, but he couldn't remember where he'd seen it before. The interior smelled as though a pack of mice had been its most recent, and prolific, occupants. "You get a new set of wheels, Leland?" He glanced around, finding a couple of sacks of horse feed in the backseat. "Most four-wheeled ponies eat gas, looks like you've trained this one to be a real traditional Indian pony."

"Ain't you the funny one tonight," Leland said, turning out onto the main road and heading for the clinic. "There's a couple of windows in the back of the clinic. I checked 'em out earlier. It won't be hard to get in through one of them."

"You're sure you want to go through with this? Haven't I already proved my loyalty to you and Bobby just by showing up?"

Leland rubbed his index finger and thumb together. "I think I'll feel better about it when ya pull the job with me. And yeah, you bet I'm gonna go through with this. For the money . . . the moneee."

Breaking one of the back windows had been easy. Getting Leland through the window had presented another problem.

Standing just inside the window, Dane tried to help Leland. "You're going on a diet, Leland. I thought Big Elk was your name, not your—"

"Shut up, White Eagle, just haul me in."

Dane gave Leland's arms another hard yank. They both landed on the floor in Claire's office. Without a word, after scrambling to his feet, Leland headed for the supply room.

"You seem to know your way around in here pretty well," Dane said.

Leland snorted. "You think this is the first time I've been here?"

"When have you been here before?"

"Don't worry about it, *kola*. It was a long time ago."

The niggling alarm that kept ringing in Dane's head wouldn't go away. A whole lot of unanswered questions kept forming in his mind. Dane watched Leland stuff box after box of syringes into a plastic bag. "Don't take them all. They're going to need some supplies to run the place until they can get more delivered."

"Ain't you the bleedin' heart," Leland said, taking the last box out of the cupboard. He held it in his hand for a moment and then dropped it on the counter. "Okay, okay. You happy now, *kola?*"

"Ecstatic." Dane turned away and walked through the clinic to Claire's office and then back to his mother's desk.

"Hey, *kola,* I need somethin' to get this cabinet open. Give me a hand, will ya?"

Dane found a claw hammer in a drawer in the utility room. "Here, give this a go."

"Perfect," Leland said. Grabbing the hammer out of Dane's hand, he wedged the claw between the door and the frame of the locked cabinet, and in five minutes he had the door open. "Eyee, lookit all the goodies. Hold that flashlight on 'em while I see what I want."

Leaning against the counter, Dane held the light and watched Leland sort through the contents of the cabinet, picking some and dropping them in the bag, leaving others on the shelf. In a far corner of his mind, a tiny sound resounded like a cannon blast. The clink of keys in a lock, the squeaky sound of the soles of sneakers on a tile floor, the sharp gasp.

Quickly turning, Dane found Claire standing in the storeroom doorway.

"Dane! What's going on?" She quickly looked at Leland and then back at Dane. "Thank God you caught him. Do you want me to call Iron Cloud?"

"That's a good one, eh *kola?* She thinks you're playin' cop tonight." Leland laughed and lunged at Claire, grabbing her arm and hauling her further into the room. "Well, ain't this a nice surprise?" He pushed Claire into the corner.

She turned to Dane, her eyes wide with fear. "I don't understand. What's . . . what's happening? Dane?" She glanced at the open narcotics cabinet, at Leland, and then back at Dane. "Please. I don't understand." She tried to move out of the corner, to go to Dane.

Leland pushed her back, sending her crashing against the wall.

"Hey, take it easy," Dane said, stepping closer. "No need to hurt her."

The look of shock that moved on Claire's face struck Dane like a freight train and tore into his soul, shredding it into tiny pieces.

"No, oh God no. Dane, please, not you . . . please. I believed in you, trusted you—"

"Shut up," Leland barked, dropping the plastic bag on the floor.

Dane stepped between Claire and Leland. "Let's just get the job done and get the hell out of here."

"It ain't that easy anymore, *kola*. Give me a hand, will ya?" He grabbed a couple of rolls of wide adhesive tape off the counter. "Hold her hands still." Leland pushed Claire against the wall, pulled her hands behind her back, and began to wrap the tape around her wrists. "We got a problem, *kola*. Your little sweet piece here, she's a witness. I don't like leavin' witnesses."

"Dane, please, stop this, help me—"

Leland slapped a piece of wide tape across Claire's mouth, turned, and pointed at Dane. "Don't try to be a hero, man." He pulled out a gun that had been hidden in the waistband of his jeans, under his shirt. "I'll hurt her right here and now if you push me. I've got a place we can take her. Ain't nobody gonna find her. Maybe we can have some fun with her for a while, if you don't mind sharin'." Leland rubbed his belly, picked up the plastic bag and, grabbing Claire's blouse, yanked her out of the corner.

Dane's blood turned to ice as he feverishly tried to think of all of his options. *Go with it. Keep Leland thinking you're working with him. You've got a better chance of keeping her safe if you're outside and moving. You've got a better chance of taking Leland down if you're outside and moving.* "Okay, let's get out of here." He pointed at the bag of narcotics. "You take care of the loot, I'll . . . take care of her." He tried to sound cold and unfeeling, but he prayed that Claire would find another message in his touch.

Leland led them out through the front door of the clinic and around the side of the building to the old Chevy.

"Put her in the back. With her hands taped, she can't pull any tricks. There's some rope back there. Tie her feet."

Dane shoved the sacks of horse feed out of the way, then, with Claire struggling to get out of his grasp, Dane eased her in the backseat. "Shh, Claire," he whispered, watching through the rear window as Leland loaded the stolen drugs and syringes in the trunk. "Trust me. Things aren't what they seem. Just stay as close to me as you can and do what I tell you."

Leland got behind the steering wheel. "Let's get the hell outta here."

"Hang on a minute," Dane said, running his hand along his belt.

"What's the problem?"

"I've dropped my cell phone somewhere. Give me a minute. I'll find it."

"Shit," Leland hissed. "Hurry up, *kola*."

Going around the corner and out of sight, Dane slipped his cell phone from his back pocket where he'd hidden it earlier. He pressed number three on the speed dial. After three rings, the voice mail clicked in. Hunkering down and speaking low, he left a message. "Damn guys, great cover you have got going for me. We're at the clinic now and are getting ready to leave. Claire Colby is with us. She came in while we were inside. I'm not sure where we're headed." He quickly looked over his shoulder, making sure he was still alone. "I'm leaving the phone on so you've got GPS and can track us. Go pick up Clement. That old buzzard knows just about every inch of this place and can guide you. Hurry, damn it. Hurry."

24

FILLED WITH FEAR, HER BODY TREMBLING, CLAIRE
fought to keep her wits about her. There was no question.
Her life depended on it.

How could I have been so terribly wrong? The excruciating pain of Dane's betrayal mixed with her fear and
anger. The agony took her breath away. The sensation was
like nothing she had ever felt before. She sobbed, praying
that Leland or Dane hadn't heard the sound. *Dane. Dear
God, what do I do with all this love? How do I take it back?
How do I make it die? How do I stop loving him so much?*
She squeezed her eyes closed, trying to hold back the flood
of burning tears. She failed to stop their slide down her
cheeks. *It hurts. It hurts so much.*

Stop it. Her anger rose, and she gave herself a mental
shake. *Stop feeling so sorry for yourself. Just figure out
how to get out of this mess. You can start with the tape.*

Pushing with her tongue, squeezing the tip between her
lips, she worked at loosening the adhesive tape that Leland
had stuck across her mouth. After the fourth try, it began to
lift. *Keep at it, rub it against your shoulder . . . you've got*

to get it off. With her hands and ankles tied, the only weapons she had left were her screams and her teeth.

She looked at Dane sitting in the front seat beside Le-land. *How could I have been such a fool? How could I have ignored the things that I already knew about him?* She shuddered to think she'd slept with a murderer . . . made love to a murderer. *Am I so cursed that any man I care about is a monster, and I am still stupid enough to believe him? That's what happened with Keith . . . Is Dane no different, just deadlier?*

His words echoed in her mind: *"Trust me . . . trust me . . . trust me." How can I? Please tell me that. How can I?*

Panic pushed her heart into a wild rhythm. *Hang on. Keep your wits about you. Think. Think of something to get out of this mess.* She rubbed her wrists against the rough burlap sacks of horse feed, hoping to loosen the adhesive tape. It didn't work. *Maybe if I can get the rope off my ankles.* She looked at Leland. *If I do, I know I can outrun him.* Her gaze shifted to Dane. *But can I get away from Dane?* She moved her feet, trying to loosen the rope. The rope held, cutting into her flesh. *Damn! Now what? Damn!*

Through another wash of tears, Claire looked up and tried to peer out the window. Where were they taking her? Seeing Leland looking at her in the rearview mirror, she quickly turned away.

"Where in the hell are you going?"

Dane's voice grabbed her attention. How odd that he'd have the same question. She looked at Leland, waiting for his answer.

"Just wait. I think you're gonna like it." He slowed down and yanked the steering wheel to the right. "Damned pot-holes, when the hell are they gonna get these roads fixed?"

A mile or two later, Leland turned off the road, steered the old Chevy through a shallow ditch and up a rough, narrow lane that cut through the hills.

Claire's panic grew, almost suffocating her, and she

knew she would hyperventilate if she couldn't calm down. She closed her eyes and took one slow, deep breath after another. *I've got to stay calm. I've got to figure a way out of this.*

The Chevy bucked and rocked across the back hills of Cold Creek for another mile. Dane thought that he knew every inch of the reservation, but this trip was proving him wrong. He had an idea that they were somewhere south of Clement's place, but that was about it.

The car careened down a hill, and Leland laughed as Dane reached out and grabbed the dashboard. "Damn, *kola,* you ain't scared of a buckin' Indian pony, are ya?"

In the next instant, Leland Big Elk jammed on the brakes, and the old car shuddered to a stop in a copse of cottonwoods. A small shed stood about twenty feet away. Dane's pulse began to rush. *Is this it? Is this the damn lab?*

"Come on," Leland said, getting out of the car.

When Leland jerked open the back door, Dane's heart leaped into his throat. "Leave her alone, Elk. I'll take care of her."

"Don't worry, *kola.* She's all yours . . . for now." Leland laughed, dragging the two bags of horse feed out of the car.

"Just make sure she ain't gonna be able to go anywhere, then give me a hand, will ya?" Leland hoisted one of the bags onto his shoulder and, without looking back, headed for the shed.

Dane watched him disappear into the small building, then turned to Claire. He could see her fear; her blue eyes were filled with it when she turned and looked at him. "I'm going to get us out of this, sweetheart, I promise. And I do mean *us."* He hunkered down beside the back door of the car. "I don't know what Leland has got planned, but until I find out what it is, I have to play along with him." He gently placed his hands on her arms. "Turn around. I'm going to try to loosen the tape on your wrists."

As he worked at the tape, trying to stretch it and give her some ease, he whispered, "Trust me just a little longer, please, Claire. I'm not working with Leland. I'm not." He kissed her cheek, knowing he would give up his life to keep her safe. He didn't blame her when she pulled away from his lips. "Claire, you've got to promise me that you won't try anything on your own. The last thing I want is to get Leland riled. I don't know what he'd do or how far he'd go." He brushed her hair out of her eyes and gently eased the strip of tape off her mouth.

"Am I supposed to thank you now?" Claire whispered with a sharp edge to her voice.

"You're welcome," Dane answered, a slight smile moving his lips, relieved there was still fight left in her. She'd need it. "Remember what I just said. Believe it." Before she could move away a second time, he placed a light kiss on her mouth, then turned and, lifting the bag of horse feed onto his shoulder, followed Leland into the shed. He prayed with each step that Claire believed him.

A camping lantern lit up most of the shed. Dane quickly looked around, and his hopes fell. There weren't any signs of the equipment the Big Elks would need to run an E lab. There weren't any mixing tubs, bottles or bags of ingredients, and there wasn't any sign of a press mold for the tablets. This wasn't the ecstasy lab.

"Put the feed over there," Leland said, pointing to the far wall of the shed. "Then give me a hand here."

"With what?" Dane dumped the sack on top of the other one.

Leland disappeared out the back of the shed and soon returned, leading a bay horse. "The saddles are over there." He pointed toward the back of the shed with a quick lift of his chin. "Bridles are with 'em. Saddle up." Handing the horse's lead to Dane, he disappeared out behind the shed again.

Dane quickly saddled and bridled the bay. Looking down, he wasn't surprised to see that the gelding wasn't shod. He suddenly thought of what Clement had said about the night riders' horses. Not shod. The puzzle pieces were tumbling into place. Were the Big Elks Clement's *wanagi* riders? *This is getting interesting.*

"Nothin' like a little moonlight ride. It's kinda romantic, eh?" Leland sniggered, returning with another horse. "Too bad this ain't that kind of trip, though." Leland threw a blanket and saddle on the sorrel he'd led into the shed. "It might be a little uncomfortable, but yer girlfriend's gonna have to ride double with one of us."

Dane looked over where the saddles were kept. Two remained. "There are four saddles. Are there other horses out there?"

"Yeah, but I don't wanna have to take three when we only need two. No point havin' an empty horse to lead back."

Dane's heart thudded in his chest, beating so damned hard it pounded against his ribs. *So that's how it's going to be. Three go, two come back.* He watched Leland tighten the cinch on the sorrel's saddle. The man looked as though he was planning nothing more than an afternoon ride in the park. Another thought hit Dane. *Maybe there's only one coming back.*

"Okay, we're ready." Leland blew out the lantern. "Go get her." Taking Dane's horse's reins, he led the two horses outside.

Stepping out of the shed, it took a few moments for Dane's eyes to acclimate to the darkness. As he walked toward the Chevy, his eyes scanned the car. In that instant the memory hit him and caused his step to falter. He remembered where he'd seen the car before. It had been on a snowy day last December as he'd driven to Rapid City with Kylee. This was the dark sedan that had followed him off the reservation. But that wasn't the first time he'd seen the car. As a teenager he used to see the black Chevy parked at the clinic or being driven around Cold Creek on house calls . . . by Martin Butz . . . Dr. Martin Butz.

If he thought he'd ever been touched by gut-burning dread before, it was nothing like what scorched him now.

Martin Butz's car in Leland Big Elk's possession could mean only one thing. Like dominoes in a child's stacking game, the facts seemed to be rapidly falling into a pattern, but some of the questions still remained.

He jogged to the car. "Come on, sweetheart." He glanced over his shoulder as Leland led the horses around to the front of the shed. He turned back to Claire. "I'm going to take the rope off your ankles. I don't know where he's taking us, but you're going to ride with me." He glanced at Leland again, and then back at Claire. "We've got a better chance of getting out of this if we work together." He waited for her to nod in agreement. It didn't happen. He tossed the freed rope aside, then looked back into her blue eyes. "We stay together, Claire . . . no matter what happens."

Under the cover of night, Leland led them along the rim of the hill. They'd already been warned not to talk, and not a sound disturbed the night. Even the horses walked quietly, the pieces of buckskin tied around their hooves muffling each step, leaving no hoofprints on the ground.

About twenty minutes into their ride, Dane looked down from the ridge. The moon offered just enough light to softly illuminate the small cabin about a half mile away at the low end of the valley. No doubt remained in Dane's mind; he even chuckled with the irony. *I've become one of Clement's night riders, one of his* wanagi.

Would the old man be looking up the hill tonight? Or would Gaines and Pardue have stopped by and picked him up, asking for his help as they tracked the cell phone's GPS signal?

Dane figured they'd ridden almost three miles. He had no idea where Leland was taking them or how much longer it would take them to get there.

They traveled across the high rocky bluffs that the locals called the Three Warriors, and then down into a gully, through Buffalo Creek, up the bank on the other side, and along a deer trail that led through the brush and into a thick stand of cottonwood trees.

Claire's arms tightened around Dane as his horse suddenly shied at something in the dark. She continued to hold on, even after he brought his horse under control. "It's okay, I won't let you fall," he said.

"What the hell is that?" Leland hoarsely whispered, pointing off to his left as his horse swung around and tried to bolt.

Moving with stealthy silence through the dense thicket of scrub brush and trees, the pack of rez dogs made no attempt to hide their presence. Periodic flashes of white told Dane that Kylee's pup, Pirate, was with the pack, in fact, was up front with the leader, once again.

"What the hell are they doin' here?" Leland croaked. "I don't like this. I ain't never seen 'em up this far before."

The dogs kept pace but faded into the night as the horses broke into a small clearing in the middle of the cottonwoods. Off to one side, Dane spied a cabin about the same size as Clement's. His pulse shot up a notch or two. "So, here it is," he whispered. "Here's the damned lab."

Almost hidden by the wide overhang of cottonwood branches and scrub brush growing in front of it, Dane realized that even in daylight, the cabin would be hard to spot from the air. No wonder the FBI's air patrols had never found it. He glanced up at the sky. *Even with the GPS, will the FBI be able to find us now?* He looked over at Leland. *I still don't know what the son of a bitch has in mind. Whatever it is, someone's not getting out of here alive. Hell, will they be able to find us in time?*

Leland guided them across the clearing to a small corral behind the cabin. He twisted in the saddle and looked across the clearing. "Where'd those damn dogs go? Can you see 'em?"

Dane looked and shook his head. Nothing moved in the

woods. He wasn't surprised. The dogs had a talent for appearing and disappearing like will-o'-the-wisps.

Trying to look relaxed and unconcerned about anything that might happen, Dane turned and helped Claire off the horse. She looked up at him, her eyes questioning. He slightly shook his head and watched helpless as her bottom lip began to quiver. He gave her arm a gentle squeeze, trying to encourage her. Would she understand?

"Come on." Leland dropped a long pole into place, closing the corral. He looked at Claire, his gaze sliding down her body. "Let's get her inside and tied up." Leland poked Dane in the ribs. "You gonna let me . . . you know . . . have a bit of fun with her."

No damn way, you son of a bitch. Dane felt Claire stiffen. He gave her arm another encouraging squeeze.

Leland opened the cabin door and led them inside. The smell hit Dane, making his nose burn. Before Leland lit a lantern, he knew without any doubt that this was the lab. Light flared from the lantern and filled the room. Across one side of the cabin a long bench held mixing tubs, bags and bottles of chemicals and, on the end, the custom mold. A gas-powered generator sat under the workbench, and a large cardboard box, filled with plastic bags full of pink tablets, was on a small table by the mold. A couple of chairs, a Coleman camp stove, and a cot filled the other side of the small room.

"Pretty neat setup, eh?" Leland stood in the middle of the room, looking like a king surveying his kingdom.

Dane knew he needed to stall for time until he could not only get the answers to a couple of questions he still had but also figure out a way to get Claire somewhere safe. "You going to show me around?"

Leland looked at Claire. "Aren't we going to have a little fun?"

"What's the rush? We've got all night. Let's give her a little chance to rest up after the ride out here. I like my women lively. So, show me the lab. You're the expert."

Dane knew Leland's ego couldn't pass up preening from any kind of flattery, even if it was a lie.

"What about her?" Leland glanced over at Claire who was sitting on one of the chairs. "You ain't gonna tie her up?"

Dane glanced around. "Where in the hell is she going to go? She can't get herself a horse without trying to lift your pole gate. She has no idea where she is, she can't out-run your gun or mine, and with those rez dogs out there looking for a snack . . . she's not going anywhere." He followed Leland around the cabin, periodically checking on Claire.

A container caught his attention. Paramethoxyampheta-mine. "I thought you were going to get rid of this stuff." Dane pointed at the bottle.

"You ain't in charge, *kola*. It's this stuff that gives the kids the high they like. It only kills 'em if they take too much." Leland shoved the container out of sight. "I dumped some in the creek. Gave the fish a nice big high . . . until it killed 'em, too."

There was the answer to Clement's puzzle about the dead animals. Dane pushed his anger down, fighting for the control he knew he'd need if Leland gave him the rest of the information he wanted. Trying to appear as though his actions were casual, Dane ambled to the door and opened it. "There's a lot of room out here." He looked back at Le-land and hard popped the first question. "Where'd you bury Martin Butz?" Claire's gasp was followed by Leland's low snigger.

"I don't know what you're talkin' about, *kola*."

"Don't try to blow smoke up my ass. Hell, you drove us halfway around the rez tonight in Martin Butz's old car." Dane snorted. "Your brother Bobby told me some interest-ing stories while I was in Wakefield."

"The hell he did! Bobby wouldn't rat on me."

"He didn't rat. You only rat if you tell a cop. . . . Tribal cops don't count." Dane forced a counterfeit chuckle. "He said you'd had to take care of some business here on the rez with the old doc." Dane casually leaned against the doorjamb.

Leland seemed to believe Dane's explanation. He shrugged. "It was kinda like tonight . . . with her." He pointed at Claire with a quick lift of his chin. "Bobby and I was doing some midnight shoppin' at the clinic, and that nosy old bastard showed up and busted in on us. He didn't want to have a giveaway so . . . we took him for a nice ride. When we found out he'd been talkin' to the cops and the FBI about E bein' on the rez, I got pissed. That son of a bitch was trying to shut us down. Well, I shut him down first." Leland laughed. He started rummaging around on the workbench. "I got a bottle of good Jack here somewhere. We're gonna have a drink."

"Do you drive Butz's old car often?"

As he reached for the bottle, Leland's hand stopped in midair. He turned and looked at Dane. "Now what are ya gettin' at, *kola?* What is this, a game of twenty questions?"

"Nah," Dane answered. He folded his arms across his chest and felt his heart thumping wildly against his forearms. *Easy, White Eagle. You've got to hold it together just a little while longer.* "Just two more questions."

"I ain't got nothin' to hide," Leland answered. His hand shook as he lifted the bottle of Jack Daniel's to his lips.

"Good, because I want to know where you went that Saturday last December when you followed me off the rez in Butz's car." Dane pushed away from the door and crossed the room, stopping in front of Leland.

The bottle slipped from Leland's mouth and spilled whiskey down the front of his shirt. "Who says it was me or Butz's car? Could've been any old Indian car. Could've been Denny Old Horn. He's always drivin' clunkers."

"Yeah," Dane replied, fighting hard to keep the sound of his growing rage out of his voice. "You're right, it could've been . . . but it wasn't, was it?" He pushed against Leland's chest, and the bottle of whiskey hit the floor. "You followed me all the way to Rapid City." He pushed Leland again. "You followed me to the I-90 exit, and you took the turn right behind me." He gave Leland another hard push. Dane leaned closer to Leland, got right into his face. "Did you kill my sister? Did you pick up my gun, hold it to that sweet, innocent child's head, and pull the trigger? Did you?" Dane shoved him again. "Did you?"

Leland exploded, his face suffused with sweat. He began to push back, striking Dane on the chest and the arms. "You're damned right I shot her," he yelled. His face reddened, and flecks of spittle fell on his chin. "You're damned right. The little bitch wouldn't die quick enough." He shrieked louder and louder. "Connie wouldn't marry me until she died. Damn it, what difference did it make? She was goin' to die anyway, but she was takin' too damned long. I took care of that. I helped her along!"

"You son of a bitch!" Dane's resolve broke, and he swung at Leland. His fist contacted with solid flesh, and Leland fell to his knees. "You damned filthy son of a bitch!" His voice had become a feral growl. Grabbing Leland's shirt, Dane hauled him to his feet and drove his fist into Leland's gut.

"Dane! Stop it! Stop it!"

Somewhere in the back of his mind, Dane heard Claire's voice, and then felt her hands on his arms, trying to pull him away from Leland. Knowing the danger he'd put her in made his rage climb even higher.

Taking advantage of Dane's distraction, Leland shoved against him, setting Dane off balance and knocking Claire to the dirt floor. The two men grappled, both falling against the chair. They lurched across the room and, tipping over the small table, sent the bags of pink pills skittering across the floor. Catching Leland off balance, Dane swung, his fist making a solid connection on Leland's jaw. Dazed, Leland careened toward the open door. With a shove, Dane pushed him outside. Leland fell, sprawled in the middle of the grassy clearing. Grabbing his shirt, Dane lifted Leland off the ground and drove his fist into him again and again.

"Dane! My God, please stop it. He's not worth killing. Not even for what he did. Kylee wouldn't want that. Please, please, stop!"

Aware that Claire had followed them outside, Dane released Leland's shirt and pushed him to the ground. He drew a quick, stabilizing breath. "Claire, get the hell out of here." He spoke in a hard, cold, and controlled tone, pushing all sound of emotion from his voice. "Take one of the horses and go."

Leland scuttled backward on the ground. Pushing himself to his feet, he took another swing at Dane, connecting with Dane's left shoulder, the shoulder that Primeaux had carved with his knife. Nausea rolled in hot tides through Dane's gut as wave after wave of excruciating pain washed over him. He stumbled and fell to his knees.

"I think the word is *checkmate, kola,*" Leland sniggered.

Dane looked up to find a little twenty-two-caliber pistol in Leland's hand. Instinctively, he reached to his side for his service revolver and his heart lurched wildly in his chest. His holster was empty.

"Didja lose somethin', *kola?* Ya must've dropped it somewhere inside, eh? That's too bad for you." Leland laughed louder, lifting his arm and wiping blood from his lip with his sleeve. "You're dead now, you bastard." He stepped closer. "What, no begging? Come on, White Eagle, beg just a little. If you ain't gonna do it for yourself, how about your little sweet piece." Leland raised the pistol. "After I off you, I'm gonna show her what a real man—"

"You're not going to show anybody anything," Claire vowed as she rushed up behind Leland and swung the large hunk of wood she held in her hand. The makeshift club hit him across the shoulders, sending him stumbling forward from the blow. He dropped the gun.

Both men dove for the small pistol, each struggling to reach it before the other. Without hesitating a moment,

Claire dashed forward and kicked the gun out of their reach. As much as she wanted Dane to get it, she was terrified that Leland would reach it first. Retrieving the pistol from the patch of weeds where it had landed, she lifted the gun above her head and fired it into the air.

The sound of the shot echoed from one side of the clearing to the other and finally faded away, leaving only the sound of Leland Big Elk's wheezing breaths and the smell of burnt gunpowder.

"You bitch," Leland gasped. Scrambling to his feet, he lunged at Claire.

Crouched low, ready to take Leland down again, Dane quietly spoke to Claire. "Use the gun if you have to, sweetheart. Don't let him get too close. Shoot if you have to."

"Give *me* the gun, sweetie," Leland coaxed. "You ain't gonna shoot anybody. Doctors ain't supposed to hurt people. You took an oath." He took one step closer, stopped, and suddenly looked up at the night sky. Leland's eyes grew wide with fear.

The sound was faint, a thud-thud-thud that grew louder and louder. Thud-thud-thud-thud. The tops of the trees began to sway, their dance growing more and more frantic. Thud-thud-thud-thud-thud. Dirt and bits of grass and twigs swirled up from the ground, blowing in a storm cloud of mini tornadoes that stung the skin like tiny bees. Thud-thud-thud-thud-thud.

Appearing out of the dark night sky, a helicopter came into view and hovered over the clearing, the thud-thud-thud-thud of its rotor blades beating the air almost deafening. A spotlight suddenly shone down, illuminating the entire clearing. A voice, its sound rising above the noise of the rotors, boomed over a loudspeaker. "This is the FBI. Leland Big Elk, you are under arrest."

"The hell I am," Leland shouted, raising his fist in the air. With a quick turn he grabbed the gun out of Claire's hand and ran toward the woods.

"Damn," Dane hissed, and followed.

In his dash for freedom, Leland stumbled twice, almost falling down. The third time he tripped, he fell forward, landing facedown in a clump of wild fern. The gun flew out of his hand and pitched into a dense thicket of thorn bushes. Rising to his knees, he froze.

Muscles bunched as if ready to spring, with their heads held low and their eyes glittering like rubies in the helicopter's spotlight, fifteen rez dogs stepped out of the woods. Inch by inch they closed in, circling around Leland like a living fence. Then, as though prearranged, none of the dogs moved as one smaller one stepped from the ranks. Its lips pulled back showing its sharp, white teeth, the black and white pup closed in on Leland Big Elk. Slowly walking around him, the dog's gait almost a swagger, Pirate taunted Leland until finally it lunged in, nipping Leland's legs, his arms, and his butt. One last insult remained and as it was being delivered, loud cheers resounded from the helicopter overhead. Lifting its leg, Kylee's pup sent a long, steady stream all over Leland Big Elk's expensive custom-made Lucchese boots.

Tilting their heads toward the moon, the rez dogs raised their voices, the sound close to laughter, and Dane's laughter joined in. Dane watched, as one by one the dogs turned and began to filter back into the woods and disappear. He glanced at Leland, elated to see the fear in the man's eyes. Then turning away, Dane closed his eyes and thought of Kylee. "For you, *Taŋski*, it's all for you." His voice caught in his throat and tears welled up in his eyes.

Dane felt Claire gently slide her hand into his. He wrapped his fingers tightly around hers, afraid that if he let go, she'd disappear.

"I think these are for you." She smiled and then pointed at Leland. "Well, actually, I think they're for him." The smile became a grin as she handed a pair of handcuffs to Dane.

Puzzled, he looked at the cuffs. "Where did you get these?"

She pointed up at the helicopter, then gently pushed him toward Leland. "Be careful. Don't get wet."

Leaning over, Dane kissed her, his mouth lingering, savoring the soft touch of her lips. "Will you wait for me?"

She kissed him back. "Always."

25

❧

"ABOUT TIME YOU FOUND THE LAB. BY THE WAY, WE found this inside." Jack Gaines held up Dane's gun, then handed it back to him. He draped his arm over Dane's shoulder. "You're the worst Indian FBI special agent I know."

"I'm the only Indian FBI special agent you know, and it's about time that you guys learn what FBI really stands for. Full-Blood Indian, which makes you guys all wannabes." Dane turned in time to see Pardue and two other men put Leland Big Elk in the helicopter. His ribs ached from the beating Leland had given him, and his shoulder hurt like hell, but seeing Leland Big Elk in custody made all the pain worthwhile. "You sure know how to cut it close. What took you guys so damned long to get here?"

Gaines shook his head, dropped his arm from Dane's shoulder, and pointed at Clement. "That tough, old bird over there. He told us that the only way he'd help us was if we gave him a helicopter ride, and it had to be this one, the one to come after you. We had to go pick up the old fart at his place." Gaines chuckled. "The wind from the rotors almost blew his old shack to Oz." Gaines glanced at the edge of the clearing where the rez dogs had been only minutes before. "The old guy knows some pretty cool stories, though. On the way over he told us one about a pack of wild dogs that followed some warrior around, helping him in battle." Gaines rubbed his arms. "I tell ya, seeing those dogs circle around Big Elk like that . . . well, it gave me the shivers, that's what."

They'd given Dane the shivers, too. So did the story that Gaines had just told him. *More damned stuff to talk to the old man about.*

Clement tottered across the clearing toward Dane and Gaines, escorting Claire as though he was taking her to a grand ball. He looked up at Dane and a scowl creased his face. "I told you to take good care of this girl, didn't I?" He lifted Claire's hand from his arm, placed it in Dane's hand and then patted Dane lightly on the shoulder. "Guard your treasures well, Grandson. This one's worth all the hard work."

Dane's gaze locked with Claire's, as he lifted her hand to his lips, turned it over, kissed her palm, and then closed her fingers over the kiss. "For safekeeping."

"Sorry to break the romantic mood, but are you two going to ride back to civilization with us?" Pardue asked. "There's room in the chopper." He pointed at the two agents who were standing outside the cabin. "MacKenzie and Gregory are staying to take inventory and pack up everything inside."

Dane looked down at Claire and then up at the starlit sky. Drawing Claire against his side, he gave her a squeeze. "No thanks. I think we're going to ride back." Claire pressed closer and put her arm around his waist. He took it as her silent approval. "Those are two nice horses that Leland has. I don't know who he stole them from, but we're taking them back to Clement's."

"Good," Clement cackled. "That means I get to sit next

to Leland in the helicopter, and maybe I'll get the chance to push the *cusu* out the door."

Gaines leaned close to Dane. "What's a *cusu?*"

Dane laughed. "It's the Lakota version of calling a guy a prick."

"Works for me." Gaines laughed, then sobered. "He's going to get what he deserves, Dane. I promise you, he'll pay for every life he took. He'll never be a free man again. There's at least four deaths we can pin on both him and Bobby Big Elk. I know it won't bring your sister back, but you've given her the best gift of justice by nailing the bastard."

A lump rose in Dane's throat, and he tried to swallow it. It didn't budge. "I didn't get him. The little white and black dog that counted coup on him did. He's your hero, not me."

THEY RODE SIDE by side in silence, neither knowing what to say, neither satisfied with the idea of small talk. They both wanted something more, a whole lot more.

Beneath the moon, beneath the stars, Dane took hold of Claire's reins and stopped both of their horses. Without a word, he dismounted and, holding his arms up, silently asked Claire to join him. She allowed him to take her off her horse and she stayed in his arms, pressing her head against his shoulder.

His hands cupped her face, his fingers plundered her hair, and he kissed her, not just with his lips but also with his soul. "I was so scared you wouldn't understand. I couldn't tell you about my job . . . not for my safety, but for yours." He kissed her again. "My mother doesn't even know."

"Oh, Dane," she whispered against his mouth. "I don't think I've ever met anyone as strong in spirit as you. I can't imagine how difficult this whole charade must have been for you, what it has cost you."

He lowered his head. The guilt had returned. "If I hadn't been so careless, if I hadn't left my gun in the truck . . ."

"Is that what you meant when you said *Tanski*'s death was your fault? My God, no, Dane. It wasn't. It wasn't your fault." She gently held the palm of her hand against his cheek. "You have absolutely no reason to believe it was your fault." She clung to him, her tears wetting his shirt. "If your gun hadn't been in your truck, it wouldn't have made a difference. Leland would have . . . done it any way he could." She stood on tiptoe and spread tiny kisses across his cheek and over his lips. "Think of the lives you've saved by putting Leland and his brother out of business. Think of the good that has come out of it all."

"*You* are the good that has come out of all this. Would you believe . . . I fell in love with you in a courtroom. You came to me in my dreams; you gave me hope and a reason to finish this damned job." He kissed her forehead, her eyelids, and her mouth. A soft chuckle erupted from his throat. "You scared me to death, though, with that damned baseball swing you put on Leland."

"I was on the all-star softball team in school." She snuggled further into his arms. "The only reason I hit him was to help you earn another reward, to give you the chance to arrest him."

"Another reward, eh?" Dane grinned. "So . . . what kind of a job did I do tonight? Good? Bad? Anything worth a big reward?"

Claire laid her index finger against her lips. A thoughtful expression played on her face for a moment. "Hmm . . . let's see." And then her mouth curved into a broad grin. "Oh, I think it's worth at least . . . three rewards."

"Come here." Dane pulled her back into his arms. "Rewards should be given as soon as possible after the good deed."

"I agree," Claire whispered. "I thoroughly agree." Her fingers quickly unbuttoned his shirt and pushed the fabric aside and she luxuriated in the hot, smooth skin she found beneath. Her hand hesitated over his heart, and she savored the strong beat that filled her palm. She moved her hands once again, drawing his shirt off his shoulders, and Dane helped her by letting it fall to the ground.

Moonlight touched him, illuminating the hard angles and planes of his body, and Claire, using only her finger-tips, slowly traced downward, exploring every inch of him. "Is this soon enough for your rewards?"

"Oh, yeah."

"I could give you one reward now and save the other two until later."

"Claire, I'm going to die if you don't shut up and kiss me."

THE CELEBRATION SHOWED little evidence of slowing down. Only a few guests had left, and those who remained seemed determined to stay all night.

Julie stood beside Claire, wrapped her arm around her, and gave her a hug. "Best wedding I've ever been to." She kissed Claire's cheek. "This one's going to last, and be-lieve me, I don't make that prediction very often."

"I'm so happy you could come. I was afraid you wouldn't, especially after the way you felt about me leav-ing Pennington and coming to Cold Creek."

"I wouldn't have missed this for anything. Besides"—she lightly struck herself over the heart with her fist—"these are my people. My mom was happy I was coming. She kept babbling on and on about coming back to my roots." Julie laughed and then glanced over at Dane. "My God, girl, I want one of those for myself."

"You can't have that one, he's all mine, but stick around." Claire laughed, pointing to a couple of the single male guests. "I wouldn't be surprised if these guys forty-nine later. I hear it's the best place to get a snag or be snagged."

Julie pointed to Denny Old Horn's brother. "That one. I want that one."

"Hmm, that's Luke Old Horn. Good choice."

"Are you corrupting my bride?" Dane asked, coming up behind Claire. He wrapped his arms around her, nuzzled her neck, and kissed her cheek.

Julie put up her hand. "Oh, no. I'll leave that to you." She pointed at Luke Old Horn. "But I think I'll get a head start on the snagging." Walking toward Luke, she turned and grinned. "See you guys later . . . much later."

Claire snuggled into Dane's arms. "What a perfect day for a wedding. I'm so glad it was ours." She scanned the crowded yard in front of Clement's cabin. "Look at Clement. He's in seventh heaven with all those kids sitting around him."

"I bet he's telling them *Iktomi* stories. Jack Gaines's kids are right in there, too."

Claire glanced around. "Where's your mom?"

"She said she needed to get something out of her car. She said it was your wedding present."

"My wedding present? But she already has done so much for us."

They both watched Connie White Eagle cross the yard toward them, Kylee's white and black pup close to her heels, never leaving her side except to chase Chewy back under the porch.

Dane watched the dog and slowly shook his head. "I still think Clement caught him that night and brought him back on the helicopter."

"I don't," Claire replied. "I think his heart . . . or somebody in his heart . . . told him to come home."

Connie reached them, out of breath, and hugged them both.

"Having a good time, Mom?"

"The best, the very best. Best wedding I've ever been to on Cold Creek." She winked at Claire. "Eyee, must have somethin' to do with the folk who're gettin' married. I'm real attached to 'em both." She smiled, and drawing Dane's head down to her, gave him a loud smacking kiss on the cheek. Turning to Claire, her face held a stern expression. "You'd better take care of my son. Keep his tipi clean. Make good moccasins for his feet. Cook his buffalo and venison the way he likes it. Clean his hides good. Carry all the firewood he wants . . . and make lots of fat, happy babies to fill his mother's arms."

Claire hugged Connie, fighting the tears that had filled her eyes. "I promise I will do all you ask, *Ina,* and much, much more."

"One more thing," Connie said. Reaching into her pocket, she pulled out a slip of paper. "My wedding present to you." She passed the paper to Claire. "Don't tell nobody I gave it to you, and don't you give it to anyone else. It's special. Only for White Eagle women."

Claire slowly unfolded the piece of paper. Written in Connie's scrawling script, the words at the top of the page— "Connie White Eagle's Special Frybread Recipe"—sent the tears tumbling down Claire's cheeks.

"Welcome to my family, daughter." Connie hugged her, kissed her cheek, and swiped at her own tears. "Be happy with my son."

"You gonna let these women stand around all day and bawl their eyes out, or are ya gonna take yer bride on a honeymoon? And not that old Lakota way in a tipi, but the good white man way . . . at the Holiday Inn." Clement shuffled across the yard toward them.

"I'm not telling you, or anybody, where we're going, you old *tatanka.* I want this woman all to myself so I can spoil her before you get the chance."

"Humph," Clement snorted and then turned and pointed at Jack Gaines and Gil Pardue. "I gotta posse and a helicopter, now. Besides I'm Lakota. I can follow tracks . . . even on asphalt."

Claire scanned the crowd of wedding guests one more

time. Dane had been afraid that after finding out he was an FBI agent, all of his friends would shun him. The only one who had been displeased was Calvin Iron Cloud, who said he was losing the best officer the Cold Creek Indian Police Force ever had. Everyone they'd invited had come.

In a shaded corner of Clement's porch Julie and Luke Old Horn were together flirting up a storm. Mattie was at the buffet table with her hand in the jar of jalapeño peppers. Jerome Rabbit was petitioning for votes for the next tribal council election. Denny Old Horn and Arvin Runs Buffalo were under the hood of Arvin's truck, trying to figure out why it wouldn't start, and Calvin Iron Cloud was showing the kids his shiny tribal police badge.

Dane took Claire's hand. "It's time to go. We've got less than two hours to get to the airport and get on the plane. Are you ready?"

She looked up at the man she knew she'd love forever. The shadows were gone from his face. The sad, haunted look had left his eyes. The secrets had all been told and forgiven. She grinned, stood on tiptoe and kissed his lips, then tugged his braids, and whispered, "I've been ready all of my life. What took you so long?"

JUDIE AITKEN is a Native American painter, a powwow singer, and an award-winning author.

The sizzling debut from
Nancy Herkness

A Bridge to Love

Kate Chilton thought she had it all. But shortly after her husband's death, she discovers a letter from another woman: his mistress.

Furious at his betrayal, Kate decides to get even and accepts a far-from-innocent invitation from a playboy millionare. And as one wild night quickly turns into another, what began as a fling becomes something else entirely.

"SIZZLING SEX, DAZZLING DIALOGUE,
UNFORGETTABLE CHARACTERS—
A BRIDGE TO LOVE IS A BOOK TO CHERISH."
—DEIRDRE MARTIN,
USA TODAY BESTSELLING AUTHOR OF *FAIR PLAY*

0-425-19126-5

Available wherever books are sold or at
www.penguin.com